The Secret Affair

Danielle Shaw

ISBN: 978-1-911445-07-4

First published by Endeavour Press Ltd in 2015.

Printed and bound in Great Britain by Clays Ltd, St Ives plc.

Endeavour Press is the UK's leading independent publisher.

Also available by Danielle Shaw published by Endeavour Press:

Love and Sacrifice

Secrets from the Past

Sunflower Morning

When Summer Fades

A Fabric of Dreams

Table of Contents

CHAPTER 1

Sally Palmer slipped the gear lever into neutral and waited. To most commuters this busy contra-flow on the outskirts of Thornhampton was a nightmare. For Sally, however, it was a chance for quiet contemplation. On Fridays it gave her time to plan her weekends and on Mondays it was a brief respite before the inevitable disasters waiting at Barrington's Department store.

As the chirpy DJ on the radio regaled listeners with tales of his disaster-prone weekend, Sally nodded in sympathy. Her weekend hadn't been much to smile about either. One blink and she'd missed it. All the jobs she'd been planning to tackle remained unfinished.Monday had begun disastrously too. First she'd dropped a bottle of shampoo, spilling its entire contents; then she'd snagged her tights and caught her zip in the lining of her skirt. Downstairs she hadn't fared any better. Armed with a pair of scissors, she found herself in combat with a milk carton, while studying the calendar. Why had she pencilled in red circles? Before Richard left—or, more to the point, before she'd told him to leave—red circles meant that time of the month. For the past fifteen months, that hadn't been necessary. Not to worry, Sally thought, pondering the date and mopping up spilt milk. It will probably come to me later.

Relieved to be closing the door on every vestige of Monday morning chaos, Sally ignored the sudden persistent ringing of her house phone and hurried to her car. Assuming it to be her sister in need of babysitting services, she shook her head in despair.

'This time, Jackie, you'll have to wait. Your big sister has a job to go to.'

'Pardon?'

Sally turned to find the postman. 'Sorry, Ray, I didn't see you there.

You've caught me talking to myself again.'

Ray grinned, handing her a bundle of letters. 'You can get locked away for that.'

'Then they should have come for me years ago. I'm always doing it.'

Ten minutes later, with traffic at a standstill, Sally glanced at the assortment of mail on the passenger seat. Airmail from Gill in Australia, wonderful cream vellum from Laura (no doubt with news of her latest business venture), and a less than wonderful collection of bills; perhaps it was just as well the lights were about to change.

Pulling into Barrington's car park, Sally acknowledged several senior members of staff. Like her they also arrived well before opening. In Sally's case it meant a much-needed thirty minutes in which to prepare for the day ahead. As the personnel officer of Barrington's department store, with its seemingly ever-increasing staff problems, there was a constant need of being prepared. To her surprise, George Fry was already at work outside her office.

'Morning, Mrs Palmer. I shan't be much longer. Just finishing the sign.'

'The sign?' Sally spied George's open tool-bag propped against the wall along with a nameplate. The nameplate that had once graced her office door. 'Oh! Am I being moved out of my office? Mr Barrington never said.'

'No, it's your new title. What do you think of that?' George pointed to the shiny new replacement. Embossed in bold gold lettering was MRS SALLY PALMER – HUMAN RESOURCES MANAGER.

'Don't tell me this is all part of the current revamping plan? What's wrong with Personnel Manager? Is this Mr Barrington's idea?'

'Not sure Mrs P,' George said, picking up a screwdriver, 'but if you ask me it's a bloody stupid idea—begging your pardon that is.'

'Don't worry, George, I think it's a stupid idea too. I suppose I should be grateful it's only my sign they're getting rid of and not me.'

'They wouldn't do that Mrs P. Mr Barrington's always saying what a valuable member of staff you are.'

'I can't think why. He's hardly ever in the store these days.' With a shrug, Sally placed her post and briefcase upon her desk. George, meanwhile, had finished his task and was buffing the newly fixed doorplate with the sleeve of his khaki overall.

'George,' Sally began, 'you've been with the firm a long time... What do you think of the rumours that Mr Barrington is going to retire?'

'It's all right for some, Mrs P. Don't I wish I could have retired in my late forties; as for the rumours...' George rubbed his chin, 'Somehow I can't see it happenin' misself, can you? Then again, Mr and Mrs B don't have any kiddies to hand this lot on to. Maybe they're going to sell up and travel the world together.'

Declining to comment—far better to keep her thoughts to herself—Sally watched as George gathered up his tool-bag and prepared to walk away. 'You could always ask him yourself, Mrs P. I did hear he's coming in this week sometime.'

'Perhaps,' Sally called after him. Then again as she was only Hugh Barrington's personnel officer—correction, Human Resources Manager—what Hugh and Serena Barrington did in their private life was none of her business.

What was her business, however, was the official looking envelope tucked between her pile of bills and Laura's letter. Alarm bells rang in her head as she ripped open the envelope and examined its contents. Those red circles on the calendar, in the confusion of spilt shampoo, and snagged tights, she'd completely forgotten: confirmation of her decree absolute! After nine less-than-happy years, she was no longer the wife of Richard Anthony Palmer.

Swallowing hard, Sally buzzed through to her assistant for a coffee.

'Make it strong and black, please. Could you also ask George Fry to save my old nameplate; I'd like to keep it as a souvenir.'

'You're not thinking of leaving?' Amy said, coming in with a tray of coffee.

'Leaving?'

'You asked for your old nameplate as a souvenir. By the way, I managed to get hold of George—he'll drop by with it later.'

'Hmm. Coming face to face with that new sign, Amy, I admit I did feel like leaving. To begin with, it sounds anything but human. Then again, as I've been with Barrington's so long, what else could I do? Besides, I need this job more than ever now. It appears I'm no longer married.'

'Oh, Sally, I'm so sorry. It hardly seems five minutes since you—'

'Started divorce proceedings? Yes, I know.' Sally pushed the offending manila envelope to one side. 'Well, this won't do will it? Me sitting here feeling sorry for myself. Looking at this pile of memos from last Saturday, it would appear I'm not the only one at Barrington's with problems.'

Sally studied the yellow slips of paper. Customer complaints about staff service – or lack of it, supervisory complaints against late timekeepers and Miss Kettle in Kitchenware (an apt name if ever there was one) with yet another incident of sexual harassment. Checking in her diary, Sally noted everything down and planned her day accordingly. By midday, pleased with her progress, she opted for an early lunch and made a mental note to stop by at Hosiery for some tights.

*

Later that evening, happy to immerse herself in culinary delights, she was in the process of adding bay leaves to a Bolognese sauce when she was halted by the ringing of the phone. Reminded of the morning call that she'd deliberately avoided, she reached for the receiver.

'Perfect timing as ever, Jackie,' she said, anticipating her sister's voice. 'In answer to last week's request, I'm already in the process of making you a spag bol. As for babysitting on– '

'Hello Sal… it's not Jackie... it's Richard.'

Sally's blood ran cold. Richard! All day long she'd forced herself not to think of him and now he…

'Sally… are you there?'

'Yes, I'm here.'

'I'm just ringing to see if you received your letter… the decree absolute?'

'Yes, I did. It came this morning.'

'That's all right then… is it?'

'All right? I don't understand.'

'I mean it's what *you* want, isn't it?'

'Of course it's what I want, Richard! You got what you wanted, didn't you?' Hearing a baby screaming, Sally stopped herself from mentioning the slip of a girl that Richard had picked up at the office party; the same office junior she'd tried to pretend didn't exist until Richard dropped the bombshell—he was going to become a father.

'Don't be like that, Sal. I thought we were friends. We still have to talk about the house and things.'

Sally willed herself to think of the three Cs. Cool, calm and collected. 'As far as I'm concerned, there's nothing further to discuss. The solicitors have sorted out our finances, and it was agreed I should stay on here at the house. Don't forget, it has been *me* paying the mortgage, and most of the bills, for years.'

'But…'

Richard got no further as the baby continued to scream and Sally overheard a young woman call, 'Here, you can take her now and give her a bottle. I'm going to bed!'

Replacing the receiver and conscious that her hands were shaking, Sally looked at her watch. It was only eight o'clock. She for one was not going to bed at eight in the evening. Instead, with hurt and anger mounting in her breast, she returned to her cooking. Savouring the smell of newly picked bay leaves, she set the timer for an hour. That way both she and the

Bolognese would have ample time to simmer.

Five minutes later, snatching up the list of outstanding jobs with one hand and a glass of red wine with the other, she climbed the stairs to her bedroom. Following this morning's disasters, it was the perfect place to begin.

'What *I* want! What *I* want! The bastard, how dare he?' Sally cried, her eyes stinging with tears. Then, taking a deep gulp of wine, she placed the glass on the dressing table, flung the contents of her undies drawer onto the bed and gave a brittle laugh. 'What I want, by the looks of it … is a complete new set of underwear.'

Against the newness of her Barrington's broderie anglaise pillowcases and duvet, the sets of undies looked horribly tired and jaded. Just like me, she mused, catching sight of her red-rimmed eyes and dishevelled hair in the mirror. Well, Sally Palmer, tomorrow *you* are going to buy yourself the prettiest sets of underwear Barrington's have to offer.

*

Roz Hughes, senior departmental manager, placed several exquisite sets of lingerie on the counter for Sally's benefit.

'These are the very latest we've had in for Christmas. Mind you, they're also the most expensive. I always boost the department's sales by stocking such frippery at this time of year.'

Fixing Sally with a wicked smile, Roz continued, 'You've no idea of the pleasure it gives me, standing here behind this counter. I'm like a beast in its lair waiting to pounce.'

Sally looked up from where her fingers had been caressing smooth pleated satin, inset with gossamer lace panels. 'Sorry, Roz. You've lost me. Waiting to pounce on what?'

'The guilt-ridden bastards who come in for late-night Christmas shopping, having first drunk themselves witless at their office parties.'

Peering over her thick horn-rimmed glasses, Roz paused, anxious there was no one within earshot. 'You can always tell the guilty ones. Those who've just had their hands up the skirt of young Sharon or Tracey in the call centre; they're the ones who spend the most… or at least the ones I encourage to spend the most.'

'Roz, you're quite dreadful! I don't know how you get away with it. One of these days someone will hear you. What if Mr Barrington—'

'Hugh Barrington, my dear Sally, already knows me to be an outrageous old woman. You're forgetting I'm not a mere slip of a girl like you. I joined Barrington's when his father was alive and our boss was simply young Master Hugh. Take it from me, behind that cool exterior and exquisite tailoring, HB possesses quite a wicked sense of humour.

Sally found it hard to think of Hugh Barrington with a wicked sense of humour. Polite yes, even charming, but humorous—no. Still, as her own contact with HB was strictly on a business level, dealing with Barrington's personnel problems, humour never really entered into it.

'I expect,' Roz said, putting another delightful lace confection on the counter, 'you've already seen the 'boss man' today. They tell me 'Hunky Hugh' is doing his rounds.'

Sally raised her eyebrows. 'Since when have the staff begun referring to Mr Barrington as Hunky Hugh?'

'Oh, that's some of the newer recruits. They think our HB is rather dishy. It's probably got something to do with that film *Pretty Woman*. I suppose you might call it the Richard Gere effect. You know what I mean, the older man and…'

Sally wasn't listening. She was still surprised that no one else had mentioned seeing Hugh Barrington in the store. Tall, good looking and immaculately tailored (complimented by handmade shirts, silk ties and the ever present yellow rose in his lapel), 'the boss man', as Roz called him, could hardly be missed.

'Well, no… I had no idea, perhaps I'd better get back to my office in case he needs to see me.'

'Oh, no you don't, Sally, not after I've got this little lot out for you.' Roz's gaze encompassed the contents of the counter. 'Besides, you've still got half an hour left of your lunch break. From what you were saying earlier, you are in desperate need of some new undies. Now, are you going to try some of these on, or do you want me to measure you?'

Sally picked up an assortment of lingerie. 'Wonderful as you are at your job, Roz, even you would find it hard to measure me as anything other than a 34B. Tell me, though, did Richard ever come in here to buy underwear?'

'No, why do you ask?'

'As it would appear he got more than his hand up Sharon's skirt, I can't help wondering what he might have bought for me.'

'Ouch! Sorry, Sally. Me and my big mouth again. I was forgetting.'

'There's no need to apologize, particularly as I'm beginning a new chapter in my life. They might say life begins at forty, but for me it's beginning at thirty three and a bit, and this,' Sally said, dangling a white satin and lace bra with matching briefs in the air, 'is just a start.'

Unaware that Hugh Barrington was in the next department, discussing millinery with Edith Hawtin, Sally declared, 'Right, Mrs Hughes, wrap them up, I'll take the lot, including the black!'

'Including the black? Goodness! What have you been keeping from me?'

'Nothing,' Sally said, wistfully running her index finger along a pleated satin bra cup, 'but you never know…?'

'Do I take it you're planning a little holiday, Mrs Palmer?'

With a start, Sally turned to face the tall, upright frame of her boss.

'W-why… have you heard that I am, Mr Barrington?'

'Well… no, but according to Mrs Hughes here, most ladies who buy themselves pretty lingerie are usually planning a romantic escape with their husbands or partners.'

Feeling herself colour, and the onset of tears pricking her eyelids, all

Sally wanted to do was escape. In desperation, she looked first at her watch and then at her friend. 'It's—um… OK, Roz, don't bother about wrapping these up now. I'll fetch them later. I have to see Miss Kettle in Kitchenware.'

Hugh Barrington gave an embarrassed cough as he watched Sally hurry away.

'Tell me, Mrs Hughes, did I imagine it, or am I to understand from Mrs Palmer's hasty departure, that I've committed a dreadful faux pas?'

'You most certainly have, Mr Barrington, and if I may say so, a most unusual one on your part.'

'Oh, dear. And there was me thinking I always had a way with the fairer sex.'

Discerning the faintest glimmer of a smile on Hugh's lips, Roz was reminded that at least twenty-five years ago, young Master Hugh had quite a reputation with the ladies. In those days of course, Roz had seen several come and go, though none had been serious, until he'd met and married the stunningly beautiful Serena Summers in the hope of living happily ever after.

Happily ever after, Roz thought to herself, placing Sally's purchases to one side. Sadly, those three little words didn't apply to her friend. As for Hugh and Serena Barrington, who always appeared to be the perfect couple, Roz Hughes was one of the very few who suspected otherwise.

'Mrs Hughes?'

'I'm sorry, Mr Barrington, I was miles away. What was it you were saying?'

'I was hoping you'd tell me why Mrs Palmer rushed off like that.'

Roz felt distinctly uneasy. It didn't seem right to discuss Sally's personal life in public; on the other hand it wouldn't take long before the news became common knowledge.

'Um… Mrs Palmer has finally received notification of her decree absolute.'

'I see, and to think I said…' Hugh Barrington fingered the yellow rose in his lapel. 'How insensitive of me! Yet, I could have sworn I saw them having lunch, only recently. I thought they were together again.'

'That was probably Sally's way of trying to be reasonable, to prevent any further unpleasantness over financial matters. Richard can get quite nasty at times.'

Hugh cast a questioning eye in Roz's direction, waiting for further information. When none was forthcoming, he nodded as if in understanding. 'Am I right in thinking there are no children?'

Roz gave a bitter laugh. 'Yes, that's right. Richard told Sally, when they first got married, that he didn't want any – hence her total commitment to work.'

'And an excellent job she's made of it too. Look, I think I should go and apologize, don't you? Can you wrap these now, and I'll take them to Mrs Palmer's office?'

Deeply hesitant, Roz picked up the sets of underwear and wrapped them carefully in tissue paper. 'Do you think that's wise? If Sally got embarrassed about you discussing her underwear, it might make matters worse having you deliver it.'

'Surely not, Mrs Hughes! I've been looking at, and discussing underwear with *you*, in this department since the days of knickers, brassieres and corsets. Now that it's all bras, briefs and those uncomfortable-looking thongs. I thought you ladies were far more broadminded.'

'Me, perhaps, Mr Barrington. Don't forget, I'm not Sally Palmer.'

There was little chance of Hugh forgetting that as he strode purposefully towards Sally's office. No two women could have been more different: Roz Hughes, who was tall and thin like a stick insect with her steel grey hair pulled back into a bun at the nape of her neck, looking every inch the schoolmistress of years gone by, and Sally Palmer, who was petite and softly rounded with expressive deep blue eyes, hidden beneath a long fringe of warm brown hair.

Knowing that Roz was almost at retirement age, Hugh assumed Sally to be in her early thirties and, other than acknowledging his personnel manager as a thoroughly dependable member of staff, he'd never given her a great deal of thought until now. Then again, what was it his father had cautioned? 'Hugh, my boy, if it's still your intention to join me in the family business, make sure you always follow the Barrington golden rule: female members of our work force must remain at all times, *strictly* employees and nothing more.'

Pausing to study the new sign on the office door, Hugh knocked and entered. Inside there was no sign of Sally. Disappointed, he placed the burgundy and gold bag containing the lingerie on her desk and was about to leave when a series of prints on the opposite wall caught his eye. A fine arts enthusiast, he stooped to get a better look, then decided to view them from Sally's chair. The pictures had obviously been hung with that purpose in mind.

It was here Sally found him, having gone not to Kitchenware but to the staff cloakroom instead. She'd needed to sponge her face and cool down following her embarrassing encounter. Opening her office door, Hugh Barrington was the last person she expected to find.

'Mrs Palmer, I do apologize, I have no right to be sitting here but I was delivering your…' Hugh rose and motioned to the bag, 'and I couldn't help but admire your delightful prints. It seemed the perfect place to view them was from behind your desk.'

Glad to be drawn into conversation on anything other than underwear, Sally regained her composure. 'Oh, yes, the pictures. A friend sends them to me; she owns a small arts and craft gallery. In fact, I had a letter from her only yesterday. She's thinking of expanding her business and asked if I'd like to help her.'

'Are you saying you intend to leave Barrington's?'

'No! Not at all,' Sally reassured. 'I'm very happy working here. It's simply that Laura knows I enjoy going to art and craft fairs; she's asked me to look out for some new artists, who might be interested in exhibiting at *Laura's Lair*.'

'Laura's Lair?'

'That's what she calls the gallery.'

'Does she indeed? Well, I confess if I was passing by and saw *that* sign, I'd think it was a den of iniquity and intrigue.'

'Exactly,' said Sally smiling. 'That's the whole idea. It draws people in, and once inside, Laura...'

'Go on.'

'I was going to say pounces; she has a certain way with her, you see. But Mrs Hughes has already used that expression today and it doesn't seem appropriate somehow... not in Laura's case.'

'Probably not. I should imagine Mrs Hughes is an entirely different kettle of fish from your friend Laura. By the way, how did you get on in Kitchenware?'

Thankful that she'd dealt with Miss Kettle before lunch (she'd merely used Michelle as an excuse to get away) Sally could at least meet Hugh's penetrating gaze.

'It's all been sorted, thankfully. A minor case of sexual harassment, I'm confident there'll be no further trouble.'

'Good! We don't want to see Barrington's splashed across the front page of the Thornhampton Gazette do we?'

'You can rest assured I'll do my best to avoid it, Mr Barrington.'

'I know you will, Mrs Palmer, which is why I've come to see you. As you're so good at arranging things, I was hoping you could help my secretary with a small retirement party for Edith Hawtin. She's been with Barrington's since my father's time, and my wife and I thought it would be a nice gesture. We were thinking of a small get-together one evening after the store closes, heads of department, the old stalwarts, that sort of thing. What do you think?'

'I think it's a lovely idea. Where would you hold it—the staff restaurant?'

'Heavens no! Miss Hawtin deserves better than that. I thought in the suite behind my office.'

From the blank look on Sally's face, Hugh explained. 'It's a suite of rooms that my grandfather had converted during the war. He used to stay there occasionally, particularly during the bombing raids when he couldn't get home to my father and grandmother. Why not pop along with some ideas for the party on Friday—about four o'clock—and I'll show you around.'

CHAPTER 2

By Friday morning, Sally had almost forgotten her distressing start to the week and the house was no longer in chaos. During the evenings, full of renewed energy, she'd turned out drawers and cupboards, filling bags for the charity shop and boxes for the tip.

'I can't believe how good it feels,' she told Roz over lunch in the staff restaurant. 'I never dreamt that getting rid of all that rubbish would leave me feeling quite so liberated.'

Roz patted Sally's hand. 'I'm jolly pleased to hear it, particularly if you're including Richard in all that rubbish. You're looking so much better than you did on Tuesday. By the way, how's the new lingerie?'

'Wonderful! It's a real treat in the mornings to put on such pretty undies. I feel almost brazen.'

Roz laughed. 'Brazen's hardly a word I'd use to describe you, but I would use it for her!' She pointed her fork in the direction of Michelle Kettle. 'You mark my words, one of these days that young woman's going to come seriously unstuck.'

Sally recalled her earlier investigation – Michelle's complaint directed at Mr Knowles of Lighting. Today, standing in the queue with Les Knowles, she appeared not to mind his wandering hands.

'What's Les having today, I wonder? Grope and chips.' Roz stabbed at the fish pie on her plate. 'Jesus! This fish pie is disgusting. I shall have to complain to the boss man.'

'Which reminds me,' said Sally, 'I've an appointment with him this afternoon; he wants to discuss Edith's leaving do. I'd better get a move on if I'm to be ready for the weekend.'

'That sounds intriguing. Are you planning anything exciting?'

Sally recognized the suspicious tone in Roz's voice. 'Hardly,' she murmured, finishing her coffee. 'If you think I've made illicit plans for prancing about in my black underwear, you're going to be deeply disappointed. I'm saving those for a special occasion.'

'Like Edith's party?' Roz teased. 'By the way, you haven't forgotten that I shall be expecting an invitation?'

'Of course I haven't. Mr Barrington said I was to invite *all* the oldies!'

'I suppose I asked for that! Serves me right for being nosy. You're right though, a couple more years and it will be *my* retirement party you're planning. What time's your appointment?'

'Four o'clock.'

'Ooh! Lucky you, it will be tea and cakes then. Just make sure you don't have the éclairs.'

Deeply puzzled but with so much still to do, Sally knew there was no time to ask Roz for an explanation. Instead, making her way from the restaurant, she paused briefly by the table where Michelle Kettle and Les Knowles were having lunch. Les was feeding Michelle chips, with his fingers. Ignoring the disapproving looks of their fellow diners, Michelle's scarlet painted mouth opened seductively to accept yet another ketchup-covered chip. Hardly a case of sexual harassment there, Sally thought, hurrying away to update Michelle's file.

*

Outside Hugh's office, Sally chatted with his long-time secretary. Anyone expecting a dollybird gracing the MD's office was in for a surprise. It was not a long-legged blond for Hugh Barrington, but instead the short squat figure of Muriel Baxter.

Of florid complexion, a haircut of the pudding basin variety and owl-like eyes, Muriel peered defensively across her desk. No one ever dared seek out *her* boss without prior appointment. A mere five foot two, in twin-set pearls and box-pleated skirt, she organized Hugh's office like a regimental sergeant major.

'Mrs Palmer, Mr Barrington won't keep you a moment, he's just taking a call from his wife. Do sit down and tell me about your ideas for Edith's farewell. I shall really miss her, your know, we've both been here so long. To think of her going off on that wonderful cruise with her sister, I was only saying to Mr Barr–'

The door to the inner office opened and the immaculately dressed man himself extended his hand in Sally's direction. 'Mrs Palmer, so sorry to have kept you, do come in. Will you make that tea for two, Mrs Baxter, please.'

Closing the door and helping Sally to a chair, Hugh said softly, 'I do hope she hasn't been boring you with details of Miss Hawtin's cruise.'

'Not exactly, but I think she was about to.'

'Mmm. Pity I can't send Muriel to keep her company.' Hugh fixed Sally with a disarming smile. 'Don't look so shocked Mrs Palmer, Mrs Baxter is a wonderful secretary, I simply don't share her enthusiasm for cruises. I prefer dry land pursuits myself: tennis, golf and walking.'

Sally followed his gaze to an array of tennis and golfing photos, gracing his desk. On all of them, and with not a hint of Savile Row tailoring, her boss looked fit, tanned and relaxed. What was it George Fry had said about him? Well, if he was late forties, he certainly didn't look it.

'Mind you,' Hugh continued, 'my wife's not averse to life on the ocean waves. She dragged me along once, but I vowed never again. Luckily her sister's only too happy to go along with her these days.'

Hugh studied the agenda Sally had compiled for Miss Hawtin's farewell and nodded approvingly. 'That looks about right, I think: a presentation in the staff restaurant at lunchtime and a small gathering of close friends and colleagues here, after the store closes. Perfect.'

Also perfect was Muriel's timing. She entered, pushing a polished brass trolley on which rested a fine Wedgwood tea service and two-tier cake stand, brimming with a selection of cakes.

'Will you be wanting me to pour, Mr Barrington?'

'No thank you, Mrs Baxter. I'm sure Mrs Palmer's quite capable. That will be all.'

Hugh's tone was firm, yet polite. Muriel left the room downcast.

'Oh dear. Is she offended?'

'Quite possibly, Mrs Palmer. Muriel's a great one for ritual, but I'm sure we can manage perfectly well on our own. Now, if you don't mind wheeling that contraption, perhaps you'd care to follow me.'

With that Hugh opened large double doors in what Sally had taken to be solid wood panelling and ushered her into a large sitting room.

'Goodness! How amazing, who would have thought…?' Sally ground to a halt with the trolley and stared about her.

'Yes, it is rather novel, isn't it? It was my great-grandfather's idea, originally and then grandfather added to it during the war. Spending so much time here—often days at a time—he filled it with several prize possessions. He felt they'd be safer here. Every day, so I'm told, he defied the bombs to fall on Barrington's.'

Sally's gaze encompassed the exquisite antique furnishings and carpets. 'It obviously worked. Aren't you worried that something will get damaged during the party?'

'I appreciate your concern, Mrs Palmer. However, we'll only be having the more senior members of staff in here for drinks and canapés. I think we can trust them not to throw their food about, don't you?'

Hugh was presumably referring to last year's staff Christmas party, when things had become unusually out of control. For a fleeting moment, Sally was reminded of another such party with serious consequences. The one which resulted in divorcing Richard!

Not expecting a reply, Hugh continued, 'Don't worry about the carpets. I'm sure they'll be fine. Besides, I think my wife would love to see the whole room ruined. Given half the chance, she'd get rid of all this. Serena, who's into all things minimalist these days, thinks the place looks like a bordello. I wouldn't know myself, but I bet great-grandfather did!'

Sally followed Hugh's gaze to a portrait on the wall. There was a distinctive presence about the sitter who, though elderly had maintained his dark good looks and glint of eye.

'Hubert Barrington the first, founder of the store on this very site. Now, how may I tempt you?'

Still pondering Hubert Barrington's handsome features, Sally turned with a start towards his great-grandson. To her relief, she discovered Hugh was only referring to the plate of assorted cream cakes and iced fancies.

Moments later, pouring the tea Sally remembered Roz's earlier warning. *Don't have the chocolate éclairs*. Still none the wiser, she passed Hugh a cup of tea and deciding to play safe, declined cakes of any description.

'If you're sure about the cakes…' Hugh said, rising from his chair, ' I hope you won't object if I take the éclairs for Stanley.'

Sally watched as Hugh walked to a cabinet, removed a plastic container and placed two dainty éclairs carefully inside.

'In case you're wondering, Stanley is my dog. Poor old chap, he might be on his last legs, but he's lately had a thing about chocolate éclairs. With these being so small, and Stanley being so old, I don't think they'll cause him too much harm at this late stage. I'd also be extremely grateful if you didn't tell Mrs Baxter; she thinks it's me who eats them.'

Fixing Hugh with a conspiratorial smile, Sally recalled another of Roz's remarks. What was it she'd said? Something about Hugh Barrington having a delightful sense of humour. He certainly had something, Sally thought, something that made her hands shake as he'd watched her pour the tea. Now, however, she made sure her hands were perfectly steady as she passed him the list of presents, suggested by Edith Hawtin's colleagues.

'I'm afraid, even though I asked around, everyone's come up with the usual things: clocks, sets of luggage, tea sets and decanters. I've been trying to think of something all week that's different.'

'Whatever you do,' Hugh grinned, glancing down the list before returning it to Sally. 'Don't buy her a camera! I've lost count of the times she's tried confronting me with photos of her umpteen cats and assorted holidays. That is one time when my secretary does have her uses. Speaking of whom, Mrs Palmer, I've a pile of letters to sign before the weekend…'

'Don't forget Stanley's éclairs,' Sally whispered, when Hugh escorted her back through his office and said goodbye.

'She's such a lovely person, isn't she?' Muriel declared, wheeling the trolley away. 'I take it with a trim figure like that, she didn't touch the cakes. Still, at least you had your eclairs, Mr Barrington. Were they nice?'

'Yes… lovely,' Hugh said deliberately, his reply suiting both Muriel's question.

*

With a final adjustment to the burgundy and gold ribbons, Sally passed Hugh the neatly wrapped leaving present. 'I know you said not to buy Miss Hawtin a camera, but I'm sure you'll be quite safe. It's unlikely she'll invade your office with this after her retirement, and her sister did tell me it's exactly what she wanted.'

Later, in the suite behind Hugh's office, Edith paused for breath (giving everyone a well-deserved break from the detailed itinerary of her cruise), while George Fry offered advice on her new camcorder. Serena Barrington, meanwhile, stunningly tall and blonde and elegant in black, walked to where Roz and Sally were admiring the late October skyline of Thornhampton.

'Hugh tells me the camcorder was your idea, Mrs Palmer. It was obviously the perfect choice, Edith hasn't stopped talking about it all evening.'

'That and her cruise,' Roz remarked caustically.

'Don't you like cruises, Mrs Hughes? Personally I adore them. All those wonderfully exotic ports of call, blue skies and open seas, not forgetting such interesting people on board too.'

Serena looked across the room in her husband's direction. 'Hugh of course simply loathes them and refuses to go anymore. In fact, he's refusing to go anywhere at the moment because of Stanley. Can you believe we were supposed to be going away with my sister and her husband for a long weekend, but Hugh won't leave that damned dog? It's such a nuisance.'

'Then why not leave Stanley in kennels?'

'*Precisely*, Mrs Hughes,' Serena clasped Roz's elbow. 'My sentiments entirely. Needless to say Hugh won't hear of it. He says it's not fair on Stanley.'

Quite why she said it she didn't know but Sally, remembering the look on Hugh's face as he spoke of his beloved dog and the eclairs, broke in softly, 'Um - I don't mind looking after Stanley. That's if you'd like me to?'

'*If I'd like you to*!' Clearly overjoyed, Serena released her grasp on Roz's elbow and reached for Sally's hand. She couldn't wait to tell her husband. On the other hand, knowing how Hugh felt about his wretched dog, telling him now was perhaps not a good idea. No, she'd wait until after Edith's little retirement do, just in case…

*

Sitting at her dressing table later that night, Serena brushed her sleek blonde hair from her face and pinned it to the top of her head like a halo. Then adjusting the triple-mirror, enabling her to view Hugh's reaction to her news as he lay in bed reading, she unscrewed a jar of cleansing cream.

'Hugh darling, you'll never guess, Sally has offered to have Stanley. That means we can still go to Devon, with Vivienne and Charles.' Serena placed a large swirl of cream on her nose, throat and cheeks and waited. 'Hugh… did you hear what I said?'

Hugh peered at her over the top of his book. 'Yes, I did, but I'm afraid I'm not quite with you. I didn't think we knew any Sally's.'

Hugh Barrington! You mean to say you work with these people for years and never get to know their Christian names. Sally - Sally Palmer!'

'Serena, are you saying you've asked Mrs Palmer to look after Stanley? Good heavens! The woman's a personnel officer, not a kennel maid.'

'It's human resources now, darling—or so Gareth tells me. You know what our nephew keeps telling us, we have to chill out and move with the times these days, and that includes Barrington's.'

Relieved to have prompted some response from her husband, for Hugh had at least put his book to one side, Serena continued massaging her face with long upward strokes.

'What Gareth plans for Barrington's will only come into being if and when I do decide to hand over to him. Until then, however, I'm quite happy to leave things as they are. As for using people's Christian names in a working environment, my father was always dead against it. I'm also convinced our customers prefer it that way too. Can you honestly say, Serena, that you'd prefer to be served by Hilda in Haberdashery or Clarice in carpets?'

'Hugh, darling, sometimes you sound just like your father. For your information I doubt very much if you'd find many Hildas or Clarices anywhere these days.'

'Don't be so pedantic. Anyway, I understand perfectly well what you're trying to do. You are trying to draw my attention away from the all-important problem of Stanley and Mrs Palmer.'

'That's just it, Hugh, can't you see there is no problem? Sally has kindly offered to look after Stanley and that's the truth. You can ask Roz – that's Mrs Hughes to you – if you don't believe me.'

Returning to his book, Hugh could stare only blankly at the pages. Yes, he did believe his wife, but quite how the subject of Stanley and the proposed weekend in Devon had come to be a topic of conversation at a retirement party… Then again, having been married to Serena for almost twenty-four years, he knew better than to start asking questions at this time of night. Far better to switch off the beside-lamp and get some sleep.

With a resigned sigh, Hugh turned on his side. Going away with Charles and Vivienne shouldn't create too many problems, should it? He'd always been deeply fond of Serena's older sister and her husband; unlike his wife they were usually charming company. Also, as the problem of Stanley appeared to have been resolved... What hadn't been resolved, he suspected, were sleeping arrangements at the holiday cottage in Devon. Having taken considerable time to convince Serena to dispense with their double bed in favour of two singles (following a recent revamp of their bedroom), Hugh only hoped a similar arrangement would be maintained in Devon.

*

Serena stood impatiently by Sally's front door, waiting for Hugh and Stanley to follow her up the garden path.

'The door looks as if it could do with a coat of paint, Hugh. I thought you paid your staff decent wages. Paint's not that expensive.'

'Serena, please! Don't forget Mrs Palmer's husband left some while ago. I suspect it isn't a question of money but more a question of time. Working full time doesn't exactly leave you free for DIY projects; neither does looking after other people's dogs!'

'Hmm. At least the house looks clean... and the garden's pretty, even for this time of year.' Serena turned round as Sally opened the front door.

'I was just saying to Hugh how pretty your garden looks.'

'Thank you. It's one of my hobbies. Won't you come in?'

Serena shook her head and, keen to avoid contact with the aging black Labrador, took a step backwards. 'It's probably better if I wait in the car. Knowing Hugh, it will take him ages to explain Stanley's routine and diet. Thanks ever so much, Sally, you're a real poppet. Try not to be too long, Hugh.'

Sally watched Serena sashay down the path like a model on a catwalk, her cashmere camel coat, worn over chocolate brown trousers and knitted silk sweater, swinging nonchalantly from her shoulders. At the gate, she turned and blew a kiss. 'Bye-bye Stanley, be a good dog.'

'Did you say it was a walking holiday?' Sally asked.

'I suppose you could say that. Charles and I do the walking, Serena and her sister do the talking,' Hugh shrugged his shoulders as Serena, dressed for anything but walking, poured herself effortlessly into the car.

Taking Stanley's basket and box of dog food, Sally led Hugh and his faithful companion into the hall. 'Where do you think he'd like to have his basket? I only have a gas fire in the lounge, but he's very welcome to sleep in there.'

'I'm sure the kitchen will do perfectly,' Hugh replied, strangely ill at ease. 'Mrs Palmer… I know you've assured me that you don't mind looking after Stanley, but he's a very old dog and his—er—bladder doesn't function terribly well. I'm still not happy imposing on you like this.'

'Nonsense, I'm sure he'll be no bother, will you Stanley?' Kneeling down, Sally put an arm about Stanley's neck. In turn, the faithful Labrador turned soulful eyes towards her and, sensing a female who cared (unlike Serena), rested a paw on Sally's knee.

'There you are. You see. Nothing to worry about. We're the best of friends already, aren't we, boy? Now off you go and enjoy yourselves. Stanley and I will have lots of walks and—'

'Don't worry about taking him for walks. I'm sure you'll have enough to do. You look as if you're going to be busy.' Hugh nodded to the paint and Polyfilla on the dresser.

'Oh that! That's been there ages. I try to do a few jobs each weekend. Richard, my—er—ex-husband, liked to think he was a dab hand at DIY. Unfortunately, he never finished one job before embarking on another. I used to joke that we should call this place Halfway House.'

'Halfway House?'

'Because the jobs were only halfway finished.'

Hugh smiled and looked down at Sally, who was still holding Stanley's paw. 'Right, old chap, here's where I leave you. Be good, won't you?'

Stanley struggled to a standing position, looked at his master and walked towards the door. 'Oh dear,' said Hugh. 'I should have warned you. Usually, if I say *be good* he takes it as a sign to go in the garden or wherever.'

Opening the back door, Sally watched Stanley amble onto the patio and head straight for her treasured bay tree in its terracotta pot. Seeing her look of concern, Hugh ventured, 'I do hope the bay tree is purely for ornamental purposes and not culinary.'

'Um – I do occasionally use the leaves in cooking, but perhaps if I take them from the top branches in future…'

Relieved to see that Sally was smiling, Hugh thanked her profusely, patted Stanley on the head and left.

*

In deepest Devon, Hugh and his brother-in-law returned from their evening stroll. Vivienne and Serena (each with a motive) had insisted on it once they'd finished dinner. Vivienne, because Gareth, her only son, had declared he had no intention of joining his father's legal practice, and Serena because she was hoping to go on a skiing trip at New Year. Her sister's company and presence was paramount.

'As you know I consider myself way too old for skiing,' Vivienne began, 'But I don't mind coming along to keep you company. In fact the thought of chilling out, as Gareth says, in that wonderful villa in Gstaad while you hurtle at breakneck speed down the slopes, will probably do me good after such a hectic summer. I'm sure Charles won't mind me–'

'What won't I mind?'

'Nothing, Charles, it's just girl talk. Now who wants a brandy and coffee before we turn in for the night?'

'Green tea for me, please Vivienne.'

Serena frowned at her husband. 'Oh Hugh, you Philistine, you can't have tea with brandy.'

'Philistine I may be, Serena, but I'd prefer tea and no brandy–'

'Speaking of turning in,' Charles interrupted, 'Hugh, old chap, you don't mind if Vivienne and I have the twin room and you and Serena the double? Not that we don't like each other, you know,' Charles said with a loving look in his wife's direction. 'It's simply because of my persistent snoring. If Vivienne and I spend the whole night together, I wake up in the morning black and blue, from where she's been kicking me.'

Hugh looked at Serena where she reclined on a cushion by the fire. The flames played delicately against her face and cast golden lights into her hair. 'No, not at all,' he lied. 'If that's OK with Serena.'

Serena stretched her long body sensuously, nodded and got up. 'I'll go and make your tea, darling,' she whispered, kissing his cheek.

Mellowed by a sense of wellbeing following an excellent meal and fine wine before his evening stroll, Hugh lay down beside his wife and waited for sleep to claim him. His peace was shattered when Serena propped herself upon one elbow and murmured huskily. 'Hugh, darling, would you mind awfully if I went skiing at New Year? Vivienne was saying how much she'd love to go and I'd hate to disappoint her. Of course, I realize you wouldn't want to leave Stanley for a whole month–'

'Are you saying your sister's prepared to leave Charles for four weeks?'

'Well, no, and perhaps we'll only go for two. You know me, I always say I need a month to perfect my skiing to black run standard again.'

Serena's words, particularly *you know me* reverberated in Hugh's head. Yes, he did know Serena only too well in fact. The photos from last year's skiing trip (that she still didn't know he'd found) bore witness to the fact. Any fool, looking at those, would know that his wife had been perfecting more than her skiing with the handsome young ski instructor. It hadn't been the first time nor, he presumed, would it be the last.

Misinterpreting Hugh's silence, Serena ran her scarlet finger nails down

Hugh's chest and entwined her long legs around his. 'If you're unhappy about me leaving you on your own for so long, darling, perhaps I can start making up for it now? As I said before, I know how much you hate leaving Stanley. I also doubt that Sally, wonderful though she is, could look after him for a whole mon–'

Mention of Sally at that moment had an unsettling effect on Hugh. In his mind's eye he saw her, crouched on her kitchen floor, with Stanley's paw resting on her knee. Muttering apologetically, he dislodged Serena's hand from his own knee, 'Sorry, Serena. I'm exhausted. One way and another it's been quite a week at Barrington's. Perhaps I should have a serious word with Gareth after all?'

Serena, not one for attempting to hide her displeasure, sat up, reached for a glossy magazine, and angrily began to flip noisily through its pages.

Blocking out the sound, by remembering Sally's delightful laughter as Stanley christened her bay tree, Hugh was soon sleeping soundly.

*

Watching her husband load luggage into the car, Serena called out.

'Hugh, don't forget, we must stop at the village shop and buy Sally something for looking after Stanley. 'Though God knows,' she said as an aside to her sister, 'what one buys a person daft enough to take on an incontinent dog for a whole weekend!'

At that moment, back at Sally's, Stanley gazed adoringly up at her as she placed his rug on the sofa and helped him to climb up. Tired after their afternoon walk, not to mention giving him a bath (more for Hugh's benefit than Serena's), she patted his head and stroked his silken ears.

'He'll be back soon, Stanley,' she said with a yawn. 'You'll be pleased to see him and I'll be sorry to see you go. We've had a great time together, haven't we?'

Once more placing a paw on her knee, as if in agreement, it wasn't long before both dog and his new found companion, were soon fast asleep.

They were both still sleeping when Hugh came in by the back door. Sensing his master's presence, Stanley stirred and wagged his tail, leaving Sally to discover Hugh, staring down at her with a look she found strangely disconcerting.

'Sorry to startle you, only when I didn't get any reply, I looked in through the window… I did ring the doorbell but it didn't appear to be working.'

'No,' came the sleepy response, 'the battery went yesterday, something else for my list of things to do. Not to worry, I'll get there in the end, I usually do.'

'That's why you're so good at your job. How's he been; any problems?'

'None whatsoever. he's been marvellous. I've enjoyed having him. How was the weekend?'

Saying nothing, Hugh was bending down patting Stanley when Serena appeared at the back door. This time the dog did not wag his tail. 'Hugh! You've been ages. Surely it doesn't take that long to collect a dog and his basket!'

Following them to the car, Sally whispered as an aside to Hugh. 'Um—I also gave him a bath, I thought it might help…' Then, giving Stanley a farewell hug and conscious that Serena was tapping her feet impatiently, she called in her direction. 'Don't forget, I'll have him anytime. He's no bother.'

Serena snorted and reached into the rear of the car. 'Oh, by the way, Sally, these are for you. I got the biggest box. Unlike me, you're probably not watching your figure.' Kissing the air on both sides of Sally's cheeks, Serena handed her a large box of clotted cream fudge.

CHAPTER 3

Switching off the ignition, Donald Hughes stepped from his car and helped Sally from the rear passenger seat. 'I trust you two girls are all prepared for an exciting evening.'

Roz groaned before joining Sally on the pavement. 'Hmph! That remains to be seen, Donald. For the moment I'm not sure which is worse: watching football on TV with you, or an evening of Edith Hawtin's holiday films.'

'It's OK, Roz. There's no need to remind me the camcorder was my idea. How was I to know that once Edith retired, we'd all be invited to a private showing?'

'You weren't, but it still boils down to the lesser of two evils, Sally. Take your pick: Donald with his lager or Edith's sister with her pea-pod wine.'

'What! You are joking?'

'Never been more serious. It'll be pea-pod, dandelion, parsnip, the lot.'

Sally turned in Donald's direction. 'You know, I think I've suddenly developed an interest in the European cup.'

Grabbing hold of Sally's arm, Roz dragged her away from the car. 'No way, José, *you* are coming with me. Anyway, it might not be that bad after all. Lillian—Edith's sister—is a bloody good cook. There's bound to be plenty of tasty morsels to go with that dreadful booze.'

When Roz ran back to kiss Donald goodbye, Sally was touched by their show of affection. They were such an amazing couple, like chalk and cheese really. The tall, brusque extrovert Roz, whose tape-measure and expert hands fitted hips and breasts of every size and description, and the ever-placid and softly spoken Donald, who dealt with figures of a different kind.

'What time shall I come and fetch you, dear?'

'I'm not sure. It depends how quickly Sally and I can make our escape. I'll ring you and let you know.

'Don't try and escape too soon then. I'd prefer to see the whole match if possible.'

'I'll do my best, Donald.'

Sally paused with her hand on Edith's front gate. 'You're very lucky, Roz. Donald's such a lovely man.'

'I know my dear. To think my mother said it wouldn't last. She told me accountants were boring. You can take it from me they certainly aren't! In fact Donald's quite a… Hey! Isn't that the boss man's car? Jesus! Edith's never invited Hugh and Serena, has she? And there was me, not having to drive for once, hoping to get rat-arsed on pea-pod *nouveau*!'

Sally ignored the departure from Roz's 'Barrington speak' into the vernacular. She was more concerned about Hugh and Serena Barrington. An evening spent watching Edith's videos of cats and cruises was hardly their scene.

When the midnight blue Jaguar purred to a halt at the kerbside, it was only Hugh who emerged. 'Good evening ladies, what a pleasant surprise. Do you think we're in for an entertaining evening?'

Sally gulped, sensing Hugh's remark was directed at her. Should she also apologize to her boss with regard to the camcorder? There was no time, however. The front door swung open, and Edith Hawtin stood there in all her glory: newly tanned and wearing a voluminous Hawaiian print kaftan.

'Edith, how charming you look, such amazing colours. You've obviously had a wonderful holiday.' Hugh bent to kiss Edith's cheek and at the same time shot a mischievous wink in Sally's direction.

She turned to see if Roz had noticed too, but she was already handing her coat to Lillian, who then ushered everyone through to the drawing room—the setting for the night's viewing.

'I'm sorry Mrs Barrington couldn't join us,' Edith said, offering Hugh a glass of straw coloured wine.

'Yes, such a shame, she was so looking forward to it. Prior arrangements, I'm afraid, but she sends her love to everyone.' Hugh took a sip of his wine and turned away. Sally thought he was going to choke.

'That's what you get for lying through your teeth,' Roz whispered to Sally. 'Still, you have to admit HB's a damned good actor. With his good looks perhaps he should have gone on the stage instead of joining the family business.'

Roz looked about the room at the weird assortment of Barrington's old stalwarts and Edith and Lillian's friends from the Parish Council and WI. 'I ask you, Sally, can you really see snooty Serena wanting to join this lot?'

In her mind's eye, Sally could only see Serena kissing the air as she'd handed over the box of fudge. The memory of it still made her seethe.

'Are you sitting comfortably and do you all have a glass of wine before we begin?' Edith studied her guests who nodded and murmured politely. 'Right, Lillian, you may switch off the lights. If we start with the cruise, we can stop for refreshments at nine and then watch the films of…'

Sally wasn't listening; instead she glanced across the dimly lit room, convinced that Hugh had just poured the contents of his glass into a nearby aspidistra.

Several films and assorted bottles later, Roz and Sally found themselves alone at one end of the conservatory. Hugh was talking to George Fry and Muriel Baxter, while Lillian and Edith were in animated conversation with a group from the WI.

Roz took a deep gulp of wine and refilled her glass from a bottle on the table. 'I still think HB's a brick coming here tonight, which is more than his lady wife would do. Prior arrangements, indeed! We all know what that means.'

'I don't.'

'Oh, come on, Sally, you can't spend all of your time tucked away in that office. Even you must have heard about Serena and her so-called *arrangements.*'

'Roz, shouldn't you keep your voice down? Someone might hear. I thought Hugh and Serena were happily married?'

'They are in a way,' Roz insisted, 'then again… there's happily married and happily married, and I've always thought it such a shame there's no kids. I can just imagine the boss man with children. I know he's got his nephew, Gareth, but it's not the same, is it? If he had a son, they could at least do things together and then leave Serena to her prior *engagements.*'

Sally thought of her own childless marriage to Richard. 'Not everyone wants children. Perhaps Hugh and Serena didn't want–'

'That's where you're wrong,' Roz said, her speech becoming slurred. 'Hugh did want… the problem, would you believe, is in his department? Serena told me ages ago, when I was fitting her for a bra.' Roz eyed Hugh lasciviously, while reaching for another bottle to refill their glasses. 'Sad isn't it, to think such a fine figure of a man can fire only blanks.'

'Roz! I can't believe Serena would divulge anything like that; besides it's not always the man who is infertile.'

'Don't you? Well, she did and he is. In fact you'd be amazed at the things people tell me in that fitting room. For instance…' Holding a finger to her lips, Roz pulled Sally closer, 'Serena's sister, Vivienne, once let slip that Serena and a young skiing instructor had… by the way have you ever met Vivienne? She's really lovely, not at all stuck up like her snooty sister. Anyway, where was I? Ah, yes, Vivienne told me–'

'Whatever she told you, I don't want to know! I also wish you hadn't started this conversation. It doesn't seem fair on Mr Barrington.'

Feeling distinctly uncomfortable, knowing that Hugh was in such close proximity, Sally looked across the room and caught his eye. He in turn, raised his glass in her direction, smiled and walked away to the table laid with an assortment of food.

Following her friend's gaze, Roz also raised her glass. 'Here's to Hugh

Barrington the Fourth,' she said, clinking her glass loudly against Sally's. 'Jesus! He's such a virile looking bastard, couldn't you just go over there and grope him all over?'

'No, I couldn't! For the past eighteen months I've managed to avoid all that unpleasant groping.'

'You don't mean Hugh Barrington's been—?'

Sally's face, that had been full of anger, creased into laughter. 'No, of course I don't stupid, I was referring to Richard!'

The two women exploded into giggles. Then, on a more serious note, Roz took hold of Sally's hand. 'I'm so sorry. I thought you and Richard had been really happy. I even remarked to Donald on one occasion that I thought the two of you were like us at that age—having a truly wild time together.'

When Muriel Baxter passed by, carrying her plate piled high with asparagus canapés, smoked salmon, scotch eggs and mini toad in the hole, Sally gave a wistful sigh. 'I suppose you could say my relationship with Richard was a bit like that: smoked salmon and fillet steak in the early days, then once he started drinking and coming home reeking of cheap perfume, we ended up with sausage and mash, if you get my drift.'

'Only too well, my dear,' Roz said, patting her hand in motherly fashion.

'I was going to offer you ladies some of these delicious canapés, but as you appear to be talking about fillet steak and sausage and mash, I doubt whether I can oblige.'

Sally and Roz spun round, aghast. Hugh Barrington was standing directly behind them. How long had he been there? More importantly, how much had he heard?

Conscious of her face flushing scarlet, Sally declined the plate of food Hugh was extending in their direction. 'N-no, thank you. I don't feel at all hungry. What about you, Roz?'

Downing the remains of her glass in one gulp, Roz fought hard for something to say. 'Me neither. I ate a huge dinner with Donald before I came out this evening. Which reminds me, I'd better ring him. If he is coming to fetch us, I'd rather it was before Edith summons us to the second half of the show. I expect the football has finished by now.'

'Apparently not,' Hugh enlightened. 'George tells me they're currently into extra time.'

Roz groaned, desperate for a means of escape. Her head was beginning to ache. 'Lord! I don't think I can stand it here any longer, Sally. What on earth can we do?'

'You could always let me drive you both home,' Hugh said with a smile, 'unless you want another glass of this delightful wine?'

'No thanks! I think we've had more than enough already. If you want one yourself, Mr Barrington, you go ahead. Sally and I can go and say our goodbyes, get our coats and wait by the front door. I could do with some fresh air.'

Hugh looked directly at Sally. 'Like you, I've also had enough. One glass was quite sufficient, particularly as I'm driving.'

Edith Hawtin stood in the hallway to wave them goodbye. 'It's so kind of you to take Roz and Sally home, Mr Barrington. You're sure it's not too far out of your way? We could always ring for a taxi.'

'Nonsense, it will be my pleasure.'

Moments later, watching Roz leaning unsteadily by Hugh's side, Sally followed them both to the car. Unlike Roz, she wasn't at all happy about Hugh taking them home, it didn't seem right somehow. On the other hand, faced with the alternative (films of Edith's cats), and as Roz was already clambering ungainly into the front passenger seat, Sally said softly, 'Perhaps you can drop me off first; that is, if Roz doesn't mind?'

Roz didn't mind at all, if it meant sitting in the luxury of leather upholstery for another twenty minutes. She even hoped some of the neighbours would still be up to see her travel home in style. Her sex life with Donald might never be boring, as for his choice of car… that was exactly like his job - exceedingly dull.

Despite her protestations, Hugh walked Sally to her front door.

'I'd prefer to know you were safely indoors,' he said, watching her take her key from her handbag. 'By the way, how's the bay tree?'

'Surviving, thank you. How's Stanley?'

'Oh, he's surviving too. The vet's suggested a course of injections, which might help. And, as long as he's not suffering, I shall be spared from making that final inevitable decision. I'm hoping when the times comes, Stanley will simply go in his sleep.'

'I hope so too,' Sally said, waving goodbye. 'I also hope Roz behaves herself on the journey home. She's still looking a bit green about the gills.'

'Don't worry,' Hugh called back. 'I'll drive very slowly, in case she needs to stop for some fresh air.'

It's not your driving I'm worried about, Sally thought to herself, closing the front door behind her. It's the beige leather interior of your beautiful car.

With a sideways glance in Roz's direction, Hugh manoeuvred his way carefully past several parked cars, overhanging branches and a tangle of overgrown shrubs. 'It would appear Mrs Palmer's neighbours don't share her enthusiasm for gardening… Are you all right Mrs Hughes? You look as if you…'

Meanwhile, in her bedroom Sally slipped off her shoes, hung up her trousers and top and sat facing her reflection in the mirror. For a brief moment she didn't know whether to laugh or cry. Roz had certainly made her laugh tonight, but there'd also been an air of melancholy to the evening. With talk of childless marriages and Serena Barrington's *arrangements*, Sally thought of the *what ifs* and the *if onlys* in relation to her own marriage.

If she'd had a child, would things have been any different? Reminding herself that it was Richard who'd been dead against having children, and that it was also too late to be having a post mortem, Sally went in search of some paracetamol. She was feeling decidedly woozy and her head ached like mad.

Tablets first, cleanser and toner later, she thought, putting aside a jar of cold cream.

Halfway to the bathroom, she was halted by the ringing of her doorbell. Had she left something in the car or, more importantly, had Roz proved to be a problem passenger in more ways than one? Alarmed, she reached for her bathrobe and hurrying downstairs hoped it would be Roz and not her boss waiting on the doorstep. The silhouette behind the stained glass panel was that of a man.

'Hello, Sal.'

'Richard! What are you doing here?'

'I've just called to say hello. Aren't you going to invite me in?'

'No, it's much too late and I have a headache.'

'That wasn't exactly what I came for, Sal—but now I come to think of it…' Looking her up and down, Richard's eyes caught sight of the delicately pleated satin and lace bra, where her robe gaped open.

'Well, well, do I detect some new undies? They look nice.'

Smelling alcohol on Richard's breath as he stepped forward and made a grab at the sash of her robe, Sally pushed him to one side.

'How dare you! What do you mean by coming here at this time of night? I do believe you're drunk!'

'No, Sal, not drunk. I've simply had a little drink to drown my sorrows. I've a slight cash-flow problem, you see. I thought you might like to help me out… for old time's sake, shall we say?'

'Old time's sake? You've had more than enough from me for old time's sake. I don't know how you've got the nerve to even ask!'

'I need some money, Sal, and as you've got yourself some rich new friends—lifts home in expensive cars, eh? I thought you wouldn't mind giving me a few hundred quid, or perhaps ask your sugar daddy to lend me some. Was it him who paid for your satin and lace?' Richard's hand reached into Sally's robe and made a grab at her breast.

This time pushing him away more forcefully, Sally screamed, her voice a mixture of anger and fear. 'Get out, Richard! Just get out! In future if you want to talk, I suggest you ring beforehand. As for giving you money… you've had more than enough out of me over the years.'

'We'll soon see about that.' Richard rubbed at his shoulder from where he'd fallen against the doorframe. 'I was only asking for a few hundred. Still, if you'd prefer, we can always sell this house.'

'Go to hell!' yelled Sally, slamming the door in his face.

With silent tears coursing down her cheeks and her heart pounding in her chest, Sally slumped to the floor, her whole body shaking.

'The bastard! The absolute bastard, how dare he? I will *not* sell this house.'

Desperate to still her trembling hands, she began tracing the shadows cast on her bathrobe: full blown roses and acanthus leaves from the stained glass panel of her front door. Suddenly and without warning, the pink and green shadows took on a different form. No longer were there delicate leaves and flowers, but instead a looming dark shape… the shadow of a man… which could mean only one thing—Richard had come back!

Frozen to the spot in terror, Sally forced herself to think logically. Whatever she did, she must not panic, nor must she open the door. Richard had been drinking, hadn't he? With luck, he would soon give up ringing her doorbell and go away. If only she hadn't replaced the battery…

Only he won't, will he, Sally told herself, her nerves at breaking point. With the ringing of her doorbell more persistent than before - and was that her neighbour's dog barking - there was only one thing to do. Bracing herself, she reached for a candlestick on the hall table, half opened the front door, and called angrily. 'Look, Richard! I thought I told you to go to hell! If you don't leave now I swear I shall ring the pol– '

Almost as if in slow motion, Sally watched as Hugh Barrington pushed open her front door and seizing the candlestick from her trembling fingers placed an arm about her shoulders.

'I thought… I thought you were Richard… H-he must have been waiting when you dropped me off… He wanted money and he tried to—'

'It's all right, Sally,' Hugh's voice reassured. 'I think I understand, but you don't have to worry any more. Richard's gone.'

Sobbing and in a state of shock, Sally fell into Hugh's arms. 'H-how do you know he's gone? H-he might still be out–?'

'He isn't. I saw him go when I pulled into the close. He took one look at my car and probably guessed that I'd come back to see you.'

'W-why did you come back?'

'Roz was concerned. She said she thought she saw Richard but wasn't quite sure. Initially, I thought it must have been Lillian's wine giving her hallucinations. However, just to be on the safe side, I thought I'd better come by and check. I would have been earlier only Donald insisted on giving me a blow by blow account of the football.'

Gulping back tears, Sally looked up at Hugh and forced a weak smile. 'T-thank you, it was very kind of you.'

'There, that's better,' Hugh said, watching Sally fumble unsuccessfully in the pocket of her bathrobe. 'Now, would you like my handkerchief? Isn't that what we men are supposed to do when we rescue damsels in distress? And… if perhaps we could go and sit somewhere warmer? There's a horrendous draught coming from this front door.'

Realizing that the door was still partly ajar, Sally locked and bolted it and ushered Hugh through to the lounge with a nervous smile and lit the gas fire. 'Excuse the muddle,' she said, moving papers from the sofa, 'I've been preparing for a seminar. Um… would you like a coffee?'

'You're sure you don't need a brandy after your unpleasant experience?'

'Oh, no! I've had far too much to drink tonight already; besides, I don't have any brandy. I could offer you a whisky.'

'Heavens no! Actually, I'd much prefer a cup of tea. At this time of night, I sometimes prefer tea to coffee. Especially since Lillian's wine was enough to destroy anyone's stomach.'

'But you didn't drink it.'

'So you did see me pour the rest of my glass into the aspidistra. I wasn't sure at the time. I simply sensed someone was watching me. Thanks for keeping mum.'

'I was hardly likely to tell. I only wish Roz and I had done the same. I'm afraid we got rather carried away.'

'Hmm. I did notice.'

Not wishing to be reminded of what had happened when she and Roz got carried away, Sally made her way to the kitchen.

'Assam, Earl Grey, fennel or peppermint,' she called, while filling the kettle, not realizing that Hugh had followed her into the kitchen.

'Earl Grey would be perfect. I prefer to leave the fruit and vegetables to Edith and Lillian Hawtin, and did you notice Muriel? I never realized she could eat and drink so m— What's wrong? You look as if you've seen a ghost.'

Sally stopped stirring her tea and let the slice of lemon float to the surface. 'I've just noticed your shirt.'

'My shirt?'

'You've got makeup on your shirt. When you first arrived and… gave me your handkerchief, I must have… Whatever will Mrs Barrington say?'

'As she's away at the moment, probably nothing. Mrs Burt, however…'

'Who's Mrs Burt?'

'Our daily help. She also does the laundry.'

Sally froze. She couldn't risk Mrs Burt telling Serena that Hugh had come home with make-up on his shirt.

'You must let me see to it,' said Sally, moving her cup to one side.

'I don't think that will be necessary. I have heaps of shirts.'

'Nevertheless, I insist. Foundation can be quite stubborn to remove. If I wash the collar now, I can dry it of by the fire in the sitting room. It won't take long.'

'As I've said already, it isn't necessary.'

Somewhat reluctantly, Hugh took off his jacket and hung it over the back of a kitchen chair. It was then Sally noticed the left lapel. 'Um- perhaps I should sponge that too. I think that's lipstick.'

Watching Sally reach for his jacket, Hugh began unbuttoning his shirt. 'I don't suppose you'd like my trousers as well?'

Conscious that her boss would soon be standing in her kitchen minus his shirt, Sally made a dash to the hallway and up the stairs. 'Mr Barrington, if you'd like to go back into the lounge, where it's warmer, I'll be down in a minute.'

Moments later, Hugh discovered the reason for her abrupt departure and the sound of hurried footsteps overhead.

Sally caught her breath, her face flushed, 'Here you are. I'm afraid this is all I could find. Richard - um - took all his clothes with him.

This, Hugh discovered, was a knee length cotton kimono. Accepting it with a gracious smile, he turned his back, removed his shirt and donned the kimono.

'There, how do I look? Probably not as dashing as Edith in her Hawaiian print. I can honestly say I've never worn anything quite like this before.'

Sally suppressed an embarrassed giggle as their eyes met.

'Now that I'm wearing your clothes, and as you are about to do my laundry, don't you think it would be more appropriate if we were on first name terms…Sally? I'd be much happier if you were to call me Hugh.'

Nodding shyly in reply, Sally took the shirt and hurried away to the kitchen.

Aware of running water and the sound of frantic scrubbing, Hugh settled back to read the Human Resources Management brochure. Sometime later, when Sally returned, he looked up in surprise. Not only was his shirt rolled up neatly in a clean white towel, but also Sally was in the process of placing it on the rug in front of the fire. He raised surprised eyebrows when she began pummelling it with her hands.

'What are you doing?'

'Drying your shirt. It's one of the best methods for removing surplus moisture. We used to do this when I was at university. It's great for drying tights and underclothes if you need them in a hurry.'

'Ah, I see, and I thought you were giving it a Swedish massage.'

Blushing at her earlier comments with regard to tights and undies, Sally felt the colour rise to her cheeks. 'I—um—suppose you've never had to…'

'Not exactly, as I don't wear tights. I don't think it's a method I've seen Mrs Burt use, either. Then again, she never seems to be in a hurry. Come to think of it… neither am I.'

Without warning, Hugh knelt down on the carpet beside Sally, ran a hand softly through her hair and took her in his arms. 'Sally, I….'

With the warmth of the fire at her back, Sally felt Hugh's lips brush gently across her eyes and cheeks, before resting fully on her mouth. Then, very slowly, he lowered her onto the floor.

Confused by the wine, her headache and the evening's revelations, before Richard's unwelcome advances, Sally struggled with the jumble of thoughts flashing through her head. What was it Roz had said earlier, when talking about Hugh? 'Couldn't you just…?' At the time she'd said a definite no. But these were not Richard's lips kissing her throat, nor were they Richard's hands caressing her body. This was Hugh Barrington and his touch was electric… he was also her boss!

Desperately freeing herself from his embrace, Sally became aware of the damp towel at her neck. She shifted uncomfortably and sat up.

'No, Hugh! We mustn't—you're my boss. It's not right—not here,' Her words poured out in an incomprehensible babble.

Making no attempt to draw her back into his arms, Hugh studied her thoughtfully and in silence. Unable to face his penetrating gaze, Sally turned away, holding her robe against her breasts. The kimono she'd loaned him lay in a crumpled heap by the settee.

'You know,' he said, reaching out for it, 'I think this probably looks better on you. Perhaps I'd better get my jacket. I'm sorry Sally… I should never have—'

'I'll iron your shirt,' she said hurriedly.

'There's no need, I can take it as it is…'

To Hugh's dismay, Sally had already disappeared, using the kitchen as sanctuary and the ironing board as defence against any further advances.

In the yellowing fluorescent light, the kitchen took on a seedy appearance, prompting Hugh to recall the weekend Sally had taken care of Stanley. How was it she'd described her home – *Halfway House* – because of all Richard's half-finished projects?

Deeply reflective, Hugh watched Sally's trembling hands as she painstakingly ironed the creases from his shirt. Then, not wishing to cause her further embarrassment, he turned his attention to the partially stripped paintwork and kitchen doors. Even the lounge with its threadbare carpet and ancient gas fire hadn't been much better, yet he knew he paid Sally a generous wage. On the other hand, as she'd told him that Richard had been here demanding money and…

Filled with an overwhelming desire not only to help Sally, but also to protect her from her bullying ex-husband, Hugh waited for her to unplug the iron. Then, as she reached out to offer him his shirt, he quickly took hold of her hand.

'No, Sally, don't pull away. I swear I won't hurt you and once again I'm truly sorry for what happened earlier. If you'll please just listen to me for a moment… I've a proposition to put to you. If, as you say, Richard's been threatening you for money, why not let me help you?'

'Help me? In what way?'

'Perhaps we could come to an arrangement? What if I were to suggest that you–'

Not wishing to hear more, the word *proposition* was more than enough. As for coming to an arrangement... Sally snatched her hand away from Hugh's grasp and glared at him indignantly.

'Mr Barrington, I'm sorry if I've given you the wrong impression. Things might be different for you and your wife; but unlike your wife's *little arrangements*, I have absolutely no intention of following suit. If you're suggesting that you want me to become your mistress and pay for my services, let me tell you, I prefer to earn my living as a personnel manager, or should that be Human Resources Manager? By the way, you never did tell me whose bloody stupid idea it was to change my title!'

Completely taken aback, it was some while before Hugh delivered his answer. Buttoning his shirt, he walked swiftly into the kitchen and returned with his jacket. 'Perhaps, in the circumstances, it's probably best if I answer your last question first. The Human Resources idea was my nephew's and I'm wholly in agreement with you, it is a bloody stupid idea! As for becoming my mistress, Sally, that wasn't exactly what I had in mind when I mentioned coming to an arrangement. What I was proposing was an interest free loan, merely to get Richard off your back. However, if you think my earlier behaviour was all part of a ploy to try the goods beforehand, then I regret to say it's me who's given you the wrong impression. Now, as it's getting very late and we're both working tomorrow, I suggest you take yourself off to bed. And by that I do mean alone.'

Ashen faced, Sally followed Hugh to her front door. How could she have been so utterly stupid? Kissing her in the heat of the moment had been one thing, and hadn't he already apologized for that twice over? Thinking that someone like Hugh Barrington would even suggest making her his mistress was quite another.

'I… I'm so sorry,' she gulped, unbolting the front door. 'It was all such a terrible misunderstanding. How can I ever apologize?'

'You don't have to, Sally,' Hugh replied, watching her shaking hands fumble with the front door key. 'Forget about everything that has happened this evening, at least for the moment; the important thing is to get a good night's sleep—or what's left of it. I'll catch up with you later at the office.'

To Sally's surprise, Hugh bent down and kissed her on the forehead. Then, brushing away the single tear on her cheek with his thumb, murmured softly, 'You know, I do think Roz was right, Edith's peapod *nouveau* has a lot to answer for. There'll be some very sore heads at Barrington's tomorrow.'

CHAPTER 4

Muriel Baxter, her eyes more heavily lidded than usual, sat nursing her aching head. Hugh, meanwhile, raged about the office like a bear with a sore one. At twelve-thirty, Roz and Sally faced each other over a frugal luncheon.

'Jesus! I felt awful this morning, how about you? Last night as I lay in bed, not only did I keep seeing the films of Edith's cruise, it was as if I was on the same bloody boat with her. The way the mattress kept rolling, and I knew it wasn't Donald being amorous… Sally, you're very quiet, are you OK?'

Deep in thought, Sally stirred her coffee. 'Shouldn't it be ship?'

'Ship?'

'Aren't cruise liners called ships and not boats?'

Roz stared at Sally's blank expression. 'I don't know, and I don't bloody care. All I care about at the moment is my head and you. Lord! I know I feel dreadful, but you most certainly look it. Here I am rabbiting on about boats—oh, all right, *ships*—and you haven't even told me what happened last night.'

'Last night?'

'That's right. I can see from the look on your face, he turned up. I was right, wasn't I? It was Richard I saw lurking in the shadows.'

Sally suppressed a sigh of relief, for one awful moment she thought Roz was talking about Hugh.

'Y-yes… it was Richard. He, um, wanted some money and tried to make a pass at me.'

'He what? He didn't hurt you, did he?'

'No, he was too drunk. I just pushed him away and slammed the door in his face.'

'The bastard, and did that work or did he come back?'

Sally wanted desperately to say to Roz, 'No, he didn't come back, but Hugh Barrington did and I made a complete and utter fool of myself.' Instead, despite the fact that Roz was her most valued and trusted friend, she shook her head as if in denial. This was a burden she must carry alone.

'Oh, Sally. You poor thing, no wonder you look so wretched. You know I nearly sent Donald round, but with the match going into extra time, and him having an extra lager or two, he would have been well over the limit. It would have been just his luck to be stopped by the boys in blue and breathalysed.'

Instead of me having my own boy in blue taking *my* breath away, Sally thought to herself. Hugh Barrington in his midnight blue Jaguar wearing…

'Look, if it happens again,' Roz began, misinterpreting the look on her friend's face, 'promise me you'll ring. Any time night or day and one of us will be round.'

Nodding and offering up a silent prayer that Richard wouldn't call again, Sally knew in her heart of hearts that he would. She also knew that she still had another four and a half hours before she could leave the office. So far today, she hadn't seen anything of Hugh, but last night he'd made it quite clear that he intended to speak to her sooner than later, which could only mean this afternoon, she concluded miserably, saying goodbye to Roz and making her way back to the office. There she discovered her secretary dealing with a phone call.

'Yes, I will. I'll tell her as soon as she's back from lunch.'

Replacing the receiver, Amy looked up at Sally's approach. 'That was Mr Barrington's secretary. Mr B wants to see you in his office at four o'clock sharp! Gracious, Sally, what have you been up to? Muriel says HB's in a foul mood, which isn't like him at all.'

'Nothing that I'm aware of; perhaps it's the end of month figures that have upset him,' Sally lied. She was hardly likely to tell her own secretary what had happened last night or that she'd woken up, still clasping Hugh's monogrammed handkerchief to her breast. If only she could get out of this afternoon's meeting.

'The end of month figures are nothing to do with us, we're human resources,' Amy said, handing Sally a large buff envelope.

Ignoring the envelope for a moment, Sally's eyes were fixed on her doorplate: HUMAN RESOURCES MANAGER. Where were her resources now? What excuse could she give to Hugh Barrington?

'It's the accommodation for your course,' Amy enlightened, pointing to the envelope. 'You were right. There is a female only annexe. It's very popular by all accounts, you've been allocated the last available room.'

Relieved that at least something had gone right today, Sally examined the contents of the envelope. At Rosebay Conference Centre, she wouldn't have to worry about unwanted male visitors knocking on her door at midnight. And, if she played her cards right, it might also be the excuse she needed to leave work early.

'Don't forget your appointment with Mr Barrington,' Amy called when at a quarter to four, Sally announced she'd got a headache and might just pop out for some fresh air.

'Just give me another fifteen minutes and I will,' Sally murmured to herself, hurrying towards the staff exit and her car.

Highly relieved that Hugh's office commanded a far better view than the staff car park, she nevertheless made a conscious effort to ring Muriel Baxter as soon as she arrived home.

'Please pass on my apologies to Mr Barrington. Tell him I have a dreadful headache and I also need to prepare for my seminar.'

'Of course I will, dear.' Muriel's hushed tone was sympathetic. 'I only wish I could finish work early. Between ourselves… Mr Barrington's been almost unbearable today, demanding all sorts of deadlines with the run up to Christmas. You're better off at home, Sally. I'll tell Mr B you're taking yourself off to bed, shall I? I'm sure he'll understand.'

Although about to remonstrate that was the last thing she wanted Muriel to say, particularly after last night's ghastly misunderstandings, Sally thought it best to say nothing at all.

Later, with her house in darkness, there was no one to hear the persistent ringing of her phone or answer the relentless chiming of the doorbell.

*

'It's very good of you to look after the children like this, Sally. A lovely surprise and so unexpected. Dave and I really appreciate it.' Jackie hugged her sister, fetched her coat and called to her husband that she was ready.

'Well, as I'm away on my course all next week, I thought I'd give you both a chance to paint the town red. Stay out as late as you like. I'll curl up in the spare room and see you in the morning.'

Trying to ignore her guilty conscience, Sally waved goodbye. Babysitting for her sister and brother-in-law had been the last thing on her mind when she'd returned home. On the other hand, they hadn't needed too much persuasion to leave their children in her care. Either way there was a positive outcome: Jackie and Dave were having a night out together and she wouldn't have to worry about Richard and Hugh calling at her door.

Glad to have something to occupy her mind, Sally went upstairs to check on her sleeping nephews before tackling what looked like the aftermath of a whirlwind in the family bathroom.

'Serve you right, Sally Palmer,' she muttered, stooping to retrieve soggy towels and an array of discarded clothes from the bathroom floor. 'This is judgement on you for your deception. And, as further penance, you can jolly well stay here tomorrow and help your sister have a blitz on this house.'

*

Exhausted by her labours and overwhelmed by the constant chaos of her sister's house, Sally returned home to the welcome solitude of her own. There, stretching luxuriously in the shower, she sighed with pleasure as needles of hot water washed away all traces of disinfectant, lavender polish and nappies.

Though feeding and changing her youngest nephew during the weekend had been a welcome experience, she still found herself wondering how Richard was coping with fatherhood. Five minutes later, totally saddened and confused, she swathed herself in fluffy pink towels, sprayed herself with her favourite perfume and concluded it was just as well she was going away. Rosebay Hall Conference Centre would be the perfect place for channelling her emotions in other directions.

Showered, refreshed and with her bag packed, Sally gathered her laptop and papers and was already on the road to Rosebay Hall half an hour before Hugh walked up to her front door with Stanley. The dog wagged his tail and looked up expectantly. Nonplussed by her absence, he ambled round to the back door, closely followed by Hugh, and once again headed straight for the bay tree.

'Well, old chap,' Hugh said, with a cursory glance in the direction of Sally's neighbours, 'perhaps it is just as well she's not at home to see that. Why don't we try again later?'

*

'The Role and Main Functions of H.R. in a Retail Environment' – discuss. Sally's eyes swam as she studied the title on the blank sheet of paper.

Seven hundred and fifty words. How am I going to think of seven hundred and fifty words when, at the moment, I can't even think of seventy! If it wasn't for the fact that tomorrow's the last day, I'd leave now. On the other hand, as I'll need my certificate for expenses…

Alone in the oppressive heat of her room, thinking of how she'd have to produce evidence of attending the seminar, Sally was briefly reminded of

Hugh. Hopefully by now he would have forgotten her non-appearance last Friday and with luck might also absent himself from the store for a while (which wasn't unusual), leaving the assistant manager in charge.

Sally doodled on her paper with her fountain pen, drawing a face in the letter O of role, and changing the 'H.R.' into 'H.B.'. From there she found herself scribbling *Hugh Barrington* in mock italic script, attempting to copy Laura's stylish handwriting.

Laura? That was it! Maybe Laura could be the answer to all her current doubts and fears. Why hadn't she thought of her before?

Remembering Laura's last letter, Sally was overcome with guilt. She had tracked down two wonderful local artists but as yet hadn't told her friend of their existence. Screwing up the sheet of paper, she tossed it into the bin. The HR project was thus dismissed; she would write to Laura instead.

That task completed, the letter was sealed with firm resolve, before she changed her mind. Moments later, and with an air of contentment, she propped it against her briefcase, walked to the far side of the room and flung open the window.

'Yes it is late,' she told her reflection mirrored in the double glazing, 'and it's also jolly dark out there, but the heat in this room is so claustrophobic…'

Reminding herself that the grounds were well lit and that she couldn't possibly get lost if she kept to the main pathway, Sally reached into the wardrobe for her walking shoes and tugged at the unyielding hanger for her coat.

Rosebay Hall, once the home of landed gentry, was set in twenty-seven acres of landscaped gardens and woodlands. The steps from the main entrance led down to a circular driveway bordered on all sides by broadleaf trees, while at the rear of the hall sunken gardens and gravel walkways led to the newly constructed accommodation block.

Tying the belt of her coat against the cold, Sally ventured past the shelter of the trees. There a penetrating north east wind tossed at her hair and stung her face. Unperturbed, she breathed in deeply and closed her eyes. This was exactly what she needed after almost a week spent in hot house conditions while people droned on and on about Human Resources.

Listening to the wind whistle and moan, as if it was breaking free of invisible chains, Sally revelled in its wildness as it spiralled its way up the hill towards the conference centre. Freedom: was that what she wanted? Freedom from Barrington's, and its myriad HR problems. Was she simply imagining it, or had things got worse since her job title had changed?

'Freedom,' Sally cried, the word seemingly tossed and caught by the wind before common sense and an inner voice intervened. '*Well, my girl, freedom might be what you want at the moment, but it certainly won't pay the bills. And, unless Laura comes up with an alternative solution—or you win the lottery—you're going to be stuck with HR for years to come.*'

Somewhat dispirited by this fact, Sally stood on the brow of the hill watching a convoy of cars head back to the conference centre. Most of the male delegates, she presumed, returning from sampling the local brew. For a brief moment, she heard their jovial voices and smelt the aroma of cigars and cigarettes as car doors opened and slammed shut. Then, when all was quiet, she continued her walk. Far better to let the men make their way, albeit noisily, back to their own quarters before she returned to hers.

Once more glad of the peace and solitude, Sally's train of thought came to an abrupt halt when she heard the sound of a church clock chiming eleven o'clock. Surely not, when she'd left the annexe it had been only… What time did the receptionist go off duty? What time did they shut the main doors?

'Please don't go off duty yet,' she gasped, running back in the direction of the hall, only to discover no sign of life and the dimmest of lights shining through the main glazed doorway.

Conscious of her legs aching and her breath rasping in the cold night air, Sally clutched at her side. To think I considered myself fit, she thought, making her way to the rear of the hall. Now, if I can work out the shortest route to the ladies' annexe…

Reaching the shelter of familiar trees, and pausing for breath against the trunk of an ancient oak, Sally started with alarm. With an agitated squawk, a roosting bird flapped noisily out of a nearby beech thicket, leaving behind… the sound of footsteps snapping on dead twigs. Footsteps that definitely couldn't be hers as she was standing stock-still!

All too late, realizing that it wasn't her presence that had startled the frightened bird, Sally felt a man's hand reach out and grab her by the shoulder. With her muffled screams silenced by her assailant, she found herself being dragged even deeper into the bushes. Terrified, she attempted to lash out in all directions and finding her arms pinioned and her mouth smothered, used the only weapon she had - her stout walking shoes. With a hefty kick, she landed a blow at what she considered to be shin height.

'My God, Sally! What are you trying to do, cripple me?'

Free from his clutches, Sally turned to find Hugh Barrington rubbing at his left shin.

'Hugh! What the… I thought you were—'

'It's perfectly clear what you thought, and if you'd only answered my calls I wouldn't have had to resort to SAS tactics. Sally, why the hell haven't you rung me? Muriel tells me she's left numerous messages for you here at reception. I would have thought from the fees this place charges, the staff aren't totally incapable of passing on a message.'

Sally said nothing, her attention was on the pain showing visibly in Hugh's face as he continued to rub his leg.

'Then again,' Hugh continued, 'according to the receptionist I spoke to earlier, you *have* received all your messages.'

'You've been up to the hall?'

'Of course! ' Hugh said angrily, standing upright once more. 'Don't you realize Amy and Muriel have been worried stiff about you? Especially since you reported in sick last Friday and what with your mobile switched off… not to mention how *I've* felt about you this past week.'

'You? I don't understand—'

'Don't you? Well you should! After what happened between us last Thursday, you could have at least given me the chance to apologize properly and explain. When you didn't come to my office on Friday afternoon as requested, and I went to your house…'

Shamefaced, knowing full well that she had ignored all Muriel's messages, Sally could only stare at Hugh in disbelief. 'Y-you went to my house?'

'Yes, I took Stanley with me—thought he might pave the way to peace. He seemed extremely disappointed you weren't at home and by the way I'm afraid he, er, watered the bay tree again.' Hugh was aware of Sally smiling in the semi-gloom. 'Hmm, it's nice to see I can still make you smile. A few moments ago… if looks could kill.'

'How is Stanley?'

'As well as can be expected in the circumstances. Speaking of which, I'd better get a move on. Serena has a habit of neglecting him if I'm not around. My guess is that he hasn't been fed this evening, let alone taken for a walk.'

'What are you doing here, then?'

'My dear Sally, I thought I'd already made that perfectly clear. I came to see you.'

Sally shivered as a gust of wind sent fallen leaves swirling about her ankles.

'You came all this way to see me? But it's over a hundred miles!'

'Exactly and now I have to drive over a hundred miles back again.'

'And have you eaten?'

'Not in the proper sense. Greasy spoon cafés and chips with everything hardly fall into my category of culinary delights.'

Hesitating, Sally said softly, 'They, um, give us hospitality trays in our rooms: tea, coffee and biscuits. I also have some fruit if you'd like it?'

'I certainly wouldn't say no to a cup of something hot.'

Allowing Hugh to take her arm, Sally led the way to the accommodation block along the gravelled walkway. 'I hope the side door is still open'

Casting a sideways look at Hugh, she studied the set of his jaw and noticed how the light from the mock Georgian lampposts accentuated the fine silver streaks at his temples. There was no doubt about it, Serena had landed herself quite a catch when she'd married Hugh Barrington. Fertile or not, he was the epitome of an attractive and desirable male.

Listening to the rhythmic crunch of their footsteps on gravel, Hugh dispensed with further conversation. Far better to wait until he and Sally were indoors. Even then he was unsure how to handle the situation. The uncertainty of this meeting had been bothering him for days.

Sally halted in front of the annexe door and pushed hard. 'Oh, no! This can't be locked too. It has to remain open, it's a fire door.'

'Open – yes,' Hugh confirmed, trying the door for himself, 'but from the inside only. You can't go around leaving doors like this unlocked at night you never know who's going to be lurking in the bushes.'

'*Oh, really*?' said Sally, with a wry glance in Hugh's direction and pressing her nose against the glass door, she began gesticulating to someone at the far end of the corridor. Presently a Muriel Baxter look-alike confronted her from the other side of the glass.

Recognizing her from the HR course, Sally pointed to the door-catch and mouthed, 'I appear to be locked out, can you open up please?'

With a scowl and a hefty push the woman raised the safety bar and the door opened wide.

Giving the woman a grateful smile, Sally hurried in to the warm. 'Thank you so much. For one awful moment I thought we were going to be locked out for the night.'

'We?'

Without saying a word, the other Muriel shot Sally a look of contempt as Hugh stepped from the shadows. Moments later, she stormed off down the corridor and slammed her bedroom door shut.

'Oh, my goodness, Hugh. I've just realized the significance of that withering look. This is the women only wing.'

'Then why not lend me your kimono again, I'll pretend to be your sister.'

'In the circumstances, I don't find that very amusing.'

'No, sorry. I suppose it isn't,' said Hugh, following Sally into her room. 'Does that mean I no longer get a cup of tea?'

Catching a glimmer of a smile in Hugh's eyes, Sally proceeded to fill the kettle. 'No Earl Grey I'm afraid, and it's that awful UHT milk, so would you prefer it black?'

With a shake of his head, Hugh deftly peeled back the corner of the tiny milk container and poured it into his cup. Sally meanwhile found the carrier bag containing apples and bananas and the remains of a packet of biscuits.

Declining the fruit, Hugh reached out for a digestive. 'If you're sure? You don't appear to have many left.'

'It doesn't matter. The course finishes tomorrow. You can take them for the journey home… if you wish. By the way, how is your leg? I'm sorry I kicked you so hard.'

'Hmm. I suppose I did ask for it, frightening you like that. I'd been waiting there for so long—I saw you go, you see—and was beginning to get desperate.'

Hugh lifted the leg of his trouser to examine the lower part of his shin. A thin streak of blood dribbled down his leg.

Sally stared in horror. 'Did I really do that? I'm so s—'

'Perhaps the England Manager should have you in his squad. Ever thought of changing your job?'

'As a matter of fact I have. Only this evening I was—'

Taken completely aback, Hugh dropped the leg of his trousers. 'Are you serious, Sally? You want to leave Barrington's?'

'To be honest I don't know what I want at the moment. After this past week dealing with Human Resources of every description…'

Reaching out for a box of tissues, Sally hurried into the bathroom, then running several under the tap, she returned and offered them to Hugh.

'I see,' he said, feigning disappointment. 'So even though it was you who inflicted this terrible wound on my leg, you don't intend to be my Florence Nightingale?'

Blushing, Sally found herself kneeling on the floor as Hugh raised the fine wool and worsted cloth once more. 'I'm afraid you're going to have the most awful bruise. Perhaps it needs more than just warm water and tissues, particularly where the skin is badly broken. What if I try and find the night porter - ask him if he has some antiseptic or iodine?'

'Oh, no you don't, sadist!' Hugh said, suddenly reminded of the school nurse and her yellow bottle. I refuse to let you—' but he got no further as a loud knock came upon the door.

'Mrs Palmer. Mrs Palmer! Will you open the door please!'

Opening the door, surprised to find the afore-mentioned night porter illuminated in the doorway, Sally noticed almost immediately that he was carrying a torch the size of a truncheon!

'Mrs Palmer, we've had complaints that you are entertaining a man in your room which, as you are only too aware, is a serious contravention of Rosebay Hall's rules. I must therefore ask–'

'But I'm not entertaining—'

'That's quite correct, she isn't,' Hugh declared, shaking down his trouser leg and striding to the door. For your information, Mrs Palmer happens to be one of my senior employees and I have just driven over a hundred miles to discuss an important business matter with her. One that cannot wait.'

Timid piggy eyes squinted up at Hugh through thick wire-framed spectacles. 'Then… if that is the case sir, this time I'm prepared to ignore it.'

'I should jolly well hope so, particularly as I don't much care for your insinuation that Mrs Palmer is *entertaining* me in her room!'

The porter shifted uneasily, still hovering in the doorway, unsure as to what he should do next.

'For your information,' Hugh concluded, beginning to close the door. 'I was about to leave, anyway. Now, if you'll allow me to finish off my conversation with Mrs Palmer… I'll bid you goodnight.'

'Very well. Goodnight, sir.'

Sally's face blazed with anger as she picked up the bloodstained tissue and threw it in the bin. 'How dare he, what an odious little man.'

'He was only doing his job. And according to Amy, you did ask specifically for the women only annexe.'

'Yes, I know, but as you said, you've come all this way to discuss Barrington's affairs with me.'

'That was merely an excuse, Sally, to save us both from an embarrassing situation. My visit has nothing to do with Barrington's. It's more to do with that other affair concerning us both last Thursday. I wanted to apologize and–'

'And I accept your apology. I'd also prefer to forget all about what happened.'

'Would you, Sally? Would you, really?' Hugh said, walking towards her and taking her in his arms, 'Because… somehow I don't think you're being entirely honest with yourself.'

Sally made no attempt at a reply as Hugh kissed her on the forehead, released her from his embrace and moved slowly towards the door. 'For my part, I definitely don't want to forget it. Let's talk again next week.'

*

Long after he'd gone, with the fragrance of his aftershave still lingering in the air, Sally was left to contemplate the significance of his parting comment.

'A hundred miles,' she asked herself. 'Why come a hundred miles simply to apologize?' She already felt bad enough about last Thursday, but one week on she'd only added to her humiliation by greeting Hugh Barrington the Fourth with a hefty kick on the shin. She was in no doubt that for the same offence, Hugh's illustrious ancestors would have had her banished to the colonies!

Watching the seconds slip by, Sally waited for the double zeros to herald the approach of midnight and another day ahead. In the semi-gloom the luminous double 00s peered eerily, like eyes in her direction. She smiled to herself, remembering last weekend's attempt at teaching her eldest nephew not only the time but also his numbers using the digital clock. Ben had been enthralled and excited by his newfound knowledge, announcing proudly to his parents at breakfast that he'd still been awake when they'd returned home at 'ooh ooh o'clock'.

Poor Ben, unable to cope with his parent's subsequent laughter and teasing, had taken solace in Sally's arms, even begging her not to leave when the time came to say goodbye.

'P-promise me you will come for Christmas,' he sobbed, 'because you're the only one who plays with me; Daddy's always too busy and Mummy's always seeing to the baby.'

Christmas, Sally thought her eyes beginning to close. She hardly dared think about Christmas.

CHAPTER 5

Clutching Laura's letter, Sally's spirits rose. It was the answer to all her prayers. She no longer need fear the daily confrontations with Hugh Barrington.

Hugh looked at her across the desk. 'You look jolly pleased with yourself. Have you won the lottery or been left a fortune?'

'Not exactly, but I have been offered another job.'

If Sally was expecting Hugh to look disappointed, then she was very much mistaken.

'I see… Naturally Barrington's will be sorry to lose you, but if you've had a better offer… How soon do you intend to leave?'

'My contract states three months' notice. I was wondering if—'

'How would the end of December suit you?'

Sally stared at him in amazement. He seemed positively delighted she was leaving.

'What about my replacement? Won't you need me to–?

'No problem at all,' Hugh interrupted, 'my nephew has been pestering me for ages to give him more responsibilities. You remember Gareth, don't you? He has a law degree but doesn't intend to join his father's firm. I'll get him to stand in for you until we find a proper replacement.'

Stunned, Sally left the office and went to find Roz. How would she react when told of the decision to join Laura at *Laura's Lair*?'

*

'Leave Barrington's to work in an arty-farty craft shop. My God, Sally, you must be mad! Can you really afford to?'

'No, not exactly, but I'll be living in the flat above the gallery, Laura won't be charging me any rent.'

'I bet she won't be paying you much in wages, either.'

Sally shrugged. 'No, but it will be enough to cover my needs.'

'What about your house?'

'I'm putting it on the market.'

'What!'

'Richard wants his share. He needs the money.'

'Hard bloody luck, he should have thought of that when he went off with Tarty Tracey.'

'Actually it was Sharon.'

'Shifty Sharon then. Sally Palmer you are a bloody fool! What on earth made you give in to Richard's demands?'

Sally emitted a deep sigh. 'I don't know,' she lied. 'Although Sharon is pregnant again and—'

'Hmph! That's Richard's fault, not yours. You should tell him to tie a knot in it!'

Still reeling from Hugh's response to her decision, and unable to defend herself against Roz's verbal salvo, Sally stood up. 'I'd better go. I've been asked to sort through some HR files for Mr Barrington's nephew.'

'Oh, you mean Gareth the Golden,' Roz sniggered. 'Well, dare I suggest that when you do start showing him around, make sure our Miss Kettle stays away from him. Otherwise she'll have her hand in his trousers before you can say Father Christmas!'

Sally hurried away. She couldn't cope with Roz in her present mood and only hoped the afternoon customers would be spared the same forthright advice.

*

On Christmas Eve an air of festivity filled the store. Garlands and bows decorated every department and last minute shoppers arrived en masse. A constant opening of doors heralded refreshing bursts of air to harassed shop assistants, and the sound of carols drifted in from the Salvation Army, who were playing on the market square.

'Merry Xmas, Mrs Palmer.'

Michelle Kettle, wearing mock reindeer antlers, waved from across a display of novelty bottle openers and oven gloves. Sally acknowledged her greeting with a gracious smile.

'Merry Christmas, Michelle.'

'Is it true you're leaving?'

Sally nodded to the questioning antlers and moved on. She had no intention of discussing her plans in public and couldn't wait for the store to close. Alone in her office she tidied her desk and studied the pictures on the walls. Should she take them down now or after Christmas?'

'Moving things out already, Sally?'

Unaware she was being watched, Sally dropped the wildflower print she'd been holding. It shattered on the floor, scattering tiny shards of glass.

Hugh rushed forward to help pick up the pieces. 'I'm so sorry. I didn't mean to startle you.'

Finding herself on her knees facing him, aware they were only inches apart, Sally lowered her gaze. She winced as a splinter of glass pierced her finger and oozed forth droplets of blood. Hugh took his handkerchief from his pocket.

'Don't you think this exchange of handkerchiefs and tissues is becoming quite ridiculous?' he murmured, wrapping the pristine white cotton round her finger. 'Now you'll have to let me hold that in place until the bleeding stops.'

'Sally, are you coming… Oh!'

Roz stood in the doorway, her bun adorned with tinsel and a sprig of mistletoe wedged between her ears and the frames of her glasses.

'Mrs Hughes, how delightfully festive you look. Have you come for Mrs Palmer? I'm afraid she's had a slight accident and cut her finger. Do you think you could go and find a plaster?'

'It's all right. I'm sure I don't need one, I'll just…' Sally felt Hugh squeeze her hand as he threw Roz a look of command.

With mistletoe and tinsel bobbing, Roz turned on her heels.

'Sally!' Hugh urged. 'There isn't much time before she comes back. Look, I'll give you the number of my mobile phone. Promise you'll ring me over Christmas.'

Sally hesitated for what to Hugh seemed like an eternity. 'What about your wife, won't she think it strange if I call you?'

'No, Serena never answers my mobile and I always carry it with me when I take Stanley for a walk, morning and evening. Ring me then, please!'

Roz's footsteps clicked down the corridor as she returned carrying a box of plasters.

Removing the handkerchief, Hugh watched as Roz fixed the plaster in position. With her back towards him, she was unaware of the small white card being placed under a potted Poinsettia. Hugh gesticulated to Sally, who in a daze merely nodded.

'A perfect job, Mrs Hughes, I'm sure I couldn't have done it better myself. Now I'd better wish you both a very Merry Christmas and be on my way.' With that, he plucked the sprig of mistletoe from Roz's glasses and kissed her cheek. 'Give my regards to Donald, won't you?'

'Well I never,' gasped Roz, after he'd gone. 'In all the years I've worked here, he's never done that before. He must be in a good mood!'

Roz put a hand to her cheek. 'Pity you didn't have any mistletoe, Sally. If only I was twenty years younger. Believe me, that was quite an experience.'

'Oh, I do,' Sally said, not needing to be told what it was like to be kissed by Hugh or held in his embrace. Even now the thought of it caused her heart to beat and her stomach to churn. Should she ring him though, as he'd insisted? That was the million-dollar question.

Watching Roz press the button for the staff lift, Sally turned sharply. 'Hold the lift for me. I've forgotten my Poinsettia. It was an early leaving present from George Fry.'

All the way down to the staff entrance, Sally kept one hand on the Poinsettia and the other fixed firmly in her pocket. Clasped between her fingers and palm was the slip of white card containing Hugh's phone number.

'Don't forget to ring…' Roz called to her across the car park. 'You promised to let me know if you can join us for supper on Boxing Night.'

'No, I won't forget to ring….'

*

On Boxing Day afternoon, Sally found herself in Thornhampton Park with her two nephews. Ben's brightly mittened hands clutched a bag of bread for the ducks and Nathan's rosy-cheeked face beamed out from a quilted snowsuit. Parking the buggy, she lifted Ben onto a nearby bench and helped him tear the bread into duck-sized pieces.

'We'll sit here and feed them; it's too dangerous to stand at the edge of the lake.'

'How much longer can we stay?' asked Ben.

'Mummy wants us home at four o'clock for tea.'

Ben scrutinized the face of his new Thomas the Tank Engine watch and grinned. 'Good, that means we can stay for a whole hour. When the little hand is on four and the big hand is at twelve…'

Sally was beginning to wonder if it had been such a good idea to buy Ben the watch. Ever since Christmas morning, almost every question he'd asked had been related to numbers and time. She concluded that was probably why Jackie had suggested this trip to the park, insisting she and Dave would stay behind to clear up the debris from lunch.

'You go and get some fresh air, Sally,' Jackie had urged, 'cooped up in that office every day, you probably need it.'

As yet Sally hadn't told them of her decision to leave Barrington's and when Dave had thrust a whole baguette at her, the moment seemed somehow inappropriate.

Nathan, who had been blowing bubbles at the ducks though berry red lips, suddenly stopped. His eyes widened with pleasure and he gurgled, 'Bow-wow, bow-wow.'

'No, Nathan', Sally corrected with a smile, 'ducks go quack, not bow-wow.'

'He's not looking at the ducks, he's seen a dog,' Ben said, sending a large chunk of bread skimming across the water.

Sally looked up. The approaching dog, sniffing at a piece of bread that had missed its target, looked familiar. 'Stanley?'

Recognition dawned in the rheumy old eyes as the animal lolloped towards her, his tail wagging furiously.

Hugh sat down on the bench. 'Well, this is a pleasant coincidence. What's this, the feeding of the five thousand?'

Sally studied the piles of bread at her feet. 'We were hoping to feed the ducks, but they seem a bit thin on the ground.'

'Not like the bread!' Hugh teased. 'I expect the ducks are like the rest of Thornhampton, sleeping off a rather large lunch.' He looked behind him. 'Apart from that fellow by the kiosk, we appear to be the only mortals in need of fresh air and exercise.'

'I thought you exercised Stanley in the mornings and evenings.'

'Ah, yes, I usually do. Why, did you try ringing me?' Hugh looked disappointed when Sally shook her head. 'Actually, I've come out to escape *The Sound of Music*. My sister-in-law and her husband are spending the day with us and Christmas wouldn't be Christmas for Vivienne without Julie Andrews, edelweiss *et al.* Is that what you're doing, Sally, escaping?'

'Not exactly, though I did get the distinct impression my sister and her husband wanted me and the boys out of the house.' Sally motioned to Ben, who was once more studying his watch, and the now sleeping Nathan.

Hugh raised an eyebrow. 'I can't imagine anyone not wanting you around.'

'Can't you, Hugh? Well, you obviously don't want me at Barrington's. You seemed positively delighted when I handed in my notice!'

'Of course I was,' said Hugh quietly, checking that Ben wasn't within earshot. 'That doesn't mean I don't want you around, Sally. Can't you see… that by resigning, you are making things so much easier for us?'

'Easier, in what way?'

'If you're no longer a Barrington's employee, it makes it easier for us to meet. Isn't that why you resigned?'

'No, it isn't,' Sally said, rising to her feet. 'I did it to avoid seeing you! Come along, Ben, time to go home.'

'But it's not four o'clock yet.'

'You're right, Ben, it isn't,' Hugh said, anxious for an ally. 'That looks like a pretty super watch you have there.'

Proudly, Ben extended his timepiece in Hugh's direction. 'Auntie Sally bought it for me for Christmas. Do you have a watch?'

Hugh turned back his sleeve to display the slim gold-strapped Rolex.

Ben seemed deeply disappointed. 'But it hasn't got any colours. Mine's red, blue and green, you see.'

'Yes, I do,' Hugh replied kindly. 'I'm afraid mine must seem very dull by comparison.'

Puzzling over Hugh's last word, Ben asked, 'And does your watch play a tune?'

Hugh shook his head. 'Sadly no, but I expect yours does.'

Ben proceeded to demonstrate how his watch played a tune, then reached for Hugh's hand as Sally walked behind with the buggy.

'You know it suits you—pushing a pushchair,' Hugh said, waiting for her to catch up. 'Who would guess you were a Human Resources Manager?'

'Not any longer, or aren't you forgetting?'

'Sally! Stop being so dramatic. Look, is it OK for Ben to have an ice cream or something? I mean, I don't want to cause problems – children accepting sweets from strangers and the like…'

Ben's ears pricked at the mention of sweets and he looked in anticipation towards his aunt. Sally nodded ruefully as Hugh gave Ben a five pound note and he headed in the direction of the kiosk by the park gates.

Hugh placed a hand on her arm. 'Please listen, and don't say a word until I've finished. As they say in that bizarre French sitcom, I shall say this only once. We haven't got much time to discuss things properly and it won't take Ben long to buy some sweets. I want you to be part of my life Sally, but what I need to know is do you feel the same about me, yes—or no? And in case you're thinking back to what happened between us, the night of Edith's film show, and also what you said at the time, being part of my life does not mean becoming my mistress.'

Shuddering at the reminder of what she had said, Sally made no reply. What about Serena, she wanted to ask, and what about the rumours that…? Hugh was right, there was no time, Ben was already on his way back.

'I got Smarties for me and Buttons for Nathan and here's the change.' Ben turned in Hugh's direction.

'Change too, eh? What an astute shopper you are. Perhaps you could put the change in your moneybox.'

'No!' Sally said. 'Sweets are one thing, money's another.'

Hugh, visibly hurt by her sharpness, accepted the change Ben emptied from the inside of his mittens.

'Don't worry, Sally, I'm not trying to buy him – or you – for that matter… if that's what you're thinking.'

At that precise moment, Sally didn't know what to think as she watched Hugh, with Stanley by his side, walking along holding Ben's hand. From their animated conversation, anyone would have thought that man and boy had been friends for years. Sally felt tears prick her eyelids as they walked out of the park.

'Auntie Sally, are you crying?'

'No, Ben darling. It's just the wind stinging my eyes.'

'But there isn't any wind.'

'I think there might be from up here, where the grown-ups are standing,' Hugh offered, glancing at Sally.

Puzzled, Ben looked up to where Hugh was towering above him. 'P'raps it might be a bit windy,' he conceded, exchanging Hugh's hand for his aunt's.

'I think this is where we say goodbye, Ben,' Hugh said, stopping by the Range Rover. As if reading Sally's mind, he added, 'Serena's banned Stanley from the Jaguar.'

As Ben knelt and patted the dog goodbye, Hugh looked anxiously in Sally's direction.

'I just need time to think,' she said in reply to his unspoken question, 'and then…I'll ring you.'

'Please do,' he whispered, 'anytime. You still have my number?'

Sally nodded and smiled as his hand brushed gently against her cheek.

'Isn't Stanley a funny sort of name for a dog?' asked Ben on the journey home. 'I've never met a dog called Stanley before.'

Come to think of it, Sally hadn't either. She would add that to the increasing list of questions already forming in her head. Questions she needed Hugh to answer.

In response to Ben's excited chattering while Sally helped him off with his coat, Jackie came running down the stairs. Spying her sister's flushed and dishevelled appearance, it didn't take long to work out what had taken place in her absence.

'We just sort of… after you left with the boys,' Jackie said, buttoning up her blouse and checking the zip of her skirt. 'I'll, um, make Dave a cup of tea and then get cracking on that.' Nodding in the direction of the kitchen sink, where the pile of saucepans and greasy dishes remained untouched, she plonked a kiss unceremoniously on Sally's cheek. 'Thanks for taking the boys out, I can't begin to tell you what a lovely afternoon we've had.'

Wishing to be spared the details, Sally pretended to ignore her sister's state of undress. Busying herself with Nathan and the buggy, she hurriedly changed the subject.

'I'll give you a hand with the boys' tea, if you like, and then I must go home. You haven't forgotten I'm going to Roz and Donald's for supper?'

'Lucky you! Civilized suppers with civilized people. I've forgotten what it's like since we had the boys. Still', she said, smiling lovingly at her two rosy-cheeked offspring, waiting for their tea, 'we can't have it all, can we? 'You're the clever sophisticated one and I'm the one that churns out babies.'

'You're not pregnant again?'

'Lord, I hope not,' cried Jackie, thinking of the past two hours.

*

Driving to Roz and Donald's, Sally recalled her sister's words. *You're the clever, sophisticated one.*

'Hmm, I wonder what she'd think if she knew I might become Hugh Barrington's mistress,' she whispered to the confines of her car.

He didn't say mistress, her conscious reminded. *And what's with the "might"? You certainly didn't say no to his proposal, did you?*

'Considering I don't even know what he *is* proposing,' Sally said to her reflection in her rear view mirror. She panicked, pulling into Roz's drive, would Hugh be expecting her to share snatched afternoons in bed, just like Jackie and Dave? Only it wouldn't be when they were free of Nathan and Ben, but free of Serena!

'Gosh! You look flushed,' Roz said, taking her coat. You're not going down with flu, are you?'

'No, perhaps it's just my age.'

'I would have thought you way too young for the menopause and haywire hormone bit. Still, I'm glad it's not 'flu. We can't have you missing your last few days at Barrington's.'

'Who's got haywire hormones?' Donald asked, coming into the hall.

Roz pinched his cheek. 'No, one, big ears! And we know there's nothing wrong with yours, don't we Donald?'

Roz turned and winked deliberately at Sally. 'Right,' she said, 'come along and meet the boring old farts we've gathered here this evening.'

Donald took Sally's arm in fatherly fashion. 'Just ignore my wife, she's been at the gin. I'm sure you'll get on well with Sheila and Gavin… and Bernard. His wife died about eighteen months ago. No, don't look so alarmed, we're not trying to match-make. It's just that Christmas can be such a lonely time if you're on your own.'

*

Later, back home again and alone, Sally reflected on Donald's words. He was right Christmas could be desperately lonely. OK, so she was luckier than poor Bernard, who appeared to have no one. She had Jackie and Dave and the boys and numerous friends, of course. But it wasn't quite the same as having someone to share your innermost thoughts with… or someone to snuggle up to on a cold night like tonight.

With a determined effort, Sally tried to erase from her mind the thought of Jackie and Dave and even Roz and Donald entwined in each other's arms. With a dry sob, she reached for a pillow and drew it close. Moments later, crying silent tears, she whispered softly, 'Oh, Hugh, I do want you, but I'm so frightened of letting it show.'

*

Early next morning, following a night of troubled sleep, Sally rose to the sound of persistent drizzle on the window panes. The weather on the penultimate day of the Christmas holiday matched her mood. Usually, with Christmas falling at a weekend, she welcomed the thought of two extra days at home. Today, however, she couldn't wait to get back to Barrington's, finish her contract and put that chapter of her life behind her.

Her enthusiasm diminished rapidly when she contemplated the next chapter of Sally Palmer, aged thirty-three and a half. It wasn't *Laura's Lair* that bothered her, but the association with Hugh. Gingerly, she picked up the phone and dialled the number. Almost immediately Hugh answered and she hung up. Terrified he might have realized who it was, and call back, she dashed into the bathroom, switched the radio to its highest volume and turned on the shower. Half an hour later when the doorbell rang, she froze.

'Richard! Won't you come in?'

Surprised not to have the door slammed in his face, Richard followed Sally down the hallway to the kitchen. His eyes took in her freshly showered appearance and the sweet fragrance of shower gel and dusting powder wafting behind her.

'Sorry to call at such an unearthly hour, only—'

'That's all right, I was about to make some coffee. Would you like a cup?'

Richard nodded and looked about the neat and tidy kitchen. 'Looks like you've been pretty busy. I see you've finished the decorating.'

'It's a question of having to, isn't it? When you rang with your good news and said you wanted the house sold…'

'Good news?'

'That Sharon's expecting again.'

Richard groaned, watching Sally pour hot water into the cafetiere, 'I don't know what's so good about that.'

'Oh, so it wasn't planned then?'

'No, it bloody wasn't!'

'Don't they say it's better to have your children close together, if you can? Sharon's still young and by the time the children are grown up, she'll be more like a sister than a mother.'

Sally turned her back, unable to suppress a giggle. She was enjoying watching Richard in his present predicament. She passed him his coffee.

'Still, I don't suppose you've come to talk about babies, have you?'

'Too right I haven't. Kylie kept us awake all last night, she's teething—and

Sharon's got morning sickness. As a matter of fact, Sal, I wanted to see you… to see if you're OK.'

'Me? As you can see, I'm fine and as I told you on the phone, the house is going on the market next week. With regard to the decorating, I merely wanted to finish as many jobs as I could – to get a better price.'

'Did you do everything yourself?'

'Of course. Didn't you think I was capable?'

'No, it's just that I thought your new man-friend might have helped.'

'What man-friend?'

Richard sensed the tone of indignation in her voice. 'Er… I thought perhaps you might have… especially as I've been trying to get hold of you. You weren't here at Christmas and last night—'

'Last night, not that it's really any business of yours, I was making up an odd number at supper. There I partnered an elderly widower, hardly a man-friend.'

Appearing to delight in this information, Richard walked round the table towards Sally. Gently fingering her fringe where it lay still damp against her forehead, he then dropped his hands to encircle her waist. Stunned, she soon sensed what was coming next and pushed him away.

'Come on, Sal. You must be lonely, if you haven't got anyone, and it must be ages since you've… There's no harm in it, is there? Sharon's always tired these days.' Richard's voice was pleading as he grabbed Sally roughly by the shoulders.

'Sally, please … for old time's sake. She won't find out.'

'What do you mean *she* won't find out? No, don't answer that, as I suspect what you're really getting at is that you're hardly likely to tell your second wife - who's pregnant with your second child - that you've been back to see your first wife, begging for a screw!'

'Sally!' Desire in Richard's face gave way to shock and indignation as she pulled away from his clutches.

'Oh, don't look so shocked, Richard, it's clearly what you came for, isn't it? I was a fool not to recognize the signs earlier. In fact I can see it all now. What was it you said? The baby's been awake all night teething and Sharon's always tired. Don't you mean too tired for sex? All I can say in response, is that you clearly still think only of yourself!'

Richard raised his hand as if to strike her, then stopped as if frozen in time. He slumped onto a kitchen chair and buried his head in his hands.

'What have I done to us, Sally? What have I done to you? I've never heard you speak like that before.'

'Perhaps not,' Sally said, opening the back door, 'but there's always a first time. As for what you've done to me, Richard – I think you've just brought me to my senses. Now, as I'm sure we no longer have anything else to say to each other, I think you'd better go.'

'But—'

'Please go!'

Outside the back door, Richard pulled up his jacket collar against the continuing drizzle and shot one last, pleading look in her direction. Lashing out in frustration with his fist, the bay tree toppled over.

CHAPTER 6

Distraught and angry, Sally dialled Hugh's number. She had no idea what to say and only hoped he was alone and able to answer his phone.

'Dear God, please let him be there,' she whispered, keeping an anxious eye on the door in case Richard should return.

Her heart lurched as the monotonous ringing tone was silenced by Hugh's reassuring voice.

'Hugh… I… it's…'

'Sally, is that you?'

'Yes, I need to speak to you. Can we meet… now?'

'Now? But Sally, I'm—'

Sally ran her hands through her hair. 'I'm sorry, I should have realized it wouldn't be convenient… it doesn't matter.'

'Sally, stop! Don't hang up, of course we can meet, it's simply that I'm in the middle of Campion Forest with Stanley, so not exactly in the area. It will take me some time to get back to the car.'

'Perhaps… perhaps I can come and meet you half way?'

'What… yes, that sounds like a good idea. Look, the line's pretty bad and I can hardly hear you. Do you know Campion Forest well?'

'Not really, there's so many paths and… but I know Campion Church.'

'Right then, behind the church is the village hall and car park. Wait for me there and I'll be as quick as I can. Sally, is everything all right? You sound upset.'

'I'm OK now, but Richard's just been and…'

Hugh's heart filled with dread at the mention of Richard's name. He remembered the night of Edith Hawtin's film show. 'Tell me when I see you, Sally. It will take me about half an hour to get out of here and…

Sally…'

'Yes.'

'Drive carefully.'

'I will,' she said, wiping her eyes and hanging up the phone.

A noise at the back door made her jump but she realized it was only the bay tree rolling around in its pot. 'Poor old bay tree,' she murmured, 'Peed on by Stanley and used by Richard as a punch bag. Righting the upturned pot, she went back indoors for her handbag and car keys. Only then did she catch sight of herself in the hall mirror. With no make-up and still wearing the jeans and sweatshirt she'd slipped on after her shower, she did a double take.

'There's no time to change and beautify yourself, just go, and if he changes his mind when he sees you, well… it's just too bad.'

With the windscreen wipers working full pelt, Sally drove out of Thornhampton and beyond to where the road forked to Campion Magna. Her delight at being in the vicinity was short-lived when she looked at her petrol gauge. It was at zero and the warning light was flashing. Why hadn't she seen it before? There was nothing for it but to keep going in the hope she reached Hugh before her car ground to a halt.

With row after row of dark coniferous plantation on either side of the road, she assumed she'd found Campion Forest and peered anxiously ahead for further road signs and the merest glimmer of a church spire. Perhaps if she opened the window, she might even hear the sound of a church bell. Sadly, there was neither sight nor sound of the church or its bells, only the rain pouring through the window and the debilitating sound of an engine gasping for petrol. Sally slumped across her steering wheel in disbelief.

'Damn! Damn! Damn! Now what do I do?'

Her immediate reaction was to wind up the window, lock the car and run. But run where and for what? There certainly wouldn't be any petrol stations here and she couldn't just run about blindly in the hope that she would bump into Hugh. Besides, she was hardly dressed for trekking through mud-filled woodlands.

'Woodlands – more like wetlands,' she muttered, watching the rain pour down the windscreen in rivulets. 'It's going to be like wading through peat-bog out there.'

Studying her trainer-clad feet, Sally peered once more into the forest. The view was the same apart from the fact the windscreen was becoming steamed up, both from the warmth of her body and the penetrating dampness. Rubbing at the condensation with a handful of tissues, she decided to open the window again.

For a brief moment the rain eased and in the distance she thought she heard… yes, she did… a clock strike! Quickly she looked at her watch. It was a quarter to nine now, so at nine o'clock, it would be striking the hour. This meant she had a quarter of an hour to collect her thoughts, concentrate her hearing and be prepared to run like mad in the direction of the chimes.

The first ten minutes passed quickly enough as she searched in her handbag for a comb and the chance of finding some make-up.

She gave a resigned sigh, looking at the base of a lipstick. *Wild Plum*, how very appropriate, the wild certainly applies in more ways than one. Not only do you look like the wild man of Borneo, Sally Palmer, but this is a totally wild and plum-stupid situation you've got yourself into. For someone who used to go to summer camp, you are anything but prepared, although… Moments later, a flash of inspiration caused her to discard both lipstick and comb as Sally remembered her winter emergency bag.

Hurrying to the boot, she cast aside assorted debris from pre-Christmas shopping trips and visits to the tip and found the holdall she was looking for. Inside was a small shovel, a torch, supermarket shopping bags - held in a roll with elastic bands - an old tartan travel rug, an ancient plastic raincoat and a misshapen bar of chocolate.

When the church clock struck nine, Sally was ready. Newly attired in an assortment of tartan, polythene and plastic, she ran as fast as her legs would carry her with the rain driving full into her face.

On seeing the church spire, the rain mingled with salty tears on her cheeks and she found herself running straight into Hugh's arms as he emerged from the Range Rover.

'Sally! Thank God. You've no idea how worried I've been… I thought I'd missed you.'

'I thought I'd missed you too,' she sobbed, 'then I got lost and ran out of—'

Hugh went to stroke her hair and found a handful of plastic. Sally's shoulders shook once more. 'There's no need to cry. You're here now. I'll take care of you.'

'I'm not crying, I'm laughing,' she said, looking up into his face through a veil of tears and laughter. 'Just look at me, Hugh, is this how you visualized our first assignation?'

For the first time since she'd arrived, Hugh studied her appearance and roared with laughter. 'Well, Mrs Palmer, I've always credited you with being a stylish dresser. Without doubt there's a certain *je ne sais quoi* about your present attire. Ralph Lauren it most certainly isn't!'

Pulling back the hood of the raincoat, previously repaired with Cellotape, Sally looked away. 'Do you… do you still want me, Hugh?'

'Want you? My darling, Sally, if only you knew. Of course I want you, more than I think you realize. Nothing would please me more than to take care of you.' Hugh said softly. Then, tilting her face towards him, he kissed her tenderly and led her to the car where Stanley was sleeping soundly after his walk.

'There is one thing, though,' he continued with a glint in his eye as he helped her into the Range Rover. 'I would very much appreciate you toning down your style of dress somewhat when we're out together… Tartan rugs around your waist and polythene bags on your feet, despite being held in place with colour co-ordinated elastic bands, are hardly conducive to—'

'You intend to be seen in public with me? Is that possible? What if Serena should—?'

'She won't. We'll be very discreet both in Thornhampton and away from it.'

Feeling distinctly uneasy, Sally bit her lip. Now that she'd come this far, in more ways than one, shouldn't she ask Hugh the long list of questions that had caused her such a troubled sleep?

Hugh put a comforting hand on her arm. 'Don't look so worried.'

'I'm not exactly worried, I simply can't help thinking that if people see us together – or if they find out about us – they will think I'm your mistress. The mere connotation of the word… conjures up…'

'Yes, go on.'

Sally fingered a frayed corner of the tartan rug, unable to look Hugh in the eye. 'Well, apart from it sounding so cheap and sordid, I can only think of peroxide blondes with scarlet mouths and false fingernails, wearing nylon see-through negligees… trimmed with marabou.'

'Good grief! Your mind has been working overtime. What a ghastly thought, I'd rather you keep your plastic bags and elastic bands in that case. Hugh reached for her hand. 'Seriously though, this is neither the time nor the place to discuss what's troubling you or the state of my marriage. Goodness! Your hands are freezing. I'll switch the heater on. The sooner we get going, the better. Have you had any breakfast?'

'No, only a cup of coffee at home and a few squares of chocolate I keep in the car for emergencies. Would you like some?'

Hugh shook his head when Sally offered him what remained of the mangled chocolate bar. Smiling, he reached into the pocket of his Barbour. 'Hmm, remind me never to get stranded with you in winter, if that's all you take by way of emergency supplies. Have a sip of this instead.'

Sipping reluctantly from the hip flask, Sally felt the liquid burn her throat. She grimaced but it had the desired effect. Before too long she felt herself not only warmed by the brandy and enveloping heat of the car, but also Hugh's presence.

'We'll collect your car later,' he said, aware of her anxious look in its direction as they drove past. 'Let's get our priorities right. First of all, you need a change of clothing and some breakfast.'

When Hugh looked about the kitchen, his gaze fell upon the two coffee cups. 'Richard must have called early. Do you want to tell me about it?'

Sally gestured to her wet clothes. 'I'd rather—'

'Of course you would. Right, upstairs with you and have a hot bath. I'll give you a call when I'm ready for you.'

Panic-stricken, Sally stared back at him. Had it come to *that moment* already? Hugh didn't believe in wasting time, did he? Yet in the car, he'd spoken of taking things slowly, perhaps having a weekend away – 'to get to know each other,' as he'd so tactfully put it.

Hugh reached for Sally's hand. 'Don't look so alarmed. I suppose what I should have said was I'll call you when your breakfast is ready. Now if you'll just show me where you keep the eggs, and if you don't mind my fetching Stanley in from the Range Rover…'

Breathing a sigh of relief, Sally pointed to the pantry. 'You'll also find the bowl and blanket that I used for Stanley, in that end cupboard,' she called making her way upstairs. 'Whatever you do, don't leave him out in the car.'

In the peace and quiet of her bedroom, Sally contemplated the morning's events. So far, she'd had a shower followed by a confrontation with her ex-husband, a drenching in the woods and an assignation with her boss. Now here she was, barely two hours later, about to have another soaking while downstairs, Hugh was making her breakfast!

*

Hugh placed scrambled eggs and toast on the table in front of her.

'Feeling better?'

'Yes, thank you. Though, I feel it should be the other way round, me getting breakfast for you.'

'There'll be time for that another day… I hope.'

Sally blushed. 'Hugh, as I said before, there's so much I need to ask you.'

'I know, but eat first,' he said, bending to kiss her cheek, 'And I promise we will talk about everything that's troubling you.'

Later, watching Sally put away the last of the breakfast dishes, Hugh cast an admiring glance about the kitchen. No longer were there tins of paint, Polyfilla and brushes adorning the work surfaces.

'You've been very busy since I was here last.'

'Yes, I've been trying to finish all of Richard's halfway projects. It's a case of having to, really. I'm putting the house on the market.'

'A good idea too, if I may say so. I think one of those flats at Elmsmarsh would be ideal for you. You deserve somewhere nice.'

Sally spun round to face him. 'Elmsmarsh?'

'What's wrong, don't you like the idea of Elmsmarsh?'

'There's certainly nothing wrong with Elmsmarsh, apart from the fact that even the smallest flat would be well out of my price range. I was planning to live in the flat above Laura's Lair.'

'You've already told your friend, Laura, about us and our arrangement?'

'Of course not. Until an hour ago, I didn't even know myself that you and I were going to be *us*. As for arrangements, I'm still not sure what you have in mind.'

Relieved, Hugh led Sally by the hand into the lounge, closely followed by Stanley.

'Right,' he said, joining her on the sofa, 'the way I see it is this. You sell your house and work for Laura as planned. That way you still have an excuse to come into Barrington's.'

'How?'

'I want to open an art and picture department on a small scale and you can advise me on prints and the like. And, in case you're wondering, it will all be above board. We shan't be taking any business away from Laura. In fact it could be the opposite.'

Sally stared at Hugh in disbelief as he continued.

'However… I'm really not keen on you living above Laura's Lair and would prefer you to take the Elmsmarsh flat. I'm getting the key the day after tomorrow.'

'You are what! How long have you been planning all this?'

'Not planning, Sally, merely hoping, since the night I called back here after I took Roz home. You seemed so vulnerable and I couldn't bear the thought of you being alone here, with Richard on the loose and him behaving so unpredictably. Of course, if you and Richard were still happily married… I don't believe in relationships with other men's wives.'

'But it's OK for me to have a relationship with another woman's husband?'

'Oh, dear! Do I detect a distinct note of sarcasm there?'

'You are still married, aren't you?'

'Yes,' said Hugh, 'but in name only, unbelievable though it sounds. Things have been very difficult between Serena and myself for many years now. I'm surprised you haven't heard the rumblings of gossip at the store – or maybe you have. As I recall, didn't you once mention Serena and her 'little arrangements'?'

'Um – I think I did, but only a short while ago, when you were talking about us and the Elmsmarsh flat, you even used the same word… *arrangement*.'

Hugh rubbed his chin. 'Ah, yes, *mea culpa* too. There is one difference however, Serena's been having casual affairs for years, usually with handsome young skiing instructors or else with–'

'Are you saying you don't mind?'

'Of course I mind, or perhaps I should rephrase that to *I used to mind.* Initially, following the unexpected death of my father, when I was forced to take over the running of the store at quite an early age, I suppose some people would say I neglected Serena, she certainly did–'

'But managing Barrington's is a huge responsibility,' Sally interrupted, 'particularly in this day and age. There's not only competition on the high street from shops selling cut-price goods, but also cheap clothes made in sweatshops and–'

'And I can see from the look on your face, Sally, that unlike Serena, you would have understood why I had to work such long hours, simply to keep Barrington's afloat, not to mention keeping our loyal workforce in employment. Some of the staff have been with us ever since they left school. Sadly, Serena was not quite so understanding. She was forever telling me I was being totally unreasonable, inconsiderate and extremely selfish when I spent so much time at the store, yet I never once complained while she went off on her numerous holidays. These days, when Serena is at home, she barely has time to think of anyone other than herself and as we've no children…'

Watching Hugh's pensive and solemn face, Sally was about to break into his chain of thought when she heard the ringing of his mobile. Gently Hugh put a finger to Sally's lips as he answered.

'Serena! Oh no, not too wet. I managed to take shelter from the worst of it. Stanley got a bit muddy though. You forgot what? OK. No, don't worry. I'll be with you as soon as I can. Bye'.

Sally looked downcast. 'I take it you have to go.'

'Afraid so. Serena's invited some very boring people to lunch and forgot to tell me.' Hugh looked at his watch. 'Getting home in time won't be a problem, but it will take me ages to get Stanley cleaned up before Serena even lets him near the house.'

'You could leave him here and I'll clean him up for you.'

'That's a wonderful idea, Sally, and one I'd love to take up. However, much as Serena loathes Stanley, I think even she might begin to wonder how he just happened to be with you.'

With Sally fetching his Barbour, Hugh thought lovingly of the past two hours spent in her company. Perhaps, before too long, they could spend more than just a few snatched hours together.

Sally was looking up at him with questioning eyes. 'Shall I ring you later?'

'That's probably not a good idea as I shall be surrounded by people for the rest of the day. However, I could meet you this evening, when I take Stanley for a walk. It would probably be safer than phoning. We don't want to end up like the Royals, do we, with people listening in.'

Sally smiled and lifted her face to be kissed. 'Enjoy your lunch and if I go for a run about nine o'clock, perhaps I might just happen to bump into you near the car park by the lake.'

'I hope you do. In fact, I sincerely hope you do.'

Later that evening, it was Stanley who first recognized Sally's approach. He pricked up his ears and wagged his tail furiously. Hugh held out an arm to steady her, as she stopped to catch her breath.

'When you said you were going for a run, I thought you meant a gentle jog around the park. You look as if you've just finished a marathon!'

'I feel as if I have. Tell me, Hugh, is there a sadistic streak in you that likes to see me looking my worst? You've obviously forgotten, as I did, my car is still in Campion Forest!'

Hugh clasped a hand to his head. 'My God! So it is; we never went back for it. My darling, I'm so sorry. But why run all the way here, why not ring me or get a taxi?'

'A, because you told me not to ring you and B, because my handbag was in the car too. If you remember when you took me home this morning, we went in by the back door and I used the spare key from under the stone trough.'

Hugh refrained from adding, while Stanley watered the bay tree again. Instead he held her in his arms and kissed her tenderly. 'You know, Sally, while this isn't exactly fulfilling your picture of me, waiting for you in a bordello, as you swathe yourself in see-through nylon and maribou, I can at least get you some petrol for your car.'

*

'It's so quiet,' Sally whispered, watching Hugh pour petrol into her tank.

'Yes, thank goodness. At least I have you all to myself again.'

'You've forgotten my chaperone.'

Hugh studied Stanley's soulful eyes gazing down at them from the Range Rover. 'Mmm, so I have. I suppose I shall just have to leave him behind when I take you away to my castle hideaway.'

'That sounds intriguing, I can't wait.'

'You think I'm joking?'

'Well…'

Putting down the can and replacing the petrol cap, Hugh stood up. 'Actually I lied about the castle, I don't own it and it's a hotel.'

'What if someone recognizes us, or, more to the point…*you*?'

'I doubt it. The weekend after New Year is bound to be quiet. I'll book us a suite and let you know the arrangements later. In case you've forgotten, it will soon be your last day at work and, as head of Barrington's, I shall be taking you out for a farewell lunch.'

The word *farewell* struck a chord in Sally's heart. Until that moment, she'd been enveloped in the almost magical presence of the fir trees, still damp from this morning's downpour. Cocooned in their gentle whisperings, she felt safe and protected from the outside world. But once she left them - and Barrington's too – what would fate have in store?

CHAPTER 7

Amy entered the office carrying two bouquets, one of yellow roses and the other of mixed flowers.

'These have just arrived for you, Sally. Goodness! This office is looking more like a florist's shop every minute.'

Sally looked up from her desk, which was already covered with assorted plants, flowers and good luck cards. 'Oh, dear, this is all so overwhelming. I never expected any of this.'

'As you wouldn't agree to an Edith Hawtin type leaving do, I suppose everyone wanted to show you just how sorry they are to lose you.'

Sally opened the cards attached to the two bouquets. Amy was watching and waiting.

'Well… who are they from?'

'The mixed bouquet is from Roz and Donald and the yellow roses are from… Mr Barrington.'

'How kind,' Amy said, peering over Sally's shoulder to study the inscriptions. 'I should have realized the roses were from HB, they are his trade mark. And of course Roz is certainly going to miss you. She always terrifies the life out of me, yet people come back year after year to be measured by her. I understand she's on her third generation of bosoms now.'

Only half listening to Amy's comments, Sally was too preoccupied reading Hugh's message. She was hugely relieved to see that it contained nothing too personal. "*Barrington's won't be the same without you. With every good wish for the future, Hugh Barrington.*"

Amy picked up a stray rose petal. 'I understand he's taking you out to lunch.'

'Yes, but it's all above board,' Sally added a little too quickly. 'Gareth, his nephew, is also joining us. Apparently he wants to pick my brains and tie up a few loose ends before he takes over in earnest.'

Amy raised her eyebrows. 'You can tell him from me that he can pick my brains and tie up my loose ends anytime he likes.'

'Why not tell him yourself next week, when you start working for him?'

'I wouldn't dare!'

'Wouldn't dare what?' came a familiar voice. 'Or is that a secret between you two ladies?'

Amy and Sally looked at each other and said nothing. Hugh was standing in the open doorway. 'Mrs Palmer, I assume you are ready for our lunch date.'

Sally could only nod as Amy passed over her jacket. 'I was just admiring Sally's beautiful roses, such a lovely colour.'

'So they are,' Hugh said boldly.' I thought yellow would be best. If I'd sent red roses, we would have really set the tongues wagging, wouldn't we, Mrs Palmer?' Hugh turned and winked at Amy, while Sally turned a delicate shade of pink.

Half way along the corridor, Hugh turned back. 'Oh, by the way,' he called to Amy, 'my nephew's just rung to say he's unable to join us for lunch after all. I was wondering therefore if you wouldn't mind working late a few evenings next week, to help him get the hang of things. Paid overtime of course.'

Amy was ecstatic, she'd have no problem with that. In fact her mind was already working overtime!

Unable to meet Hugh's gaze, Sally contemplated the menu,

'Have I said something wrong, Sally? You seem very subdued.'

'It was your comment about setting tongues wagging. Do you think that was wise?'

'In the circumstances I couldn't have said anything better. Didn't you see the way Amy reacted? She thought it was a huge joke. Only you and I know otherwise.'

'Maybe, but at risk of offending you, I'd rather you didn't treat our, er, situation as a joke.'

'Rest assured I'm not, that's the last thing I want to do. And I apologize if I've upset you. That wasn't my intention when I suggested we have lunch together. You do want us to have lunch together, don't you… or have you changed your mind?'

Sally's fingers played with the yellow silk tassel on the menu, it was the same colour as Hugh's wonderful roses. 'Yes, I do still want to have lunch with you. I also think it's a shame that Gareth couldn't join us.'

'Perhaps it's just as well he couldn't, I'd hate him to think I'm the cause of the sadness in your eyes.'

Sally gulped away a tear. 'I'm sorry, Hugh. It's not really you who's upset me. This last week has been such a strain. I hadn't realized how much I was going to miss everyone.'

'But you'll be coming back into the store to see them from time to time and when you do, I promise no more cryptic comments. Does that make you feel better?'

Relieved to see a smile flood her face, Hugh caught the attention of a nearby waiter, 'So… Mrs Palmer, if you've finished shredding that tassel on the menu, perhaps you'd care to order. We don't want to arouse suspicion by being out of the office for too long.'

'I expect you think I'm becoming paranoid.'

'No, I think you're lovely and I'd give anything to reach across the table and kiss you, but it's far too risky. There are people here I recognize. Don't look so worried, if they're still here when we leave, I'll introduce you.'

'You'll what!'

'I'll introduce you as my Human Resources Manager and also explain why we're having lunch together… that this is your very last day at the store.

Don't forget Barrington's possesses an excellent reputation for looking after its staff, there'll be no reason for them to think otherwise.'

With her final hours at Barrington's drawing to a close, Sally began to relax. She'd given Hugh strict instructions not to come to her office again, and even refused his offer of help with all her flowers and gifts. Roz had volunteered Donald. Reliable as ever, he was there to organize the removal of what appeared to be a market garden into the staff lift and out to the car park.

'Thank you both so much for the flowers,' Sally said, watching Roz and Donald set off up her garden path laden with blooms. 'You shouldn't have done it, you know.'

'Of course we should. Just think of all the years you've put up with my acid tongue.' Roz peered through a cluster of cream and gold spider Chrysanthemums, placed them unceremoniously on the kitchen table and reached for her handkerchief. 'Christ, Sally! What am I going to do without your company during lunch? When I think back to Edith Hawtin's farewell do, I was convinced it would be me leaving next, not you.'

Sally watched the tears well behind huge tortoiseshell glasses and gave Roz a hug. 'It isn't as if I won't be coming back, Mr Barrington's very keen to get this new art and picture project off the ground.'

Roz gave a brittle smile and blew hard into her handkerchief. 'Well, just make sure you do come back, Sally Palmer!'

'And I have to remind you that you're coming to the New Year's concert with us,' Donald added, trying to raise both women's spirits. 'Bernard's really looking forward to seeing you again.'

'Hmph! I'm not so sure Sally wants to see *him*!'

Donald turned to his wife. 'There's no harm in it, you know.'

'Maybe not,' Roz said, screwing her handkerchief into a ball and tucking it up her sleeve. 'As long as you make it perfectly clear that Sally is *not* looking for a husband. God knows Richard was bad enough, but

Bernard…'

Donald shifted uneasily, coming to Bernard's defence was probably not conducive to the current situation. 'I'm sure Bernard means well, he's probably just lonely that's all. Anyway, don't you think we'd better go? Sally looks all in. It will probably take her the rest of the evening to arrange all these flowers.'

Pausing at the door Donald turned and whispered, 'Don't mind Roz, she's simply so upset that you're leaving. Rest assured, Sally, I have absolutely no intention of marrying you off to Bernard.'

*

Sally was arranging Hugh's flowers when the phone rang.

'Are you alone?'

'Yes, and I'm just seeing to your beautiful roses.'

'That's good because I'm ringing to let you know I have the key to the Elmsmarsh flat. I thought perhaps we could go and look at it tomorrow evening.'

'Tomorrow?'

'Isn't that convenient?'

Sally felt the familiar panic rising in her breast. If Hugh genuinely intended to help set her up in this flat, it was something she would have to come to terms with. She took a deep breath.

'Tomorrow will be fine.'

'So… shall I call for you or would you prefer to meet me somewhere?

'If you've got to walk Stanley, I could meet you by the lake as before.'

*

The road to Elmsmarsh was thinly populated with the occasional cottage and pub. Hugh studied the milometer.

'It's quite amazing, we've done these twenty five miles in less time than it takes me to get into Thornhampton in the morning.'

Sally stared out of the window, her eyes catching site of a filling station.

'At least there'll be no excuses for me running out of petrol.'

Hugh laughed, recalling their time in Campion forest and the confusion over her car. He reached across and squeezed her hand. 'And you certainly won't starve. I did a reconnoitre of the area a few days ago. In that group of 'olde' world shops to my right, you'll find a bakers, grocers, post office and a pretty decent fruit and veg shop. So… if you're ready, here we go… Next turning on the left and we're almost there.'

Sally was entranced. Hugh's face was like a child on Christmas morning as he slipped the key into the lock, opened the door, switched on the hall light and waited for her reaction.

'Don't look so worried,' he said, 'there's no one in there. Shall I wait here in the hall while you have a look round on your own?

Venturing forward, Sally switched on the lights as she went. The door immediately in front of her led into a galley kitchen, while the archway to her right led to an unexpectedly large lounge/diner. Beyond was a corridor with fitted cupboards on one side and a bathroom door on the other. At the far end was a door leading to what she assumed was the bedroom.

Sally hesitated with her fingers on the door handle and looked back at Hugh. 'I take it this is the bedroom.'

Hugh waited for her to open the door and go inside. Slowly he made his own way along the corridor and found her peering from the bedroom window.

'Well, what do you think? Do you like it?'

'It's incredible, not another house in sight for miles.'

Hugh smiled as she pressed her face against the glass to study the rural landscape.

'Yes,' he said, peering over her shoulder, 'you'll find the view quite enchanting - when you can see it in daylight - but what about the flat, Sally?'

'It's amazing, almost like a dream. Everything's so wonderful and new. Are you… are you really sure about this, Hugh?'

'Seeing you standing there like that, I don't think I've felt this sure about anything in years. And as long as you don't think the flat is too small or you won't mind climbing the stairs... I know the flats round the corner are bigger and they have a lift but I thought you'd prefer this block because of the view.'

Sally nestled against Hugh's shoulder, 'I might have been gasping for breath when I had to run all the way to the park to meet you, but I think I can cope with one flight of stairs. I'd also prefer not to sleep on the ground floor. It's going to be strange not having a garden, though.'

'Ah! But there is a balcony,' said Hugh, taking her hand and leading her to the far end of the lounge. A glass door led onto a small balcony.

'That's why the kitchen's so small,' Hugh explained, 'but I thought you'd want somewhere to put your bay tree. I also thought you might have room for a few window boxes and, who knows, there might even be room for Stanley's basket too.'

'Definitely not! I'm not having Stanley banished to a balcony. I want him indoors with us.'

Hugh put his hands on Sally's waist and drew her towards him. 'No wonder Stanley and I both adore you. I can't wait for you to move in. Speaking of which, I'm afraid I have to get a move on.'

Locking the door, they heard muted voices and the sound of soft music coming from the neighbouring flat.

'I haven't had a chance to vet them yet,' Hugh whispered, 'but the agent assures me they're a very nice couple.'

Sally gave Stanley a reassuring pat and stroked his ears when she climbed back into the Range Rover. 'Well, old chap, you can be my first dinner guest.'

'Oh, really! And what about me?'

'Well… I might invite you too. Would you like me to stroke your ears as well?'

'Sally Palmer! That is a very leading question. Now, as it's far too late to drop you by the lake, would you like me to take you all the way home?"

'No on the corner will probably be better, just in case…'

Studying Hugh's profile in the semi-gloom, Sally found herself wondering what it would be like to spend more than just a few hours with him.

'Penny for them.'

'Sorry, Hugh, they're not for sale – not tonight anyway.'

A short while later, watching his comforting silhouette as the Range Rover disappeared into the night, Sally hurried indoors clutching the large brown envelope he'd taken from the glove compartment. Carpet samples he'd said.

Studying her own threadbare carpet as she sat in front of the gas fire clasping a welcoming mug of hot chocolate, Sally felt tears prick her eyelids. Tonight, however, these were not tears of sorrow and despair. Instead she was suffused with the most wonderful glow of contentment. Not only was she to have a new flat and new carpets, but also – and most importantly of all – she was to begin the New Year and a new stage in her life with a simply amazing man!

Thinking of that amazing man and draining the last of her hot chocolate, Sally gave a gasp.

New Year! She'd forgotten to wish Hugh a Happy New Year!

*

In the foyer of the concert hall, Roz, Donald and Sally waited anxiously for Bernard to arrive.

'I'm giving him another five minutes, Donald,' Roz snapped. 'And if he hasn't arrived by then, I'm going in without him. I can already hearing the orchestra tuning up in there!'

Roz nodded in the direction of the door to the stalls, where the few remaining latecomers hurried to their seats. An usherette stood in the open doorway, her supply of programmes severely depleted.

'Here he is!' Donald said brightly and waved his hand in greeting as Bernard arrived completely out of breath and dishevelled.

'So sorry I'm late, I couldn't find a parking space. I've been driving around for ages.'

'And you've been driving us mad for ages,' Roz hissed under her breath to Sally. She studied Bernard critically over the rim of her glasses. His dinner suit was obviously a relic from the past: wide lapels, enormous velvet bow tie and flares.

Sally watched Roz's look of disbelief as she scanned Bernard from top to toe, like a probe. '*Please don't say anything, Roz*,' her innerself was pleading, willing Roz to look in her direction. When she did, Sally held a finger to her mouth and shook her head.

'Hmph!' was all Roz said as she gave Bernard a look that would kill. She turned on her heels in a swish of taffeta, snatched a programme from the startled usherette and left Donald fumbling for some money.

'Don't mind Roz,' Sally said kindly, watching Bernard struggle to adjust his bow-tie, 'she's a stickler for punctuality. She'll be OK by the interval.'

For once Sally was wrong. By the interval, Roz was still fuming. It had been bad enough making their entrance just before curtain up, but the fact that their seats were in the middle of the row made the situation worse. Disgruntled concertgoers - comfortably installed – shuffled to their feet, their eyes full of contempt and their mutterings painfully audible.

To add to their embarrassment, Bernard had trodden quite heavily on the feet of a daintily shod female and added insult to injury by passing round a bag of peppermints before the conductor even had a chance to warm his baton.

'Remind me, never again, Sally! Donald can plead "poor bloody Bernard" till the cows come home, but I absolutely refuse! Now, let's find a corner of this bar where we can hide during the interval. I've never felt so embarrassed.'

'I'm sure he means well,' Sally said, trying to placate her. 'He's obviously not used to this sort of occasion.'

'Hmph! He's made that perfectly clear from that suit. My God! The last time I saw one like that was on some would-be Frank Sinatra at a talent concert, when Donald and I had that ghastly weekend away. I'm sure I told you about it. That geriatric medallion man, complete with hair piece and gold chains, attempting to croon his way through *Strangers in the Night*.

Roz laughed loudly, causing heads to turn in her direction.

'What's so funny?' asked Donald, returning from the bar with drinks. 'Oh, Bernard's just bringing yours Sally.'

'I was just telling Sally about that chap at the dreadful holiday camp, remember? The one with the appalling "dooby-dooby-do's".'

Roz giggled and winked at Sally as Bernard struggled through the crowd, clutching Sally's gin and tonic in one hand and a pint of lager in the other.

'I wonder what his dooby-do's are like, Sally. Let's hope he never gives you the opportunity to find out!'

Struggling to suppress a smile, Sally turned away. Lifting her glass to her mouth, familiar eyes met hers across the crowded bar. Hugh Barrington!

Sipping nervously at her drink, Sally watched as Hugh turned to Serena, tonight clad in exquisite black lace, whispered something in her ear and then made his way towards Roz and Donald.

'Roz, Donald… and Mrs Palmer too. What a pleasant surprise.'

Hugh turned to face Sally. His look, as he glimpsed Bernard by her side, was cold and questioning.

'This is - er - Bernard, he's an old friend of Donald's.'

Hugh extended his hand in Bernard's direction. 'Hugh Barrington,' he said, accepting Bernard's limp and clammy handshake.

Seconds later, Serena was also by their side. 'Hugh, dah-ling. Come along now, they'll be ringing the bell soon and you haven't even finished your champagne. Charles was going to order another bottle, but there's no time now.' Serena put her arm on Hugh's and looked back in the direction of her sister and brother-in-law and the rest of their party. She waved and turned quickly to Roz and Sally.

'How lovely to see you both, but you don't mind if I drag my husband away, do you? Poor thing, it appears Barrington's follows him wherever he goes.'

Sally watched as Serena bent forward to proffer the perfunctory mid-air kiss of the cheek.

She searched desperately for something to say.

'How's Stanley,' she asked feebly.

'Oh, my dear, don't ask! Unfortunately he's frightfully hale and hearty… almost with a new lease of life.'

'Erm – well don't forget I'll take him any time you like…'

'I wish you would, Sally,' Serena whispered in her ear. 'I wish you would take him – period!'

Suddenly spying Bernard standing by Donald's side, Serena's face said it all. Her left eyebrow shot up and clasping Hugh's arm, she wished them all a Happy New Year and hurried back to her sister. Hearing shrieks of laughter, Sally realized only too well who was the butt of Serena's cruel outburst.

Deeply uncomfortable and dispirited, Sally reached for Bernard's arm.

'Come along, Bernard, let's get back to our seats before everyone else, shall we?'

Bernard looked down at what remained of his pint glass. Still half full, he hesitated and looked to see if Roz and Donald had finished their drinks. Roz was chewing on the flesh of her lemon slice. Drawing in her mouth at its sourness, she deftly dropped the remaining peel into Bernard's lager and smiled sweetly.

'Yes, come long, Bernard, there's no time to finish that now.'

Cheered by Roz's change of humour, Donald duly obliged by putting down his glass and followed Sally through the door. As the lights dimmed Roz's voice was heard to echo, 'And no more peppermints, please!'

*

Sally stirred sleepily and reached for the phone. It had to be a mistake; no one would ring her at this time of the morning, unless… Jackie or the children… Panic gave way to relief as she recognized Hugh's voice.

'Hugh! It's a quarter to three in the morning.'

'I just wanted to wish you a Happy New Year…'

'Where are you?'

'At home.'

'Won't Serena be suspicious?'

'No,' Hugh laughed wryly. 'She's only halfway through her beauty routine and I'm in the garden. I'm waiting for Stanley to do the necessary.'

'Oh, I see.' Sally rubbed at her eyes and yawned sleepily.

'I'm sorry, I obviously woke you up.'

'Yes, you did. I've been in bed for ages.'

'Alone?'

'Of course, alone! Hugh, what are you implying?'

'I was wondering… your escort at the concert.'

'Bernard's just an old friend of Donald's. He's a widower. You didn't honestly think he and I were…?'

'No. I simply didn't like seeing you together. It made me feel terribly jealous. Why didn't you tell me you were going to the concert with—'

'Because I didn't think it was important. Besides, I don't even know Bernard's surname. That's why I couldn't introduce him properly. I didn't know you and Serena were going to the concert either; perhaps *you* should have warned *me*. I too can get very jealous.'

'Oh, dear, Sally, are we having our first row?'

'No, not row, more a misunderstanding and Bernard probably did us a big favour.'

'How's that?'

It's probably good for me to be seen in another man's company – a bit like you putting Amy off the scent with your comment about red roses.'

'Touché. I suppose I asked for that.'

'I'm sorry. I'm not at my best when I'm tired.'

'I'd better let you get back to sleep then.'

Reluctant to say goodbye, Hugh looked towards the bedroom window. Serena had just switched off her bedside light. Only the dim glow of his own remained in an otherwise dark and starless night. He whistled softly for Stanley.

'Hugh, are you still there?'

'Yes, still here my love, waiting for Stanley to make his way from the bottom of the garden.'

'Wish him Happy New Year from me then.'

'I will and Sally… make sure you get plenty of sleep between now and Saturday, because you and I will be spending next Saturday night together…'

The significance of Hugh's statement, prompted by his slight overindulgence of champagne, was lost on Sally. She was already fast asleep. It was only the following morning, when she made the comparison between Hugh in his immaculately tailored dinner suit, and Bernard in his flares, that the memory came flooding back. What was it Hugh had whispered, before she'd hung up her phone?

CHAPTER 8

As dusk fell on the wintry January afternoon, Hugh swung the Jaguar into the tree-lined driveway of Cedar Court. Sally felt her stomach lurch; there was no turning back now. She bit her lip and brushed an imaginary piece of fluff from her skirt.

'Nervous?' Hugh said softly.

'Does it show that much?'

'Afraid so. Try and relax; the staff at Cedar Court are extremely discreet.'

'Oh! You've been here before then.'

Hugh watched her face fill with disappointment. 'Yes, I have been here before… but not as an overnight guest. I was here for a golfing tournament – with Charles, my brother-in-law. There's a superb course on the periphery.'

'How do you know the staff are discreet then?'

'Just something Charles said in passing.'

'Has he stayed here with another woman?'

Hugh laughed. 'Good Lord, no! What is this the third degree?'

'No, I'm merely curious, that's all.'

'Well,' said Hugh, giving her hand a reassuring squeeze as he helped her from the car. 'Dare I suggest you become curious about the interior of Cedar Court instead? They serve wonderful teas in the library and their dinner menu is amazing. And Sally…'

'Yes.'

'As I said before, relax. It's going to be a wonderful weekend… I promise.'

Unable to look the receptionist in the eye, Sally studied her immediate surroundings. Beyond the oak-panelled hallway she glimpsed an enormous log fire burning in what appeared to be the library. Wasn't that where they served afternoon tea? Gingerly she stepped sideways to view the interior. Row upon row of amazing books lined the walls, and comfortable armchairs and what Ben always described as 'squidgy settees' were placed in welcoming groups.

'Will you be requiring afternoon tea, sir?' The receptionist was handing Hugh a key.

'Sally, shall we have tea or would you prefer to go to our room first?'

She turned abruptly, aware of two pairs of questioning eyes. She'd heard the word 'tea' and 'our room'. 'Oh, I think I'd prefer tea first, please.'

'*Coward!*' the voice in her head murmured. '*You can't put it off forever, you know. Sooner or later you'll have to walk up those stairs.*'

And what a staircase it was. Quite the baronial hall, with its sweeping oak panels and intricately carved banisters. Sally stared in wonderment at the ornate carving, galleried landing and walls adorned with oil paintings so vast that just one would have covered her entire bedroom wall.

As if from nowhere a young man in livery appeared at the foot of the stairs. About to remark that someone else must have a tapestry suitcase exactly like hers, she realized it was *her* suitcase and the same young man was also reaching out for Hugh's luggage. She felt a hand upon her arm.

'Shall we go through for tea then?'

Watching the reflection of twisting, red and gold flames from the fire, dancing on the silver teapot and hot-water jug, Sally registered Hugh's questioning gaze.

'I was thinking, it's not quite like my old brown earthenware, is it?'

'Not exactly, but shall we see if it tastes as good?'

Surprised by the weight of the teapot, Sally was glad of Hugh's steadying hand.

'Careful, we don't want you burning yourself. Now you know why women were so well-built years ago.' He gestured to a portrait of a grand dame, of ample bosom, swathed in yards of gold brocade.

'Mmm,' Sally smiled in response. 'I'd say she looks as if she could do with some assistance from Roz.'

'Most definitely, now what about something to eat?'

Contemplating the plates of neatly cut finger sandwiches and cakes, not to mention dinner and the evening ahead, Sally hesitated. 'I don't know if I could.'

'Well, I think you should, because if we're reasonably quick with tea, there might also be time for a walk in the grounds before dinner. The fresh air will do wonders for your appetite.'

Appetite for *what* or for *whom*, Sally thought, reaching for a smoked salmon sandwich. When her eyes alighted on a selection of tiny eclairs, she thought immediately of Stanley.

'Stanley's favourite. He will be all right with Serena, won't he? She won't mind looking after him tonight?'

Hugh gave a brittle smile. 'Oh, she minds all right, but as she's going away on one of her skiing trips, she can hardly begrudge me one night away from home.'

'Did she ask where you were going?'

'Sally, we didn't come all this way to talk about Serena – did we? So… why not try one of those dainty meringues and just this once I will have an éclair.'

'I'll tell Stanley.'

'And I'll tell him how delicious it was, so… how about that walk?'

Reaching for her coat, Sally's eyes rested on their room key with its elaborate key fob in royal blue and gold. Hugh's long, fine fingers swept it away deftly into his pocket, but not before she read the bold gold leaf on leather inscription *King Charles II Suite.*

Thoughts of Roz sprang immediately to mind. Had *she* been here no doubt there would be some reference made to Nell Gwyn. Tying the belt of her coat Sally followed Hugh back into the panelled hallway, where the receptionist called from her inner office. 'Excuse me sir, will you be dining with us this evening?'

'Most definitely. We're just popping out for some fresh air to give us an appetite. Are you expecting to be busy?

The receptionist smiled warmly and shook her head. 'Not like last weekend. You couldn't move in here for haggis and bagpipes. As for this evening,' she said, studying the book on her desk, 'we've a party of ten booked in for nine thirty but before then it's—'

Hugh didn't wait for her to finish her sentence. Looking in Sally's direction he announced,

'Oh, we don't like to eat late, do we, darling? I think we'd prefer seven thirty.'

Outside in the dampness of late afternoon, Sally shivered and breathed in the faint smell of wood-smoke, spiralling above the many fluted chimney pots. Taking Hugh's arm a smile crept across her face.

'What's so funny?'

'Oh, we don't like to eat late, do we, darling?' she mimicked.

'Well, we don't, do we?'

'No, I suppose we don't.'

'At least you nodded in the right place, Sally. Right, let's have that quick walk around the block – or in this case the gravelled walk. I would imagine, like most women, you would prefer plenty of time to dress for dinner.

*

Pausing at the foot of the stairs, Sally stared up at the galleried landing in both wonder and trepidation. Flickering candle-bulbs in sconces illuminated the stained glass windows, which in turn cast delicate hues across the deep pile carpet and dark oak carving. Hugh took her hand and led her forward.

Logs the size of tree trunks had been placed on the fire below and for that she was deeply grateful. While fresh flames licked their way noisily up the chimney at least the thumping of her heart was drowned out by the crackle and spit of wood.

With her feet sinking into the pale smoky-blue carpet, Sally was conscious of Hugh closing the door behind them. He murmured appreciatively. 'Yes, I think even Old Rowley would have approved of this setting.'

'Old Rowley?'

'Charles II's nickname… so-called after a stallion at the time, renowned for its prowess at stud.'

Sally wished she hadn't asked; she was only glad Hugh was a Hugh and not a Charles! Moving to a corner of the room she studied three miniatures on the wall. Hugh moved to her side.

'Charles II, Catherine of Braganza - his wife – and of course dear Nell.'

Sally recognized Nell Gwyn instantly, one of Charles' favourite mistresses. She was less familiar with Catherine of Braganza , his Portuguese wife. How strange that all three should be hanging side by side. Would Hugh ever consider hanging his own photo between those of Serena and herself? Keeping her thoughts private she turned and whispered, 'It really is a magnificent room, isn't it.'

Hugh nodded approvingly at the four poster bed with its heavy gold brocade hangings and, taking Sally by the hand, led her to a settee by the window. Sitting down, he motioned her to join him, patting the gold chintz by his side. 'Five minutes,' he said softly, drawing her into his arms, 'then we must get ready for dinner.'

Sally closed her eyes as his lips met hers.

Released from his embrace, she looked at her watch just as Hugh announced, 'We've got an hour. Would you like to unpack and use the bathroom first?'

Unzipping her suitcase, Sally removed several layers of tissue to reveal the simple, navy-blue crepe dress she'd bought specially for this evening. She smoothed out the long fitted sleeves and went to the wardrobe for a hanger. Selecting one in gold chintz – the same fabric as the settee – she smiled. Her own wardrobe at home contained a selection of wood and plastic.

Hugh, she noticed, was feeding the trousers of a lounge suit into the trouser press, pulling levers and setting dials with well-practiced dexterity. She recalled Richard's first attempt with a similar contraption, only to discover the creases in his best suit ran not vertically but diagonally.

She suppressed a smile. How strange it was that this past week she'd hardly thought of Richard. Yet, in a way, she supposed she should be grateful to him now. If it hadn't been for Richard's behaviour on the night of Edith Hawtin's party, she wouldn't be here - showering and dressing for dinner.

At a quarter past seven, Hugh adjusted his silk tie and fingered his left lapel.

'No yellow rose?' Sally asked, her gaze taking in the assorted floral displays distributed across the room. The arrangements were all creamy white.

Hugh shook his head. 'No, that's just for Barrington's,' And with eyes that reflected warmth and approval he walked slowly towards her. 'Sally, you look perfectly lovely.'

For a brief moment, she thought he was going to brush his fingers through her hair. Instead he stopped and gently stroked her left shoulder.

'Fluff?' she asked, 'I did use the clothes brush.'

'No,' he said softly, 'I just wanted to touch you, but I didn't think you'd thank me for spoiling your hair. Now, are you ready to eat?'

*

As she finished her aperitf, Hugh nodded in the direction of the maître d' and they made their way from the bar to the restaurant. There, at Hugh's request, they were shown to a corner table, by the window and, although it was dark, they were still able to look across the formal floodlit gardens.

'Of course they switch off the fountains and waterfall in the winter months,' Hugh announced, 'so we'll have to come back again in the summer.'

There was something comforting in those last words. The mere thought that Hugh was already thinking of them sharing a summer together filled Sally's heart with hope. She smiled at him across the table and watched his eyes sweep unobtrusively in the direction of other diners. Seeing no one he recognized, he gave her his attention once more.

'And is the wine to your liking with your starter?' he asked, squeezing lemon juice on his seafood ravioli. 'I confess I stopped ordering French wine when the French started burning our sheep. But better not tell the sommelier; I understand he hails from Bordeaux!'

Dismissing the wine waiter once the main course was finished, Hugh studied Sally's empty wine glasses. Although the white wine glass was empty, she still hadn't quite finished the red.

'You're sure you don't want any more red wine?'

'Positive, thank you. Too much red wine gives me a headache.'

'Hmm. We can't have that then, can we? Not tonight.'

Even in the subdued lighting of the restaurant, with the candlelight casting golden glints on her hair, Hugh discerned the gentlest glow brush Sally's cheeks. Tenderly, he reached for her hand. 'Sorry, would you rather I hadn't said that? I hope that doesn't mean I've put you off choosing one of Cedar Court's irresistible puddings.'

Sally fixed him with a forgiving smile. 'I think it would take more than that, Hugh. I'm afraid I have a very sweet tooth when it comes to anything made with chocolate.'

'Really? I would never have guessed that from looking at you.'

With the confection of milk, white and dark chocolate placed before her, Sally watched wide-eyed as the waiter presented Hugh with his pear and Stilton strudel. He grinned at the look of sheer disbelief on her face.

'Fruit and cheese course in one,' he said, 'and not, thank goodness, a hint of raspberry coulis anywhere. Would you like to try some?'

Looking round surreptitiously, Sally leaned forward and allowed Hugh to feed her the tiniest morsel of filo pastry and filling.

'Well, what do you think?'

'I'm afraid I don't much care for it, I think I'll stick with the chocolate.'

'You don't have to be afraid for that, come to think of it, I don't want you to be afraid of anything while we're here. Oh, look, the party of ten has arrived. In which case shall we have coffee in the library?

Relaxed and sitting by the fire, Sally whispered softly. 'That was a wonderful meal, Hugh, simply perfect and just the right amount. I really dislike it when food is piled high so high on to plates that it looks almost obscene.'

Hugh was looking towards the library door, where he was smiling at someone. 'Well… I hope you have just a little more room left, especially as you like chocolate.'

Sally watched as the waiter placed a tray of coffee on the delicate lace cloth and turned the silver salver of *petits fours* towards her. The first thing she noticed were tiny chocolate cups filled with fresh wild strawberries.

'Enjoy Madame, Monsieur thought you would like zem.'

'Thank you. I'm sure I shall.'

Sally's eyes met Hugh's as she reached for a dainty chocolate cup. 'You've obviously had these before.'

'Yes, the summer I was here. I wasn't sure they would have them in winter though. I expect they have the strawberries flown in from exotic parts.'

'Mmm, summer in January, how wonderfully decadent. I think you're spoiling me, Hugh. Aren't you going to have any?'

'I prefer the physalis myself,' Hugh added, reaching across for the golden orb of caramelized fruit.

'Hmm. After that superb white wine—not to mention the red—I don't think I'd even dare attempt that pronunciation.'

Hugh laughed, peeling back the papery petals of the fruit and moments later, placed the stalk in the saucer of his coffee cup. Looking across at Sally, he was deeply moved to see her so contented and relaxed.

'Are you ready to go up?' Sally heard him whisper, as the sleeping butterflies in her stomach suddenly took flight.

Rising from his chair, Hugh held out his hand. 'Come,' he urged gently, leading her to the foot of the stairs. 'It's going to be all right.'

*

In the bedroom, the drapes had been drawn and the bedspread turned down to reveal ivory damask sheets. Sensing her unease, Hugh switched on lamps, turned off the main light, reached for a magazine and sat down on the settee.

'I can read while you're getting ready for bed,' he announced tactfully. 'Or would you prefer me to go for a walk for ten minutes?'

Joining him on the settee, Sally hugged her knees and stared down at the toes of her navy suede shoes. 'I'm sorry, Hugh, I don't appear to be much good at this game.'

'Sally, darling,' he murmured, and laying down the magazine, placed his hand gently under her chin and tilted it towards him, 'I want you to know, this is no game… this is serious.'

Comforted by his very presence when his lips brushed her eyelids and her cheeks, Sally straightened her shoulders and rose from the settee. 'There's no need to go for a walk, I'll just get my nightdress and if I could use the bathroom first… Oh!'

'What's wrong?'

'I can't find my nightdress.'

'Are you sure you packed it?'

Sally peered into the depth of her suitcase, pushing aside layers of tissue paper. 'I know I didn't take it from the suitcase before dinner, but I certainly remember it being on my bed at home, because I was in the middle of packing when the estate agent rang and…'

Sally cast her mind back to the morning when, having completed most of her packing, she'd received the unexpected phone call. The young couple who'd been to see her house the previous evening, wanted to come back for a second viewing before heading back to Milton Keynes.

It was a company move the agent had said, and as they were first-time buyers they were every vendor's dream. Not wanting to miss out on such an opportunity, Sally had already closed the lid of her suitcase, and concealed it beneath her bed, when she'd caught sight of the new cream satin and lace nightdress, purchased especially for tonight. The same satin and lace confection that she remembered bundling up and pushing under her pillows! She turned to face Hugh with a shrug of her shoulders.

'No problem at all,' he said, assessing the situation and heading for a chest of drawers. 'We can share these.'

Hugh held up a pair of navy-blue silk pyjamas, piped with red. You can have the top and I'll take the bottoms. How's that?'

Sally stepped forward and accepted the top gracefully. Even in its folded state it was quite clear Hugh's pyjama jacket – with its long sleeves – was going to cover more of her than her nightdress.

In the bathroom she ran her fingers over the fine silk and lifted one of the sleeves to her cheek. She closed her eyes and sighed; it felt sensuously smooth and smelt of Hugh's aftershave.

'Well, Sally Palmer,' she murmured, opening her eyes again to face her reflection in a large mirror, 'this is where you join the ranks of Nell Gwyn and Lily Langtry!'

Stepping out of her dress she hung it back on the chintz hanger and slowly removed her bra, holding it to her modestly as she unfastened the hooks. Quite why she did so, she wasn't sure. Although, as there were so many mirrors in the bathroom, she felt exposed from every angle. Yet there was no one to see and Hugh was hardly likely to come bursting through the door.

All the signs so far indicated he was the perfect gentleman and she had no doubt in her mind they would remain that way. He'd even gone so far as to suggest he went for a walk while she got undressed! Sally smiled nervously and put on the jacket, counting each button as she drew the edge together. There were four.

As expected the sleeves of the jacket were far too long, so she turned them back to her elbows, as she did with her casual cotton shirts in summer. The effect was pleasing and she ran her hands over the silky fabric, downwards over her breasts and on to where the silk met the less than smooth fabric of her tights. Quickly she stepped out of those and felt the cold marble of the floor against the soles of her feet.

With only her panties left it was decision time. Once more she turned to the many mirrors and Hamlet style, asked her reflection. 'To wear or not to wear?

Whilst deliberating, she brushed her hair and fingered her fringe into place, sprayed a fine mist of perfume onto her throat and wrists and reached for the door.

Hugh stood up and smiled appreciatively.

'Do you know, I've often heard it said that men's pyjamas look better on a woman and you've certainly proved that.'

He bent and kissed the top of her head, breathing in her delicate scent and only briefly was reminded of Serena. Her taste in perfumes of late had become incredibly sickly and cloying.

In art and beauty, inanimate and human, Hugh had always preferred a more subtle approach to things beautiful. Serena was beautiful right enough, and at one time had always gone for a more natural approach to makeup and clothes. These days, however, her mere presence in a room had been about as subtle as a London doubledecker in the desert!

Sally on the other hand, well, Sally was… Aware of his hand stroking her hair and the gentle warmth of her body pressed against his, Hugh said softly, 'I won't keep you long.'

For the first time since they'd arrived, Sally sat on the bed and ran her hands along the damask sheets. She'd only once heard of damask sheets. Hadn't Roz told her one lunchtime, ages ago, that they had them on the Orient Express. They'd sighed enviously, thinking of their own poly cotton.

'Still, just think of all that bloody ironing,' Roz had declared, trying to make them feel better.

I don't think I'd mind the ironing, Sally thought, slipping between the sheets. She could hear discreet movement in the bathroom and thought of Hugh minus his pyjama top. Feeling her pulse race, she concluded that perhaps she was already warm enough and it might be a good idea to open the window for some fresh air.

On the far wall her attention was caught once more by the trio of miniatures. Charles, Catherine and Nell; who all appeared to be looking down at her—Nell even more so. It was almost as if they knew why she was here… That she was waiting to be seduced by her lover!

'Don't look so smug,' Sally hissed under her breath to the king's paramour, just as she reached up to unfasten the window. At that moment, Hugh opened the bathroom door and caught a glimpse of satin and lace navy panties. Sally froze, her hand moving down fleetingly. Thankful that she had opted for her undies, she remained convinced that Nell was still grinning at her.

'Contemplating the lasciviousness of the seventeenth century, Sally?'

With beating heart, she turned to face Hugh where he stood, tall, tanned and handsome in the doorway. Charles II's father had lost his head, now Sally had lost hers. As Hugh crossed the deep pile carpets, she even noticed a bowl of oranges on the table by the window and smiled. How very appropriate!

CHAPTER 9

Woken early the next morning by the cooing of doves outside their window also seemed appropriate. Sally stirred sleepily. Vaguely aware of unfamiliar surroundings, she felt her hand brush accidentally against Hugh's naked torso. Alarmed that she may have woken him, she hugged her arms to her breasts and lay quiet and still, almost without breathing.

The room was silent and full of shadows. There were shadows on the walls from the pictures; shadows on the canopy above her head; shadows from the heavy folds of fabric (enveloping each of the four carved bed posts), and shadows of the man who, last night, had taken her in his arms and made love to her so gently and so lovingly that she'd wanted to cry.

Feeling tears from such contentment well her eyelids, Sally closed her eyes and thought of Hugh. What was it he'd said, helping her from the car when they arrived. 'It will be wonderful… I promise.'

How could he have known? How could he tell? Last night could have been a complete disaster. But it wasn't a complete disaster, was it? Hugh had been right, it was wonderful. She smiled to herself. Well, it was once she'd got over her initial nerves and shyness.

Turning to face the side table, Sally reached out with one finger to touch the cool, smooth stem of the empty champagne flute.

'A perfect cure for nerves,' Hugh had announced, having first carried her to the bed.

Her initial reaction had been for no more alcohol. An aperitif followed by a glass of both white and red wine had been more than enough, but Hugh had insisted.

'It's good for headaches too,' he said, watching her reaction as the bubbles burst in her mouth and made her nose tingle.

'But I haven't got a headache.'

'Just goes to show how good it is then!'

She'd laughed and passed Hugh her empty glass before he slipped into bed beside her. Drawing her close, she felt his hands slide down her silk-covered arms and across her breasts, while her own bare legs curved against his silken trousers.

'Sally,' he'd murmured softly, 'my own beautiful Sally,' and she'd counted in her head, one – two – three – four – as he found each of the four buttons and edged the pyjama jacket gently from her shoulders.

Feeling his lips on her mouth, throat and breasts, Sally fingered the tiny hairs at the nape of his neck and sighed. Hugh was right, champagne was exceptionally good for nerves and headaches! Later – much later in fact – in a tangle of silk sleeves and pyjama legs, Hugh released her briefly, reached to the side table for a small green packet and switched off the bedside lamp.

'Something tells me you'd prefer the light off,' he'd whispered in her ear, stroking her hair as he did so.

In the darkness, Hugh discerned the gentle nodding of her head and heard the softly murmured, 'yes,' – silenced by his mouth on hers – followed by the giving of herself… completely.

Sally stirred dreamily and felt Hugh's hand reach for hers.

'I take it you are awake,' he said, 'I hope you weren't disturbed by the doves.'

'No, I think they sound lovely. They remind me of a Christmas carol I once sang at infant's school.'

'Sing it to me then,'

'No,' she replied shyly. 'Because I can't remember all the words. It was something about bowing and curtseying and jubilation.'

'Do doves bow and curtsey?'

'They did in the carol. They flew around too, and made pigeon and dove noises, like coo-coo and croo-croo.'

'Did they indeed! Well, fancy that!'

'I think you're teasing me,' Sally said, pulling away.

'No, I'm not. I'm merely interested to have learnt something new this weekend. They certainly didn't have that carol at my school.'

Drawn back into his arms, Sally remained silent. There was no way she was going to tell Hugh what *she'd* learned this weekend.

'What time do we have to leave?' she asked, when Hugh reached out to peer at his watch.

'Oh, not for ages yet. Do you realize it's only six o'clock. Tell me, Mrs Palmer, do you always wake this early in the morning?'

'Mostly, especially when I'm going into Barrington's.'

'Well, you won't be doing that for a while.'

Sally was deeply reflective. No, she wouldn't, she would be going into Laura's Lair.

'I hope you're not too hungry,' Hugh said, breaking into her thoughts. 'If you remember we've ordered breakfast for seven thirty which means we have another hour and a half, unless I ring downstairs…

'Or we could always go for a walk – although I expect it's still dark outside. As far as breakfast is concerned, I don't mind waiting, especially when I think about last night and that wonderful meal.'

Hugh stroked his hand gently down her bare arm and lifted her fingers to his lips. 'I do hope the food wasn't the only wonderful thing about last night.'

Sally blushed and felt her mouth go quite dry. Hugh's hand was caressing her thigh… When at last she found her voice, she heard herself saying softly, 'I suppose we could always go for a walk after breakfast.'

Later, hand in hand, Hugh led Sally through the formal gardens and beyond to the woodland walk. On the periphery a magnificent cedar of Lebanon stood defiantly, its sweeping branches held out in proud display.

It was almost as if it was saying to the distant avenue of oak and ash, now stripped naked of their leaves, 'look at me; aren't I a fine specimen?'

'The cedar of Cedar Court, no doubt,' Sally remarked.

Hugh nodded and scanned the distant hedgerows, where a few remaining berries stood out brightly against bare twigs. There had been a slight frost during the night and a dampness hung eerily above the ground.

'Wonderful,' said Hugh, breathing in the chill morning air. 'Just look at it, not a soul for miles. You won't have quite the same view from the flat, but at least you won't be plagued by people and cars.'

'I can't wait to see the flat and the view in daylight.'

'By the way, did you decide on a colour for the carpet?'

'I hadn't until this morning, then I thought pale smokey-blue, like the carpet in our suite. I know Elmsmarsh isn't exactly Cedar Court, but the colour seems right somehow.'

Silhouetted against the skyline, Hugh took Sally in his arms and kissed her tenderly. You know something… you seem right too, somehow. What isn't, however, is the fact that we now have to leave this place… Although, we could perhaps stay for lunch and go home later.'

Sally shook her head, trying to hide her disappointment. 'No,' she said, turning for one last look across the fields, 'we must keep to our original plan. Didn't you say Serena's arranged for you to have drinks with friends this evening? Besides, if we go back inside Cedar Court I shall only want to stay.'

Walking back to the car in silence, Sally studied the set of Hugh's jaw in profile. Unlike last night and this morning, there was no hint of a smile. And even for the first part of their journey home conversation was subdued. Pulling into the lesser-used corner of Thornhampton station, it was Hugh who spoke first. 'Won't you let me drive you home?'

'No. For the simple reason, my car is parked here. If someone sees it or me, they'll assume I've been away by train. However, if anyone were to see you dropping me off outside my house, then… I think you know the answer to that just as well as I do.'

Hugh's face was pensive and his knuckles white against the steering wheel. 'It doesn't seem right, Sally, just leaving you here.'

'It's not really leaving, is it? At least not like Brief Encounter. I do know when I'm going to see you again and as it won't be long before I move into the flat… then you won't have to leave me at the station or meet me in the park.'

Hugh's face brightened at the prospect. He opened the passenger door and then took her suitcase from the boot of the Jaguar. Fleetingly, their hands touched against the suitcase handle, the only physical contact before their eyes said their sad farewells. In her rear-view mirror and through misted eyes, Sally watched Hugh drive away. He had one more call to make before returning to his wife.

*

Serena looked up from where she'd been compiling her holiday list. 'Hello, darling. How was Uncle Bertram?'

'Much the same as ever. We had our usual game of chess and he still insists I'm his favourite nephew'

'I'm not surprised, as you're the only one in the family who bothers about the old fool. Everyone else steers well clear of him—smelly old man!'

'For your information, Serena, Uncle Bertram does not smell! His generation are not into using colognes and after-shaves, that's all.'

'Considering you insist Stanley doesn't smell either, that's exactly the sort of comment I'd expect from you.'

'By the way, how is Stanley? Where is…?'

'In the laundry room and I didn't bother to take him for a walk as I knew you'd be back soon.'

'I'll take him now then,'

'You've only just got in! Don't forget we're going…'

'How could I, Serena, when you obviously take great delight in arranging these evenings without even consulting me?'

Hugh strode grimly from the room, glad to escape the unnecessary heat and the heavy scent of Serena's perfume.

From the other side of the laundry-room door, Stanley stood whining.

'Hello, old boy, has it really been that grim?'

The dog nuzzled his master eagerly and watched as the familiar leather lead was taken from its hook on the wall. Feeling in his pocket for his car keys, Hugh realized they were for the Jaguar and not the Range Rover.

'Oh, well, what the hell,' he announced to Stanley. 'Why shouldn't you go in the Jag, too? It's Sunday!'

Looking out of the window, Serena threw down her pen and pad in disgust. 'Bloody dog! And bloody Uncle Bertam! They're both long past their sell-by date and should have been put down years ago.'

Turning back to her holiday brochure, Serena's imagination got the better of her. In her mind's eye she saw herself strapping both Uncle Bertram and Stanley into a cable car and taking them to the highest mountain. From there it would be perfectly simple… all she had to do was push them both off! She gave a sardonic smile.

Hmph! She thought, and it would be just my luck for both of them to land in a fresh fall of snow, brush themselves off and walk away unscathed. 'Still,' she said smugly, pouring herself a large whisky, while focusing once more on chocolate-box style chalets, 'two more weeks and Vivienne and I will be in Gstaad.'

*

Sally meanwhile was pouring hot water onto the solitary Earl Grey teabag. 'Back to earth with a bump,' she mused, replacing the lid on the brown earthenware teapot.

Taking her tray into the sitting room, she lit the gas fire and sighed deeply. As the pungent smell of bergamot wafted into the air, she bit her lip until it hurt.

I mustn't, I mustn't, I mustn't, she told herself. You knew it wasn't going to be easy, Sally Palmer! You said you'd be able to cope with the goodbyes but you can't, can you? In fact after one night away with him, you can't cope at all!

The shrill ringing of the telephone caused her heart to leap and she ran frantically to the phone. Out of breath she called, 'Hugh!'

'Er no,' the male voice replied. 'It's Jason… from the estate agents. Look, I'm sorry to bother you on a Sunday… I did try ringing yesterday afternoon…'

'I was away,' Sally said, trying to hide both her disappointment and the fact she could have made life very difficult for herself, simply by mentioning Hugh's name. What if it had been her sister on the phone, or even Roz, when she'd made a special point of buying her pretty satin and lace nightdress (the one she'd never got to wear), from a rival department store.

'…Well, it's good news. The Taylors… they like your house and want to make you an offer. The only problem is they want a quick completion.'

'That isn't a problem,' Sally said, once more in control of her emotions.

'So you haven't got to consult your, er, ex-husband?'

'No. I haven't got to consult him at all anymore.'

Sally's sprits lifted, not only were the Taylors prepared to offer the full asking price in return for a quick completion, but also this meant she could sever all contact with Richard.

'I'll get back to the Taylors and give you a buzz about a proposed completion date…' Jason was saying, but Sally wasn't really listening. She already had a buzz from the deep glow inside her at the thought of Hugh and the wonderful weekend they'd spent together, not to mention the buzz of satisfaction she'd have when telling Richard that the house was sold.

It didn't matter now that it wasn't Hugh who'd telephoned; she'd be seeing him soon anyway. Just like the song, Ray the postman was always singing, this weekend she'd taken the first steps along life's highway. Her next steps would be to Laura's Lair!

*

Laura Maitland carried a tray of coffee and biscuits from the tiny kitchenette at Laura's Lair into the front gallery. She passed Sally a red mug decorated with a question mark.

'What's the question mark for? In case I've forgotten who I am?'

'Oh, that,' Laura smiled. 'They were a new line I got in for Christmas. You always get mugs with initials on, but I thought the question mark covered a whole gamut of things. Useful for the unexpected guest, when you can't remember a name, or – ' she grinned wickedly - 'on those rare moments when you'd love to hand someone a mug with something really sarcastic printed on it. On such occasions, my imagination runs riot and that simple question mark becomes an array of expletives.'

'Not in my case, I hope.'

'Definitely not, Sally. In your case, it was the first one I grabbed hold of!'

Laura peered from the bay window, watching large flakes of snow fall and settle. She turned and reached for a biscuit. 'The weather's just as I thought, which is why I'm glad I decided not to open for another week. I never do much business after Christmas.'

'Are you sure you really need me, then?' Sally asked, running a finger along the curve of the question mark.

'Good Lord, yes! You're the answer to a maiden's prayer.' Laura brushed biscuit crumbs from her ample bosom and laughed hoarsely, setting a mass of apricot curls a quiver. 'Mind you, it's quite some time since I was a maiden!'

Sally smiled warmly and munched on her biscuit.

'However,' continued Laura, 'I have to confess I was delighted when you said you wouldn't need the studio flat, after all. At least it means I'll be able to give Marion a roof over her head.'

'What did you say happened to her husband?'

'Simon? Oh, cancer, I'm afraid. It went through him like the proverbial dose of salts. Poor chap never really knew what hit him. Which was just as well in a way.'

'Why's that?'

'Well, by all accounts he'd run up a load of debts, the house was in danger of being repossessed… In fact, I suppose you could say everything happened for the best. Laura's green eyes misted with tears and she dabbed at them with a blue spotted handkerchief before reaching for another biscuit.

Through a fine spray of crumbs, she explained, 'When I told Marion she could have the upstairs flat, she simply handed the keys back to the building society. Now she can't wait to start painting again.'

Laura nodded to where a series of wild-flower miniatures hung in rows. Delicate snowdrops, dwarf daffodils, crocuses, scillas and golden aconites blossomed from the oval frames, filling the shaded corner of the gallery with a breath of spring.

Sally put down her coffee and walked towards them. 'These are Marion's? But they're beautiful! Why did she stop painting in the first place?'

'To help Simon with all his mad-cap ideas and the children…'

'She's not entirely on her own then, if she's got children?'

'She might just as well be,' Laura said. 'Mind you, it's her own fault for encouraging them to be free spirits and do their own thing. They certainly did that all right—all five of them.'

'Five! No wonder the poor woman hasn't had time to paint. And just where are these free spirits?'

'Oh, scattered my dear. Australia, Canada, Oxfam projects in Africa and the last I heard of Fern, she was living in a tree trying to halt the construction of a bypass.'

Laura hesitated before reaching for a third biscuit. 'Yes, I know I shouldn't, Sally, but it's so jolly cold out there and I feel as if I need all the calories I can get. I shall be on the road next week, don't forget, so there'll be plenty of time for dieting then. Now, if you've finished your coffee, I'll show you round the rest of the studio and explain all the stock.'

Taking another look at the miniatures, Sally recalled those hanging on the walls at Cedar Court. She thought of Hugh; only a few more days to go before Serena left for her skiing trip and they could be together again.

Reminded that it wasn't only Serena going away but also Laura, which meant she was going to be left in charge, Sally picked up a feather duster.

'I have to say, I think your friend Marion has the right idea,' she said, flicking the duster across the wildflower picture frames.

'Really? In what way?'

'By starting with early spring flowers she can then progress through the seasons; violets, primroses, auriculas, sweet peas and so on. They'd all be suitable subjects, and you know how people like collecting things. Remember "The Country Diary of an Edwardian Lady"? I know you were saying earlier that you were pleased to see the back of Christmas, but next Christmas if Marion could produce a series with holly, mistletoe, cyclamen and Christmas roses…'

'Sally, you are a genius,' Laura said, grabbing hold of the feather duster. Then as if bestowing a knighthood, she tapped Sally gently on both shoulders. 'In this business you have to think months ahead, and with you here to encourage Marion out of the doldrums, that's one thing less for me to worry about. Well done, you!'

Later that afternoon, when the two women went upstairs to prepare the studio flat for Marion le Sage's arrival, Sally was secretly glad that she wouldn't be living here after all. With the layers of dust, dingy paintwork and faded wallpaper it certainly wasn't very inspiring. She wiped at a mildewed window frame with a J-cloth and smiled. At least at the

Elmsmarsh flat she would…

'Sally you're dripping.'

Sally looked up, startled as a pool of dirty water dripped from her bright yellow rubber gloves onto the windowsill.

'Sorry. I was miles away, thinking about decorating the flat.'

'Well, if you've got any more bright ideas, especially with regard to brightening this place up for Marion… What exactly did you have in mind?'

Sally didn't have the heart to say it wasn't Marion's flat she was thinking of. It was her own – as to how she was going to explain about her flat and even the relationship with Hugh…

Deciding she'd have to face that hurdle as and when it arose, she dabbed at the sleeve of her blue sweatshirt where the drips were creeping from the rubber gloves and said without thinking, 'How about blue and yellow?'

'Brilliant,' replied Laura. 'That should cheer her up, blue sky and sunshine all day long.'

'Good, then I can get some paint and start tomorrow if you like.'

Laura nodded enthusiastically. 'I was forgetting you were a dab hand at DIY, what with Richard and all his unfinished projects. Are you sure you don't mind? I thought you'd be pleased to get away from all that.'

'Put it down to withdrawal symptoms. Besides as the Elmsmarsh flat is brand new… Can you believe, there's not a hint of lead piping or old wiring anywhere.'

Laura placed a comforting hand on Sally's shoulder. 'I don't mind admitting I was quite worried about you a few months ago. Now you look a completely different person. It must be no longer having to worry about Richard, the mortgage and the house. I expect it will be quite a wrench leaving it, especially the garden, but at least keeping the flat going should be a darned sight easier.'

Sally toyed with the fingers of the rubber gloves and the J-cloth. There hadn't been any awkward questions about the flat after all. And if Laura wanted to believe she was buying it, then so might everyone else. There would be no need to discuss it further. Her only worry was that she might receive unexpected visitors when Hugh was with her.

CHAPTER 10

Pasting the last piece of wallpaper and fixing it in place, Sally stepped back with a sigh of satisfaction.

'There, what do you think of it, Hugh?'

'Very nice. I only wish you'd let me send George Fry round to see to these finishing touches.'

Wiping a blob of paste from her fingers, Sally stood on tiptoe to kiss Hugh on the cheek. 'It's kind of you to offer, but it's only one feature wall that I've papered. Besides, I don't think sending George round would be a good idea. Are you usually in the habit of sending Barrington's maintenance staff to help ex-employees?'

'No, I suppose not. However, it doesn't seem right, coming here to find you doing this when, you've not only been working in the gallery, but also spending the past few weeks decorating Laura's flat for… what's her name?'

'Marion—Marion le Sage; her brother's an opera singer apparently. And by the way, you're going to love some of her pictures. Laura will sell the originals of course and I was thinking, perhaps the prints will be ideal for your new department at Barringtons.

'Whilst on the subject of painting -' Hugh gestured to the decorating brushes, '- do I take it you've finished for the day?'

Sally nodded and gathering up her tools, took them through to the kitchen. 'Of course,' she added cheekily, 'you could just help me finish hanging the curtains, while the casserole is cooking.'

Hugh smiled and took her in his arms. 'Actually, I had something else in mind. I was going to suggest going to bed.'

His face dropped when Sally passed him a packet of curtain hooks.

'Don't look so forlorn; if you can put the hooks in here – like this – I'll go and have a quick shower and wash of the Polycell.'

Wedged together in her single bed, Hugh murmured, 'I was beginning to think I was never going to drag you away from your paste brushes.'

'And I thought you were never going to ask!'

'Sally Palmer! If I didn't know you better, I'd say that was an extremely brazen statement.'

'Funny you should mention that. That's a word Roz said she'd never use to describe me. If only she knew…'

'She doesn't though, does she?'

'No, nobody knows. There's no need, is there? But Laura thinks I've changed and as Roz is so perceptive, she might think I've changed, too.'

'No, Sally, you haven't changed. You've merely woken up to life.'

Hugh reached out and drew her close, until their lips met. Moments later as he turned to switch off the bedside light, she hear him mutter jokingly, 'Why didn't you tell me you had a single bed?'

'Because that was one thing you didn't ask me!'

Stroking her hair and caressing her bare shoulders, he continued, 'Well, much as I love you, I intend to get us a double bed as soon as possible.'

*

The next morning after breakfast, when Hugh announced he had to leave, Sally found herself staring down at the bowl of diminishing soapsuds with unfocused eyes. It was as if her bubble had burst too. Hugh placed a hand on her shoulder.

'I shan't be long. I'm only going to see Uncle Bertram.'

'Oh, I thought you had to go and fetch Serena from the airport.'

'I do, but that's not until this evening. I thought if I go to see Uncle Bertram now, it still gives me time to come back later… that's if you want me to?'

'If I want you to? As if you need to ask.' The shuttered look lifted from Sally's face as she emptied the bowl of soapy water and rinsed the breakfast dishes. 'By the way, who exactly is Uncle Bertram?'

'Uncle Bertram was my alibi for Cedar Court. I try to see him most weekends and as Serena loathes him, and is convinced most of the family also share her opinion, it can be quite convenient. Sometimes I take him out to lunch or we have a game of chess and on occasions, if his asthma is bad, I've even stopped over with him. So as you can see, Uncle Bertram has his uses. Actually… I think you'd quite like him.'

'Why is that?'

'Because he's quite a character. If Uncle Bertram decides he doesn't like a person in the first instance, he makes sure they don't like him in return. That way he never has to entertain them at his home or attend what he calls ridiculous family gatherings.'

Sally was beginning to feel deeply uneasy. What if Hugh suggested taking her to meet…

'Yes, he's a crafty old devil is Uncle B,' Hugh continued affectionately, 'I suppose you could say he was the black sheep of the family; he was my father's middle brother – Uncle Stanley being the youngest.'

At the mention of his name, Stanley looked up from his basket at his master.

'Anyway,' said Hugh, 'the story goes that when Bertram was a young man he had a bitter row with his father – my grandfather – and he left home. Grandfather then cut him off without a penny but, just to spite him, Uncle Bertram made a fortune anyway.'

'And Uncle Stanley, what about him?'

'Oh, Uncle Stanley was the complete opposite. The dutiful younger son, and epitome of respectability. The only trouble was, he always looked a picture of abject misery. That's why Stanley here got his name.'

'That's not fair!' Sally said, reaching down to pat her second favourite visitor to the Elmsmarsh flat. 'Stanley doesn't look a picture of abject misery. Do you, boy?'

'Not now maybe, but he certainly did when he was a puppy.' Hugh looked at his watch. 'Sally, I'm sorry, I really ought to go. If you are sure about me coming back, will it be OK if I leave Stanley with you?'

'Of course, and why shouldn't it be all right for you to come back?'

Hugh shrugged his shoulders. 'I thought perhaps you might want to have friends round or perhaps go and see your sister.'

Sally lowered her eyes and whispered. 'When I know you're free, I only want to see you. I can see Jackie and the others when you have to be with… Serena.'

'Oh, Sally! Things between Serena and myself… well, let's just say they're different from when you and I are together. To begin with, we no longer sleep together. In fact we haven't…'

Sally placed a finger on Hugh's lips and looked up into his face. 'Please, Hugh… I think I'd rather not know.'

'Don't worry, I wasn't going into graphic details. I was merely hoping I could explain things. I'd hate you to compare me with some of those men who write to the problem pages protesting that their wives don't understand them.'

Managing a weak smile, Sally asked, 'And does Serena understand you?'

Taking her hand in his, Hugh kissed her tenderly before replying. 'Let's just say Serena and I understand each other perfectly.'

Returning from a walk with Stanley, Sally was surprised to find an enormous basket of fruit outside her door. Puzzled, she carried it through to the kitchen to examine the gift card wedged between a pineapple and a bunch of black grapes. She certainly hadn't been expecting visitors, and who would deliver fruit on a Sunday?

The card read simply. 'Welcome to Elmsmarsh. We hope you'll be very happy in your new home. Terry and Julie.' In a different hand someone had scribbled in brackets: 'Your neighbours across the landing, come and have a drink with us sometime.'

Her immediate reaction was to call straight away, just to say thank you – but she'd heard no sounds from their flat as she'd climbed the stairs with Stanley and hadn't Hugh said he intended to come back?

*

'Gracious! It looks like Covent Garden market in here. What happened while I was away?'

Sally handed Hugh the card from the basket of fruit.

'How very kind… and have you met Terry and Julie yet?'

'No, I think they must have gone out. I thought I'd pop in and say thank you one evening when you are busy.'

Hugh read her thoughts and nodded in understanding. 'As I recall, the estate agent told me they were a very nice couple. It's always useful to have one decent set of neighbours you can turn to in an emergency.'

'Hmm. Let's just hope I don't have too many emergencies, even if the neighbours are nice. Now, can I tempt you with some of this wonderful fruit while you tell me all about your wicked Uncle Bertam.'

'Sally, you can tempt me with anything you like – but first of all I want you to come here.

Hugh reached in his pocket, brought out a tiny sprig of mistletoe and held it above his head.

'Where did you get that? It isn't Christmas.'

'Uncle Bertam's garden. He has an old apple tree with a wonderful clump of mistletoe and I thought, as I didn't get the opportunity to kiss you under the mistletoe before… You probably won't remember, but Roz had that ridiculous tinsel in her hair and mistletoe wedged in her glasses.'

'Oh, I remember! Do you know, you quite made her day'

'Really? Well, come here and make my day,' said Hugh, reaching for her hand.

*

At the airport Hugh studied the arrivals board only to discover Serena's plane was delayed by almost an hour. Annoyed at having to wait unnecessarily when he could have been spending time with Sally, he set off on a tour of the airport. It could be useful to study other people's merchandise, and airport shops were invariably up to date with the latest trends.

After half an hour and about to head back to arrivals, Hugh's attention was drawn to a dainty silver box in a display case. Smiling, he approached the sales assistant. It was just what he'd been looking for. Putting the small gift-wrapped box in his pocket, he hurried to find Serena and Vivienne.

He noticed Vivienne almost immediately but was unable to attract her attention. She appeared worried and kept looking behind her anxiously. Of Serena there was no sign until…

Hugh saw her companion first. At least to anyone else, the tall and tanned Lothario by Serena's side would have passed as her companion. Hugh, however, knew otherwise. No wonder Vivienne was looking furtive. Serena usually left her *companions* behind in Gstaad. Changing positions and deliberately averting his gaze away from his wife, Hugh called to his sister-in-law.

'Vivienne! Over here.'

Vivienne looked flushed as Hugh relieved her of the luggage trolley and swung it away from the crowds.

'I expect Serena's having the usual problems with her luggage,' Hugh said, feigning ignorance of what he'd just witnessed.

Vivienne only nodded, relieved that Hugh had his back to her. Quickly she turned and gesticulated to her sister. Serena and her companion parted instantly, but not without an exchange on whisperings and knowing looks.

'Sorry we're so late, Hugh,' Serena said, catching up. 'There was a fresh fall of snow and it took simply ages to clear the runway. You must be bored stiff, darling. I know how much you hate airports. Still, I expect you found time for a drink or something.'

Taking his hand briefly from the handle of the trolley, Hugh touched his pocket reassuringly. Yes, he thought to himself, he had been able to find something!

With Vivienne safely home, Serena studied the newly spring-cleaned sitting room. The smell of beeswax and lavender mingled with her perfume. Hugh sighed as the cloying smell met his nostrils.

'You look tired, Hugh. I expect you've been busy with pre- and post-Christmas figures, while I've been away. And, if the immaculate state of this house is anything to go by, no doubt also banished by Mrs Burt.'

'Exactly,' acknowledged Hugh. 'You know what Mrs Burt is like for early spring cleaning the minute you're away. Anyway, it wasn't too bad, I stayed over with Uncle Bertram a couple of times. I thought it best to keep out of the way.'

'And how is Uncle Bertram and Stanley too, are they well?'

Biting his lip, Hugh struggled to keep his tone casual. Serena's sudden contrived concern for Uncle Bertram was always a sure-fire giveaway of her infidelity.

'Oh, they're fine, Serena, Bertram's asthma hasn't been helped by the damp weather and Stanley…'

But Serena wasn't listening. She was already crossing the floor. Pausing at the door, she blew Hugh a kiss. 'You don't mind if I go up, do you, darling? Only I'm simply exhausted.'

Relieved, Hugh watched her go then, flinging open a window, took a deep breath before making his way to his study. He switched on his green desk lamp and opened a file. Yes, Serena had been partly correct; he had been studying pre- and post-Christmas figures, but at this precise moment, would far rather be studying Sally's.

*

Before preparing for bed, Sally tied the small sprig of mistletoe to her dressing table mirror with a piece of white ribbon. Hugh had given her strict instructions to do so.

'You must put it somewhere high and do not let it fall.'

Smiling, she'd turned to face him with questioning eyes. 'Why is that?'

'Because it's Norse legend. When Freya, the goddess of love, cried for her lover, it is said that her tears turned to pearls when they dropped to the ground, just like the berries on the mistletoe. A string of pearls was then given to her for safekeeping and she hung them between heaven and earth for safekeeping.'

Making sure she'd tied the ribbon securely, Sally promised herself that she wouldn't let her mistletoe fall.

How very strange, she thought, turning to her reflection in the mirror. Perhaps that's why my mother used to say "pearls for tears". If only she was still alive, I could tell her about Freya and the legend.

Pearls of a different kind filled Sally's eyes as she thought of her mother. Had she really been dead for five years? It was amazing how time flew. At least she'd lived to see her first grandchild born to her youngest daughter and mercifully been spared the demise of her eldest daughter's marriage.

Opening a dressing table drawer Sally took out Hugh's navy blue silk pyjamas. She'd kept them ever since that first weekend together at Cedar Court. When she felt particularly sad and he wasn't with her she wore the jacket, wrapping the silk arms around her body. Tonight, wiping fresh tears from her eyes, she also counted the pearlized buttons. Just like the mistletoe berries, there were four.

'Pearls,' she murmured to herself, reminded not only of Freya's tears but also her own as she dabbed at her eyes, thinking of Hugh at home with Serena. She recalled his earlier words. 'We have single beds…'

Sally looked towards her own single bed where only hours earlier they'd lain together, locked in each other's arms. Swallowing hard, she forced herself to put Hugh and Serena out of her mind and think of Marion le Sage instead. Not only had she promised Laura she would look after Marion in her absence but also she must make a mental note to thank Julie and Terry for the fruit.

*

The following morning, Sally watched Marion squeeze yellow paint from a tube onto her palette, add the merest touch of green and apply it to the petal of a primrose.

'Are you sure you don't mind me watching you?'

'Not at all, I was always used to having one of the children hovering behind me or else playing at my feet. Besides, it's nice to have company for a bit.'

Transfixed, Sally gazed in wonderment as Marion's large hands, holding such delicate brushes, deftly filled in petals and leaves in the minutest details. Wasn't it Redouté, she thought, who'd painted all those wonderful pictures of roses? Yet he too, like Marion, gave the appearance of being large and clumsy.

Her long salt and pepper hair, worn in a thick plait, held flat against her head with two plastic hair slides, only served to accentuate her angular face. And the body beneath the flowing kaftan could have been anything from a size eighteen to a size twenty-four. Behind her, Sally seemed positively dwarfed in comparison.

Cleaning her brushes, Marion sat back to scrutinize her work with a critical eye. 'What do you think, Sally?'

'I think it's beautiful. I expect Laura's already told you that the earlier ones have been a huge success. We already have people placing orders for your summer selection.'

Marion laughed cynically. 'So I gather. She also tells me a store in Thornhampton might be interested in producing a series of prints. What was it she said… Bravington's?'

'Actually, it's Barrington's. It's where I used to work and, yes, I think they will be interested.'

'Oh,' said Marion, turning to look at Sally. 'You know the buyer at Barrington's, then?'

'Not exactly, because they don't have a buyer as such, but it is something the MD is hoping to set up.'

'And this MD, is he a decent sort of chap; I mean he wouldn't cheat me, would he? Only I fell foul of an unscrupulous dealer years ago and vowed never again.'

Trying desperately to remain nonchalant, Sally heard herself saying, 'Oh, Mr Barrington. Yes, I think you'll find he is a decent sort of chap.'

Anxious to escape further questioning, Sally made an excuse to return to the gallery.

*

That night, returning home, she heard music and voices coming from the neighbouring flat. With Hugh not expected for another four days, now seemed the ideal time to introduce herself.

'Hello,' she said, extending her hand, 'I'm Sally Palmer. I've come to thank you for the fruit.'

'Well, hello at last. Come in, Sally. I'm Terry. Look, we're just about to eat, why don't you join us? That's if you haven't eaten already?'

'No, I've only just come home from work, but won't Julie…'

A mouth-watering aroma wafted into the hall from the kitchen, reminding Sally how hungry she was. The prospect of not having to cook this evening was very tempting.

Terry was offering to take her coat. 'Don't worry, Julie always makes far too much and I'm in danger of getting a paunch.'

Terry patted his stomach with short pudgy fingers, gestured to Sally to take a seat and, opening the kitchen door, called through. 'Julie, it's Sally, our new neighbour. I've invited her to dinner.'

'Smashing,' came the reply, 'I'll be with you in a minute.' Through the steam of bubbling saucepans, Sally caught the rear view of slender hips in blue denims, a pink gingham shirt and a shock of curly blonde hair.

Terry poured Sally a glass of red wine. 'Italian,' he said, 'like the meal. Julie's a dab hand at Italian. Hence this' —and he pointed to his stomach yet again. 'Mind you, we do try to make up for all the pasta with the fruit.'

'Speaking of which,' Sally said, glancing towards a large Mediterranean terra cotta dish at the end of the dining table, brimming with fruit, 'you've certainly guaranteed me my dose of vitamin C for days. It was very kind of you.'

Raising her glass to her lips, Sally studied the immaculate setting of the room, with its blue and green tartan upholstery and rosewood furniture. She also made a mental note of the relaxed atmosphere Terry and Julie had created by the addition of numerous lamps. Perhaps, the next time she went into Barrington's to see Roz, she could also look for lamps.

'Terry,' a soft voice called from the kitchen, ' I'm OK with the small casserole dish, but can you please give me a hand with the large one, you know my wrists aren't strong enough.'

Terry stood up. 'I don't know,' he laughed. 'I get pestered to buy him a set of cast-iron cookware and then when I do, he complains he can't even lift them.'

Sally took a long gulp of wine. Terry had referred to his flatmate as male. Thankfully, that gentle hint helped disguise her surprise when Julie came through the door.

With the steaming chicken dish set upon the table, Julie removed his bulky oven gloves and held out a delicate white hand.

'Hi, Sally,' he said nervously. 'Nice to meet you at last. I'm Julian but as you've probably gathered people call me Julie.'

Pale blue eyes in a fine-boned face searched Sally's for signs of disapproval. There were none. Instead she shook his hand warmly and continued, 'I'm not surprised you can't lift those dishes, Julie. I can't either. In fact I gave mine away to a charity shop only last year. You obviously need biceps like Terry's to carry a dish that size.'

Sally nodded in the direction of the kitchen doorway where Terry was holding a large pan of tagliatelle. Stepping back to let him pass, she watched the two men glance fleetingly at each other and smile.

'So, Sally…' Terry said, placing the pasta on the table, helping her to a chair and passing her three plates, 'as you're our honoured guest for this evening, would you mind being mother?'

Towards the end of the meal, with the dishes soaking in the sink, Sally studied the enticing array of fruit.

'No wonder you have such an amazing selection. I had no idea the greengrocer's shop in Elmsmarsh belonged to you. I confess I haven't been in yet; I've been so busy sorting out my flat and also helping a friend with hers. Now that I know it's yours, I'll certainly make a point of calling in to see you both.'

'You can always leave us an order, if you don't want to carry it,' Julian insisted, 'and we can bring it home with us.'

'Thank you. That's very kind. By the way, who thought of the name, *Pots and Posies*?'

Terry smiled. 'Originally we were going to call it Potatoes and Posies, but Julie thought that sounded a bit too earthy.'

'Well, it did, and wasn't it you who said you wanted to get away from the image of a market stall?'

'Too right, I did! I've had enough of standing on market squares in all weathers. I need a bit of comfort in my old age.'

Sally fixed both men with a bemused smile. Terry could only be about thirty-five and Julie possibly in his mid-twenties. 'I think Pots and Posies is a super name. Very original.'

Terry nodded proudly at a dried flower arrangement of flowers, fruit and seed heads, standing in the bay window. 'The posies also refer to Julie's decorations. We—or should that be he—started doing them just before Christmas. Not only is he clever in the kitchen, he's a dab hand with oasis and flowers too.'

'Your mother doesn't seem to think so,' Julie said tartly. 'She threw the one I gave her at Christmas in the bin!'

'Like I said before, don't you go taking any notice of my old mother. Unlike some people, she just doesn't understand.' Terry turned and smiled at Sally and pushed the dish of fruit in her direction. 'Now, why don't we eat some of this up before it goes off.'

Later, while Julie busied himself in the kitchen with the last of the clearing up, Terry accompanied Sally on to the landing. He waited as she opened her front door.

'Thank you both for a wonderful evening,' Sally said softly.

'Don't mention it. In fact it's me who should thank you… for being so understanding about Julie. He gets a bit – well, you know, when he meets people for the first time. He hasn't lived with anyone before.'

'That's OK. I quite understand. Please tell Julie I thought the meal was superb and perhaps he'll let me have the Italian chicken recipe… I'll try it out on Hugh sometime.'

'Who's Hugh… your husband or partner?'

'Hmm,' Sally sighed. 'I suppose this is where I'm like Julie and I also get a bit – well, you know… Hugh's not only my ex-boss but also he's still married. We have an arrangement of sorts… I suppose in certain circles people might see me as Hugh's mistress.'

'So your relationship with Hugh is quite public, then?'

'Gracious, no! In fact, I haven't told a soul about Hugh…'

Sally clasped a hand to her face. Despite having made a conscious decision not to mention Hugh to anyone, including her sister and Roz, she'd just told Terry – the neighbour she'd only met a few hours ago…

'Don't worry, Sally,' Terry reassured, 'your secret will be quite safe with me and Julie, and if you ever want a shoulder to cry on, I'll always be here for you.'

'Ditto,' said Sally, fixing him with a wan smile, before she closed the door behind her.

CHAPTER 11

With the memory of grey winter months fading into spring, Sally found her relationship with Hugh blossoming like early spring flowers. Her earlier uncertainties about *their arrangement* disappeared as rapidly as the morning mists. The flat - now complete with double bed – was exactly as she wanted, Terry and Julie were the perfect neighbours and at Laura's Lair, Marion le Sage's miniatures were proving to be a huge success.

'All's well with the world,' Sally murmured, drawing back the bedroom curtains on a brilliant spring morning, 'and it's going to be a *wonderful* day.'

Ben thrust a bunch of daffodils into Sally's hand as Jackie wheeled Nathan through the front door in his buggy.

'I must say, you've got this place looking really nice, Sally. I admit I had my doubts at first. Somehow I never imagined you living in a flat. You being the gardener in the family.'

Filling a Poole pottery vase with water and quickly arranging the daffodils, Sally motioned to some seed packets on the kitchen work surface.

'As you can see, I haven't completely given up on gardening. Those are for the tubs and hanging baskets I'm planning to have on the balcony. I thought Ben could help me with them this afternoon, when Nathan has his nap.'

'Rather you than me,' Jackie said. 'You know my thoughts on gardening. If I had my way I'd have Dave concrete the lot! Speaking of whom, I'd better get a move on if we're going to make it to the matinee on time. Thanks again for offering to have the boys.'

Spreading out the seed packets after his mother had left, Ben asked, 'What seeds are they?'

'The red, yellow and orange ones are nasturtiums and the trailing yellow one on that packet is Creeping Jenny.'

'Why is it called that?'

'Because it creeps everywhere - like a spider!' Sally ran her fingers up Ben's arm and onto his shoulder.

He giggled, then added thoughtfully, 'I don't think I want to plant the creepy one… can I plant the 'sturtiums instead?'

After lunch, Sally took Ben onto the balcony where she spread out sheets of newspaper and filled the baskets with soil.

'Mummy has seeds but she told daddy she didn't want them watered,' Ben announced solemnly.

'I'm not surprised,' Sally said, pressing seeds firmly into moist compost, 'your mummy has never liked gardening. Now… how about you planting the nasturtium seeds?'

For a moment Ben looked confused, shrugged his shoulders and peered into the packet of seeds. They didn't look at all like his mother's; in fact, apart from the colour, they looked more like the shrivelled frozen peas she was always sweeping from under the freezer.

'Are you sure they'll grow?' he asked, wide-eyed.

'Yes, but only if they're watered regularly,' Sally said, stretching to fix the baskets onto hanging brackets, 'which means I'm going to need a special watering can if I'm to reach right up there.'

'P'raps we can go and buy one.'

'What a good idea. We'll go when Nathan wakes up.'

Ben scurried off to search for her handbag, then skipped back along the hallway. 'Found it,' he cried, waving it in the air. 'It was on the table by the bed.'

'Right then, let's go on a watering can hunt and… who knows, we might even find some Smarties as well.'

After making their purchases, she decided on the long route home. Sally led the way with the buggy across the fields to the rear of the flat, pointing out as she did so the frenetic gatherings of nesting birds. Stopping to pick some sprigs of pussy willow, she was surprised to find Terry coming in the opposite direction.

'Make the most of it while you can, Sally, it won't be here for much longer.'

'Sorry, Terry, what won't be here?'

'This lot for a start,' he said, waving his arms to encompass the fields beyond.

'You're not serious?'

Terry ran a hand through his closely cropped hair and designer stubble. 'Let's just say I heard a rumour.'

'What sort of rumour?'

'One of our customers – her husband works in the planning office – tells me there's going to be a new housing development.'

Sally's heart sank; her lovely view and all these beautiful fields may soon be gone. 'I suppose it's inevitable, isn't it? It all gets built on in the end.'

Terry toyed with the gold sovereign ring on his finger and gave a sardonic smile. 'Yes, and they call it progress. Anyway, if I were you I'd ask H-'

Before he had time to finish, Sally shook her head and darted a glance in Ben's direction. Terry got the message and changed the subject before they went their separate ways.

'Auntie Sally, is that man a pirate?'

'A pirate? Why, did you think he was?'

'He had a gold ring, necklaces and an earring and pirates have earrings and lots of treasure, don't they? '

Sally smiled, reminded of Terry's blue and white striped T-shirt, swarthy complexion and designer stubble. 'Sorry to disappoint you Ben, Terry's a greengrocer, not a pirate.'

There was a resounding, 'Oh, well, never mind.' But Ben felt in his pocket just to make sure his tube of Smarties and his other treasures were still there.

*

On the Monday before Easter, Sally received a phone call at the gallery from Muriel Baxter.

'Mrs Palmer, Mr Barrington has asked me to call you. He'd like to see the latest set of Marion le Sage's prints and suggested Thursday afternoon, if that's convenient?'

Confused, Sally replaced the receiver. If Hugh wanted to see her, he usually rang himself. Why get Muriel to ring her, instead? And more to the point, why Thursday, when he knew early closing at the gallery was Wednesday afternoons. There just had to be a reason, one she hardly dared contemplate.

Leaving Marion in charge at the gallery, and entering Barrington's, Sally avoided both the escalator and the lift and climbed the lesser used stairs with trepidation. She'd already decided Hugh was summoning her to the store to end their relationship and wished Thursday hadn't arrived so quickly. At the top of the stairs she heard a familiar voice.

'Sally! What on earth are you doing here?'

'Roz! You're late back from lunch. Have you been drinking?'

Roz held a finger to her lips and emitted a loud, 'Sshhh… not a word. Everything's under control, Sally dear. My junior's in charge of boobs and bums this afternoon and I've just been for a little drink with…'

'Mrs Hughes! Have you been drinking?' Hugh's voice echoed down the stairwell. Roz looked up at him from where she clung unsteadily to the banister. 'And, Mrs Palmer, I thought we had an appointment!'

Sally reached sheepishly for her portfolio containing Marion's pictures, unable to look Hugh in the eye. His tone was ominous as he told Roz to take the rest of the afternoon off and ordered Sally to follow him to his office.

Muriel Baxter beamed in greeting. 'Will you be requiring tea, Mr

Barrington?'

'No, Miss Baxter, I will not. In fact I would suggest you take an extended teabreak, I wish to talk to Mrs Palmer in private!'

Sally watched as Muriel's obsequious smile turned to a scarlet gash in an otherwise ghostly face.

'And, Mrs Baxter,' Hugh called after her,' absolutely no interruptions and you may bring my letters for signing at five o'clock!'

With panic rising inexorably in her breast, Sally followed Hugh through to his office. Expecting him to sit down behind his desk, she became even more anxious when he strode towards the doors of his private sitting room and motioned her inside. She stood with baited breath and closed her eyes until she heard the door slam shut.

'Right,' he announced, 'Now that we're alone, you can get undressed!'

Whirling round to face him, Sally saw that he was smiling.

'But I don't understand…'

'Don't you, my darling,' whispered Hugh, walking towards her. 'Well, I had to get rid of Muriel somehow, didn't I?'

'And Roz… what about Roz?'

'That,' Hugh chuckled, 'just happened to be pure coincidence.'

Sally fell into Hugh's arms, tears welling in her eyes. 'Y-you had me so worried. I thought you'd called me here to end our relationship.'

'Far from it,' he murmured, leading her to one of the settees, where he dried her tears. 'I simply couldn't bear the thought of not seeing you until next week.'

'We're supposed to be seeing each other this weekend.'

'I know,' Hugh said glumly, 'but I can't make it, I'm afraid.'

'I suppose Serena's made other plans for…'

'No, this time it's nothing to do with Serena. It's Uncle Bertram. He's become rather frail of late—so much so that he thinks he's dying. I don't think he is, mind you, but nonetheless he's asked me to take him to

Harrogate for Easter. He's anxious to spend some time with his old army friend.'

Reaching reassuringly for Hugh's hand, Sally noted the time on his Rolex. 'And I'm anxious to spend some time with you. Don't forget, you asked Muriel to come back with your letters at five o'clock.'

Heading for the customer cloakroom, Sally came face to face with Muriel Baxter. Her face was still ashen and she approached Sally cautiously. Acknowledging Sally's red-rimmed eyes (had Mr Barrington actually made Mrs Palmer cry?) and her flushed appearance, Muriel shook her head sadly.

'Oh, my dear! I'm *so* sorry, he's been in such a terrible mood, ever since he heard about his Uncle Bertram. You look as if he gave you quite a dressing down.'

Suppressing a smile, Sally bit her lip and reached for her handkerchief. Holding it across her mouth she feigned distress and murmured through the delicate folds of fabric, 'Yes, he did. Quite a dressing down.'

*

Jackie shifted uneasily in the chair, watching Sally pour the coffee.

'I mustn't stay long, Sal, as I've left Dave with the boys. It's just that I've got a confession to make. Well, not me exactly but Ben… the Saturday you had the boys, so Dave and I could go to the matinee…?'

Bewildered, Sally looked up. 'I don't understand. Ben was perfectly well behaved, as usual. We had lunch, I put Nathan down for his nap, then Ben and I planted some seeds before we…'

'Yes, but Ben went into your bedroom…'

'Did he? That's not unusual, I probably asked him to fetch my handbag or my keys. Anyway, nothing's been broken or damaged. Why are you so anxious?'

'Sally… Ben took something from your bedroom. Since he's been watching that pirate thing on kiddies' TV, he's been gathering all sorts of worthless odds and ends for his treasure chest, which in his case is only an old biscuit tin. However, this isn't worthless, is it? It looks like silver to me.'

At the mention of the word 'silver', Sally emitted a tiny gasp. Fortunately for her, Jackie hadn't noticed, she was too busy delving into the depths of her bag for the chased-silver box Hugh had purchased at Heathrow airport. The same silver box that he used for the condoms he kept in Sally's bedside drawer. 'So much nicer than seeing those bright green packets,' he'd remarked at the time, in an attempt at sparing her blushes.

Trying to spare her own blushes, Jackie continued as she clicked open the lid, 'Um - not only did Ben help himself to your box—and he said he was only borrowing it until he saw you again—he also found what was inside.'

Sally's mouth gaped open. 'Oh! How stupid of me.'

'What do you mean, how stupid of you? Of course it wasn't stupid. It's been such a long time since Richard left, I expect you'd forgotten all about those condoms. Besides Ben had no business to…'

'Well, I – er – suppose there's no harm done,' Sally said, eyeing the sealed green packets. 'At least he didn't open them and he won't know what they're for.'

'Oh, but he does. We told him some time ago.'

'You did what!'

'We told him what condoms are for.'

Sally stared at her sister in disbelief. 'Why, for heaven's sake, Ben's only a child. Whatever happened to innocence?'

'He found a packet of Dave's,' Jackie said, struggling to keep her tone casual, 'one Sunday morning when he came into our bedroom.'

'Are you saying he saw you and Dave…'

'No, thank God. Mind you if he'd come in ten minutes earlier…'

Sally gave a shudder; there were occasions when she simply couldn't understand her sister's carelessness, especially when it came to her children. 'OK,' she said, matter-of-factly, 'so, as you and Dave appear to have told

Ben the facts of life, perhaps you'd better tell me, too.'

'Don't be stupid, Sal. You already know. Crikey, you were married to Richard for long enough!'

'Of course I know. The point I'm trying to make is what did you tell Ben, exactly? Just in case he starts talking to me about making babies, or in this instance *not* making babies.'

'It all worked out quite well, really, as Ben already knew I had seeds in my tummy – we had to tell him something when I became pregnant with Nathan. We also told him that mummies can only have babies when daddies water the seeds and when they don't…'

'And when they don't?' Sally asked intrigued, almost dreading what was coming next.

Jackie shrugged her shoulders, 'Well, on those occasions daddies wear special wellingtons

that come in tiny packets.'

'And did Ben accept that?'

'Of course he did, wasn't it you who said a few minutes ago that he's only a child! We'll give him the full biology lesson and tell him about STDs when he's older.'

Lost for words, Sally recalled the conversation she'd had with Ben the afternoon they'd planted the seeds. No wonder the poor child had appeared so confused. However, watching her sister empty the contents of the silver box onto her lap, there was something that still niggled at the back of her mind. She gestured to the green packets. 'Taking into account all you've said, didn't Ben think it strange to find those in my bedroom?'

'Not at all. We told him Richard must have left them – mind you, it's a pity he didn't have them with him when he met Sharon! By the way, how long is it since he left?'

Sally didn't reply. She was only too relieved to be saved the embarrassment of having to explain why she had a box of condoms in the bedroom of her new flat. What did irk her however, was the fact that Jackie should assume she was no longer interested in having a sexual relationship.

'Don't look so hurt, Sal. After all Richard got his comeuppance, didn't he?'

'Yes, I suppose so…'

'And, as you won't be needing these,' Jackie said with a wink, scooping the condoms into her handbag, 'Dave and I might as well make use of them. Oh, and yes, while I remember, Ben said I was to give you these Smarties, by way of an apology for you know what. He saved you all the orange ones. As you know they're his favourite.'

'Then tell Ben thank you very much and that I'm not at all cross with him.'

'Will do,' said Jackie, plonking a kiss on her sister's cheek. 'And do cheer up, Sal, you don't seem your usual bubbly self today. Look, if you're lonely, why not ring that widower friend of Roz's? The one you met at New Year. What was his name, Bernard?'

*

Later that evening, Sally tipped the Smarties onto the table and counted them. There were ten. Poor Nathan, she mused, it must have been quite a sacrifice relinquishing all his orange Smarties. With her thoughts turning from her nephew to her sister, she considered Jackie's parting comment, 'If you're lonely…'

I'm not lonely, she told herself, sitting down on the settee and clasping a cushion to her breast, I'm simply missing Hugh and I have absolutely no intention of ringing Bernard!

Although Bernard had rung a couple of times following the never to be forgotten New Year's Eve concert, Roz had already forewarned her of Bernard's intentions. Sally was thus able to decline politely, both his invitation to dinner and the cinema. Grateful for Roz's intervention, Sally wanted desperately to tell her about Hugh. Keeping quiet about their relationship was proving to be such a strain. It was bizarre really; only Terry and Julie shared her secret. As for Hugh, at least he had dear old Stanley…

*

In Harrogate, driving past The Stray, resplendent with its spring blooms, Hugh headed back in the direction of the Ripon Road and Uncle Bertram. On the front passenger seat of the Range Rover was Uncle Bertram's prescription. Stopping for traffic, Hugh drummed his fingers thoughtfully on the steering wheel.

Bertram wasn't going to die, but the young doctor who'd been called out in the night said it had been a particularly bad asthma attack. He'd also advised against driving back to Thornhampton until Bertram was much improved. To do so at this stage would have been foolhardy. Besides, Cyril, Bertram's old army colleague, and his sister Rose appeared to be giving the old chap the best attention possible.

It wasn't staying away from Barrington's that bothered Hugh. A couple of phone calls to Muriel Baxter and his nephew Gareth had resolved those problems. It was not seeing Sally and having to cancel their plans yet again that bothered him. There was also the problem of Stanley.

Serena had made it abundantly clear that she was far from happy having to look after Stanley as it completely cramped her style. Admittedly Hugh had left her the Jaguar, but she refused to take 'the wretched animal' out in that and her sporty hatchback was hardly conducive for what she described loosely as Stanley's 'walks'.

Seeing a young mother pushing a baby in a buggy, with a toddler on one side and a black Labrador on the other, Hugh thought longingly of Sally. It reminded him so much of last Christmas when he'd come across the delightful trio in the park, while taking Stanley for a walk.

'Sally, my love,' he sighed, pulling into Cyril's driveway, 'oh, how I miss you.'

*

'Hugh old chap,' wheezed Bertram from his bed, 'so sorry to put you to all this bother.' He placed the spacer in his mouth, pressed down on the inhaler and breathed in as deeply as he could.

'Don't worry about it, Bertram. Things appear to be running smoothly at Barrington's. You know what Muriel Baxter's like. As for Gareth, I expect he's running round like a dog with two tails.'

'Speaking of dogs, Serena rang while you were out fetching my prescription. Rose took the call—something about Stanley and the vets?'

'Oh, Lord! I'd forgotten all about that. Stanley's due for one of his injections. I'd better ring Serena right away.'

'Hugh darling!' Serena said with relief when she heard his voice. 'So you did get my message. I wasn't sure. You know I couldn't understand a word that Rose – or whatever her name is – was saying. Yes, that's right. I just happened to look on your desk in the study and saw Stanley's appointment card for the vets. No, don't worry I'll take him for his injection.'

Returning to Bertram's bedside, Hugh shook his head.

'Everything OK?' Bertram enquired.

'Yes, surprisingly, Serena's offered to take Stanley to the vets. That's one thing less to worry about. Funny, I was expecting her to read the riot act.'

'Well, I expect she'll be wanting something in return, Serena can be such a scheming bitch at times!'

Hugh raised an eyebrow in his uncle's direction.

'I always sensed there was no love lost between the pair of you, but you're quite right, she's asked me to try and locate a piece of Moorcroft pottery for her collection.'

Bertram chuckled wheezily from his frilly pillows. 'You know me, my boy, as I said to Cyril while you were out, I am a bloody good judge of character. Oh, I'll admit Serena's a stunner, but has she made you happy? Has she, Hugh – has she really made you happy?' Bertram's voice had that inflection which usually meant he had no intention of giving up on the subject.

Hugh toyed with the fringe of the antimacassar on the bedside chair. For once he felt strangely vulnerable. Here he was in his late forties, being interrogated about the state of his marriage as if he was an errant schoolboy.

'Serena and I have a good relationship… I mean we've been married for almost twenty-five years. We understand each other.'

'Bah!' said Bertram angrily, sending his medication flying. 'Good relationship and understanding, my foot! Hugh, as my dearest nephew, I'll tell you something. You are a Barrington through and through and we Barrington's need more than just good relationships and understanding. Know what I mean, my boy?'

Hugh slanted a curious sideways look at the old man cocooned beneath layers of pink woollen blankets and a floral print eiderdown.

'Well, put like that, Uncle, I don't quite know what to say.'

'Don't you, Hugh? Well, I do! I'd be prepared to bet that young filly of yours, that you've got hidden away somewhere, is a damn sight better for you than Serena!'

'Whew!' Hugh whistled. 'That's quite a broadside you've fired.'

'I'm right though, aren't I? You can't keep much from me, Hugh. I've been around way too long.'

Bertram turned his rheumy old eyes in his nephew's direction. Hugh merely nodded, before saying softly, 'Yes… but I've told Sally I'd never leave Serena…'

'"Never" is a word I'd never use,' Bertram replied solemnly.

Hugh roared with laughter and patted his uncle's hand.

'What's so funny?'

'You are. Don't you realize what you've just said?'

With a sibilant splutter the old man's face creased into a grin and, patting the eiderdown in rhythm with his laughter, he sent a fine cloud of dust into the air.

Through his renewed coughing spasm, Hugh heard him beg to be taken away from all the 'damned lace, flowers, feathers and frills!'

CHAPTER 12

Scooping Nathan's Smartie offering into a Susie Cooper dish, Sally placed them in the middle of the coffee table and went to answer the phone. The distant male voice seemed strained yet familiar.

'Sally…'

'Bernard…?'

'No, it's not Bernard. It's Hugh.'

'Hugh, you're back! But you sound so different. Where are you? '

'I'm in a lay-by, on my way back from the vets. Are you alone, is it OK for me to come…?'

'Of course, but why have you been to the vets? Stanley, is he -?'

'Yes, it is Stanley,' Hugh said, his voice choked with emotion, 'but I can't explain now. I'll tell you when I see you. I'll be with you as soon as I can.'

He arrived not long after. Alarmed by Hugh's dishevelled appearance, Sally cradled him in her arms. He struggled to speak, trying to recount all that had happened in his absence.

'I can't believe Serena could do such a thing,' she whispered at length.

'Oh, she could all right! You don't know Serena as I do, Sally.'

'But why? Are you suggesting she did it deliberately… that she'd planned it before you went away?'

'Perhaps not before I went away – more like when I rang and asked her to take Stanley to the vets for me. I can still hear her voice now, all sweetness and benevolence, insisting I stay with Bertram.'

Hugh shuddered. 'How the hell was I to know Serena's idea of "taking good care of Stanley" was to have him put down the minute my back was turned!'

'That's unforgivable!'

'Unforgivable is right, Sally. Oh, I knew Stanley was old, and heaven knows, I would never have let him suffer, but the vet said he'd be good for a while yet.'

Sally stroked Hugh's head as he stared numbly into her eyes.

'What hurts the most,' he continued, 'is that I wasn't even there to say… goodbye.'

Sally eyes filled with fresh tears at the very thought. Poor dear Stanley bundled off to the vets by Serena, no doubt thinking he was going on an outing or else going to meet up with his beloved master.

Pulling away from her embrace, Hugh banged his fist on the coffee table, sending the dish of Smarties scattering across its shiny polished surface. His face was a suffusion of hurt and anger and his eyes flint hard as he remembered Bertram's description of his wife.

'Do you know what that bitch had the gall to say, in an attempt to appease the situation?'

Sally shook her head.

'She told me that at least Stanley had travelled in style… She took him in the Jaguar! And that, Serena assumes, makes everything OK.'

Stifling a sob, Sally also wanted to make everything OK, but how? In his current state of distress there was no way Hugh could drive anywhere tonight. As for returning home to Serena, that too was probably out of the question. Instead, she rose from the settee, took hold of Hugh's hand and whispered, 'Come along… come to bed.'

Resisting, Hugh said lamely,' Sally, my love, I don't really feel in the mood. I'm sorry.'

'I didn't mean for that, I just want to hold you in my arms and make the hurt go away; besides…'

'Besides?'

'Nothing,' said Sally. Now seemed not the time to tell Hugh about Nathan, her sister and the missing contents of the silver box…

In silence, Hugh allowed himself to be led into the bedroom and while he slept a troubled sleep. Sally found her thoughts drifting back to the early days of their relationship. The night of Edith Hawtin's retirement party (when she'd first offered to look after Stanley), and the never to be forgotten night of Edith's film show when Richard had appeared without warning and Hugh had come to her rescue.

Before that, however, there had been something else that evening; something that had woven its way into the darkest recess of her mind. She and Roz had not only over imbibed on the home brewed wine, but also Roz had insisted on divulging too many home truths as far as Hugh and Serena's marriage was concerned. At the time Sally had done her best to ignore them but now…

*

In the stillness of early morning, Sally stared into the blackness, aware of Hugh lying awake in her arms. Stroking his bare shoulders, she asked softly, ' Hugh… what about the vet?'

'What do you mean?'

'I presume you told him it was all a mistake. Stanley should never have been…'

'Oh, yes. The poor fellow was mortified when he discovered the truth. Apparently, Serena told him that I was too upset to take Stanley myself. She put on quite a convincing act by all accounts.' Turning to face her, Hugh held Sally's arm in a vice-like grip. 'You know, I've forgiven Serena for many things during our marriage, but I shall never forgive her for this… Never! You're all that matters to me now, Sally.'

Feeling the blood rush back through her arm as Hugh released his hold on her, Sally was also aware of him slowly and deliberately unbuttoning her nightdress. Minutes later, when he reached for the silver box, she faltered. 'I'm afraid it's empty…'

In the fervour of the moment, it was as if Hugh wasn't listening anyway. He loved Sally so much and was desperate to take her utterly and completely as his own. Other than that, nothing mattered any more.

*

Watching Sally appear with a tray of coffee, Hugh surveyed the scattered sweets on the coffee table. 'What's this, the morning after pill?'

Sally laughed and scooping up the Smarties, popped one into her mouth. 'Just in case,' she said.

Hugh laughed wryly. 'Hmm, I think you know you're quite safe from that – and other things.'

Wondering if by 'other things' Hugh was simply anxious to prove he'd used contraception as a way of protecting them both, Sally wasn't sure. Instead, she found herself asking. 'Won't Serena be wondering where you are? She's probably worried about you.'

'If she is, then it's too damned late! I'm sorry, I didn't mean to snap, it's just…'

'I know,' Sally said, smoothing the discreet silver hairs at his temples. 'I do understand. I loved Stanley too.'

Taking immense comfort from the love he saw reflected in her eyes, Hugh drew her into his embrace. 'Thank God I have you, Sally. Uncle Bertram was right. You are good for me.'

'Uncle Bertram! You've told him about me?'

'I didn't have to. The old chap is so perceptive, he'd already guessed.'

'Then... you don't think Serena knows too?'

'Lord no! She's much too interested in herself and her cronies to bother about us.'

Hugh stood up reluctantly. 'Speaking of which, I suppose I ought to be getting back, though God knows I'm dreading coming face to face with her. But I've some paperwork to catch up with before I head back to the office again.'

'You won't do anything rash will you?'

Hugh smiled. 'No, my love, I give you my word, I won't do anything rash… However, one of these days I might just take you to see Uncle Bertram. I think the pair of you would get on extremely well.'

'Why do you say that?'

'Because he absolutely loathes Serena!'

*

One look at Hugh's rigorously solemn face was enough to put Serena on her guard. Panic rose inexorably in her breast and her mouth and throat went dry.

'Hugh darling, you look all in. All that driving, to Yorkshire and back for Uncle Bertram – how is the poor man? Come and sit down and I'll get you something to eat. You must be quite ravenous.'

'I'm not hungry, Serena,' Hugh said, his tone icy.

'Well, a drink then, let me fix you a drink. I expect you could do with one.'

'Could I? Could I really? And why, pray, do you think I could do with a drink?'

Serena's eyes darted nervously in her husband's direction. With trembling fingers she picked up the decanter and poured two large whiskies. Offering one to Hugh she said feebly, 'I thought it might help numb the pain. I mean… I know you must be absolutely devastated about Stanley, but it was all for the best, my darling. The poor dog could barely walk from his basket to the back door…'

Hugh took a deep gulp of his drink. Feeling it burn as he swallowed, he paused before asking, 'And did you give Stanley a shot of whisky before you took him to the vets?'

Serena slanted a puzzled look in his direction. 'I- I don't understand.'

Placing his glass on the mantelpiece, Hugh turned towards her with cold assessing eyes. 'If you don't understand, then perhaps I'd better rephrase that. Before you took Stanley away, did you give him a shot of whisky to ease his pain?'

Anxious to change the subject, Serena made for the door.

'Well, if you're sure about not wanting anything to eat, Hugh, I think I'll go and have a bath and an early night. No doubt you'll want to check your mail before you come to bed. It's all on your desk in the study. Don't be too late yourself, darling.'

Sifting through the piles of letters, Hugh found his attention drawn time and time again to the photos of Stanley. What was it Serena had said? 'The poor dog could barely walk from his basket to the back door.' Surely not – the vet hadn't said anything about such difficulties. Slumped at his desk, Hugh put his head in his hands and wept.

Upstairs in their bedroom, Serena paid particular attention to her beauty routine, only tonight having removed all her make-up, she reapplied the merest touch of blusher and lipstick. Then brushing her hair until it shone like burnished gold she admired her reflection in the mirror.

Addressing a photo of Hugh on the dressing table, she traced her fingers across the antique silver frame, 'I'll soon make you forget Stanley, my dearest,'

Reaching down and opening her bottom drawer, Serena cast aside silks and satins in stained-glass colours, until she found what she was looking for. Though not originally meant for Hugh's benefit, she was desperate to make amends for Stanley's demise in the only way she knew how. Moments later, slipping into the wisp of black lace, she sprayed herself liberally with perfume, switched off all the lights, except the one on Hugh's side table, and waited anxiously for her husband.

*

Hugh woke with a start, sending papers tumbling to the floor. The green desk lamp cast an eerie glow about the study and he looked at his watch. It was almost one o'clock and he must have dropped off. Hardly surprising, he thought, as he got up to check the house for the night.

In the utility room, he automatically opened the back door, as if to let Stanley out for his late night stroll round the garden. But there was no Stanley, only an empty basket and the familiar lead hanging on its hook. Feeling a lump rise in his throat, Hugh bent down to pick up the dog's water bowl.

Though still half full, the dust of the past few days had collected on the surface. Tipping the water away, Hugh rinsed out the bowl and wiped it clean with kitchen paper. Then refilling it with fresh, clean water, he placed it back on the floor by Stanley's basket.

'Just in case,' he murmured. 'Perhaps it's all just a bad dream and in the morning you'll be here, old chap.'

The moment he opened the bedroom door, Serena's presence was more than enough to remind him it was not a dream after all. Hugh watched, as she got out of her own bed and slipped unceremoniously into his own.

'You don't mind, do you, darling?' she whispered huskily

The reply, when it came, shocked her beyond belief. 'Sleep in any damn bed you please, Serena, only don't expect me to share it with you!'

Removing his toilet bag from the still unpacked suitcase he'd taken with him to Harrogate, Hugh turned his back on Serena and strode towards the bedroom door. From now on the guest bedroom would suit him perfectly.

'You're simply over-reacting, Hugh!' Serena called after him. 'Stanley was only a dog, remember. And, if having a dog is that important to you, I'm sure we can find another one just like him…'

Over-reacting, am I? Hugh thought to himself, slamming shut the guestroom door. We'll soon see about that. As for finding another dog like Stanley…

Sitting on the bed, Hugh began to undress. Then, just to be on the safe side, he got up and locked the bedroom door. If Serena had come through the door at that precise moment… On the other hand, however, Sally had pleaded with him not to do anything rash.

'God knows I've never hit a woman,' he said, running his hands through his hair, 'and I've certainly no intention of starting now.'

Thumping the pillows in anguish, Hugh thought of Serena alone in his bed. What a pathetic figure she'd made in that ridiculous nightdress, if you could call it a nightdress. He'd never seen her wear anything like that before; whereas Sally, wearing his silk pyjama jacket at Cedar Court, had looked an absolute delight…

*

With a glance at the ominous thunderclouds forming across the fields, Sally closed the bedroom window and went in search of a damp cloth. There were thunder flies all over the windowsills and white paintwork. Rinsing out the cloth, the first clap of thunder echoed overhead at the same time as the ringing of her doorbell.

'Terry. Won't you come in?'

'No thanks, Sally. I've only dropped by to see if you're OK.'

'Yes, fine thank you. Did you think there was a problem?'

Terry rubbed at his stubbled chin. 'I didn't, but Julie was wondering if you'd like to come and sit with us; he thought you might be frightened of the storm'.

Sally smiled kindly. 'That's very thoughtful of him but tell him no, I'm not at all afraid of thunder; in fact quite the opposite. I rather enjoy a jolly good storm. At least it will clear the air. What about Julie, is he OK with thunder?'

'No way! He's absolutely terrified of it, poor thing. It's just as well I don't have to go out for another half an hour or so.'

'When you do, please tell Julie he's more than welcome to ring my doorbell. He can help me with all these wretched thunder flies.'

Sally held up the cloth impregnated with tiny black spots.

'Little buggers,' said Terry,' they get everywhere, don't they? We've even got them in the picture frames.'

'Mmm. That's one of the joys of living in the countryside, I suppose. Oh, I told Hugh about the rumours you mentioned—building across the fields—and he's going to look into it for us.'

'Cheers, Sally. How is Hugh by the way? I don't suppose he'll ever get over Stanley, will he? I won't tell you what my old mum said when I told her about Hugh's wife having the poor old dog put down.'

A slightly guarded look came into Sally's eyes; she knew Terry's mother lived in Thornhampton. 'You didn't actually mention Hugh and Serena by name?'

'Definitely not! Mum's the word in every way. I merely said a friend of a friend. Don't worry, your secrets are perfectly safe with Julie and me.'

Sally breathed a sigh of relief. 'Thank you so much. You don't know how much it means having someone to talk to about Hugh.'

'Hmm. I think I do,' Terry said, as another clap of thunder rent the air and a flash of lightning streaked through the curtains. 'Only too well in fact.' He nodded to where Julie was now peering into the hallway with terrified eyes. 'Believe me, I had a pretty rough time keeping Julie a secret, but now I don't give a damn! People can think what they like.'

'If only it was that easy for Hugh and myself,' Sally said, closing the door.

Returning to her task of dealing with the dreaded thunder flies, Sally tackled each and every surface in the bedroom. Pausing as she lifted the empty silver box from the side table, she was reminded not only of the last time she and Hugh had made love, but also the time before that when she'd been summoned to his private sitting room. He certainly hadn't kept any condoms there, so did this mean the delicate silver box was no longer needed…?

*

'Talk about "Flaming June",' Laura groaned in Sally's direction. 'If it gets any hotter I shall melt! I also know, because Marion keeps telling me, that I'd probably feel a whole lot better if I lost some weight.'

Helping Laura lift the box containing the latest stock delivery, Sally replied, 'Marion's not exactly sylph-like though, is she?'

'No, but considering she's almost six foot tall and I'm a mere five foot three, I feel twice as wide!'

Laura studied Sally's trim figure in navy floral print calf-length skirt and white silk blouse. 'It's really quite sickening, Sally. You eat like a horse and never put on an ounce. What's your secret?'

'Quite possibly all the masses of fruit and veg I eat, courtesy of my two wonderful neighbours.'

'Oh, yes. The two delightful homosexuals.'

Sally shot Laura a disapproving look.

'Sorry, Sally. I was forgetting Terry and Julie's relationship is quite a sensitive subject with you. Don't get me wrong I don't have a problem with their sexuality. It's simply that I was at school with a girl named Gay and she was such a pretty thing. It doesn't seem right somehow to refer to people as being gay.'

'Do people have to be categorized? Why can't adults have friends, partners or lovers, whatever their sexual preference?'

Laura regarded Sally thoughtfully. 'And what about your lover, my dear?'

'I… I… don't know what you mean.'

Placing a comforting hand on her friend's arm, Laura said simply. 'Shall I assume then… that you simply don't want to talk about him?'

Sally shook her head. 'If you don't mind, I'd rather not at the moment. It's not that I don't trust you. It's just that the situation is somewhat complicated, that's all.'

'Well, as long as he's not spinning you along, telling you that his wife doesn't understand him and he can't bear to leave his children.'

'It isn't like that at all, ' Sally said a little too quickly, 'besides he doesn't have any children.'

'Ah, but he is married? So why doesn't he leave his…'

'Laura, please! I've already said I don't want to discuss this.'

'OK. OK. I'll say no more. I'm only concerned because I don't want to see you hurt in any way. I apologize for prying.'

'And I apologize for biting your head off! I expect it's the heat or my hormones. Roz is forever warning me about the approach of middle age.'

'Middle age? Good grief you're not even forty. You've a long while yet before middle age. By the way, how is Roz?'

'Oh, just as outrageous as ever. She keeps begging me to meet her for lunch one day. I really do miss her company. She's such a character.'

'Not like Marion and me then. After Roz and Barrington's, we must seem a right pair of boring old farts in comparison!' Laura laughed and dabbed at the beads of perspiration on her top lip. 'I'll tell you what, next early closing, why don't we all go into Thornhampton and have lunch with Roz? Heaven knows, if this heat continues, I'm going to need some summer dresses. Marion tells me Barrington's summer stuff is lovely.'

Knowing that since Stanley's demise, Hugh was spending more time in the store, Sally became distinctly uneasy. Not only that, Barrington's had also been mentioned twice in the past five minutes. If she was to suddenly try and dissuade Laura from going ahead with this proposed lunch date and shopping trip, she could quite easily arouse suspicion.

Concluding it was far better to go along with the suggestion and anxious to avoid further mention of Terry and Julie, Barrington's and her mystery lover, Sally ripped off the Cellotape from another cardboard box. 'Right,' she said, a determined expression on her face, 'Let's get this stock unpacked, shall we? If we don't get a move on, they'll soon be delivering for Christmas!'

*

Clutching their acquisitions, Sally, Laura and Marion met up with Roz and made their way

across the market square. The sticky heat of the oppressively hot June day hit them full in the face. Laura ran her fingers through her thick apricot curls and sighed, envious of Sally's new-look shorter hairstyle.

Sally watched as beads of perspiration collected on the bridge of Roz's nose, causing her glasses to slip forward. Pushing them upwards, Roz looked about her for a spot of shade. Where to eat—that was the problem. The decision to avoid Barrington's restaurant had been unanimous. Now it was not so much a question of dying from hunger, but wilting from thirst.

'This is a spot of luck,' Roz said, sitting down under a red, green and white striped parasol. 'I'd forgotten all about this place opening.'

Four bank clerks, with their identity cards swinging, came scurrying round the corner and stopped abruptly, their faces crestfallen.

'Looks like we got here just in time then,' Marion agreed, 'we appear to have found the last free table.'

'They're young,' Roz announced. 'They've got more stamina than us. It won't hurt them to walk a bit further to find somewhere. Now you three, are you going to show me what you've all been buying?'

Watching them display their purchases, Roz gave a wicked grin and winked at Sally. 'If I didn't know otherwise, I'd think you were all going on a camping holiday. At least I'll know where to come if Donald and I ever need a tent.'

'Take no notice of her,' Sally said, 'she's only jealous because she has to wear that uniform all day long.'

'Too right I am, duckie.' Roz pulled at the waistband of her skirt. 'The last thing you want to wear in this heat, even with Barrington's air conditioning, is fitted clothing.'

Marian toyed with her spritzer, watching large cubes of ice melt without trace. 'I don't suppose this heat is exactly helping business though.'

Roz shrugged her shoulders. 'You wouldn't have thought so, but I gather from Muriel Baxter that sales figures are up. At least with summer starting early, people are rushing out to buy their holiday clothes. Unlike last year when we were in winter woollies practically all year long.'

Roz gulped thirstily at her drink and crunched on the remains of an ice cube. 'That's something to please the boss man anyway. I expect you heard about him losing his dog—the poor chap looked gutted. That's the trouble with having pets…'

Watching the waiter place the tempting dish of antipasto on the table, Roz enquired, 'Whilst on the subject of things tasty and exotic…'

'I wasn't aware that we were,' Laura said with a knowing grin, following Roz's gaze as the young Italian flashed a brilliant white-toothed smile in her direction. 'Sorry, Roz, do continue.'

'I was only going to ask where you're all going for your holidays?'

Sally shook her head. 'At the moment, I'm going nowhere, but Laura's doing the Shirley Valentine thing and going off to Greece and Marion…'

'I'm going to Cornwall,' Marion continued, 'to stay with friends, so I shall come back bigger than ever, which is why I need my "tent".' She patted the vast multi-striped garment on her lap, folded it over several times and popped it back in its Barrington's bag. 'You see, I have a terrible weakness for Cornish cream teas.'

CHAPTER 13

Sally stared dejectedly from the bedroom window across the fields of scarlet poppies. At any other time their bright silky blooms would have lifted her spirits. With Hugh away, however, it was like being in the slough of despond. Feeling tears prick her eyelids she recalled his last visit.

'I'm so sorry, Sally. I knew nothing about it. Serena arranged it all with Charles and Vivienne behind my back. According to Serena it's a belated birthday surprise, but I know it's simply another of her schemes to put things right since Stanley. By involving her sister and brother-in-law, she knows damn well it makes it hard for me to refuse. Charles and Vivienne are such decent people and…'

Hugh paced the floor in despair, his dark eyes filling with anger. 'Look, I'll make it up to you when I get back, I promise.'

'You don't have to make it up to me, Hugh, or make any promises. I have no claim on you and Serena is still your wife.'

'In name only, and she needn't think this outrageous suggestion of hers is going to put us back in the same bed!'

Sally said nothing and fixed her gaze numbly on the dried flower arrangement Julie had made for her at Easter. Hugh drew her into his arms and whispered. 'That wasn't very tactful of me, was it? But it is true, my darling. Serena and I will not be sleeping together; I've made that perfectly clear and she knows it.'

'But it might not be that easy if you're with Charles and Vivienne. Won't they expect you…'

'Oh, I can assure you it will be very easy. The villa sleeps eight and I intend to get up early and play as much tennis and golf as I can. Serena's a late riser. My excuse will be separate bedrooms so as not to disturb her.'

Stroking Sally's hair, Hugh continued. 'Anyway, let's not talk about that, I have some good news for you.'

'Good news. In what way?'

'The proposed building plans Terry alerted us to, they won't be affecting you after all. There's a new development right enough but it won't encroach on your view. Actually, it all sounds quite tasteful, a type of mews setting in keeping with the local yellow sandstone.'

*

Now, forcing thoughts of Hugh and Serena's holiday from her mind, Sally was suitably mollified. The bright yellow JCBs, lying in wait with their gaping jaws ready to gorge on virgin meadows had all trundled off in the opposite direction. She could at least go to work in better spirits.

Sorting through the post at Laura's Lair, Sally found the postcard signed SV 2. She laughed and handed it to Marion.

'I suppose by that she means Shirley Valentine the second and has no doubt met her Costas or Dimitri.'

'Heaven help us when she returns then, you know what Laura is like for holiday romances.

'Dear Laura,' Marion sighed, 'she hasn't changed a bit in all the years I've known her.'

'People don't though, do they—despite their promises.'

'That sounds a very deep statement, Sally. Is it prompted by anything in particular?'

'Not really, but I was sorting through some old photographs at the weekend and came across early photos of Richard. Looking back, I suppose I must have been really naïve when I met him.'

'Meaning?'

'Meaning, I thought I could change the little things that annoyed me about him, after we were married.'

'Oh, Sally! And pigs might fly my dear!'

With a wistful smile, Sally fixed Laura's postcard onto the gallery's kitchen door. 'Whoever he is, Laura, make the most of him and all that lovely sunshine.'

Marion studied Sally carefully. 'Are you beginning to wish you'd gone with her? You could have, you know. She's closed the gallery for a fortnight anyway, so there really was no need for you to come in.'

'I know,' Sally conceded. 'I suppose I was feeling restless and I also wanted to ask you something.'

'Ask away then.'

'I was wondering if you could paint a miniature of a dog - that's if I gave you a photo to copy? Reaching into her handbag, Sally brought out some photos of Stanley. 'It's for a friend, you see, and it is, at least it was, a very special dog.'

Marion took the photos and laid them on the table where she could see them better. As she did so, her thick plait fell over her shoulder. Standing up, she pushed it to one side. 'Hmm. It's not something I usually do. I much prefer flowers to animals, but as it's you, this time I'll make an exception.'

Sally hugged Marion warmly. 'Oh, that's wonderful! Thank you. Thank you so much!'

'I wouldn't get too excited if I were you, my dear. You haven't seen the end result yet. It might be far from perfect.'

'I doubt it… and in case you were wondering there's no hurry but…'

'You'd still like to know how long it will take me?' Marion unclipped and refastened her brown hair slides. 'It's difficult to say, really. The flowers don't take too long as a rule but as it's a dog… Tell you what, Sally, if you don't mind me taking these photos on holiday with me, I could do it while I'm away.'

*

Emerging naked from the shower, Hugh was surprised to find Serena standing in his bathroom. She was holding two glasses of chilled white wine.

'I thought you might like a drink, darling. Charles said it was a pretty exhausting tournament.'

Hugh nodded, fastened a towel round his waist and murmured an almost inaudible thank you.

Struggling to keep her tone casual, Serena said softly. 'Hugh, don't you think we could forget this silly business over Stanley…' She stopped abruptly when she recognized the now familiar look in his eyes.

Setting one of the glasses on the bathroom shelf, Serena choked back a sob. 'Shall I go away for a while and come back when you're dressed?'

'That won't be necessary, Serena. Just tell Charles and Vivienne I shall be out in ten minutes!'

Hugh heard the champagne cork before he reached the terrace.

'Hugh, old chap. Here, have a glass of champagne. After all it is your birthday we're supposed to be celebrating and if you can pass a glass to your good lady wife…'

Hugh turned to face Serena, who stood draped in a fuchsia-pink and purple sarong, with matching bougainvillea blossoms entwined in her hair. What was it Uncle Bertram had said about her in Harrogate? 'Oh, I'll admit she's a stunner but has she made you happy—really happy?'

Holding out the champagne glass, Hugh saw not his glamorous sun-tanned wife, standing against the exotic backdrop of Moorish arches and azure-blue ocean, but Sally, dressed in his navy-blue silk pyjama jacket, nervously sipping champagne.

Seeing Hugh smile in her direction, a glimmer of hope stirred in Serena's breast, but it was extremely short-lived. When Hugh heard the clink of glasses and the resounding 'Happy Birthday, Hugh!' he was immediately transported back from Cedar Court and Sally to the villa in Spain with Serena. As she raised her glass in her husband's direction, only Hugh noticed how her sculptured mouth twisted with displeasure.

'Right everyone, let's eat,' announced Vivienne, appearing with an enormous dish of paella. 'And while we tackle this little lot, you two must tell us how you plan to celebrate your silver wedding anniversary. I trust you're really going to celebrate in style!'

*

While Marion scooped the contents of a pot of clotted cream into a glass bowl, Laura cut up squares of halva and placed them on a dish in the middle of the table. Sally looked at them and smiled.

'It looks as if my offering is the healthiest of the lot. Mind you, if I eat any more of these I shall end up looking like a strawberry.'

'Another contribution from the neighbours?' Marion enquired.

Sally nodded. 'Yes, they spoil me. All these wonderful summer fruits, I can't stop eating them. I had thought of making some jam, but as it's way too hot to stand over boiling jam pans, we might as well indulge.'

On her plate Laura had a heap of caster sugar and a generous dollop of cream. Sally and Marion watched as she dipped a large strawberry into the sugar and then the cream before popping it into her mouth. 'Mmmn,' she sighed,' Wonderful. It reminds me of…'

'We don't want to know!' Marion interrupted with a grin. 'You already look like the cat that got the cream.'

'Yes, and you're becoming almost as bad as Roz!' Sally teased.

'Not for much longer, I've too much work to do. Before we know where we are, the kiddies will have gone back to school and Christmas will be upon us.'

Sally groaned. 'Don't remind me. In last week's Thornhampton Gazette, they even had a feature on this year's pantomime!'

'Well, I shall love you and leave you two to finish the rest of this.' Laura's be-ringed hand motioned to the remains on the table. 'I shan't be back until late, Sally, so if you can lock up…'

The two women watched her go and shook their heads.

'Whoever he was, it certainly looks as if he did her the power of good. That will keep her going until Christmas.'

Sally got up from the table with Laura's empty plate. 'Mmm… and she looks simply amazing in that colour.'

Marion watched as a flash of green walked past the window. She sighed enviously, 'Not everyone can wear that acid green. You know it always makes me think of spurge and those wonderful lime-green tobacco plants. Which reminds me, I must try painting some one of these days.'

'Oh, you mean Euphorbia and Nicotiana.'

Marion laughed. 'Of course, I was forgetting you were the gardener in our midst. How are the hanging baskets and tubs by the way?'

'Coming along nicely, I'm really pleased with them. I must take some photos.'

'And how about you, Sally… are you coming along nicely?'

Sally looked up, bewildered, unsure of what Marion was implying. Her thoughts had been elsewhere. 'I'm not sure I'm with you, Marion.'

Toying with a strawberry stalk in the remains of the caster sugar, Marion said softly, 'Well, you are pregnant, aren't you?'

'No! Of course I'm not! What makes you think that?'

'You just look it that's all. Having had five of my own, I thought I'd recognized some of the symptoms… obviously I was mistaken - sorry.'

'But I haven't been sick, isn't that the first sign… morning sickness, I mean?'

'Not necessarily. The first sign is missed periods.'

'I haven't actually missed any, they're just a bit irregular.'

'OK… and feel free to tell me to mind my own business here, but when was your last period? Can you remember?'

'Yes, I can. It was at Easter and I even remember thinking what a stroke of luck because…'

Sally bit her lip. She was just about to say, that's when Hugh was in

Harrogate with Bertram.

'You were saying,' Marion coaxed.

'Oh, nothing, it doesn't matter.'

Sally smoothed her hand over her breasts and down onto her abdomen. Through the folds of the loose summer frock she'd bought at Barrington's there was only the gentlest curve. She regarded Marion with questioning eyes.

'You really think I am pregnant?'

Marion nodded and pulled her chair closer to Sally's. 'Accidents do happen you know. Even I can vouch for that – and even if you are taking precautions. I take it you were…'

'Yes, of course but since…' Sally wanted to say, since Stanley died we haven't… But she daren't risk any mention of Hugh. Instead she said softly, 'We haven't recently and as he's infertile…'

'Oh, Sally!' Marion cried. 'Don't tell me you fell for that one! I admit it's novel, my dear, as usually it's "I've had a vasectomy so I'm OK!" But if you want my advice, you'll get yourself a pregnancy kit asap!'

'But it's true. Ages ago even Roz told me…'

Marion patted Sally's hand. 'Take my advice, it's best *not* to believe everything people say.'

In numbed silence, unable to comprehend the conversation that had just taken place, Sally rose from the table and looked about her. 'I'd better clear these plates and dishes away and then get back to the gallery.'

'Oh, don't worry about this place. If I were you, I'd go home and rest,' Marion urged. I'll keep an eye on the gallery as I'm reasonably up to date with my painting. Speaking of which…'

Marion reached into her folder and brought out not one miniature of Stanley but two. Placing them on the table she said, 'I hope they'll be all right. I did that one first – just the dog on his own – but I couldn't resist having a go at copying one of the other photos you gave me.'

'But that's me!' Sally said through misted eyes. 'You've painted me as well. Oh Marion, they're beautiful, thank you.'

Marion smiled modestly. 'I'm glad you like them. I have to confess even I'm pleased with my efforts. After I painted the first one, I thought why not try one of you and the dog together. Perhaps your friend might like that one too?'

'Y-yes. Perhaps he will. I'll get them framed as soon as I can.'

Wrapping the miniatures in tissue paper, Sally placed them carefully in her bag and headed for the door. 'If you're sure about me leaving early…?'

'Positive,' said Marion.

Sally waited anxiously for Hugh's arrival, wondering quite how and when to tell him her news. Even now she still couldn't believe the result of the pregnancy testing kit. As for what to do next…

Thinking back to her sister's two pregnancies and the arrival of Ben and Nathan, the prospect of motherhood already appealed to her. The very thought of holding Hugh's child in her arms brought tears to her eyes. But would Hugh share her enthusiasm? In recent weeks he'd made it abundantly clear that he and Serena were married in name only, yet the word divorce never entered the conversation. Even now Sally didn't expect Hugh and Serena to divorce – but would she be able to keep the baby's paternity a secret?

Reminded of one of her friends at university, Sally recalled how she'd had a baby by a married man and that somehow they'd managed to keep the child a secret for five whole years!

'A lot can happen in five years,' Sally sighed. 'I've got to get through the next five months first.'

She took down at her calendar and counted back to the time when she presumed she had conceived. Four months, she really was four month's pregnant! Gracious! She must buy a book or something, and also make an appointment to see a doctor.

Holding both hands across her gently swollen stomach, she suddenly felt the urge to know what this tiny being - growing miraculously inside her - was like. Jackie had referred to her embryos in stages; spot, blob and tadpole, yet this didn't feel quite right to Sally. Her gaze wandered to the two neatly wrapped packages, waiting for Hugh.

'There's only one thing I can call you,' she murmured, patting her stomach, 'I shall call you baby Stanley.'

Walking to the bathroom door, she declared brightly, 'Right, Stanley, this is where you and I have a refreshing shower before your daddy arrives and we tell him the good news!'

*

At the mention of breakfast, Hugh stretched lazily and watched as Sally drew back the bedroom curtains to let in the early morning sunshine.

'That was a wonderful meal you cooked last night, Sally. I don't think I could manage breakfast just yet. Can I suggest you come back to bed instead?'

Slipping back between the sheets and into his arms Sally said, 'I notice you didn't go in for naked sunbathing while you were in Spain.'

'Apart from tennis and golf I didn't go in for anything else, either, which is why I missed you, and want you so much now.' Turning on his side, Hugh reached out to caress her breasts. She flinched visibly. 'Are you all right? Did I hurt you?'

'No,' she lied, turning on her back, ready to receive him – now was not the time to explain her tender and swollen breasts. 'It was nothing… nothing at all.'

Later, running her hands down the fine hairs on his chest, bleached by the sun, Sally fixed him with a curious smile. 'Do you know what I think we look like?'

'No, tell me.'

'I think we look like that wonderful chocolate dessert I had at Cedar Court. The one with the white, milk and dark chocolate… remember.'

'Why, so we do, me with my deep suntan, you with your pale-golden arms and smooth, white body. We really must go back to Cedar Court sometime,' said Hugh, his right hand straying to the silver box on the side table, 'But that's one thing we won't be taking with us. You'll have to think of another use for that from now on.'

'I already have. Well… not for the moment but perhaps in five months' time.'

Hugh frowned hard. 'Why can't you use the box until then? What's so important about five months' time?'

'I thought I could use the box for the contraceptive pill. You see… I'm, er, four months pregnant.'

'You're what!' Hugh gasped, drawing away from her.

Sally saw his eyes go cold, and felt the muscles in his body go rigid.

'I know it must be a shock, Hugh—it certainly was to me—and I know you don't have any plans to leave Serena, but I did wonder if you might be remotely pleased… You've always taken such an interest in Ben and Nathan.'

'Pleased!' Hugh's dark eyes flashed with anger as he moved from the bed and reached for his clothes. 'Pleased? Why should I be pleased that while I've been keeping you, you've got yourself pregnant by another man?'

'But I haven't! It isn't another man's child, it's yours, I swear. Apart from Richard and until I met you, I'd never slept with another man.'

'Hmph! And since you met me, by the sound of it, you've certainly made up for it!'

'Whatever do you mean?'

'Look at the time I came here and found… whats-his-name from next door in your arms.'

'You mean Julie? But he was only here because he and Terry had had a row and he was upset.'

'And you expect me to believe that? What were they rowing about then?'

'I don't know,' Sally said, exasperated. ' What do gay couples row about?

'Certainly not about being pregnant, that's for sure!'

'Well, just because they're gay doesn't mean to say they don't have arguments!'

Hugh was putting on his trousers; his mind was in turmoil. Something else that he couldn't quite pinpoint was niggling away in his head. What was it? Moments later, his gaze fell on the miniatures Sally had given him last night before they went to bed; Marion le sage's delightful paintings of Stanley on his own, and Stanley and Sally together.

That was it! The day he came from the vets and he'd telephoned Sally… when she'd answered the phone she'd called him Bernard. Bernard… that unassuming but embarrassing fellow from the New Year's concert? Surely not!

'Well, one thing's for certain, Sally, the child you're expecting definitely isn't mine – or had you forgotten I'm infertile!' Picking up his jacket, Hugh strode angrily to the bedroom door. 'And if it isn't Julie or Terry's or that fellow who accompanied you to the New Year's concert, I suppose you could always try your ex-husband?'

'Richard! But that's preposterous; you know that as well as I do.'

'Do I? Well he seems to be making quite a name for himself as a stud by all accounts.'

'Hugh' Sally sobbed, 'please! You're making a big mistake.'

'Not making – more like made,' Hugh said, momentarily unmoved by her tear-filled eyes. 'I'm sorry, Sally, as far as I'm concerned, we've nothing more to say.'

Covering her nakedness with the lace-trimmed ivory sheet, Sally held out the two miniatures. Slowly and deliberately Hugh picked them both up. The one of Stanley on his own he placed in his pocket, the other of Stanley and

Sally together, he placed face-down on the side table next to the silver box. Without even pausing to look at her again, Hugh walked down the hallway and let himself out of the flat for what he determined to be the very last time.

Hearing the door slam shut and wrapped in a tangled mass of sheet, Sally ran to the window. With tears streaming down her face, she was in time only to see the midnight blue Jaguar speeding away from the car park in a cloud of dust.

In a daze, she righted the painting of herself and Stanley and placed it lovingly by her bed. Then, when she was showered and dressed, she went to the balcony and picked a spray of bay leaves. These she wove like a miniature laurel wreath and fixed them carefully to the top of the picture frame.

'Oh, Stanley,' she cried, as her eyes brimmed with fresh tears, 'What on earth are we going to do?'

Crushing a solitary, stray bay leaf with her fingers, Sally reached for her address book and searching through the pages, one at a time, realized there was no one she could phone and confide in unless…

Terry stood at the door, bleary-eyed and in his dressing gown.

'I'm sorry,' Sally said, choking back a sob, ' I forgot, you don't get up 'til late on a Sunday. Perhaps I can come back later?'

'No, you won't!' Terry declared, pulling her inside. 'You'll come in now. What's the problem, Sally? If you don't mind my saying so, you look bloody awful!'

'Thanks, that's probably because I feel it. Oh, Terry… remember the time you said if I ever needed a shoulder to cry on… Well I need it now. The trouble is I'm pregnant and Hugh doesn't want to know.'

'The bastard! And there was me thinking what a decent chap he was.'

'Oh, he's decent all right,' Sally continued. 'It's simply that he won't accept the baby is his. Even I have to confess, I can't understand how it happened.'

Terry fixed Sally with a peculiar look in his eyes and his fingers rubbed rasp-like against his chin. 'Well… if you sleep together, which you do, then isn't it obvious how it happened? Or is there something my old mum didn't tell me about the birds and the bees?'

Sally smiled weakly and allowed Terry to take her by the hand and lead her to the sofa. 'Right,' he said, placing a cushion behind her back, 'let's just make you comfy and then you can tell your Uncle Terry all about it.'

At that moment Julie emerged sleepily from the bedroom. With his pale blue eyes, mass of golden curls and dressed in a pristine, white bathrobe, Sally thought he looked like an angel.

If he was surprised to see her sitting on the sofa with Terry's arms comfortingly around her shoulders, he didn't show it. Terry answered the unspoken question. 'Sally's going to have a baby.'

'Oh, how lovely! Shall I make us all a coffee and put some champagne in the fridge for later – when Hugh comes round?'

'Hugh won't be coming round, Julie,' Terry said softly. 'But if you could just make the coffee…'

CHAPTER 14

During the following weeks, an air of gloom and despondency descended on Laura's Lair.

Marion and Laura exchanged knowing looks when Sally was there and when she wasn't, their conversation turned to acute concern for her wellbeing.

'Has she seen a doctor yet?' Laura asked.

Marion shook her head sadly. 'No, I keep telling her to go, but it's almost as if she's on another planet. She seems in a daze most of the time.'

'Perhaps she wishes she was… as far away from that bastard as possible.'

'Laura! You'd better not let Sally hear you call him that.'

'Well, he is, a complete and utter bastard! If I knew who he was, I'd certainly find him and tell him.'

Marion was hugely relieved that Laura didn't know; the situation was bad enough already. Sally was clearly still deeply in love with the fellow, yet the pain and anguish on her face was enough to make anyone weep.

No, Marion decided Sally didn't need anyone to go and bully the man responsible for her distress; she needed someone to guide her gently through her pregnancy… unless of course she was considering an abortion. But wasn't that already too late?

Convinced Sally would never consider this as an option, Marion was desperate for Laura to leave the gallery. The place was far calmer without her these days. 'Look,' she said, motioning to the wall clock, 'you go off and do your rounds or whatever else it is you do, and leave me to worry about Sally and the baby.'

Laura fingered her curls into an apricot-froth round her still-suntanned face and nodded thoughtfully. 'OK. Hint taken. I've probably too fiery a temperament to deal with the situation and as you're much calmer than me...'

'I've also had five babies of my own.'

'Crikey! So you have. You know I find it impossible to think of your brood as ever having been babies. I always visualized them being born carrying knapsacks and Greenpeace banners. I just wish...'

'Yes?'

'I just wish I knew who the bastard was, that's all – are you sure Sally didn't tell you?'

'Positive, and don't look at me like that, either, Laura! In fact, when I see you all set to do battle, I'm glad you don't know.' Marion sighed, 'All I can tell you is that on one very rare occasion, when Sally was talking about you-know-who, she also mentioned Roz's name in the same sentence.'

'Oh, so he could be a friend of Roz's,' said Laura, picking up her car keys, 'then perhaps I should go and see R-'

'Laura, if you do!' Marion threatened.

*

Charles and Hugh picked up their tennis racquets and walked back to the pavilion and its changing rooms.

'Whew, that was a good game, Hugh, I enjoyed that.'

'You mean you enjoyed beating me?'

'Have to admit, I did, 6:2- 6:4- 6:1. Why, I feel just like what's his name when he beat that Spanish chappie for the gold medal at the Olympics.'

Charles studied his brother-in-law's dark countenance and patted his shoulder genially. 'Don't look so glum old chap. After all, it's ages since I've beaten you. Usually it's the other way round.'

'I'm sorry, Charles, I was miles away.'

'Now, don't go and spoil my victory by saying you weren't concentrating on your game,'

Hugh smiled weakly. 'No, of course not, that wouldn't be very gentlemanly of me, would it?'

Standing in the shower, Hugh recalled the painful parting with Sally. That hadn't been very gentlemanly either. But how else did she expect him to behave, faced with such a shock announcement? Surely she wasn't that naïve to think she could tell him the problem of his fertility had been resolved almost overnight. Hugh groaned audibly.

Charles' voice called out from the neighbouring shower cubicle, 'Hugh, are you OK?'

'Yes,' said Hugh, 'nothing to worry about,' and he turned the shower to its coldest setting. With luck the icy needles of water would numb the pain and desire he still felt for Sally.

There was also the problem of Serena. For days she'd been pestering him, not about returning to their bedroom – she'd conceded on that point, weeks ago – but about this wretched business of their wedding anniversary. Egged on by Vivienne, Serena was desperate to make it a pretty spectacular occasion. Left to Hugh, he would have preferred to forget it. He had other things on his mind.

Back in the drawing room, Serena sat with a drink in one hand and a pen in the other. 'Hugh darling! Just the man I need. I've been making some lists.'

'Lists?'

'Yes. Lists of guests, menus and likely venues.'

'Guests and menus, I can understand, Serena, but why venues?'

'Well, this house isn't really big enough, is it?'

Hugh raised an eyebrow and looked about the expansive drawing room, which in turn led to a rather spectacular Victorian conservatory. As for their dining room where they never had had any problem seating people…

'And of course, being January,' Serena continued, breaking into his train of thought, 'we can't really have a marquee in the garden.'

Hugh walked to the patio doors and stared thoughtfully across the expanse of manicured lawns and borders. A clouded blue butterfly hovered near the buddleia. Dipping and closing its wings, the colour reminded him of something. The carpet at Sally's flat. They'd even made love on that carpet – just after it had been laid and before Sally's furniture had arrived.

'That makes two of us then,' Sally had whispered shyly.

'Two of us?'

'Yes, me and the carpet, we've both been laid today!'

He'd smiled and taken her in his arms, caressing her body as he did so.

Hugh suppressed a sigh and shivered. Serena was standing by his side. She placed a concerned hand upon his arm.

'Are you all right, darling? Is there something bothering you?'

Hugh shook his head. 'No, I'm fine, thank you. Someone's just walked over my grave. Isn't that what they say when you shiver for no reason at all?'

Serena gave a wry laugh and linked her arm in his. 'I would say you're simply feeling cold. There seems to be a distinct chill in the air this evening. When Mr Burt was cutting back some of the shrubs and summer bedding, he even mentioned a distinct smell of early autumn in the air and suggested having a bonfire.'

Taking hold of Hugh's hand, Serena led her husband to the sofa and her piles of lists and brochures. 'We can't have you talking about graves at a time like this. We've a guest list to sort through!'

Hugh perused the lists of names, while Serena scribbled down menus and had conversations with herself about people with special dietary needs, until he could stand it no longer. When she began a tirade on colour schemes and table settings, he placed pen and paper on the table in front of him and stood up.

'Serena, by the looks of it, our wedding anniversary is in danger of turning into a fiasco. There are people on these lists we haven't seen in years. In fact, I thought half of them were dead! If you want to have a celebration, fine, but let's at least keep it simple.'

Seeing the crestfallen look on her face, Hugh felt a tiny pang of guilt and sat down by her side. 'Look,' he said gently, 'I'm only suggesting we cut down on numbers, that's all. Why don't we restrict it to twenty-five couples and have it here?'

'Why twenty-five couples?

'We've been married for twenty-five years, isn't that reason enough? One couple for each year… and if you pick our dearest and closest friends and/or relations, what could be nicer?'

'Oh, Hugh,' Serena sighed, 'darling, what a wonderful idea.'

She turned to kiss him and he shivered again.

'I definitely think you're getting a chill,' she announced, feeling his forehead and running her hand gently down his cheek. Nuzzling against him, she whispered seductively, 'You know, if you're cold, we could always go to bed to keep warm. Do you remember how freezing it was on our wedding night, how we went to bed early and your fingers were so numb with cold you could hardly manage the zip on my wedding dress?'

Looking all dewy-eyed, Serena continued. 'My beautiful wedding dress, all those yards of wonderful white velvet and the cape and hood. Perhaps I should wear velvet for our anniversary, not white of course, but black perhaps. What do you think, Hugh?' Serena placed a hand on his knee. 'Shall we go to bed?'

At the mention of bed, Hugh rose abruptly. There was only one person he wanted to go to bed with and the last time he'd seen her… With a perfunctory look at his watch he strode to the door. Stunned, Serena ran after him.

'Hugh, where are you going? I thought we were…'

'Sorry, Serena, I promised Charles a drink as he completely slaughtered me at tennis this afternoon.'

*

'I must say, this is pretty decent of you,' Charles replied in response to Hugh's invitation as he opened the front door.

'You're sure Vivienne won't mind me dragging you away?'

'Good Lord, no! I'd better just check to see if she's got her box of tissues.'

'Why? Does she have a cold?'

Charles chuckled warmly. 'No, she's watching one of those *Heart Surprise* thingies and it always ends up with her in tears.'

Hugh frowned. 'I must confess my ignorance. What's a *Heart Surprise* thingy when it's at home?'

'Oh, just one of those programmes where they find long-lost relations that you haven't seen since the year dot.' Charles gave a cynical smile and lowered his voice to a whisper. 'Mind you, I wouldn't mind betting that half these people probably hate each other and have no wish to be reunited… yet they all end up crying in each other's arms.'

Charles motioned to the sitting room door, 'You'd better pop in and say hello to Vivienne while I go and fetch my jacket. Won't be a tick.'

'Hello Vivienne. How are you?'

Vivienne turned a tear-filled face in her brother-in-law's direction.

'Good programme is it?' Hugh enquired.

'Wonderful!' Vivienne sighed ecstatically. 'You see that poor woman there. Well, in the 1950s she was deserted by a GI – there used to be an airbase at…'

'And let me guess,' Hugh broke in, remembering Charles' earlier description of the programme, 'they've just been reunited.'

'Oh, no, Hugh! Far from it, he must have been horrible anyway. I doubt she'd want to be reunited with him – that's if he's still alive. No, he deserted her when she told him she was pregnant and she had to give the baby up for adoption – we've all heard what it was like in those days. Anyway, they've just reunited her with her long-lost son. Isn't that amazing?'

Vivienne's eyes filled with tears once more. As she reached for a box of tissues and blew her nose hard, Hugh turned his attention to the television screen. There an elderly white-haired lady was being comforted in the arms of an athletic middle-aged man.

Leaving the room, even Hugh felt a lump in his throat. When Charles appeared in the doorway, he called goodbye to his wife and followed Hugh to his car.

'What's it to be, the golf club or the Melbourne Arms, Hugh?'

'The Melbourne if you don't mind, Charles. I not in the mood for the golf club set tonight.'

'Problems at home with the good lady?'

'Not exactly what you'd call problems. It's simply that Serena's got this bee in her bonnet about our wedding anniversary. I mean it's not exactly a Royal Wedding, is it?'

Charles gave a laconic smile. 'If you care to think about it, as far as some of the royals were concerned a few years back, a silver wedding would have been quite an occasion. At least the younger ones appear to be more committed to matrimony.'

Hugh nodded in agreement and swung the Jaguar into the pub car park.

Handing Charles a beer once they were inside, Hugh raised his own glass. 'Here's to Thornhampton's Andre Agassi. And thanks again for the match, Charles, you played well.'

Heartened by his brother-in-law's praise, Charles replied, 'And here's to your anniversary plans.'

'Don't remind me. No doubt Serena will have covered the entire dining-room table and floor with her lists by the time I get home.'

'I take it she doesn't watch *Heart Surprise* then?'

'*Serena*? You've got to be joking, Charles! You know Serena; she's not at all like Vivienne and definitely not a sentimentalist.'

Charles sipped his beer thoughtfully and wiped a fine layer of froth from his moustache.

'You know, he said, turning in Hugh's direction, 'it's peculiar really – Serena and Vivienne, I mean. There they are, two sisters, complete opposites in every way, yet they're the best of friends and always have been.'

Hugh was studying his own reflection in his glass, his face looked strangely sallow and distorted.

'Mind you,' Charles reflected, 'that's probably why they do get on. Although, I have to confess… when Serena had dear old Stanley put down, Vivienne was extremely cut up about it. She'd already told Serena not to make any rash decisions until you'd got back from Harrogate. But you know Serena…'

Hugh nodded. He did, only too well.

*

When Roz met Sally for lunch, it was far too cold to sit under gaily-striped umbrellas. They opted for the aromatic warmth of the trattoria instead. Nibbling on a breadstick, Roz faced Sally across the table and a look of concern spread across her face. Sally looked different somehow, yet she couldn't quite pinpoint why. Tiredness perhaps – she certainly had deep circles under her eyes – and as for the deeply unflattering baggy top that she was wearing under her coat… Sally never used to wear clothes like that when she worked at Barrington's. Assuming it was because there was insufficient heating at the gallery, Roz snapped another breadstick in half and said brightly.

'Right, tell me about everyone and everything at the Lair. Has Laura trapped anyone recently?'

'No,' Sally smiled. 'Not since Costas when she was on holiday.'

Roz's eyes scanned the restaurant for the young waiter who'd served them on their last visit. 'Hmm. I was wondering… as I can't see him, you don't think she's scared off our handsome Luigi, do you? He doesn't appear to be here today.'

'Who?'

'Luigi, the gorgeous young thing who served us before. Laura kept giving him the come-on, remember?'

Sally shook her head.

Forty minutes later Roz reached for her handbag. 'Well, Sally Palmer, if you've finished playing with that plate of lasagne, and you don't want coffee or dessert, how about coming with me to buy a pair of shoes? It won't take long, as I even tried them on a couple of days ago. I've still got twenty minutes left of my lunch break, so I'll still get back to Barrington's on time.'

Leaving the shoe shop, Roz grabbed at Sally's arm. 'Why didn't you try on that lovely pair of high heels? They were so pretty and you've got such dainty feet. Unlike me, who needs shoes the size of kipper boxes!'

Sally turned to Roz with a forlorn look in her eyes. 'There's no point in me buying pretty shoes, Roz. To begin with I don't think I'll be able to walk in heels that high, and in a couple of months I probably won't be able to see my feet. You see… I'm, er, pregnant.'

'You're what? You dark horse! No wonder I haven't seen you in a while.' Dropping her shopping, Roz flung her arms around Sally in the middle of the market square. 'Sally that's wonderful!'

As astonished shoppers passed by, Sally's eyes brimmed with tears and she clung onto Roz's shoulders.

'Hey!' Roz declared. 'What's all this? You're going to have a baby and you're crying. Surely you must be over the moon? I am, even though you've obviously been keeping a certain special man a secret from me. Who is he by the way and where did you meet him? No, don't answer that here – it's way too public. Perhaps tell me on the way back to Barrington's. Which reminds me they've got some gorgeous new things in their baby department… Oh, I can't wait to tell Donald… Is there going to be a wedding before or after the baby's born…?'

Roz's burst of enthusiasm diminished rapidly when she saw Sally's crestfallen face. 'Oh, dear! Me and my big mouth, yet again. Have I been jumping to all the wrong conclusions here?'

'Yes, Roz. I'm afraid you have.'

'So I take it there are problems and I'm not going to need a new hat?'

'You could say that, I suppose.'

Roz looked at her watch. 'And do you want to talk about it? There's still time before I head back to…'

'Not at the moment. All I really wanted to do today was tell you about the baby and apologize for keeping it a secret until now. Believe me I had been intending to tell you…'

'And I'm jolly glad you have told me, after all we've been friends for so long. Better late than never, as the saying goes,' Roz said, grabbing hold of Sally's arm.

'Where are we going?'

'To Barrington's to buy something for the baby.'

'No, Roz,' said Sally, wracking her brain for an excuse. 'I know too many people there. I don't want them to know about the baby just yet.'

'Oh, right. Point taken. In that case, we'll just have to go over there to *Les Enfants*. I'm not having you going home empty handed today. What do you need?'

'What do you mean, what do I need?'

'Well, what have you bought already?' Roz asked, nudging Sally through the door of the exclusive baby boutique.

'Nothing.'

'Nothing! Sally Palmer!'

Armed with bags from Les Enfants, Sally found herself being led towards Barrington's after all.

'Roz… I've already told you…'

'I know and don't worry. We're not going to babywear, we're going to my department. One thing you're really going to need is a decent maternity bra!'

In the confines of the changing room and the baby purchases concealed in a large Barrington's bag, Sally found herself in a more relaxed frame of mind.

'Tell me, 'Roz whispered, reaching for her tape measure, 'aren't you just the teeniest bit happy about all this?'

Sally rubbed lovingly at her bump. 'Yes, I am, honestly. It's just that…'

'Just what?' said Roz, taking the first measurement.

'I wish the father was happy too.'

'No doubt he'll come round. I expect, if it wasn't planned, that he was a bit shocked when you told him.'

In her mind's eye, Sally relived Hugh's unexpected outburst when she'd told him about the baby. "A bit shocked" was hardly how she would describe it!

Emerging from the changing room with Roz, Sally was mortified to see Hugh coming in their direction. For a brief moment he looked as if he was going to ignore her and walk the other way, but seeing Roz nod in greeting, he had little choice but to approach.

'Mrs Palmer. How nice to see you and are you well?'

'Yes, thank you, Mr Barrington.' Sally felt her throat go dry. What else could she say to the man she'd known so intimately?

Hugh stared at her with flint-hard eyes before turning to Roz. 'Mrs Hughes, I understand you have a complaint about one of our suppliers. Perhaps, when you've finished serving Mrs Palmer, you will come and see me? Ladies, if you'll excuse me.'

Watching him nod curtly and turn away, Sally choked back a sob.

'Whew!' whispered Roz. 'What's got into him?'

Quickly regaining her composure, Sally gathered up her shopping. 'I'd better be going and you'd better not keep him waiting.'

'Suppose not,' Roz said, hugging her goodbye. 'Muriel says he's been extremely irascible of late. It's probably his hormones. Male menopause or something.'

'Or something,' Sally whispered to herself, making her way to the escalator. Still at least that was one hurdle over. Roz had been a real tower of strength. Next on her list was her sister!

*

'Right then. Leave it with me, Mrs Hughes. If they can't guarantee their deliveries, we will tell them we'll find another supplier. I shall expect a full report from them in forty-eight hours.'

Roz was deeply impressed with Hugh's no-nonsense way of dealing with her complaint. For months she'd been trying to get LDL to improve on their delivery times. Even old established family firms like Lady Daisy Lingerie had to function effectively if they were to keep up with their competitors, particularly as the company had been endorsed by Barrington's. Long-standing customers were beginning to lose patience and some, Roz knew, had even deserted them for the High Street chain stores.

'I've told them to email me,' Hugh announced sharply.

'Hmm. I doubt whether LDL even know what that is,' said Roz. 'They probably burn up all their discontinued stock of brassieres and corsets and send smoke signals instead.'

A brief glimmer of a smile flickered across Hugh's face. Roz breathed a sigh of relief, and made as if to leave.

'You didn't have any trouble serving Mrs Palmer, I take it?'

'No, Mr Barrington. LDL cater for the more mature woman and fuller figure. Sally's far too young. Besides…'

'Besides…?' Hugh stood up to escort Roz to the door.

'Well,' she said in hushed tone, 'perhaps I shouldn't tell you this but I'm sure you'll be as thrilled as I was when I heard… Sally is pregnant. Isn't that wonderful news?'

'Yes, wonderful,' Hugh responded weakly, 'and what is the, er, father's reaction to the good news?'

'Oh, not very favourable at the moment, I'm afraid. I don't know who he is, mind you, but I'm sure he'll come round in time.'

'Really, Mrs Hughes. What makes you say that?'

'It stands to reason, doesn't it, Mr Barrington? What man doesn't want a son to dandle on his knee, or to take to cricket or football?'

Roz bit her lip. Spying the photos on the wall of Hugh Barrington playing tennis and golf, she realized only too late, she'd made another classic Roz Hughes *faux pas*. The poor chap could only fire blanks! Hurrying to the door, all she wanted to do was beat a hasty retreat but HB was barring her way.

'And how does Mrs Palmer know it's a boy. Have the doctors told her?'

'No, because she still hasn't seen a doctor. I tried to persuade her, but I think she's frightened of doctors and hospitals in general. Sally really ought to go you know,' Roz said hurriedly, trying to cover up her earlier *foot in mouth* episode. 'I mean, having a baby at her age, there could be a problem.'

Watching Roz scurry away, Hugh closed the door of his office and returning to his desk, buried his head in his hands.

*

'You're *what*!' Jackie spun round from where she was standing at the sink, peeling potatoes.

'I'm pregnant.'

'But how?'

'Jackie, I hardly need to tell you *how*!'

'OK, *who* then?'

'I'm not prepared to say.'

Angrily, Jackie threw a peeled potato into a bowl of water, where it bounced up and splashed her face. At that moment Ben came running into the kitchen. Seeing the water dripping down his mother's cheeks, he enquired anxiously, 'Mummy, why are you crying?'

'I'm not crying, the potato splashed me when I dropped it in the water. Although, heaven knows, I've plenty to cry about.'

'Why?' Ben's voice pleaded.

'Your Auntie Sally is pregnant. She's going to have a baby!'

Ben left his mother's side and walked over to Sally. He peered at her inquisitively and placed a tiny hand, stained with felt-tip pen, on her tummy. Turning his head to one side he said, 'Oh dear. What happened?'

'What makes you say that, Ben?' Sally asked kindly.

Ben twisted his mouth from side to side thoughtfully, before replying. 'Because you don't have a daddy to water your seeds, do you?'

Sally and Jackie's eyes met in alarm across the kitchen.

Bending down to her nephew's level, Sally stroked his hair away from his face. 'Well, Ben, it's like this. I did have a "daddy", but he just sort of disappeared!'

There was a gasp from the kitchen sink as the knife slipped in Jackie's hand and she cut herself. Grabbing a piece of kitchen roll to stem the bleeding, she turned to Ben, urging him to wash his hands before tea.

'What are we having?' he cried, running to the cloakroom.

'Sausages, mash and spaghetti.'

'Is it 'ghetti from a tin or a packet?'

'A tin.'

'Oh,' came the voice, muffled by running water. 'I don't like 'ghetti from a tin. I like Auntie Sally's 'ghetti best. She puts leaves in hers.'

Jackie raised her eyebrows in despair towards her sister.

'He means bay leaves in spaghetti Bolognese,' Sally enlightened, briefly reminded of Stanley, her bay tree and Hugh.

Later, with the boys in bed, and in a much calmer frame of mind, Jackie turned to face her sister. 'Um, from what you were saying earlier, do I take it because Jack took those condoms from your bedroom you…'

Sally nodded. 'You could say that. Until that time we'd always taken precautions.'

'Oh, Sally! I'm so sorry! Why on earth didn't you say something when I put them back in my handbag?'

'To begin with, I didn't like to. It seemed mean somehow, particularly as you made it very clear that you and Dave didn't want any more babies at the moment. I was also a bit cross with you for assuming that I was past having a sexual relationship.'

'Phew! And you've certainly proved me wrong on that score, haven't you? What have you decided to do about the baby? Will you still keep it, particularly as the father appears to have abandoned you?'

'Of course!' Sally said angrily, reminded of just how outspoken her sister could be. 'I certainly don't intend to have an abortion if that's what *you're* implying. This baby is very special to me.'

CHAPTER 15

Returning home, Sally drove to the garage block behind the flats. Far better to put her car away, rather than wait until later. It had been a somewhat emotional and tiring day. First Roz, and then her sister. Now all she wanted was a warm bath and an early night. Locking the garage door she was startled by a familiar figure hovering in the shadows.

'Hugh! What are you doing here?'

'I came to see how you were.'

'You know that without having to ask. You've already seen me once today!'

Hugh's eyes scanned the discreet swelling of her tummy where her coat gaped open. 'You're still pregnant then?' he asked clumsily.

'Yes. Why, were you hoping I wouldn't be?'

'No, it's just that I'm concerned. I understand you haven't yet seen a doctor.'

'What makes you say that?'

'Mrs Hughes told me.'

'Well, you don't have to worry, Hugh. I didn't tell her anything else!'

'Sally, please, why won't you see a doctor?'

'It's none of your business why.'

'Isn't it? I thought it was from what you'd led me to believe.'

Objecting to the inference in his voice, Sally responded angrily. 'In which case, do I take it you're offering to come to the doctor's with me? Perhaps we could ask Richard and Bernard – not forgetting Terry and Julie – to come along too. Then we could put all your names in a hat and the first one I pull out could be the lucky father!'

'I don't think this conversation is getting us very far, do you, Sally?'

'I never expected it to!'

Hugh put a hand out to touch her but seeing her flinch, put his hand to his head instead. Running his fingers through his hair he murmured softly, 'I get the distinct impression I'm unwelcome here.'

'How positively astute of you. I thought you of all people would realize that I entertain my friends in my bedroom, not a draughty garage block!'

Though her tone was acerbic, in her heart Sally was longing to reach out and touch him—feel his lips on hers and be warmed by his embrace. Instead, from the sombre look on his face, just his cold icy voice saying, 'Regardless of what you think of me and what's been said this evening, I am deeply concerned for your welfare and would suggest you go and see a doctor.'

Choking back tears, she nodded and watched him walk away, only to run blindly after him, just as he reached the Jaguar.

'Hugh!' she called breathless.

Opening the car door, he looked up, wondering what else she could possibly have to say.

'Hugh… I know you'll probably think it's none of my business but your… inability to have children… how did you find out? I mean, did you ever have any tests?'

'Isn't the fact that Serena had a child before I met her test enough?'

Sally watched him shake his head as if completely nonplussed by such a foolish question. It seemed there was nothing more to be said between them.

*

Serena studied her morning post critically. She was waiting for revised menus from the caterers. On reflection, Hugh's suggestion for close friends and family at home was proving to be a far better idea than she'd thought.

She would be able to decorate their feature staircase with garlands of flowers of her own choosing, have a horseshoe-style table (decorated with more garlands), set up in the dining room and after dinner people could drift in and out, chatting about old times. She emitted an appreciative sigh. It would all be so wonderful.

Hugh, who was reading the morning paper, spied yet another list being thrust in his direction. He removed it carefully from where it was in danger of being stuck to the dish of ginger marmalade.

'Serena, please!'

'Sorry, darling. I just wanted you to have that one. It's the menus.'

'What do I want with menus? I thought that was your department.'

'It is. But I'm sure you'd rather see to the wine. To do that, Hugh, you'll need to know what we're eating. And when you've finished your breakfast, I'd very much appreciate it if you would call in to see James before going into the store.'

'James? James who?' Hugh enquired, folding his newspaper. It was obvious Serena had no intention of letting him read it.

'James from the wine merchants, of course!'

With an air of impatience, Serena began loading breakfast dishes onto a tray. Watching her stack the dishwasher, Hugh enquired thoughtfully, 'Serena… have you never wondered what happened to your James?'

'*My* James? Whatever do you mean?' Serena's mind clicked away like a computer, searching for a relevant programme. In all her 'little arrangements' there'd never been a James.

'James – your baby. Wasn't that what you called him, before he was handed over for adoption?'

With a resounding crash, the plate Serena was holding dropped to the floor. Her face was ashen.

'I'm sorry,' said Hugh, stooping to pick up the pieces, 'I should have realized what a shock it must be, hearing his name mentioned after all this time.'

Clinging onto the dishwasher Serena whispered, 'Yes, yes, it is, but why? I mean what made you mention him now?'

'It was when you mentioned the name James. It reminded me of something Vivienne was watching on television the night I called for Charles.'

Unable to see the significance, Serena waited for Hugh to explain.

'There was this programme, where a woman was reunited with the son she'd given up for adoption years ago. I merely got to thinking…'

'Thinking what, Hugh?'

'Thinking how nice it might be to try and find *your* James for you, a sort of anniversary celebration, if you like.'

Keeping her back to her husband, Serena answered quietly, 'No, Hugh, I really don't think that would be a good idea. Just think how distressing it could be for him after all this time. Anyway, he's probably perfectly happy with his adoptive parents – and it wouldn't be fair to rake up the past.' As an afterthought she added, 'Besides, how would we find him?'

'I would have thought quite easily. Apparently they do it all the time on these TV programmes.'

'Hugh, stop please! It was all such a long time ago. Years in fact, before I even met you, and much too painful to remember. I handed James over for adoption and that was that. I really don't think we should start interfering in his life now.'

Hugh shrugged his shoulders. 'OK, if that's what you want. It seems such a shame, that's all, especially when you think we've no children of our own and there's a great deal to inherit. Perhaps the boy could do with some financial help.'

'Hardly a boy!' Serena said tetchily. 'As we're about to celebrate our silver wedding, he must be nearly thirty and should have made his own way in the world by now.'

Taking the menus from the breakfast table, Hugh made his way towards his study. Serena followed him nervously.

'Hugh, darling. I'm sorry. I shouldn't have bitten your head off like that. It was a wonderful gesture on your part – truly – but I think we should leave James where he belongs, in the past, don't you?'

In a rare moment of compassion, Hugh bent and kissed Serena's cheek. 'Perhaps you're right. I won't mention it again.'

*

In trepidation Sally got up from her seat in the waiting room and made her way towards the door marked Dr Jeremy Mason. She knocked timidly.

'Mrs Palmer, do come and sit down.' Motioning her to a seat by the side of the desk, Dr Mason studied his computer screen.

'I see you're a new patient to Elmsmarsh. How long have you been living here?'

'About eight months.'

'And you've only just registered? You've obviously had a healthy start to life in Elmsmarsh… so how can I help? What's the problem?'

'The problem,' said Sally, looking into grey-green eyes, 'is that I'm pregnant. Well, it's not exactly a problem in that I don't want the baby, because I do, but…'

'But what…?

'The baby's father says he can't be the father because he's infertile and his wife's already had a baby by another man and…'

'Just one moment, Mrs Palmer, you've lost me, I'm afraid. Can we go through that again but this time a bit slower please?'

Explaining the situation Sally watched Dr Mason scratch his head and jot down some notes, before looking at his computer screen.

'I take it then that the father of your baby is not your husband?'

'No – I'm divorced.'

'And there are no children from your first marriage?'

Sally shook her head. There seemed little point in recounting why she and Richard were divorced and had no children.

'Right then, and when was the date of your last period? Can you remember?'

'Yes. Good Friday, April the fifth.'

Doctor Mason's rainbow-shaped eyebrows shot up. They were copper-coloured and wiry like his hair and reminded Sally of the sisal doormat they'd had at home when she was a child.

'April fifth! Why haven't you been to see me before?'

'I don't like doctors and hospitals. When my father was dying…' Sally's eyes filled with tears. 'My mother couldn't cope, you see, and my sister was too young…'

'I understand. But as we're dealing with birth here and not death, the situation should be greatly improved. Now let's see, how old are you Mrs Palmer?'

'Thirty-four.'

'And as a point of interest, how old is the father?'

'I think he's forty-seven.'

The sisal matting arches shot skywards again. Dr Mason stroked his chin. 'And this is your first pregnancy, no miscarriages…' getting up from his chair he motioned to the examination couch. 'If you'd like to go behind the screen, take of your pants and tights, I'll come and examine you.'

Concentrating on Dr Mason's head as he probed and prodded gently, Sally decided his shape resembled the copper urn Jackie had standing in her hearth… broad at neck and shoulders and narrow at the hips. Strange, she mused, even his eyes she associated with copper; they were the colour of verdigris.

Dressed and back in the chair, Sally waited anxiously.

'EDD January tenth,' said Dr Mason, studying a printed chart.

'Pardon?'

'I'm sorry, I was forgetting this is your first baby. EDD – estimated delivery date. In your case January tenth, does mid-April ring a bell?'

'Why – should it?'

'That's when you possibly conceived.'

'Oh,' was all Sally replied, wondering if Dr Mason thought her a complete simpleton. She hadn't been aware of bells ringing the first time they'd not used… yet at the same time she remembered mid-April very well. How could she ever forget seeing Hugh in such a state of shock, when he'd just come from the vets, this time without his beloved Stanley. She let her fingers trail to where her own Stanley lay curled up inside her body and felt a warm glow of contentment.

Dr Mason looked up from where he'd been keying information onto his computer. 'Now… what was it you were saying earlier about the baby's father claiming to be infertile?'

Sally told him all she could remember, which in fact wasn't a great deal. When she'd finished the verdigris eyes took on a mischievous twinkle.

'Mrs Palmer, please don't take this the wrong way, but much as I'd like to believe in miracles, take it from me, we're not contemplating another immaculate conception here. If your, er, partner is interested, please tell him I can arrange for a routine seminological analysis, or if he was to come with you for your next appointment…'

'No,' Sally said determinedly. 'I don't think he'd want that at all.'

'Very well then,' Dr Mason began tapping away at his keyboard again. 'But as you've left things a little late, we really ought to arrange for triple-testing or AFP.'

Sally's face fell; all this medical jargon meant absolutely nothing to her. Perhaps she should have brought her sister along to help explain things. What was it Jackie had said to her months ago? 'You're the clever one and I just have the babies.' Not any more, Sally thought to herself.

'Don't look so worried, Mrs Palmer,' a kindly voice was saying. 'You look a perfectly healthy specimen and I'm sure baby is, too. The tests are simply routine and just a precaution. They determine the risk of spina bifida or Down's syndrome. Older mothers can be more susceptible, that's all, which is why it would have been better if you'd come to see me earlier. You should have been taking folic acid for the first twelve weeks of your pregnancy.

'Oh, but I did!' Sally said brightly. 'My neighbours run a fruit and veg shop and have probably kept me in folic acid for the past eight months.'

'Splendid.' Dr Mason reached into a drawer and pulled out a booklet. 'The midwife would usually have given you this… so as you've got quite a bit of reading to catch up on, can I suggest you go home and put your feet up. And don't forget… if baby's father wants to come and have a chat…'

Sally nodded, and clutching the pregnancy and baby booklet, made her next appointment and left the surgery full of renewed hope and optimism. It was short-lived however, parked alongside her own car, was a midnight blue Jaguar.

'Hugh!'

'Hello, Sally. How was your appointment with Dr Mason?'

'How did you know… Have you been spying on me?'

'No, I did some detective work. I rang the surgery and told them that I was your husband and that you'd forgotten the time of your appointment.'

'You did *what*? How dare you!'

'I was worried about you, Sally. Is… is everything all right with you and the baby?'

'Yes,' she replied curtly. 'Stanley and I are just fine.'

'Stanley?'

'Oh, didn't you know that's what I'm calling the baby? You see, the doctor asked me if mid-April rang any bells with me? That's when I conceived apparently and I thought Stanley seemed appropriate. Perhaps you'd like to look back in your diary and see what you were doing in mid-April.'

For one usually so composed, Hugh looked decidedly unsure of himself.

He found Sally's abrasive manner so alien to the sweet-natured woman he remembered. With a sudden determined set of jaw he drew himself up and announced, 'Well, I'd better be going. I'm so pleased everything is all right. Take care.'

*

Walking into his office the last person Hugh expected to see was his sister-in-law. 'Vivienne! What are you doing here? Is anything wrong?'

Vivienne cast an anxious look in Muriel Baxter's direction.

'Mrs Baxter, perhaps you could get us some coffee.'

Relieved to see Muriel busying herself with a coffee machine, Vivienne followed Hugh to his private sitting room.

'I get the feeling you'd prefer somewhere quieter. Rest assured these walls don't have ears.'

Vivienne forced a smile, unbuttoned her suit jacket and rubbed her hands together nervously. 'You're not expecting Serena, are you?'

'No, why, should I be?'

'No, but it's because of Serena I'm here.' Vivienne looked furtively about her.

'You're quite safe you know…' Hugh reassured, 'Now, what is all this?'

'Oh, dear! It's all very difficult, Hugh, and I'm not very good at this sort of thing, so I suppose I'd better come straight to the point. Serena confided in me that you'd mentioned trying to find the, er, baby she had adopted.'

'You mean James?'

'Yes – James, that's right. Well, she doesn't want you to.'

'I already know that, Vivienne.'

'You do?'

'Yes, didn't Serena also tell you that? Because she got so upset about it, I told her I wouldn't.'

'Wouldn't what?'

'Try to find James, of course!'

Vivienne breathed an enormous sigh of relief and unclasped her hands.

'So is that it then?' Hugh asked.

'What? Oh, yes, that's it.'

'Good. So let's see if the coffee is ready, shall we. You certainly look as if you could do with a cup.'

Later, ushering her to the door, Hugh said softly, 'I know Serena didn't think it a good idea to contact James, yet I can't help feeling it's such a shame. After all, he can't be that much older than Gareth. And with Gareth an only child too, they could have been great company for each other.'

Vivienne thought fondly of her son, now happily installed at Barrington's and glad to be away from his father's law practice.

She gave a wistful sigh. 'Gareth's very happy here at Barrington's.'

'I know, and I can't help but wonder… If James was that way inclined too, who knows – perhaps I could have semi-retired by now and left both boys to run the show.'

Vivienne stood on tiptoe to kiss Hugh's cheek. 'You're so sweet and thoughtful, Hugh, and I know Serena's my sister, but sometimes I don't think she realizes just how lucky she is to have you.'

Embarrassed by her sudden burst of sentimentality, Hugh watched as his sister-in-law wiped a tear from her cheek. 'It's very kind of you to say so, Vivienne, but I'd be the first to admit I'm not perfect.'

'I know dear, but then I also know my sister! And as I'm supposed to be meeting her for lunch, I'd better get a move on. I can also put her mind at rest about you know who.'

Sitting at his desk, Hugh turned back the pages of his diary to Easter and mid-April. In bold letters he found 'HARROGATE WITH UNCLE BERTRAM'. On his return, nothing much else had been pencilled in, but the thick black circle around April the eighteenth was a grim reminder of Stanley's passing.

What was it Sally had said about mid-April ringing any bells? To Hugh, at that moment, in a particularly melancholic state of mind, it could only be the mourning bell that was tolling for Stanley. As for Sally referring to her baby as Stanley… Taking a tiny key from his pocket Hugh walked to the mahogany cabinet and turned the lock.

Inside, wrapped in tissue, he found the delightful miniature of his beloved dog, Lovingly, he ran his finger round the rim of the frame and regretted bitterly the fact that he'd left its partner—the one of Stanley and Sally together—on the side table in the bedroom at the flat.

'Oh, Sally, my love!' he murmured, 'and to think I don't even have a photo of you.'

Re-wrapping the miniature in tissue paper, Hugh placed it back inside the cabinet, where it rested against the urn that contained Stanley's ashes. Hugh shuddered and felt a lump rise in his throat. What did you do with a dog's ashes?'

It didn't seem right to have them on display like some tennis or golfing trophy, and he certainly didn't want them scattered in the garden, where Mr Burt was constantly digging, raking and hoeing. Besides Serena would never have approved. Closing the door of the cabinet and turning the key, Hugh realized the only person who would know of a sensitive solution was Sally, yet he could hardly ring and ask her advice.

Replacing the key in his jacket pocket, Hugh's sombre thoughts were interrupted by Muriel Baxter.'

'Mr Barrington, your brother-in-law is on the line, will you take his call?'

'What? Oh, yes, all right. I was in fact just going out but…'

'Hugh, old chap. It's Charles. Look I need to speak to you urgently. Any chance of meeting up for a spot of lunch?'

'Lunch? Well… I was just on my way out. There's something I need to attend to…'

There was a note of urgency in Charles' voice as he broke in, 'Can't it wait, Hugh? This is very important.'

'What is?'

'Um, I'd prefer not to discuss it on the phone if you don't mind. It's a bit sensitive—you know.'

Hugh didn't know, but he supposed he ought to find out. Perhaps Charles was in financial difficulties; he was once a Lloyd's name and had come unstuck on a couple of occasions. 'OK, Charles. Where do you want me to meet you? At the club or…'

'I thought Thornhampton Park, by the boating lake…'

'Good God, Charles! What is all this? Have you committed a murder?'

'No. Let's just say it's all to do with a gross miscarriage of justice.'

Puzzled, Hugh hung up the phone; his other proposed plan would simply have to wait.

CHAPTER 16

With children enjoying the last weeks of school and summer holidays, there was a hive of activity by the boating lake. It wasn't quite how Hugh remembered it from last Boxing Day afternoon. Then, he'd watched Sally and her nephews feed the ducks and Ben had proudly shown him his new watch, while Stanley…

Lost in thought, Hugh looked up to find Charles standing before him. He was carrying two brown paper bags and extended one in Hugh's direction.

'What's this, the evidence?' Hugh joked.

'No,' replied Charles, without a glimmer of a smile. 'It's lunch. Cheeseburger and fries, at least, I think that's what I ordered. I also got one coffee and one tea. I wasn't sure which you'd prefer.'

Hugh peered surreptitiously into a polystyrene carton and grimaced.

'It's only for effect,' Charles explained, 'just in case anyone sees us.'

'And I suppose all that's missing are the dirty old raincoats!'

Hugh studied both his brother-in-law and himself. Each attired in Savile Row tailoring, they looked ridiculously out of place sitting in Thornhampton Park where half-naked children and their equally scantily-clad parents played and sunbathed.

'Look, Charles. What is this all about? I really can't see why we couldn't have a had a proper lunch elsewhere.'

'Can't, old chap. Far too risky. Vivienne's meeting Serena for lunch and as I don't know where, I thought here would be safer.'

'Would it really matter then if we bumped into our wives over lunch?'

'Yes, Hugh, it would… especially today.'

Slightly exasperated, Hugh wrenched open the polystyrene container and took a mouthful of the almost-cold cheeseburger. It was quite disgusting and didn't make him feel any happier. He watched Charles chew thoughtfully on a chip.

'Well, if I can possibly tear you away from this gastronomic delight, perhaps you could tell me why I'm here. I do have a busy schedule this afternoon, Charles.' Hugh refrained from saying that he'd already had a surprise visit from Vivienne today, and that coming just after his brief encounter with Sally outside the surgery…

'It's about Vivienne.'

'Why? What's she done?'

'Nothing. That's just the problem.' Charles shifted uneasily.

'Hugh looked at his watch. 'Charles, if this has anything to do with my idea of contacting Serena's adopted baby, you can forget all about it and tuck into your burger. For your information Vivienne's already been to see me about that today. In fact, I'm now beginning to wish I'd never even thought of it. First Serena putting me off, then Vivienne and now you!'

'I haven't exactly come to put you off, Hugh.'

'You haven't?'

'No, I've come to tell you the truth. Vivienne wanted to, but couldn't bring herself to do so because Serena made her promise.'

'Tell me *what*, Charles? Because this is becoming more like Inspector Morse with every minute.'

'I wish I could see the funny side of it, old chap, but I'm afraid I can't. What I have to say is no laughing matter.'

'So… if it's not a problem with Vivienne, is it Serena? Because at the moment, I'd say she's positively glowing with the prospect of all our anniversary celebrations. She certainly hasn't given the impression of anything being untoward. Is Serena in any kind of trouble?'

'No, not now. But as we all know she was before she met you… when she became pregnant.'

'That was years ago, Charles. Serena was very young when she went off on that sixth form skiing trip. We all make mistakes when we're young, don't we? It didn't bother me then, or at least when I eventually heard about it, and she told me how she'd had the baby adopted, and it doesn't bother me now. In fact, if it hadn't been for that programme Vivienne was watching, I doubt if I would have given any thought to tracing James.'

'Hugh, I don't quite know how to say this... but there was no baby and there is no James to trace.'

'That's preposterous! If there was no baby in the first place, why on earth would Serena pretend otherwise? Why confess to your husband-to-be that another man had made you pregnant—albeit years ago—when in fact he hadn't?'

'Oh, Serena was pregnant all right, Vivienne will vouch for that.'

'For Christ's sake, Charles! Will you please tell me once and for all what happened, because I'm slowly in danger of losing the plot here. I'm also getting tired of sitting here with a bag of plastic food on my lap, trying to solve riddles, when I've a business to run. First you say there was no baby and no James and in the next breath you talk about Serena being pregnant. Are you saying my wife lied to me?'

'Not exactly… because Serena had an abortion. An abortion that went horribly wrong, one of those awful back street affairs that you used to hear about. These days, of course, things are quite different. Anyway… it left Serena unable to have any more children.'

Charles' last words were barely audible amidst the laughter and cries of excited children and, like a film in slow motion, they moved their way in stilted fashion into Hugh's consciousness. Quite how long he sat there in stony silence he couldn't remember. It was only when Charles placed a hand on his arm that he found a voice to his thoughts. His mouth was dry and his voice husky when he asked Charles to repeat what he thought he'd heard the first time.

In anguish Charles related how Serena, too frightened to tell her parents of her predicament, had confided in Vivienne and with the help of a 'so-called friend' had found herself in some dingy back street. When the abortion went horribly wrong and the family GP was called in, her parents had to be told.

'Quite ironic when you think of it,' Charles was saying, 'because Gerald and Margo, anxious to keep things quiet, whisked her away to a private clinic immediately - but of course by then it was too late.'

'Too late?' Hugh repeated lamely.

Charles patted Hugh on the shoulder. 'The doctor chappie told Margot that Serena would never be able to have children, which didn't seem a problem at the time. However, several years later when Serena met you, Margot realized your intentions with regard to her daughter could be serious. She thought you might not want to marry Serena if you knew the truth and Gerald…'

'Stop!' cried Hugh, crushing the brown paper bag and its contents into a twisted mess. Angrily he got up and threw it in the nearest bin. All the while, Charles watched him nervously, relieved that *his* ordeal was over. For Hugh, however, his was just beginning.

Taking the remains of his own lunch to the bin, Charles noticed Hugh's gaze drift from child to child, pushchair to pushchair. There was no doubt in his mind what Hugh was thinking.

'Of course you can't really blame Serena,' Charles said feebly. 'It was Margot after all who persuaded her to tell you a white lie. As we both know our dear departed mother-in-law was a force to be reckoned with.'

'A white lie! Christ, you call that a white lie, Charles! Well I bloody don't. The bitch! To think that all these years Serena's led me to believe it's my fault – yes, *my* fault, do you hear – for not having children!

'Hugh, old chap…'

'Don't *old chap* me, Charles! When I think of all the stick I took in the early days: poor Hugh Barrington, hasn't got it in him you know, can't even give the beautiful Serena a child!'

'Yes, but Hugh, even you said yourself you didn't mind about not having children and Serena was so madly in love with you… She even condoned your…'

'I might have known you'd bring that up, Charles! The one very brief affair when Barrington's and the rest of the country were going through a bad patch financially, and all Serena wanted to do was spend money, that we could ill afford, on exotic holidays, expensive furniture and ridiculously fast cars. And do you know what she said to me at the time, because it was on one of those exotic holidays that she took alone, that she began the first of her 'little arrangements'?'

Charles shook his head.

'She said that as long as I made sure I never had, and I quote "unprotected sex", she'd turn a blind eye to any future affairs that I might have. Which is a joke, isn't it? I had one very brief and foolish affair twenty years ago, whereas she's had a whole string of them. All of which I've tried to ignore, simply because I thought I'd failed her by not giving her a child. My God! Now, when I think of it, no wonder she made such an issue out of that. She didn't dare risk me having unprotected sex with anyone in case I fathered a child and found out that she'd been lying to me all these years!'

All the time Hugh was talking, Charles was leading him from the main path, away from the crowds and out of earshot. It was probably best, he decided, to let Hugh vent his anger and hopefully lessen the verbal salvo when he returned home to Serena.

Finding himself back at the main gates and the sweet kiosk, Hugh remembered sending Ben off for his Smarties. There had been orange Smarties in the dish on Sally's coffee table. Sweets that Ben had given her as a peace offering for… Sweets that Sally had jokingly popped into her mouth. 'Oh, dear God, I can only hope it's not too late to put things right.'

Misinterpreting Hugh's anguished groan, Charles added brightly, 'I'm sure you can, Hugh. Just think of the wonderful time we're all going to have celebrating your anniversary.'

At that moment a black Labrador puppy came bounding along the path by the boating lake. Trailing his lead and with no owner in sight, he was heading straight for the park gates and the main road.

'Stop him, mister!' a young boy yelled and Hugh deftly put out his foot and stood on the trailing lead.

'Cor thanks,' a breathless voice panted, taking the lead from Hugh's grasp.

Oblivious to the dusty pavement, Hugh knelt and patted the dog affectionately, whilst it wagged its tail and ignored the scolding of his young master.

'What do you call him?' asked Hugh.

'Charlie. An' 'e is an' all, a proper Charlie,' the boy laughed and, taking firm hold of his wayward charge, walked back through the park to join his friends.

Grateful for a diversion from their earlier conversation, Charles smiled and shook his head. 'I expect he reminds you of Stanley.'

'When he was a puppy, yes – but not when he got older.'

'I don't know,' said Charles, 'when you were in Harrogate and Serena was looking after Stanley, and my good-lady wife popped over to see her, I remember Vivienne saying how sprightly he seemed for such an old dog, especially when he was playing with his ball in your garden.'

Dusting off the knees of his trousers, Hugh's hand hung suspended in mid-air. As if hearing about Serena's duplicity wasn't enough for one day, Charles had now dropped another bombshell, albeit unintentional. So, according to Vivienne, Stanley had been in fine fettle even to the extent of playing in the garden. Whereas… according to Serena, Stanley could barely walk from his basket to the back door!

Unaware of the significance of his statement, Charles waved goodbye and walked back to his office. Hugh, meanwhile, remained frozen to the spot and felt his blood run cold.

*

With a flourish, Roz drew back the fitting-room curtains and was surprised to find Marion le Sage standing by a display of cotton nightdresses. She held up five fingers, indicating five minutes. Later, with yet another satisfied customer on her way, she joined Marion.

'Mrs Harrison – delightful woman, she's been coming here for years. Poor dear has a hiatus hernia so she has to find a bra that's just right.'

'And I'm trying to find a nightdress that's just right for Sally when she has the baby. I know it's not due for a few more months, but she's been a bit down lately. I wanted to buy her something to cheer her up.'

'There's nothing wrong, is there?'

'No – It's just that she's worried about the amniocentesis test. Laura has taken her in for it today.'

'Oh God!' Roz sighed, 'I do hope everything's going to be all right. I don't suppose you're any the wiser about the father. If I knew who he was, the bastard!'

'You and Laura both. In fact I'm surprised she hasn't been in to see you. She keeps threatening to.'

'Why?'

'Something Sally said seemed to imply you might know the father.'

'You're joking!'

'No, I'm not.'

Roz curled one end of her tape measure that was hanging round her neck.

'Someone I know? Surely you don't mean Bernard?'

Marion shrugged her shoulders. 'Haven't a clue, my dear. Now what do you suggest I buy for Sally?'

*

Unable to sit in his office with the revelations concerning Serena and

Stanley still fresh in his mind, Hugh took it in his head to patrol the entire store. Seeing Roz absentmindedly winding and unwinding her tape measure, he was ready to pounce.

'Nothing to do, Mrs Hughes, no pricing or displays to rearrange?'

'As a matter of fact, Mr Barrington, I've just finished serving a customer, Marion le Sage.'

'Oh, the wildflower artist. What a pity I missed her. How was she?'

'She was fine; she came in to buy Sally a nightdress for hospital.'

As calmly as he could, Hugh enquired, 'Mrs Palmer is in hospital?'

'Well, she is at the moment. Her friend Laura took her in. Poor Sally, it can't have been easy making the decision to have it done.' Roz looked at her watch. 'Anyway it should be over soon, they don't keep them in too long, do they?'

Reaching for the yellow rose in his buttonhole, Hugh crushed it beneath his grasp. What was happening today? First Serena, then Stanley and now Sally! His whole world was crumbling apart. All he wanted to do was get in his car, go and find Sally and drive miles away to where they could be alone together. Unfortunately, Serena had arranged yet another of her dreadful pre-anniversary soirées. Still, he brightened, perhaps if made a detour and called at the flat on his way home...

Finding the flat in darkness, Hugh was filled with a deep sense of foreboding. Why wasn't Sally there? Recalling Roz's word, 'It should be over soon' he could only assume Sally's abortion, like Serena's, had also gone horribly wrong.'

Tucked up in bed at her sister's, Sally contemplated the events of the past few days. She felt both physically and emotionally drained. It had been bad enough having to make her mind up about the amniocentesis test, let alone preparing herself mentally to cross the threshold of the hospital.

Dr Mason's surgery had been one thing, Thornhampton General quite another.

Of course everyone had been so kind and helpful, telling her to relax, but how could she when she relived the nightmare of last night. Finishing the mug of Horlicks Jackie had insisted on making for her, Sally closed her eyes and re-lived the moment when she saw Terry, waiting for her outside the flat.

'What is it, Terry, you look as if you've seen a ghost. It's not Julie, is it – there hasn't been an accident?'

'No, it's nothing to do with us, Sally, it's Hugh.'

'Hugh! Oh my goodness! Is he all right?'

'Hmph! He's all right, Sally. It's you I'm worried about.'

'Why should you be worried about me?'

'Hugh's selling your flat, there's been an estate agent round.'

'I don't believe it,' Sally gasped. 'I mean… h-he wouldn't, would he?'

'Afraid so. The agent knocked at ours by mistake – oh, here's his card by the way – Julie saw him first and I don't mind saying it fair put the wind up him. He thought it was me, selling my place without telling him!'

In stunned silence, Sally hung on to the stair rail in utter disbelief.

'Careful,' Terry said in an attempt to steady her, 'we don't want you falling downstairs, especially in your condition.'

'My condition,' Sally whispered to herself, hearing her sister lock the front door for the night and climb the stairs. Perhaps it would have been better if, in her condition, she *had* fallen downstairs. That way all her problems would be solved.

'Sally, are you asleep? Mind if I come in…?'

Sally made room for her sister to sit on the single bed, fitted with its Thomas the Tank Engine duvet and pillowcase. It being Ben's favourite, it seemed only fitting that Auntie Sally should have it while he shared a room with Nathan.

'How are you feeling, no aches and pains?'

'No, just tired, that's all and looking forward to a decent night's sleep.'

'Hmm. I don't suppose you got much last night, what with worrying about the test.'

And other things, like being forced to leave your flat, thought Sally to herself.

'Still,' Jackie, continued, 'at least it's over and I'm sure the results will be OK.'

'I do hope so,' Sally murmured, resting her hand on her tummy.

'Well, you get a good night's sleep and tomorrow night, when Dave gets back from his course, I'll get him to pop round with the bassinet and baby bath. I know it's still early days but you might as well try and sort out a few bits and pieces for the baby now, while you still have the energy.'

And while I still have a roof over my head, Sally thought miserably.

Hugh, she decided, had obviously intended to make things as difficult as he could. When she'd rung the estate agents, before leaving for the hospital, she'd had yet another shock. Explaining that she would like to negotiate buying the flat for herself, she'd been told there was a couple already interested.

'But surely I should have been allowed first refusal? I have been living here for…'

'Sorry Madam, Mr Barrington said nothing about offering you the flat; in fact, I distinctly recall him saying you wouldn't be interested!'

Crying silent tears, Sally became aware of Thomas's smiling face becoming quite damp.

*

When Dave finished carrying the last of the baby items into the flat, Sally stared in amazement. 'I thought Jackie was only sending a few bits and pieces.'

Dave grinned cheekily. 'This is only a few bits and pieces. You wait, Sally, you're going to need a lot more than this, believe me! Mind you, I don't even know where you're going to put this lot. You've only one bedroom, haven't you?'

Sally nodded and moved the bassinet away from the front door so her brother-in-law could get back home to his family.

'Perhaps you could look for somewhere bigger,' Dave said, stepping over the baby bath.

'Looks as if I shall have to,' Sally said cryptically.

Half way down the stairs, Dave called back, 'What about those new places they're building round the corner, they look very nice.'

'They are, very nice – and so are the prices!'

When the doorbell rang again, Sally assumed it was Dave with more baby things that he'd forgotten. 'It's OK, Dave, the door's still open, come in.'

'Erm, as I'm not Dave, I don't know if I am welcome to come in,' a familiar voice began.

Sally looked up to find Hugh standing in the open doorway. He looked dreadful, almost as if like her, he hadn't slept for days.

'Sally, I need to speak you,' he begged, 'so *please* don't tell me to leave.'

Her first feelings of compassion gave way to bitterness at the memory of her conversation with the estate agent.

'I suppose you'd better come in,' she said, her tone icy. 'Just be careful you don't trip over the baby things. I don't want you suing me for broken limbs as well as evicting me.'

'What on earth do you mean?'

'Oh, please don't play the innocent, Hugh, as if you don't know what I'm talking about. I don't know how you could be so cruel. It's quite obvious why you're here and rest assured the estate agent has already done your dirty work for you. I just think it's pretty despicable that you didn't have the guts to tell me yourself that you wanted me out of this flat!'

'But I don't want you out of the flat… well, not exactly.'

'And what's that supposed to mean, because…?'

Struggling to reach her, Hugh caught his shin on the baby bath. Sending it skimming across the carpet he reached for her hand. 'Sally, please! Before you say anything else will you please answer me one question, have you had an abortion?'

She looked coldly into his pleading eyes. 'No! I leave the killing of innocent creatures – like your dog - to your wife! And if you've come here to offer to pay for one, you're way too late, not that I would ever have entertained the idea. You might not care about this baby but I do. And as I've already told you, I want nothing from you, Hugh, absolutely *nothing*!'

Stunned, Hugh sank to the settee, still clinging grimly to her hand. 'Thank God!' he whispered, his voice catching in his throat, 'oh, thank God!'

Feeling herself dragged to the settee by his side, Sally found herself thinking, thank God for what? The fact that she hadn't had an abortion or the fact that she didn't want anything from him?

Hugh turned to face her and placed a finger on her lips. 'Please, hear me out. There's a great deal I have to say. Firstly, if you think I'm going to say your comment concerning my wife was uncalled for, then you're very much mistaken. It's Serena who has behaved badly and Serena who has been cruel. Sally, whatever else happens, promise me you *will* have our baby…'

Sally's eyes filled with tears. 'But you said it's not your baby and you want me to leave the flat, when Terry and Julie have been so good to me… they want to look after me and…'

'*I* want to look after you, Sally! You and the baby – now please will you stop crying and let me finish what I've been trying to say.'

Sobbing and allowing him to take her in his arms, Sally could only keep repeating, 'I don't understand, I don't understand…'

'Neither did I until yesterday, and even when I tell you what I discovered, I hardly dare think what your reaction will be.' Reaching into his pocket, Hugh pulled out the familiar white monogrammed handkerchief. 'Hmm. I seem to remember doing this somewhere before.'

Struggling to stretch his legs to the side of the blue gingham-lined bassinet, Hugh stood up and rubbed his shin. 'I think we could do with some fresh air; go and get your raincoat. It had stopped raining when I came in, but just in case it starts again…'

Slipping on her raincoat, Sally's eyes welled with tears once more. 'It doesn't do up. Nothing fits me anymore. I'm getting fat.'

'Nonsense, of course you're not getting fat, you're just growing in all the right places and you look positively lovely.' Hugh tilted her chin upwards, wiped tears from her eyes and kissed her full on the mouth.

'Forget the buttons on the raincoat,' he said, 'we're not going far.'

In a matter of moments after leaving the flat, Hugh swung the Jaguar onto a grass verge.

'But why have we stopped here, it's just a-?'

'Patience,' he urged, 'now just wait there for me to come and open the door, I don't want you tripping. It's pretty dangerous out there.'

Gingerly, Sally allowed herself to be helped from the car and led across shingle, planks, piles of bricks and scaffolding.

'Just make sure you keep hold of my hand, by day this is a hard hat area.'

'And by night,' she whispered, 'what then?'

Hugh laughed softly. 'Hopefully by night it becomes the answer to a maiden's prayer.'

'Aren't you forgetting something? I'm no maiden.'

'Ah, then let's say you're the answer to my prayers. Now close your eyes.'

Sally felt Hugh's hands firmly on her shoulders as he turned her in the opposite direction. 'OK, you can open them now.'

'But I still don't know why you've brought me to a building site.'

'No, of course you don't. I suppose everything must seem confusing at the moment, so let me explain.' Pointing to the far corner of the building site, Hugh announced, '*That*, Sally, is why I want you to leave the flat. It might not look much at the moment but that pile of bricks and scaffolding is to be your new home. A proper home for our baby, not a tiny one-bedroomed flat where you wouldn't be able to move.'

In the beam of security lighting from the site office, Sally studied Hugh's face critically. 'Why,' she whispered, 'why, after all this time, are you prepared to accept Stanley is yours?'

Hugh sucked in his cheeks. 'It's a very long story and one which I'd prefer to forget, but I will tell you on the way home. I only hope you can find it in your heart to forgive me.'

'I'll certainly try,' she sighed as their two silhouettes became one.

Hearing footsteps on the stairs, Terry popped his head round his front door, Spying Sally and Hugh together he became deeply anxious. 'You OK, Sally?'

'Yes, I'm fine thanks, Terry, there's nothing to worry about.'

'Well, if you're sure?' Terry glared angrily at Hugh. 'Don't forget, just call if you need me.'

'Gracious!' muttered Hugh, 'what's got into Terry?'

'Do you really want to know? In his words he thinks you're a complete and utter bastard!'

'Along with everybody else, I suppose. No wonder my ears have been burning. I suppose I do deserve it.'

'Mmm,' Sally agreed, leaning against him. 'Roz, Laura and Marion are all of the same opinion. In fact had they been Macbeth's witches, you would have been turned into a toad weeks ago.'

'And they still don't know I'm the father?'

Sally shook her head.

Hugh rubbed thoughtfully at his chin. 'They'll have to know sometime, I suppose, but for the moment if you could prevent me being turned into a toad or a frog for a little while longer, I'd appreciate it.'

'I suppose a frog would be better.'

Hugh looked perplexed.

'If you were a frog,' Sally said, tilting her head to one side,' and I just happened to let you sleep on my pillow and I kissed you… who knows, you might even turn into a prince!'

'That's highly unlikely!'

'What is?'

'Letting me sleep on your pillow after the appalling way I've behaved.'

'Oh, I don't know, we'll have to wait and see, won't we? But not tonight, as I'm exhausted and I've had more than enough excitement for one day. Besides, you look all in too.'

Hugh reached out and held her close, almost as if he was afraid of losing her again. 'Sally, if only you knew. These past weeks I feel as if I've been to hell and back on a daily basis. In fact, I think you and I need some time away together. Give me a few days and I'll see what I can arrange.'

CHAPTER 17

Trying to compile her shopping list, Sally found her thoughts drawn constantly to Hugh's revelations about Serena's abortion, her subsequent lies, and Stanley's untimely death. How anyone could be so cruel and deceitful was quite beyond her. Small wonder Hugh had looked so dreadful. As for how he would deal with it all – that wasn't going to be easy. For the moment, he'd decided, now was not the time. But when it was, what then? What would Hugh say, exactly, and how would Serena react?

Sally shrugged her shoulders and returned to her shopping list; she had more important things to think about. After weeks of careful planning, Hugh had decided they should go away for a long weekend. The Cotswolds, he suggested, not so far to drive and there was this wonderful cottage he'd heard about from a friend. It would mean self-catering, but with plenty of eating places in the vicinity, that shouldn't be a problem. If Sally would just shop for the basics for breakfast, she could leave everything else to him. They would get up when they liked, eat when they liked; and above all, she was to rest, Hugh had insisted.

Standing by the delicatessen in Sainsbury's, Sally recognized a familiar figure. Richard! Quickly she turned her back, chose her selection of cheeses, pate and cooked meats and moved to the bread counter. There, poised with tongs in her hands, ready to grip the first of her croissants, she felt a tap on her shoulder.

'Sally, it *is* you! I wasn't sure at first. How are you?'

'I'm very well, as you can see, Richard.'

Richard's eyes moved swiftly down from Sally's face to the now prominent curve of her stomach. His face registered complete and utter shock.

'You're pregnant! But…'

Unsure as to whether he was going to say *'but how'* or *'but who'*, Sally said simply, 'I suppose it must be catching. How are Sharon and the children? She had a little boy I understand.'

Richard nodded numbly, still unable to believe his eyes.

'Yes – Damian,' he muttered, 'he's three months now and thank God is sleeping better than Kylie did at that age.'

'And you're doing the shopping, I see,' Sally looked down at Richard's trolley, heavily laden with junk food.

'Yes, Sharon gets tired, so she gives me a list.' He gestured to the list written in childish script on the page torn from an exercise book.

Sally's initial reaction had been to say something sarcastic—she certainly would have done at the time of their divorce—but that was all behind her now. Besides, Richard was looking so ridiculous. Not only had he developed a paunch, but also in his tight jeans, T-shirt and bomber jacket (more suited to a man half his age) he seemed such a pathetic figure. He even had a chain round his neck. Sally fixed him with a sympathetic smile. The only thing missing was the lead!

Returning to the croissants, Sally was surprised to hear him say. 'You're out at Elmsmarsh now, aren't you? Perhaps I could call round and see you sometime?'

'I don't think that would be a good idea, do you, Richard? Besides, I shall be moving again soon and I'm also going away for a few days.'

His face fell as he watched her tie the knot on a bag of croissants, reach for a baguette and head off down an adjoining aisle.

Humming to herself Sally swung her trolley into the car park and narrowly missed hitting another shopper.

'I'm terribly sorry, I didn't see you. I'm afraid I was miles away…'

'Sally…Sally Palmer? I hardly recognized you. You look sort of different.'

'Hello, Bernard,' she beamed, 'that's probably because I'm going to have a baby. I thought perhaps that Roz might have told you.'

'No…no,' came the stunned reply. 'I haven't seen Roz and Donald in ages. I was going to suggest going to another concert together but I see you are...' Bernard nodded to Sally's left hand, where she'd taken to wearing her mother's wedding ring. At least, she hoped, it gave her an air of respectability. Though what Bernard would have thought if he's known the truth. Sally Palmer… an unmarried mother!

'Um – perhaps I can help you with your shopping?'

'That would be very kind of you, Bernard. I'm parked just over there.'

With Bernard helping Sally load carrier bags into the boot of her car, neither of them noticed Roz and Donald arriving for their Friday-evening shopping.

'Donald, stop the car!'

'What? Here? I can't just stop here, Roz! I've already got some impatient idiot on my bumper.'

Craning her neck to look back at the row of parked cars, Roz gasped, 'I don't believe it. I've just seen Bernard loading shopping into Sally's car. Oh, my God! You don't think… because if he is, I don't think I could bear it.'

*

Finishing off her packing, Sally heard the frantic ringing of her doorbell. She looked at her watch; it was too early for Hugh.

'Roz! What's wrong? You look as if you've seen a ghost.'

'I suppose you could say that,' Roz panted, out of breath. 'Goodness, I didn't realize how unfit I was, until I ran up those stairs.'

'What's the rush – why run up the stairs? The place isn't on fire is it?' Sally teased.

'Well, I'm pleased to see you in such good spirits. You look positively blooming, pregnancy is obviously suiting you.'

'Mmm, I really think it is and –'

'Sally,' Roz interrupted, 'you can call me a nosey old cow if you like, but can I ask you something?'

'It depends what it is.'

'We, Donald and I, saw you in Sainsbury's carpark. Bernard was helping you put shopping in the boot.' Roz pushed anxiously at her glasses, until they were practically embedded into her forehead. 'Oh, blast! How am I going to put this? I mean, is Bernard the father of your baby and if he is, is he going to marry you?'

Sally shook her head. 'The answer to both questions Roz, is no. Bernard is *not* the father, and as for marriage that's out of the question at present. You see the baby's father is already married.'

Without further ado, Roz's eyes filled with tears and she flung her arms around Sally's neck.

'Oh, sweet Jesus and praise the Lord! For one bloody awful moment in that car park, I thought it was Bernard. You know I even said to Donald… Hey, why are you laughing, what's so funny?'

'You are,' said Sally, hugging her friend. 'If only you could see the look on your face. By the way, where is Donald?'

'Downstairs in the car, I hope. Although he threatened to drive away and leave me stranded.'

'Why?'

'He said I had no right to ask you such an impertinent question and that it was also none of my business. I suppose he's right, really, but when I saw you with Bernard, I just sort of flipped.'

'Well, flip no more, Roz. Rest assured Bernard is not the father. Let's just say the baby's father and I sort of bumped into each other on that Human Resources course I went on ages ago. In time no doubt you will get to meet him, but for the moment we have to be discreet.'

'I suppose by that you mean because of his wife. Does she know about you and the baby?'

'I sincerely hope not. I can also tell you I'm not the cause of their marriage breaking down, either. So… why don't you go and put Donald's mind at ease.'

In somewhat calmer frame of mind, Roz caught sight of Sally's suitcase. 'Oh, have I called at a bad time? Are you going away?'

'This time it's yes to both questions.'

'Really? Somewhere nice? What time are you leaving?'

Sally smiled. 'Oh, no you don't! You're not going to catch me out like that, Roz Hughes! And just to be on the safe side, I shall come down to the car with you to make sure Donald takes you home!'

Waving goodbye, Roz turned to her husband. 'We could always drive round the block for five minutes, then come back just in case her mystery man turns up.'

'We could quite easily,' announced Donald, 'but we won't. It wouldn't be fair. Do you really want to jeopardize your friendship with Sally… how long have you known each other? No, my dear, you'll simply have to exercise a little patience. Didn't Sally say you'll find out soon enough?'

'My goodness, I thought they were never going to go,' Hugh gasped, when Sally opened the door to his gentle knocking.

'Who?'

'Roz and Donald.'

'You saw them! Did they see you?'

'No, luckily I parked round the back, as I thought it would be easier to load up the car. Then I just hid in the shadows until I heard you call goodbye and I was aware of them driving off.'

'We'd better get a move on then; you take the food, I'll get my suitcase.'

'No, I'll take the food and your suitcase, the only thing I want you carrying is our baby.'

Sally gestured to the carrier bags. 'I got you some pâté, Stilton and dolcelatte for your supper. There's a nice baguette too.'

'My supper? And what about yours, what are you going to eat?'

'Oh, I'll probably have a bowl of cornflakes and a glass of milk.'

'Cornflakes?'

Yes. According to my midwife, I shouldn't eat soft cheeses and pâté; it's not good for baby Stanley.'

*

Sally watched Hugh cut another wedge of Stilton. 'You'll have nightmares,' she joked, 'or else you won't be able to sleep.'

'Who says I want to sleep?' Hugh said, reaching for her hand. 'Tell me, if the midwife says pâté and cheeses are bad for the baby, did she tell you what's good for the mother-to-be?'

'She didn't have to, I already know.'

'Really… and what's that?'

'You are.'

'Then shall we go to bed?'

Cocooned beneath a rose patterned duvet, Sally studied the matching wallpaper and curtains. It was almost like being in a rose arbour.

'Have you any idea how old this cottage is?' she asked Hugh when he emerged from the bathroom.

'Part of it dates back to the sixteenth century, I believe. And looking at the angles of some of the walls and doors, I'd say that's probably right. Even the bed looks ancient. Are you sure you're comfortable?'

Sally stretched out fully in the bed until her feet almost reached the end of the iron bedstead.

'Wonderfully comfortable. It reminds me of a feather bed Jackie and I shared when we were children. We were staying with some elderly relations in Norfolk.'

'And was that comfortable?'

'Yes, but for some reason I always ended up at the foot of the bed by morning.'

'And if we're not careful we shall probably end up on the opposite wall.

Have you noticed how the floor slopes down?'

'That's what gives it so much character, Hugh. I think it's perfect. It's a real chocolate-box cottage, isn't it? Roses round the door, log fires, herbaceous borders, a wonderful compost heap and space for an autumn bonfire.

Hugh fixed her with a curious smile. 'And there was me thinking the new house at Elmsmarsh was just what you'd prefer; central heating, modern plumbing and en-suite facilities. Perhaps I should have found you somewhere with a tin bath and a chemical loo!

'Ah,' Sally sighed, as he slipped into bed beside her. 'You're forgetting, there's romantic and there's practical. This is romantic, but Elmsmarsh is practical and ideal for baby Stanley.'

'And how is baby Stanley?'

Sally reached for Hugh's hand and laid it gently across her stomach, where a tiny heel wriggled in her abdomen. 'Very active as you can feel.'

Hugh swallowed hard. 'You know, I still can't quite believe it. To me, it's like a miracle. To think after all those years of believing…'

Watching the familiar shuttered look creep across his face, she murmured. 'Sshh, that was then and this is now.'

'And you're sure the midwife said it's OK to make love…?'

'Positive. Not only the midwife, it's also in all the books. In fact one woman at the clinic declared that her sex drive had increased so much her husband was walking about with a grin on his face just like a Cheshire cat! It was a real case of Saturday night and Sunday morning!'

'I expect her husband's a great deal younger than me. You forget I'm…'

'Rubbish! You know for a fact you don't look it; you're also ten times fitter than most men half your age.'

Hugh stroked Sally's hair and looked earnestly into her eyes. 'And you've no regrets?'

'None,' she murmured, turning on her side, 'and as for worrying about

Saturday night and Sunday morning, let's deal with Friday night first, shall we?'

Hugh laughed, and she felt his warm breath on the nape of her neck.

*

Driving back to Thornhampton through the magnificent Cotswold autumn, Sally reached into her handbag for her diary.

'Everything OK?' Hugh asked.

'Yes. I needed to check a few dates in my diary and then count how many weeks to Christmas.'

'As you've probably gathered, it's been Christmas at Barrington's since the children went back to school after the summer holidays.'

'I think that's all wrong. Do people really want to buy Christmas things in September?'

'According to our sales figures they do. They're even up on last year. Speaking of buying things and at risk of offending your sister, would you mind if we send those baby items back?'

'Why? I know they're not exactly new…'

'That's precisely why, Sally. I would prefer baby Stanley to begin life with everything new, We have some super babyware products at the store.'

'I know, Marion and I have positively drooled over them on more than one occasion. She even offered to buy a bassinet, but I told her I'd already got Jackie's.'

'Send Jackie's back and get a new one. Pop into the store one day; make a list of what you need and let me have it.'

Sally slanted a sideways look at him. 'I couldn't do that.'

'You can and you will,' Hugh said, gently but firmly. 'This is my responsibility too, you know. Make a note in your diary now.'

Pencilling in Hugh's instructions, Sally gave a wistful sigh. 'Do you realize it's almost a year since I looked after Stanley for you, when you and Serena went to Devon. By the way, you never did say where Serena was going this weekend.'

Hugh gave a wry laugh. 'She's gone to London with Vivienne, to buy an outfit for our anniversary celebrations, which I'm sure are in danger of turning into a complete farce.'

'What's wrong with Barrington's?'

'You're joking! I expect it will be a designer outfit. I understand she's looking for something in black velvet.'

'That sounds glamorous. I'm sure she'll look lovely,' Sally said, trying hard not to think of Serena's elegant body swathed in black velvet. As for the mention of anniversary celebrations…

Hugh pulled off the main road and into a side street.

'Why have we stopped?'

'Because I want to kiss you.'

'But, Hugh. People are looking; that woman in the florist's window, she's staring at us!'

'Let her! She doesn't know who we are. We're still miles from Elmsmarsh and Thornhampton.' Hugh turned to where the florist was placing buckets of roses in the window. He smiled in her direction then got out of the car.

'Where are you going?'

'To get you some roses. What colour do you want – red?' he asked, preparing to shut the car door.

'No! Definitely not red.'

Hugh slid back into the driver's seat. 'Why not red?'

Sally shifted uneasily. 'I think red roses should only be bought for wives and fiancées. I mean…when people have really made commitments to each other. I'm sorry, you probably think I'm being very silly.'

'No, not at all. I think you're perfectly lovely. Who else would find it in their hearts to say something complimentary about Serena for a start, especially after that incident with the clotted cream fudge, not to mention…'

'Heavens! You've got a good memory. Fancy you remembering that.'

'How could I forget… that's when I fell in love with you, Sally. The same afternoon I came through your back door to find you and Stanley asleep.' Taking her hand and holding it to his lips, Hugh said huskily, 'Black velvet may be glamorous, but believe me, you can look just as lovely in jeans and a sweatshirt.'

'What about maternity dresses?'

'Those too,' Hugh called back, exiting from the car for a second time.

Sally watched as the florist went to the window and removed an entire bucket of white roses.

'Hugh, you must be mad!' she laughed, when he returned. 'Where on earth shall I put them all?'

'How about in your bedroom, then you'll think you're back at the cottage. Anyway, don't they say white roses for peace?'

'But we haven't had a row, or is this in case we do?'

'No,' he smiled. 'It's simply to reiterate how much I care and to remind you how bad I feel about not believing you when…'

Sally placed her finger to his lips. 'Sshh, remember what I said at the cottage? That was then, this is now.' Ignoring the cheerful bemused face of the florist, it was Sally's turn to take Hugh in her arms.

*

Four weeks later at breakfast, Serena asked casually, 'Hugh, have you been into Elmsmarsh recently?'

Masking his shock behind the morning paper, Hugh merely grunted. 'Not recently, why do you ask?'

'Mrs Burt tells me there's a super greengrocers and florist's over there. Apparently they do amazing floral displays. I thought I might use them for some of our anniversary flowers.'

Breathing a sigh of relief, Hugh turned yet another unread page of his newspaper. 'I suppose you could always give them a ring first, if you didn't want to drive out that far.'

'Yes, I probably will. I'll ask Mrs Burt to write down the name. I'm sure she said it was something like Pots and Pansies.'

'Never heard of them,' Hugh said, feeling in his pocket to make sure he had the list of baby items Sally had reluctantly compiled. He wasn't going to make things too easy for Serena by telling her it was Pots and Posies.

'By the way, Serena, don't make any plans for this weekend if you don't mind. I said I'd call in on Uncle Bertram. I take it, as usual, you won't want to come along?'

'Definitely not, Hugh! I shall be far too busy.'

*

In Barrington's baby department, Hugh handed Sally's list, now written in his own hand, to the departmental manageress, Mrs Murray.

'For a family friend,' Hugh explained. 'The baby's not due until January, so I'll take some of the items before Christmas and I understand we keep things like the pram until after the birth.'

Mrs Murray nodded and studied the list. 'Always a wise precaution, Mr Barrington… just in case.'

Hugh bit his lip. He knew what the 'just in case' implied and prayed with all his heart it wouldn't be used in relation to Sally and the baby. Baby Stanley, he mused; was he really going to become a father in little more than eight weeks? Certainly Sally was blooming more each and every time he saw her. With the earlier anxiety of the amniocentesis test now behind her, she seemed perfectly content.

It was Hugh, however who had the problem. It wasn't easy keeping quiet about impending fatherhood. Apart from Sally, he could only mention the baby to Julie and Terry. Although, even with them, there had been some earlier embarrassing silences. The situation having improved only when Hugh managed to convince Terry and Julie that his intentions were honourable – or as honourable as they could be in present circumstances –

where Sally and the baby were concerned.

In the end as proof of their forgiveness, Terry had invited them to dinner (a belated celebratory dinner for the baby, he said) and Julie had handed Hugh a Pots and Posies business card, with a reassuring message on the back. 'Hugh, don't forget to ring if you need me, Julie.'

'It's in case you're ever worried about Sally,' Julie had said, running his fingers through his long blonde curls. 'Only I'm at the flat more than Terry, and I can always pop in and keep an eye on her, day or night.'

With Christmas looming, Hugh realized he may well have need of Terry and Julie. This Christmas it wouldn't be quite so easy to disappear. He no longer had a dog to take for a walk, and Serena had already promised Vivienne and Charles that they would spend the time with them.

*

Sally stood nervously at Hugh's side as he pulled the heavy brass handle by Uncle Bertram's front door. In the far distance she heard a series of bells jangling.

'It will take him quite a while to answer it,' Hugh explained. 'He always gets rid of Mrs Bailey if he knows I'm coming.

'Who's Mrs Bailey?' Sally whispered.

'His housekeeper—and there's no need to whisper. Bertram won't bite, you know.'

'I'm not so sure from all the horrendous tales you've told about him. I mean, Serena never comes, does she?'

'No… that's quite simply because they loathe each other. Something tells me however, that you'll both get on like a house on fire.'

Hearing approaching footsteps, Sally reached for Hugh's hand and clung on grimly.

'Oh, by the way,' Hugh said,' just in case you're interested, the place used to be a rectory.'

'Hugh, my boy! Why didn't you use your key? You might as well, you know; after all this place will be yours as soon as I've departed this mortal coil.'

'Which won't be for a long while yet, Bertram, so in the meantime can I introduce you to Sally Palmer?'

'You can indeed,' said the old man, welcoming them in, 'but we'll have our introductions inside in the warm, if you don't mind. This special lady of yours should not be left standing on the doorstep.'

Sally looked up into kindly brown eyes, surrounded by a froth of white hair. To her surprise, she no longer felt terrified and found herself led into a flagstone porch and through to a large reception hall. She gazed about in her in wonderment where numerous family portraits graced a magnificent feature staircase.

Bertram followed her gaze to the first group of paintings. 'Well, what do you think of us, Sally, we're a rum looking lot, aren't we?'

'That's not a fair question to ask, Uncle, considering I'm the only Barrington Sally knows.'

'Hmm, and judging from her condition, Hugh, I would say she knows you pretty well!'

Aware of Sally's flustered appearance, Bertram held out his arm. 'You must forgive me, my dear, I've never been known for my tact and I suppose I'm too old to change now. If you'll just take my arm, Sally, we'll go through to the drawing room.'

Turning to look at Hugh, who only nodded for her to go ahead, Sally was escorted to a comfortable settee, in an equally comfortable room. Motioning Hugh to sit by Sally's side, Bertram returned to his own upright armchair by the fire.

Now, let me look at you both,' he announced, peering at them through rheumy eyes, as if he were studying a pair of teenagers. 'Yes, just as I thought,' he said, gleefully banging the arm of his chair, 'quite charming and a perfect match.'

Smiling, Hugh reached for Sally's hand. 'Well, Uncle, I'm glad you approve and before you ask, I can assure you the baby is mine.'

'Didn't doubt that for a minute, my boy!'

'You didn't?'

'Course not! All that earlier cock and bull stuff about you not being able to do the necessary in the man's department; didn't believe that for one minute!'

'Yet you never said…'

'None of my business, Hugh, to interfere in other people's marriages, even though I was pretty damned certain; just hoped and prayed—yes, even your wicked Uncle Bertram has been known to pray on occasions—that one day you'd find out for yourself. So… tell me, when's Baby Barrington due?'

'The tenth of January,' Sally said shyly.

'Is it, by jove! Well, I shall have to insist that my GP pumps me full of pills and potions to keep me going until then. Just think, the next generation of Barrington's. What a delightful prospect.'

Warmed by his uncle's response, Hugh turned to the neatly laid tea tray, laden with Mrs Bailey's homemade scones and Victoria sandwich.

'Shall I put the kettle on, Uncle?'

Bertram was staring thoughtfully at Sally. 'What? Oh yes, Hugh, if you will, my boy.'

Sally made as if to move. 'If you'd like me to make it… and Hugh shows me where the kitchen is… perhaps you'd like to talk.'

'Good Lord, no!' Bertram's voice boomed. 'I've spent years talking to my nephew; now that he's brought a decent young woman to see me, and a very pretty one at that, I'd far rather talk to you. Perhaps I could even show you the garden. That's if you're interested.'

'I'd like that very much, but first you must get your coat. It's getting quite damp out there.'

Returning with his Crombie overcoat, Bertram led Sally though the casement doors and into the garden.

CHAPTER 18

While Sally and Bertram took a tranquil stroll around the garden, elsewhere Serena's mood was anything but tranquil. Angrily, she kicked at the wheel of her car with the toe of her Gucci loafer. It had no effect whatsoever. The tyre was well and truly flat and did nothing to improve her temper. In disgust she slammed the garage door shut, breaking a scarlet-painted finger nail as she did so. There was only one thing for it, she decided, storming into the house; she would have to take the Range Rover, but where had Hugh left the keys?

With no one in the house to respond to her vocal outburst as she banged and slammed endless drawers and doors, Serena retired to the kitchen. Defeated, she made herself a coffee.

'I suppose I could ring Hugh at Bertram's', she muttered, watching a swirl of cream whirlpool its way from the dainty porcelain jug into tar-black coffee, 'but the very thought of speaking to that odious old man…!'

Stirring her coffee, Serena tried to remember what jacket Hugh was wearing the night before last when he'd gone out in the Range Rover. Assuming it to be his Ralph Lauren tweed and hoping to locate the car keys, she ran upstairs, pausing only briefly to check the clock in the hall.

The once familiar guestroom now had Hugh's stamp all over it. Serena ran her fingers over citrus-smelling bottles that had once stood alongside her own heavily scented ones. Why hadn't Hugh returned to their bedroom? After all, it had been months and months since they'd last…

Walking to the wardrobe door, Serena told herself the situation couldn't possibly last. It hadn't bothered her too much at first; she still had her memories from her wonderful skiing holiday and later still there had been two heavenly weekends spent with Carlo.

Recently, however, Carlo was beginning to bore her. He'd also been extremely rude, telling her she talked of nothing but her anniversary preparations. He found that very dull.

Perhaps he's right, she thought, putting her hand in Hugh's jacket pocket, talking about her wedding anniversary hadn't been very tactful in the circum…

In stunned silence, Serena withdrew her hand from the pocket of the Ralph Lauren. It contained not the keys for the Range Rover but a business card from Pots and Posies at Elmsmarsh!

'You told me you'd never heard of the place, so why lie to me?' Serena said, addressing the jacket, almost as if Hugh was standing in front of her. Then, turning the card over, she emitted a horrified gasp when she read the message. 'Hugh, don't forget to ring if you need me - Julie.'

So that's it, is it! Serena thought angrily, confronting one of Hugh's golfing photos. 'That's why you've been staying away from me - because of this Julie. Really, Hugh, I thought you had better taste than that. Taking up with a common greengrocer's assistant!'

Flicking the card against the jagged edge of her broken fingernail, Serena made her way to Hugh's bedside phone and dialled.

'Pots and Posies, can I help you?'

'I'd like to speak to Julie please.'

'Sorry, luv,' came the male voice, 'Julie's away for the weekend. Gone to visit relations.'

Slowly replacing the receiver, Serena looked about the bedroom. Who was this Julie and was there any more incriminating evidence hidden away? Had Hugh got any photos of her and, more importantly, whose relations was Julie visiting: her own or Hugh's wretched Uncle Bertram?

Glaring distractedly at the inscription on the card, Serena struggled for comprehension. Almost twenty years ago, when she'd discovered Hugh's one brief affair, she hadn't wanted to know the identity of the woman concerned. Today, however, things were different. In fact, the more she thought about it, Hugh was *different.* Ever since Stanley…

Conceding that perhaps she had stepped way over the line with Stanley, Serena still couldn't understand why Hugh was unable to move on. Why was he was still sulking about it? Or *was* he still sulking about it? Was Stanley simply a front to disguise this relationship with Julie? Stanley was only a dog and as for Julie… this trollop who served cabbages and onions to the people of Elmsmarsh. In her mind's eye, Serena conjured up a picture of a woman with henna-coloured hair, heavily pencilled eyebrows and dirty fingernails, just like that woman on Thornhampton market.

Bracing herself, Serena did what she'd never done before. She opened each and every one of Hugh's drawers and searched through all his jacket and trouser pockets. At every stage she drew a blank. Dejected, she was on the point of giving up when she remembered the brass casket, given to Hugh by Bertram many years ago.

Encrusted with semi-precious stones, it was a pretty garish object bought in some far-flung place known only to Bertram and his cronies. Not wishing to offend, Hugh had announced at the time he'd use it for cufflinks and the like. Now with her heart pounding, Serena wasn't interested in cufflinks, but she was interested in 'the like'!

Paying scant regard to the mess she was making, Serena rummaged through the wardrobe until she found what she was looking for. With trembling fingers she lifted the lid and peered inside. Initially disappointed at finding merely cufflinks, her heart missed a beat when she located what she presumed to be a small photo frame, wrapped in tissue paper, resting on one of Hugh's monogrammed white handkerchiefs. A handkerchief which bore the merest trace of lipstick!

'Got you!' she cried. 'Now what have we here?'

Disappointed for the second time in five minutes, Serena could only stare in bewilderment. This was no photo of a woman but a miniature of a dog

– Stanley!

'Infernal animal! This is your bloody fault! Why couldn't you have just died years ago like most dogs, instead of hanging on and on…. And as for being good… I don't know what was so good about being an incontinent dog. Goodness knows why Hugh wanted that inscription written in French. You were a bloody Labrador not a French poodle!'

The so-called inscription was the second of Serena's misunderstandings that afternoon. The first being Julie's sex and relationship to Hugh, and the second relating to the two words painted in the bottom right hand corner of the miniature. Le Sage, being the artist's surname and not - as Serena remembered from far-off school days and French lessons - *the good.*

Returning the business card, miniature and box to the safety of the wardrobe, Serena acknowledged that it was now far too late to go into Thornhampton. The table napkins and candles that she'd hoped to buy to match her anniversary colour scheme seemed almost irrelevant. At six-thirty on a dreary Saturday afternoon, she could only think of Julie from Pots and Posies.

Back in the kitchen, confronted by a cup of cold coffee, Serena shuddered and threw the contents into the sink with the force of a fast spin-bowler.

'Damn!' she cried, watching dark splash marks seeping across her beige cashmere sweater. Angrily she tugged at the kettle, then stopping midway between plug and tap, muttered bitterly. 'I don't need a coffee, I need a drink and a cigarette!'

Knowing that Hugh frowned on people who smoked, Serena always kept some hidden for those of her friends who did. In desperation she pulled out a tin that had once held Fortnum and Mason's Assam tea and lit a menthol cigarette with trembling fingers.

With a whisky in one hand and a cigarette in the other, Serena paced the floor. Eventually, with curiosity getting the better of her, she dialled

Bertram's number and waited.

'Come on, you stupid old man. Answer the bloody phone, won't you! Oh!'

'Hello, who is that?'

'Hello, Bertram, it's Serena. How are you?'

'Serena! This is a surprise. It's kind of you to ask but...'

While Bertram paused for breath, Serena had no intention of waiting for his reply. Even though he was wheezing, she could tell from the way he'd answered the phone that he was still reasonably hale and hearty.

'Look, sorry to disturb you Bertram, but I've had a spot of bother with my car. I need the keys for the Range Rover and can't find them anywhere, so could I speak to Hugh.'

'I'm afraid he's not here, Serena.'

'But he told me he was coming to see you...'

'He did, but he's not here now.'

There was a lame, 'Oh!' while Serena collected her thoughts. Anxious that Bertram shouldn't hang up the phone, she asked hurriedly. 'Uncle Bertram, was Hugh alone when he came to see you?'

'Actually, no,' Bertram began, 'he...'

'Oh, there's no need to continue, I know perfectly well who he had with him. That little trollop with her cabbages and onions!'

Bertram stared into the now silent mouthpiece. 'Well, well, well, what do you make of that father?' He turned with quiet satisfaction to one of the family portraits. 'You always said I was a no-good scoundrel. Even you'd have to admit that little episode might mean Serena's on her way out. And... if I've helped in the slightest bit, I'm absolutely delighted!'

Bertram was still chuckling merrily to himself when Hugh and Sally returned with steaming bags and cartons from the Chinese take-away.

'You look jolly pleased with yourself,' Hugh said, placing foil containers on the stripped pine kitchen table,' what happened in our absence? Did you win the lottery?'

'No, better than that, I've just spoken to Serena.'

'Are you saying you rang her?'

'No, quite the opposite, she rang me, which has to be a first. Tell me, Sally, my dear, have you ever worked in a greengrocer's?'

Sally shook her head and for a few very bewildered and anxious moments, she and Hugh listened while Bertram recounted the very brief phone call.

'First she asked if you were here, then when I said you weren't, she asked if you'd come alone… and I told her no.'

'And I wish you hadn't' Hugh said despairingly, watching Sally slump onto a chair, her face etched with worry.

'Look, my boy, I only told her you weren't alone and if you want my opinion – although by the look on your face – you probably don't, Serena suspects something. Why else would she ring? And why mention cabbages and onions, unless of course she'd been drinking. Think, Hugh. Your wife loathes me, always has and always will and knows the feeling's mutual.'

Hugh placed a reassuring hand on Sally's shoulder. 'Don't worry, it will be all right.'

'But what if she knows about the baby? What if she comes to the gallery or even Elmsmarsh?'

'Somehow I don't think that's likely. We've been so careful. Apart from Uncle Bertram who knows about us?'

'Only Terry and Julie that I'm aware of. You know they wouldn't say a word.'

'Ahem… If I might say a word,' Bertram broke in. '*Food.* I know you two are in a bit of a dilemma but take it from me, things will turn out OK in the end. Following that walk in the garden, I'm starving. And that Chinese smells damned good!

Nodding and walking to the table, Hugh opened up assorted steaming cartons. His uncle was probably right, *things* were no doubt moving to an inevitable conclusion.

Whist Bertram ate with solid concentration, Sally's thoughts were elsewhere. Hugh caught hold of her hand and held her fingers to his lips. 'Cheer up, it might never happen.'

'I think you're forgetting something, Hugh,' she said with a wan smile, patting her baby bump, 'it already has. In two months' time…'

'In two months' time,' he assured, 'everything will be resolved, I promise.'

Making eye contact with his uncle, Hugh asked. 'Would it be OK if I took Sally up to the room I use when I stay over? She's looking tired and a short rest will probably do her good.'

'Of course, my boy. You do that, then perhaps you and I can have a little chat. I've one or two suggestions that might be of interest to you.'

Covering Sally with the counterpane, Hugh stroked her hair and kissed her forehead. 'Just you rest, my darling, and I'll talk to Uncle B.; he might be a bit of a rogue but most of the time he talks a great deal of sense.'

Sally sighed sleepily. 'I really like him. We had a most interesting walk in the garden. He even showed me the old apple tree – the one with the mistletoe – and I told him what you said about Freya and the pearls…'

'Ssh,' murmured Hugh, caressing her hand and placing it beneath the covers, 'sleep now and we'll talk later.'

'How is she?' Bertram enquired, when Hugh returned to the kitchen to clear away the remains of the meal.

'Tired. We'll let her sleep for a bit; so how about a game of chess?'

'Only if you'll be able to concentrate. You've got an awful lot to think about. Sally and the baby – not to mention Serena.'

Following Bertram into the drawing room, Hugh watched the old man move the games table into position and motion his nephew to draw closer.

Some time later Hugh asked, 'What would you do in my position, Uncle?'

'Hmm, at the moment I'd worry about protecting your queen, I'm sure you don't want to lose her.'

Hugh studied his chess pieces and seeing the vulnerable position he was in, nodded ruefully. 'Actually, I didn't mean the game, I meant in relation to Sally and Serena.'

Bertram chuckled. 'Then my advice remains the same. However, what you have to decide is, who do you want to be your queen? Have you made your mind up yet? Which one can you afford to lose?'

Conceding defeat, Hugh moved towards the fire. Running his hands through his hair he turned to face his uncle. 'Oh, my mind is quite made up. I made my choice months ago. The problem is how to deal with everything in the best possible way. I haven't said too much to Sally of course but the silver wedding anniversary celebrations – all of which, in my opinion, are a complete farce – more or less coincide with the arrival of baby Stanley.'

'Good Grief! You're never going to call the baby after my dour-faced brother and your dog!'

'No, it's simply that Sally thinks she conceived about the time Serena had Stanley put down. That's how we found out that I wasn't – um - infertile after all.'

'I always knew Serena was a bitch,' muttered Bertram. 'I also know she's not going to give you up that easily. Or, to put it another way, she won't want to give up her extravagant lifestyle.'

'Which means,' Hugh said, 'it all boils down to what you said a few moments ago. Who can I afford to lose? Financially, I could lose a great deal if Serena and I divorce… on the other hand, Sally's always said, she never expected me to leave Serena.'

Bertram looked downcast and replaced the chess pieces in their original positions.

'Don't look so worried, Uncle, it's not what you think.'

'It's not?'

Hugh moved back to the games board and picked up the two queens.

'This,' he said, holding up the ebony queen, 'is Serena, and this is Sally.' Placing the ebony queen in his left hand and the ivory queen in his right, Hugh closed his fingers round both pieces.

'Now,' he said softly, aware of his uncle's concern. 'If I say goodbye to the black queen, I lose a considerable fortune and no doubt my standing in the community for a while. But if I say goodbye to the white queen, what I lose then is beyond price. A financial loss I can cope with…'

'Hugh, my boy…'

'I hope you're not going to tell me I can have both'

'No. Though I have to confess at one time I might have considered that an option.' Bertram shook his head sadly. 'I'm older and wiser now and I've made my mistakes – too many of them in fact – all I would ask is that you don't do the same.'

Laying the black queen face-down on the chess board, Hugh reached for Bertram's wrinkled and trembling hand, turned it over until the palm was uppermost and placed the ivory queen in an upright position. 'Hold on to this one very carefully, Uncle, and I promise I will do the same with Sally.'

Moments later, when Sally opened the door, she sensed there was something almost magical about the scene before her. Yet the two men were only playing chess. Hugh turned round and gazed at her adoringly, while Bertram reached for his handkerchief and blew his nose hard.

'Have you had a good game?' she enquired.

*

Returning Sally to the flat, Hugh was suddenly reminded of Bertram's earlier comment about a greengrocer's. And hadn't Serena mentioned something about cabbages and onions? At the time they'd all been utterly confused. Now however…

Hugh paused outside Julie and Terry's front door. 'It's only a long shot,' he said, in answer to Sally's puzzled frown, 'and I don't want to worry you unduly, but a few weeks ago Julie gave me a Pots and Posies business card.

He'd written a message on the back – offering to help if you went into labour - in case I wasn't around and….'

'And?'

'And… as I forgot to take it out of my jacket pocket, and if Serena went hunting in my wardrobe for the Range Rover keys, she might have found it and jumped to all the wrong conclusions.'

'In what way?'

'Well… as far as I can recall the message was along the lines of, "Hugh, don't forget to ring if you need me – Julie". Perhaps we should knock and ask if Terry and Julie had an unexpected customer this afternoon.'

Discovering that Julie had gone to visit his sister, who was far more open-minded than Terry's mother; Hugh and Sally were relieved to hear that Terry had only served his usual run of customers during late Saturday afternoon. 'Although,' he said, as an afterthought, 'I did take a phone call from a really snooty sounding woman, who hung up the minute I told her Julie wasn't there. Oh! Sorry, Hugh, didn't mean that to sound quite so rude…'

'That's OK, no offence taken,' Hugh called back, following Sally inside to her own flat.

'Don't frown,' Hugh said, taking Sally in his arms, 'it doesn't suit you.' He ran his forefinger across her forehead.

'I can't help it. Serena's probably wondering where you are.'

'If she has, wondering about it until morning isn't going to make any difference now, is it?'

'You intend to stay the night here?'

'Don't you want me to?

'It's not that. I merely thought that perhaps you ought to go home.'

'And I thought I ought to stay here, so that's settled.'

Leading Sally through to the bedroom, Hugh noticed a book and a DVD lying on the bed. 'What's this? I didn't know you were into women's pornography?'

'I'm not. Roz gave me the book. She's just finished it and thought it would take my mind off being pregnant. Which is highly unlikely, considering I can barely see my feet, so it will take more than that. As for the DVD it's what they used to call a birth tape. I borrowed it from the midwife.'

'What's a birth tape?'

'It shows you what to expect when labour starts and baby arrives. They showed it last week to all the prospective mums-to-be, but I didn't go.'

Hugh recalled Sally's earlier fear of hospitals. 'Why, because you didn't want to know what happens?'

'Oh, believe it or not, I really would like to know what happens, but I didn't fancy the prospect of sitting there on my own while all the other mums had their husbands and partners for support.'

'I'm so sorry, Sally. This is all completely new to me, I'm afraid. Is it so awful having to face things like that on your own?'

Sally shrugged. 'I suppose I'm getting used to it now – then I never expected things to be any different. I mean it can't be – can it?'

Moving the book and DVD to one side, Hugh pulled Sally gently onto the bed and cradled her in his arms. 'It will be different, you'll see. For the moment, I can't tell you exactly how—because I don't even know myself. I still haven't decided when and how I'm going to confront Serena about her duplicity – but while you were resting, I had a very interesting talk with Bertram and between us I think we've found a solution.'

'That sounds intriguing.'

'Mmm – but perhaps not as intriguing as the plot of this book,' Hugh teased, perusing the cover.

'Would you like to read some of it while I have my bath and get ready for bed?'

Hugh shook his head. 'How about if we watch that DVD instead?'

'You might not like what you see.'

'I'm prepared to risk that, if it means it might help us both discover what becoming parents is all about.'

Later, in the darkness, listening to Sally's peaceful and rhythmic breathing, Hugh sighed and laid a hand gently across her stomach. She was right, he hadn't liked what he'd seen. It had been bad enough watching a complete stranger go through that ordeal, but to think of Sally in a similar situation made him nervous. Beneath his hand, Hugh felt a gentle movement, presumably Stanley getting comfortable for the night in Sally's womb...

*

Arriving home after breakfast, Hugh was greeted with a look of complete and utter disdain.

'And how was Uncle Bertram?' sneered Serena.

'Very well, considering his age. And before you say anything, I gather you rang. Trouble with the car or something?'

Something was right, thought Serena. But how did Hugh know that she'd rung, when that stupid old man had said…

'I'm sorry I missed you. I'd only gone out to get us a Chinese; you know what Bertram is like for Chinese. He says it always makes a change after Mrs Bailey's cooking.'

'I would think anything's a change after Mrs Bailey's cooking!' Serena poured herself yet another strong black coffee. She'd overindulged on the whisky yesterday evening and her mouth tasted dreadful, full of stale tobacco and alcohol.

'What was the trouble with your car?'

'A bloody flat tyre. And as I couldn't find the damned keys for the Range Rover… I looked everywhere: the study, your bedroom...' The words slipped out unintentionally, and Hugh cast a suspicious look in her direction. It was as he'd thought, Serena had gone through his belongings. Slowly he made his way to the utility room.

'Why didn't you ring the garage or the breakdown service?'

'Because I spent so long looking for those bloody keys in the first place. By the time I remembered the recovery service it was too late, the shops were shut and–'

'And you'd probably had too much to drink,' Hugh added, noting the empty whisky bottle on the floor of the utility room. As he turned to face Serena he held up a bunch of familiar keys.

'And where the hell were they?' she glowered.

'On the same hook as Stanley's lead. I still do that sometimes. Force of habit, I suppose. Placing the keys on the table in front of her, Hugh left his wife muttering something about 'the damned dog' under her breath and went to examine his bedroom.

A quick check on his drawers and wardrobe confirmed his suspicions. The Pots and Posies card had been tampered with. It even bore the tell-tale signs of Serena's nail polish. She'd often remarked how her favourite brand left tiny red marks if she caught her nails at a certain angle.

Pondering the situation, Hugh breathed a sigh of relief. Thank goodness he'd only picked up the miniature of Stanley, following that never to be forgotten nightmare morning at the flat. Had he picked up its partner, the one of Sally and Stanley together, things could have been far different this morning. To think he'd only brought the picture home from his office two nights ago.

Hugh placed the Pots and Posies card in his wallet for safekeeping and made a mental note to keep it with him at all times. Having watched last night's DVD with Sally, and not wishing to think of there being no one they could call on, he was even more grateful for Julie's offer of help.

Julie with his delicately boned features and wonderful blonde curls that many young women would simply… Julie! That was it! Hugh told himself, reminded of a saying he'd heard on the radio – something about having a light-bulb moment. That's why Serena had rung Bertram. That's why she was still in such a foul temper. Serena had not only found the Pots and Posies card and message, but also she'd assumed Julie was a young woman! In current circumstances what could be more perfect!

CHAPTER 19

Helping Sally with yet another packing case, Hugh mopped his brow.

'Whew! I'm glad that's it and we're leaving the rest to the removal men.'

Sally handed him a coffee. 'I'm sorry, I know they would have seen to everything, but I wanted to pack those bits and pieces myself.'

'What time are they coming in the morning?'

'Eight o'clock.'

'Are you sure you'll be able to cope? You don't want me to be here?'

'Hugh darling, it's very sweet of you, but we've managed so far without drawing too much attention to ourselves. If you're here when the removal men arrive, it would be just our luck that someone recognizes you.'

'Promise me you won't attempt any lifting or do anything silly.'

'I've already done that by letting you persuade me to move two days before Christmas. Before you say anything, yes, in the circumstances it is better to move now, rather than wait until after the baby is born. Marion keeps telling me I won't have time for anything then.'

'Not even for me?'

Sitting by his side, Sally rested her head against his shoulder. 'I'll always have time for you.'

Hugh kissed her cheek and murmured. 'If only Serena hadn't said we'd spend Christmas with Charles and Vivienne.'

'You must go. They'll be expecting you. Besides, they sound a lovely couple and as you've always got on well…'

'Yes, I suppose we have. It might also be the last Christmas I spend with them. Next year they'll probably give me the cold shoulder.'

'Do you think Serena's said anything to Vivienne?'

'Definitely not, as she's determined to go ahead with the anniversary charade. What I can't understand is the fact she's never even mentioned finding that Pots and Posies card. I was convinced she thought Julie was female. I must have been mistaken.'

'Perhaps Serena doesn't want to admit she'd been looking through your wardrobe. And as you haven't stayed over with me since the night we came back from Bertram's, she might think your presumed affair with Julie was just a flash in the pan. With your anniversary less than a fortnight away, she's not going to risk spoiling the celebration at this late stage.'

Hugh shook his head in despair. 'Perhaps not, as she's spent weeks planning it, but what is there to celebrate?'

'Twenty-five years is a long time for a couple to be together, Hugh. Much as I want to be with you, I don't know if I could live with the fact that I've destroyed your marriage. That weekend when I offered to take care of Stanley, I never envisaged…'

'You haven't destroyed my marriage, Sally. Serena managed that all by herself – both with Stanley and her despicable lies.' Hugh studied Sally's heavily pregnant state, and was suffused with a warm glow of contentment. 'As for what you envisaged, I never envisaged that all these months later, I would be sitting here with the soon-to-be mother of my child.'

Sally eased herself from the settee with a smile. 'Well, this mother and child had better get a move on if she's going into Laura's Lair. Don't look so horrified, I shan't be doing anything silly there, either. To begin with, Laura and Marion won't let me, and it will also help to pass the time. The days are beginning to drag.'

Hugh reached for his jacket and his car keys and kissed her goodbye. 'Promise me you'll take care then.'

'I promise.'

'And you'll ring if you need me?'

'Yes.' She smiled. 'I'll ring if I need you.'

*

On Christmas Eve morning, Serena decided to call at Barrington's for her last minute Christmas shopping. She'd organized the main presents weeks ago but remembered Vivienne liked everyone to open one small present after supper on Christmas Eve.

'Don't ask me why we do it. It's something Charles' family began years ago,' she'd told Serena, 'something to do with Scandinavian tradition, I believe.'

Standing on the escalator, Serena considered her sister's surname and supposed Anderson could quite easily have Scandinavian connections. Strange how she'd never thought of that before. What she had to think of now however, was what to buy Vivienne and her nephew's girlfriend. Gareth and Charles hadn't been a problem, neither had Hugh. It had been a case of personalized golf balls all round.

Wandering from department to department, Serena found her attention drawn to some pretty silver and gilt handbag mirrors. Their size was perfect, but which ones should she choose? Selecting three, she held each one up in turn, admiring her reflection as she did so. At the same time she also saw reflected something that looked vaguely familiar.

Placing the mirrors back on the counter, Serena turned to where a selection of Marion le Sage's miniatures were on display. Now she remembered! The frames were identical to Hugh's picture of Stanley, the one he had hidden away in his wardrobe. Only these pictures - apart from two of robins in the snow – were of flowers, not animals. Had the person who painted these also painted the one of Stanley?'

'They're quite charming, aren't they Mrs Barrington.'

Serena looked up in surprise. This member of staff obviously knew her, but…'

'I'm sorry, I don't expect you remember me, I'm Celia Murray. I'm the manageress of babyware.'

Serena raised her eyebrows, never having to visit babyware, she didn't remember the woman at all. Added to which, why was Mrs Murray here in this department and not in babyware?'

In answer to the unspoken question, Celia explained. 'I've only come down to help for a couple of hours, as they're so short staffed here today. Last minute Christmas shopping, you know, and as my department's pretty quiet at the moment, I've left my junior in charge. I noticed you were admiring Marion le Sage's artwork, they really are quite delightful, aren't they?'

Serena wasn't listening; she was peering at the bottom right-hand corner of the miniatures. le Sage—that was the artist's name! It hadn't implied that Stanley was good after all.

Serena sucked in her cheeks. 'Mrs Murray, I don't suppose you happen to know if this le Sage woman undertakes commissions?'

'I'm afraid I don't. All I do know is that these are only signed prints and the originals are for sale at a gallery on the other side of town, between Thornhampton and Elmsmarsh, I believe. I suppose you could always go to the gallery yourself, or else ask Mr Barrington. I understand the setting up of this department was his baby, so to speak.'

Serena nodded thoughtfully. No, she wouldn't ask Hugh, but she might go and have a word with Marion le Sage. She was curious to know just who had commissioned the miniature of Stanley: her husband or his onion-selling friend, Julie!'

'By the way, speaking of babies,' Mrs Murray's shrill voice echoed, 'how's your friend? The one who's having the baby? I know Mr Barrington said she wants us to keep the pram until after the baby is born. As I told your husband, when he gave me the list of baby requisites to order, it is so much safer to wait just in case…'

Bewildered, Serena faced Celia Murray in silence. What was the woman prattling on about. They hadn't got any friend expecting a baby!

Biting her lip, Serena thought long and hard. No! It wasn't possible, was it? Julie couldn't be pregnant! Did that mean Hugh had discovered how she'd deceived him all those years ago? Feeling a knot in her stomach, all Serena wanted to do was get out of the store. Vivienne's Christmas Eve presents would simply have to wait!

'Damn,' muttered Serena, slamming her car into gear, 'where did that stupid woman say the gallery was – Elmsmarsh? 'No,' she whispered with an ominous tone, 'it's not the gallery that's at Elmsmarsh, it's our friend Julie. Perhaps I should go there first!'

*

At Pots and Posies, the early morning scramble for Christmas fruit and vegetables had eased and Terry had despatched Julie to the kitchen to make them both a well-deserved cup of coffee. When Serena entered the shop, there was only one other customer, an elderly woman whose clothes smelt of mothballs and tobacco smoke.

'Hello, Mrs H! How's the old rheumatics?'

'Drivin' me up the wall, Terry my dear. I just thank Gawd our Shane and Debbie are havin' me for Christmas dinner.'

Serena winced at the very thought of this wizened old woman being served up for Shane and Debbie's Christmas dinner!

'Very nice too,' continued Terry, 'and I expect you'll have a good old knees up in the evening?'

Trying to ignore not only the old woman's cackling but also the smell of mothballs, Serena glanced surreptitiously for any signs of Julie. She'd already heard movement coming from the rear of the shop, and even caught a glimpse of a slim figure in denim jeans, with a mass of fine blonde curls.

So… Serena thought bitterly, you've gone for another blonde have you, Hugh, but one who is presumably younger than me. However, unless she was mistaken, Julie's hips were not those of a heavily pregnant woman. Perhaps Mrs Murray had been mistaken. Perhaps Hugh had been doing a favour for Muriel Baxter's niece. She'd certainly remembered Hugh mentioning Muriel's delight at the prospect of becoming an aunt for the very first time.

'Anyways,' began Mrs H, breaking into Serena's chain of thought, 'what about you two, what are the pair of you doin' this Christmas? I bet you 'aint goin' to yer mum's.'

Terry shook his head. 'We're still undecided. I'd prefer to stay at home but we could go to Julie's sister if we wanted to. The thing is, as she's pregnant, and still suffering from morning sickness, I don't expect she'll really be up to having visitors.'

Serena did a double take. So, it was Julie's sister who was pregnant, which probably meant that the skinny blonde with the frothy curls had somehow managed to twist Hugh round her little finger and provide her and her family with anything they asked for! She tapped her feet impatiently, wishing A: Julie would hurry up and put in an appearance, so she could tell her just what she thought of her, and B: that this prattling old woman would simply shut up and go away.

'Well, wotever you do, ducks, don't you go takin' Julie's sister one of them there enormous melons.'

'Why ever not?' Terry enquired.

'Because,' the old woman laughed coarsely, 'don't they always tell you at those baby-clinic places that havin' a baby is like tryin' to pee a melon!'

'Oh, I wouldn't dream of doing that, Mrs H.,' a soft voice broke in. 'This being her first baby, she's frightened enough as it is.'

As if in slow motion, Serena turned in the direction of the voice, delaying for as long as possible the first glimpse of Hugh's Julie. Slowly her eyes moved upwards from the Nike trainers to the slim blue-denimed hips and Naf Naf sweatshirt – with no trace of a bust – until she reached the face surrounded in a froth of angelic golden curls. Julie was a…!

Giving an audible gasp, Serena fled towards the door, causing three pairs of eyes to stare after her in bewilderment.

'I dunno,' said the old lady, 'some people can't even wait five minutes to be served, can they?'

Watching the elegantly dressed woman rush to her flashy hatchback, Terry nodded knowingly in Julie's direction. Minutes later, when Mrs H left the shop, Julie heard him murmur, 'Something tells me we ought to ring Hugh.'

In shock and driving with unfocused eyes, Serena drove aimlessly for miles until she realized she was hopelessly lost. In desperation, she called at a service station for petrol and cigarettes and also asked the way back to Thornhampton. Following the attendant's instructions, she passed one hamlet after another until, as predicted, she came to the first set of crossroads.

'Now,' she asked herself. 'Did he say left or right?'

To the left she noticed, was just another nondescript country road but half way down on the right she saw a black and gold sign announcing *Laura's Lair.* With a violent screech of wheels and a smell of burning rubber, Serena turned right.

'Oh my God!' Sally gasped, glancing out of the window. 'I'm going to have to go!'

'You don't mean the baby's started!' Marion cried, rushing from the kitchen.

'No, it's that woman. I don't want to speak to her. If she asks for me, tell her I'm not here!'

'But…' Marion watched as Sally rushed to the loo and locked the door.

Walking through the door, Serena caught sight of Marion's paintings and was reminded she still hadn't bought anything for Christmas Eve. Vivienne's stipulation for after supper presents was for nothing wildly extravagant. OK, so the prints in Barrington's weren't wildly extravagant, but as these were originals…

'I'd like the Christmas Rose, Winter Jasmine and Cyclamen.'

'You mean to take all three!' Marion asked in amazement.

'That's what I said!' Serena snapped. What did it matter how much she spent. It was only Hugh's money after all, and how much had he been spending on that – his *boyfriend* from the greengrocers. Feeling a sickening sensation in her stomach, Serena put a hand to her mouth.

'Do you feel all right, you look quite pale,' Marion asked. 'Perhaps I could get you a glass of water?'

'No! No thank you, I think it's the perfume from all these scented candles and potpourri in here that's all. If you could just wrap the pictures.'

Watching Serena drive away, Marion walked to the loo door and knocked gently. 'It's OK, you can come out now, she's gone.'

Ashen faced, Sally emerged and reached for a stool. 'W-what… did she say?'

'Apart from buying three of my pictures—and can you believe that?—she didn't say much at all.'

'So she didn't ask for me?'

'No. Were you expecting her to?'

'Um – I just thought perhaps she…'

Marion studied Sally carefully. Why should she have panicked so much, unless the woman who had just left in such a hurry, was connected in some way to Sally and the baby? Slowly Marion opened the till and drew out the copy of the credit card receipt. The signature was indistinguishable but the name on the card imprint was perfectly clear – S. Barrington.

'Oh, dear,' sighed Marion, holding the receipt in Sally's direction. 'Could this explain everything? I do believe your secret is out, my dear.'

Not moving from the stool, Sally said nothing as she watched Marion push the credit card slip to the back of the till and close the drawer deliberately.

'I think we should have a cup of tea,' Marion said softly, 'then if there's anything you want to talk about, I am a very good listener.'

Numbed, Sally was aware of the mug with the question mark being placed before her.

Marion smiled warmly. 'I thought the question mark seemed appropriate; somehow I get the feeling you are very confused.'

'Oh, Marion! What on earth am I going to do? What if Serena comes back? What if she knows?'

'If you mean, what if she knows about you and the baby, I'd be prepared to say that from her behaviour when she came in here that she doesn't. Mind you, she seemed pretty upset about something. At one point I thought she was going to pass out. I even offered her a glass of water.'

Sally looked aghast. 'I'm glad she didn't accept. I was getting desperate in there. That loo is barely big enough for one person, let alone a heavily pregnant one, and Stanley was beginning to complain.'

'Who's Stanley?'

'Oh that's what I've called the baby until it arrives.'

'I see... and wasn't that the name of the dog you asked me to paint? Somehow, Sally, I think you've a great deal of explaining to do.'

Half an hour later, as Marion unclipped and refastened the familiar brown hair slides she emitted a low whistle. 'My goodness! By the sounds of it, you and Hugh have had quite a year. How have you managed to keep things so secret?'

'With great difficulty, and this,' Sally said, pointing to her bump, 'has made things decidedly awkward of late. Naturally we've always tried to be discreet and most of the time Hugh came to the flat. Terry and Julie have been terrific and I shall miss them, although they're still only round the corner.'

'And am I right in assuming Hugh has bought your new house?'

Sally nodded. 'Yes, but I didn't ask him to; in fact, I haven't asked him for anything. He insisted, that's all.'

'And I should jolly well think so too!'

'You do? You don't think it makes me appear cheap and sordid, like a little bit on the side?'

Marion roared with laughter. 'Sally, my dear, from the state of you, I'd say you look anything but a little bit on the side!'

Seeing the joke, even Sally managed a smile. 'True to your name as ever, Marion. You're a real tonic.'

'You mean le Sage? Well, Mrs Barrington seems to think my work is good. Fancy buying three! Even though I suppose it will mean Hugh footing the bill. Laura, no doubt, will be delighted.'

'Speaking of Laura, I'd really appreciate it if you didn't mention any of what I've just told you. I know she'll find out about Hugh sooner or later, but for the moment I'd prefer for us all to have a peaceful Christmas. I don't much relish the thought of Laura confronting Hugh on Christmas day with a carving knife!'

'Then it's probably better if you go home. I'll tell Laura when she comes back that you were feeling tired after the move and everything. By the way, you've not been lifting those heavy packing cases have you?'

'No. In fact the removal men were really sweet and helpful, and as Hugh had already had a new carpet fitted, everything went like a dream.'

Marion gave a wry smile. 'Some people have all the luck. My removal experiences have always been nightmares, never dreams. By the way, what about the nursery? Is that all ready and waiting?'

'Yes, it is, a bit like me I suppose. Hugh brought everything round last night and we set most of it up together. Luckily, none of the residents have moved in yet. According to the builder, they all want to wait until after Christmas. New Year, new house, I expect…'

'You really love him, don't you Sally…? I can tell that just by looking at you.'

'Yes, I do. I don't expect things are going to be easy for us but…'

'In that case, we'll all have to say a little prayer this evening when we go to midnight mass. You are still coming with us?'

'Mmm, that's if it's still OK for you to come and fetch me. I don't fancy driving there on my own.'

When she got home, Hugh was standing on the doorway of the new house, half-hidden by a large pink poinsettia.

'Hugh! What are you doing here? I thought you were going to Charles and Vivienne's?'

'I am, but I wanted you to have this. I thought the house looked a bit bare, and I needed to see you, if only for five minutes, not knowing when I'll be able to get away over Christmas.'

'It will have to be five minutes, I'm afraid. Roz telephoned and asked if she could call in on her way home. She wants to see the house and give me my Christmas present.' Sally placed the poinsettia in the middle of the dining table and turned towards him. 'Come,' she said softly, 'I've something to show you.'

Taking Hugh by the hand, Sally led him upstairs to the nursery and opened the door. 'I came home from work early and managed to get the last few bits and pieces organized. What do you think?'

Hugh's gaze took in the new bassinet with its broderie Anglaise trim and white nursery furniture. He'd been overcome with emotion when he and Sally had set things up last night, but this evening, he noticed the bassinet had been made up with fresh white linen, and piles of tiny baby clothes graced the top of the drawers. There was even a blue teddy bear. 'The layettes and teddy bear are a present from Marion and Laura. They gave them to me last week, but I didn't want to put things out until the furniture was in place.'

Swallowing hard, Hugh drew Sally into his arms and held her close. 'Oh, my love… '

Hearing a loud rapping at the front door, it was Hugh who took control.

'Don't panic, just leave everything to me.'

'To you?' Sally hissed, 'but if Roz finds you here…'

'Trust me. That won't be a problem.' Hugh placed a finger on her lips, 'Luckily there's no glass in the front door, so if you go downstairs, no rushing mind, I don't want you falling over, and I'll just pop into the downstairs cloakroom…'

Sally approached the front door and braced herself .

'Merry Christmas!' called a voice from behind yet another poinsettia, only this time it was red. 'Housewarming present,' said Roz, holding forth the plant as she followed Sally into the dining room.

'Oh, you've got one already - well, never mind, you can stick mine in the kitchen, as it's nowhere near as impressive as the pink.'

'Actually, the pink one is a present from Mr Barrington, 'Sally said, trying to appear calm. 'He's, um, only just brought it. In fact he's…' she motioned to the hallway and the cloakroom door. From within came the flushing of the loo followed by a running tap.

'Oh, I see,' Roz nodded. 'I'd better be on my best behaviour then.'

At that moment, the cloakroom door opened and Hugh, feigning surprise, reached for Roz's hand. 'Mrs Hughes, well I never! I take it we're both here to wish Mrs Palmer a Merry Christmas and every happiness in her new home. I must say it's a charming house and I can certainly vouch for the plumbing!'

Roz laughed whilst Sally, with her back to them, reached for a bottle of wine and two glasses. 'Can I offer you both a glass of wine?'

Hugh looked at his watch. 'Thank you, but no, I must be going I'm afraid. We're spending Christmas with my sister-in law and her family. If I don't get a move on, I shall be late for supper. Well… thank you again for all your sterling work with the gallery, Mrs Palmer. I shall look forward to seeing what Marion le Sage has to offer Barrington's in the spring. If you'll excuse me.'

Walking to the front door, Hugh turned and addressed the two women. 'Are you both spending Christmas at home?'

Roz spoke first. 'You bet. You'll never get Donald and me away from home at Christmas. What about you, Sally, you're not spending Christmas here on your own, are you?'

Directing her reply more at Hugh, Sally replied, 'I'm spending Christmas Day and Boxing Day at Laura's. I was going tomorrow but I've decided to go tonight instead. We're going to midnight mass and Laura and Marion are calling for me at half past ten.'

Hugh acknowledged this information with a brief nod, while Roz removed her coat and made her way to the sofa. 'Good, that means I've got time to join you in a drink.'

Sipping at her wine, Roz nodded in the direction of the pink poinsettia. 'That was kind of HB, wasn't it? I bet you were surprised to find him standing on your doorstep.'

'Yes I was,' said Sally in all honesty.

'Still, as HB said, the gallery has done amazingly well, and that's largely thanks to you.'

'Hardly. I think Marion's pictures have been the main draw, but it was kind of Mr Barrington to acknowledge my involvement in setting up the gallery.'

'Well, he's always had a soft spot for you… surely you must have noticed?'

Sally took a large gulp of her drink and stood up. 'Roz, would you like to see the nursery?'

Without warning, Roz was on her feet and heading for the stairs. 'You bet! You know Donald and I can't wait for this baby to arrive.'

With her friend drooling over the nursery furniture and the contents of each and every drawer, Sally thought of Hugh's reaction when they'd stood in the same room barely fifteen minutes ago. What was Hugh going to say before Roz had arrived so abruptly? She'd been convinced he was going to say something. Sadly, that would now have to wait. She wasn't expecting to see Hugh again until after Christmas.

With the examination of the nursery completed, Sally took Roz to show her the master bedroom.

'I see you're still reading that sexy book I gave you. How are you getting on with it?'

'At the moment finding it hard to work out how they manage to get themselves into all those amazing positions.'

'Ah! That's because you're pregnant. You wait until after you've had the baby and then I'll give you the one I'm reading at the moment. It's enough to make your hair curl. It's set in ancient Greece and they're at it day and night. I only wish Donald and I had half their energy.'

Sally was deeply reflective. 'What amazes me is why these characters never get pregnant.'

'Quite possibly,' said Roz, peering from the bedroom window into darkness, 'because they stuffed their vaginas with vine leaves or something.'

Sally smiled and folded her hands over her bump. 'Maybe that's what I should have used. Only if I remember correctly, there weren't any handy at the time.'

Roz followed Sally's gaze to the double bed, 'Are you saying that you weren't using… but I thought, ages ago, you told me the baby's father was married, wasn't that a bit risky? I take it he is still married? I also presume you're still seeing him, as you seem so much happier lately.'

'Gosh Roz, so many questions, but as you're one of my very best friends… Yes, he is still married, in name only, and please don't look at me like that, because I know that for a fact. And yes, I am still seeing him. As for contraception, we had always been very careful, only on this occasion, as I said a moment ago, we were completely out of vine leaves.'

'Blimey, Sally! Well at risk of sounding even more like a nosey and interfering old cow, can I suggest that you watch yourself after baby number one is born, because… if you're not careful this time next year you'll be expecting baby number two!'

Sally's eyes widened in horror. 'Let me just concentrate on this one first, Roz. I'm terrified enough as it is; besides, I'm not sure if H… he, the baby's father would like…'

Sally turned to face Roz with panic in her eyes. Had Roz noticed her brief slip of the tongue? She'd almost said Hugh and changed it to he at the last minute.

Roz turned from the window and placed a comforting arm on Sally's shoulder. 'Christ! I'm so sorry. Big feet and big mouth as my mum used to tell me. Here I am rabbiting on about ancient Greeks and virile men and you've got the whole birth thing ahead of you. No wonder you look scared.'

'Hmm, and as usual, your choice of word is spot on.'

'Why? What did I say?'

'Rabbiting.'

Laughing, the two women made their way downstairs and into the dining room, where Sally placed a finger on the potting compost of the pink poinsettia. Hadn't Hugh said it might need watering?

'What I can't understand,' said Roz, 'is why he bought a pink one. I mean red are far more Christmassy, aren't they?'

Remembering the incident with the roses, Sally knew only too well why.

Saying goodbye, Roz hugged her friend warmly, patted her bump and whispered in her ear. 'Now, have a lovely Christmas with Laura and Marion and let's hope next year you'll be able to spend it with you-know-who.'

For a brief moment Sally was filled with renewed panic, before she realized Roz meant *who* and not *Hugh*! It was just as well that Roz was leaving.

'And another thing,' Roz said, realizing there was no need to whisper, 'I want you to promise you'll let me know the minute the baby arrives. I want to be your first visitor, that is, after the baby's father of course. Is he… will he be with you for the birth?'

'I doubt it. You see as yet his wife doesn't know about us or the baby, and I don't really see…' Deciding it was safer not to continue, Sally knew that Hugh was still waiting to find the right moment to break the news to Serena. A: because he wanted nothing to upset Sally, prior to the birth of baby Stanley, and B: because the baby's anticipated arrival was hardly conducive to Serena's wedding anniversary plans.

CHAPTER 20

Struggling to behave as if there was nothing untoward, Serena waited for Hugh to open the car door. Then deliberately avoiding his outstretched hand, she swept past him to her sister's front door.

'Hello you two,' beamed Charles, 'Vivienne was getting worried. She thought you weren't coming.'

'Hugh was late home!' Serena snapped icily.

Charles watched as Serena tossed her mane of golden hair and sauntered off in the direction of the kitchen. He turned raised eyebrows in Hugh's direction.

'Search me,' said Hugh, 'she's hardly spoken a word since I got in.'

'I shouldn't worry, old chap, she's probably overwrought with all the plans for your anniversary. It's not long now, is it?'

'The actual anniversary is two weeks tomorrow, as you know, and we're having the celebrations three days later on the Saturday.'

'Going to be quite an occasion then. Vivienne's been talking about it for weeks. I only hope she doesn't expect something similar next year for our pearl anniversary.' Charles helped Hugh with the luggage and called to his wife from the hall, 'Vivienne, where are we putting these good people?

'In the pink room, Charles,' a voice called from the kitchen

Vivienne replaced the lid of a saucepan and turned to her sister, winking as she did so. 'That is what you wanted, isn't it?

'Pardon?'

'Several weeks ago, when you mentioned your little problem with Hugh, you asked if I'd put you both in the pink room. The one with the double bed.'

A look of horror crept over Serena's face; she'd quite forgotten her original request. Now it was the last thing she wanted. The mere thought of sharing a bed with Hugh, especially if he and that skinny blonde boy with angelic curls had…

'I'm sorry, Vivienne, I've changed my mind since then.'

'So you'd prefer single beds? Well, that's not a problem. I'll tell Charles to take your luggage to the blue room and...'

'No!' Serena broke in. 'I'd rather Hugh and I were in separate rooms.'

'Serena! What's made you change your mind?'

'I don't want to talk about it – not now. Later, perhaps, when you and I are alone. Only don't put Hugh and I in the same room. For all I care he can sleep on the sofa!'

Laying down the wooden spoon she was holding, Vivienne placed a comforting arm on her sister's shoulder. 'Things aren't that bad, surely. It's so near your anniversary.'

'Oh, they're bad all right.' Serena glanced towards the kitchen door where Charles hovered, nervously.

'Vivienne, my dear, could I have a word?'

Leaving her sister to watch the simmering saucepans, Vivienne followed her husband into the hallway and closed the kitchen door.

Charles coughed discreetly. 'Slight problem, old thing, Hugh's not happy with the sleeping arrangements. You should have seen his face when I opened the door to the pink room and he saw the double bed. Of course I immediately suggested the blue room with the singles but…'

'He didn't want that either,' Vivienne finished with a shrug of the shoulders. 'Oh, Charles, I don't know about you, but as Serena's just said more or less the same, I can only assume something's gone horribly wrong with them both since we were last together. Did Hugh give you any clues?'

'None at all. I know they have separate beds at home, but when we went to Devon they had a double room, didn't they?'

'Yes, dear, but that was over a year ago and so much can happen in a year.'

Charles fingered his moustache, recalling the time he'd met Hugh in Thornhampton Park and told him about… 'You don't suppose it has anything to do with Serena putting old Stanley down and that business over the abortion. Hugh was pretty cut up about it.'

'And quite rightly too,' Vivienne hissed under her breath. 'I told Serena years ago to… Oh! Anyway what's the use of going over that now? The important thing is to sort out where they're both going to sleep because, if you ask me, this doesn't exactly bode well for a very Merry Christmas!'

Deciding to leave Serena in the pink room, Charles took Hugh's luggage to the blue one, leaving Vivienne to explain the revised sleeping arrangements. Later, with Hugh and Serena unpacking, Charles poured two large gin and tonics and took them through to the dining room. He found his wife making a few last-minute adjustments to seating arrangement.

'I though in view of what's happened, they probably don't want to sit next to each other either!'

Charles nodded in understanding and offered Vivienne her drink. 'I was going to open a bottle of Moet, but in the circumstances decided against it, do you mind?'

'No, the only thing I shall mind is if the two of them keep up that stony silence throughout supper. It's going to be pretty embarrassing for Gareth and his new girlfriend if they do.'

Checking the place settings one last time, Vivienne nodded approvingly and picked up her drink. 'Thank goodness we have a circular dining table.'

With Charles and Vivienne facing each other and Hugh and Serena, Gareth and Lucy sitting diagonally opposite each other, the meal got off to a promising start. It was only when the main course arrived on the table that the atmosphere deteriorated.

With the precision of a surgeon, Charles carved the clove-studded gammon into slices and passed the first plate to Lucy who sat nervously on his left. 'My relations in Sweden always have gammon on Christmas Eve,' he said kindly.

'And they also follow it up with a very special rice pudding,' Vivienne continued, placing tureens of assorted vegetables on the table. 'But don't worry Lucy, we only follow Scandinavian tradition as far as the gammon and we only open one present on Christmas Eve. Now, please be careful all of you. The dishes are very hot and also quite heavy.'

'In that case,' said Hugh, sensing Lucy's unease at eating amongst strangers, 'will you allow me to help you?'

Lucy looked anxiously at the dish Hugh was offering. 'I'm afraid I don't much like vegetables. I only eat potatoes and peas. I don't know what some of those are.'

Taking a large gulp of wine, Serena raised a disapproving eyebrow and looking in Lucy's direction said sarcastically, 'Well, my dear, you are in luck, Hugh knows all about vegetables, don't you darling!'

Completely nonplussed, Hugh ignored Serena's remark. He explained each vegetable in turn to his bewildered neighbour, who was beginning to wish she hadn't accepted this evening's invitation. It wasn't so much sitting apart from Gareth that bothered her, or even having Gareth's father and uncle on either side – both men had been charming and attentive. The object of Lucy's discomfort was his Aunt Serena.

During the first course, Lucy had noticed Serena drink far more than her share of white wine, and once again her glass was empty. Oh, well, she supposed, it *was* Christmas after all. Her parents only opened a bottle of wine on high days and holidays. Toying with the haricot verts that Hugh had persuaded her to try, Lucy felt Serena's penetrating gaze once more.

'Of course, Hugh's not only a gourmet when it comes to vegetables, he's pretty good with exotic fruits, too!'

Attempting to hide his embarrassment, Charles refilled Serena's empty glass and looked to his wife for support. In desperation she offered Hugh more vegetables. He declined gracefully and turning to Lucy, said kindly,' Don't eat the beans if you don't like them; you can fill up on dessert. Vivienne makes the most wonderful chocolate roulade and crème brûlée.'

Seeing the puzzled expression on the young girl's face, Serena broke in without warning, 'To you Lucy, that's probably best described as chocolate Swiss roll with a fancy filling and custard with burnt sugar on the top!'

At that moment you could have heard a pin drop and laying down his napkin, Gareth turned to his mother. 'If you don't mind, Mum, I think we'll give pudding a miss. We said we'd meet up with some of the others at the wine bar. That OK with you, Lucy?'

Lucy's relief was palpable as she smiled warmly at Hugh, who stood up to help her from her chair.

'I hope you all have a very Merry Christmas,' she said shyly.

Serena raised her wine to her lips and with a resounding, 'I'm sure we shall, *Lacey*,' emptied another glass.

With the table cleared and Vivienne and Serena in the kitchen, Hugh watched Charles fetch brandy and four glasses.

'Not for me, Charles. I might pop out later, but not before I've had a word with Serena about her disgraceful behaviour. That poor girl! Goodness only knows what she must have thought.'

Charles frowned as he filled three of the glasses. 'Mmm, I have to admit old chap, Serena did go a bit over the top tonight. I know she's always been the feisty one and Vivienne's the big softy, but her comment about the Swiss roll was particularly out of order.'

'What's out of order,' Serena demanded, coming in to the room. She reached for a brandy.

'Your behaviour!' Hugh said tersely.

'My behaviour? That's choice coming from you, Hugh! You're a fine one to talk.'

Attracted by the raised voices, Vivienne hurried in with a tray of coffee.

'Now you two! Don't forget it's Christmas Eve and it will soon be your anniversary!'

'How could I forget!' Serena called, storming from the room.

Watching her go, Hugh turned in Vivienne's direction. 'Look, I'm truly sorry about all this. Leave it to me and I'll see if I can talk to her. If not, Serena and I might just as well pack our bags and go home. As you're expecting Gareth and Lucy again tomorrow, there's no point in spoiling everyone else's Christmas.'

Pacing the floor of the pink room, Serena drew heavily on the cigarette she held with trembling fingers. 'Out of order indeed! How dare he!'

Hugh knocked abruptly on the door and, not waiting for Serena's response, opened it and went inside.

'I don't recall saying you could come in!'

'Don't worry, I'm not stopping and this will only take a moment. All I have to say, Serena, is that I think you should apologize not only to Charles and Vivienne, but also to Gareth and his young lady.'

'Young lady! You think Lucy is a young lady? Well, I don't! Goodness, she hardly knew what piece of cutlery to use, let alone recognize a vegetable.'

'Then, instead of sneering at her, why the hell couldn't you have helped the poor girl out? Surely you saw how nervous she was. Can't you ever remember being in a similar situation when you were young?'

'No! Because no doubt I was better educated than her. I always knew how to behave in public and what to do…'

'Of course you did, Serena, how stupid of me to forget. Well, if Lucy ever needs a back-street abortionist—although from the look of her I very much doubt that she will—you'll be able to tell her where to go! And if she ever needs someone to look after her dog…'

From where she had been pacing the floor, Serena stood motionless, as if rooted to the spot. 'How dare…!'

'Yes… go ahead and scream, Serena, how dare I *what*?'

Watching Serena's sculptured mouth gape open, Hugh turned on his heels.

'Remember! It had better be an apology to everyone, otherwise we might just as well go home. And if you have anything else to say, can I suggest you say it now.'

For what seemed like an eternity, there was silence. Then, seeing Hugh's hand on the door, Serena announced flatly, 'I want a divorce.'

'Really? Well that's fine by me – but tell me, would you prefer to announce it before or after our wedding anniversary?'

Serena gave a brittle laugh. 'Oh, I'm not joking, Hugh. If you think I want to remain married to you after what I discovered today…'

Still with his hand on the door and keeping his back to her, Hugh asked quietly, 'And what exactly did you discover today?'

'To begin with I found out all about the lover you've been keeping from me, the reason for all your so-called visits to Bertam and even all the purchases from Barrington's babywear department. I never thought you could stoop so low.'

Puzzled by her last remark, Hugh rubbed his chin. Why would Serena accuse him of stooping so low over Sally? Sally was an attractive and educated young woman. Deciding to err on the side of caution Hugh said, 'To accuse me of stooping so low is a bit beyond the pale, isn't it? And if you didn't like what you discovered today, then perhaps you've only got yourself to blame.'

'I'm to blame? How dare you Hugh Barrington! How could you humiliate me so! If it had been another woman, I might have forgiven you – just – but to discover that you've been having an affair with that – that pretty blonde boy in the fruit shop is enough to turn anyone's stomach. My God! He has to be at least half your age!'

Turning, Hugh stared at his wife wide-eyed. 'What did you just say?'

'Oh, don't look so shocked, Hugh. You no longer have to pretend. You see I went over to Pots and Posies today; I wanted to see for myself who exactly had been sending you messages.'

'Julie hasn't been sending me messages.'

'Hah! So you're not going to deny that you know him?'

'No, but he hasn't sent me any messages.'

'Then how do you explain the card I found in your jacket pocket, the one that read, "please ring me if you need me Hugh". How *very* sweet… and as for him getting you to pay for all his sister's nursery furniture as well, then I'll only add that it looks as if you've been properly screwed in every direction! I wonder what the divorce court will make of that!'

With a face as black as thunder Hugh strode towards Serena until their faces were only inches apart. 'Very well, Serena, if divorce is what you want, you can have it, but I would think very carefully about using the same accusations in court.'

'Don't think you can threaten me, Hugh. Just wait 'till I tell them about all your clandestine meetings and those gifts hidden away.'

'Gifts? Whatever do you mean?'

'The picture of Stanley for a start. The one you had hidden away. You should think yourself lucky I never destroyed it.'

'Like you did with my dog and your baby, I suppose.'

If at that moment he'd wanted to strike Serena where it hurt, Hugh certainly succeeded. Serena slumped onto the pink king-size bed that only days ago she'd hoped to share with her husband.

Opening the bedroom door, Hugh announced coolly, 'I'm going out and, in case you are wondering, I shall explain why to Vivienne and Charles. You can tell them what you wish, of course.'

Determined to have the last word, Serena called after him, 'If you're going out for a quick grope with your golden-haired Julie, why not ask him for one of his special dried flower arrangements as a present for Lucy. I'm sure you'll find him very obliging!'

Choosing to ignore her remark, Hugh made his excuses to Vivienne and Charles and left the house.

'Whew! What do you make of all that?' Charles said, finishing his brandy.

Vivienne shook her head sadly, 'I don't know, dear. I honestly don't know. But if Hugh's left to be with another woman on Christmas Eve, then it must be serious.'

'Another woman? Is that what he told you?' Serena sneered, standing on the threshold of the drawing room, 'My God, Vivienne I always said you were far too gullible.'

'That's what he said,' Vivienne replied nervously. 'Hugh said they had been seeing each other for about a year and that it's serious. He also said you've asked him for a divorce.'

Serena's eyes were flint hard and assessing as she regarded her sister. 'Oh, it's serious all right and yes, I do want a bloody divorcee. So would you, if you'd just discovered your husband was a homosexual!'

*

Easing herself from the front passenger seat of Laura's car, Sally breathed in the chill night air and listened to the sound of bells welcoming them to midnight mass.

'Isn't it simply perfect,' she sighed. 'A clear, crisp night, the sound of church bells and…'

'Three overweight women trying to extricate themselves from one tiny car,' Laura volunteered.

'Sally's not overweight, she's simply pregnant.'

'Point taken, Marion, but looking at her now, we could have our own real live baby to put in the manger if we're not careful!' Laura shook her apricot curls, wrapped a multi-coloured shawl about her shoulders and regarded Sally carefully. 'Are you sure this is a good idea?'

'Positive. There's only one birth we'll be celebrating tonight and that's baby Jesus. Now, are we still going inside while we have a choice of pews?'

Readjusting her shawl, Laura whispered to Marion, 'You lead the way, but just make sure we sit near the back—just in case!'

The scene inside the church was charming. All the electric lights had been switched off and every pillar had been decorated with creamy white candles. They shone brightly and flickered each time the ancient wooden doors opened to admit even more worshippers. To the side of the pulpit, near the central aisle, Sally noticed the newly decorated crib, with its layer of straw and baby Jesus wrapped in swaddling clothes. Feeling tears prick her eyelids, she thought lovingly of how, only a few hours ago, she'd taken Hugh by the hand and led him to baby Stanley's bassinet in the newly decorated nursery.

Touching Sally gently on the elbow, Marion murmured softly, 'Are you OK, Sally?'

'Yes, wonderful thank you… just thinking.'

At half past eleven, the organ began to play and a side door opened. From within came the procession of choirboys with freshly scrubbed faces and neatly combed hair. Holding candles, they began to drift forward and a solitary voice sang the opening verse of *Once in Royal David's City*.

Standing, the congregation joined in at the second verse, aware only now and then of the usual straggle of latecomers.

At midnight, with the clock striking twelve and most of the congregation kneeling, Sally sat with her head in her hands and offered up silent prayers.

Outside once more, with the bells heralding a new day and the birth of the Christ Child, Laura's jovial vicar greeted each departing worshipper with a smile and a warm shake of the hand. Face to face with Sally, he grinned even more broadly, adding, 'I'm glad you made it through the service, my dear. For one moment I thought I'd have to call on the expertise of my wife.'

'She's with St John's Ambulance,' Laura explained as they set off towards the lych gate, 'and once helped deliver a baby during the church fete! In fact, she's never stopped talking about it. I expect she would have welcomed the opportunity of a repeat performance.'

'I'm only sorry I couldn't oblige,' Sally teased, stepping sideways through the gate. 'Oh!'

'Sally!' Marion made a grab for her arm, 'are you OK? Is it the baby?'

'N-no, it's not the baby. It's Hugh. He's standing by Laura's car. What shall I do?'

'Go over and talk to him, silly! After all, that's probably why he's here. There's no point in trying to hide things anymore… is there?'

'Don't worry about Laura,' Marion nudged Sally gently in Hugh's direction. 'By the looks of it, she's been cornered by the vicar's wife. She probably wants to know where you're spending Christmas Day…'

'I'm hoping Sally will be spending Christmas Day with me,' Hugh said, stepping from the shadows to take Sally's hand.

'Go on,' Marion urged, kissing Sally's cheek. 'Off you go, both of you. I'll explain to Laura.'

Struggling to get through the lych gate, Laura stared in amazement. Was that really Sally being helped into the front passenger seat of a Jaguar? 'Where's Sally going?' she asked, 'and why is…'

'She's going to spend Christmas with the father of her baby.'

'But wasn't that…?'

'Yes, that's right, Laura, it was Hugh Barrington. Isn't it wonderful?' Marion cast her eyes towards the heavens and whispered softly. 'Thank you Lord; at least you answered my prayers.'

*

Nestled in Hugh's arms, Sally listened as he recounted the disastrous evening spent with Vivienne and Charles, followed by Serena's outburst and her eventual demand for a divorce.

'I don't believe it,' she said softly. 'Are you sure she meant it?'

'Oh, she meant it all right.'

'But that's because she thinks you and Julie… well, you know.'

'Yes, I do. Only too well.'

'And yet you didn't tell her she'd made a mistake.'

Hugh gave a wry smile. 'Sally, with Serena in that frame of mind, no one would be able to convince her. The very fact that I admitted to knowing Julie, was enough for her to put two and to together and make five. I won't even repeat the worst of what she said. Besides…'

'Besides what?'

'It makes it easier for us at the moment, doesn't it? Gives us more time to think about the future… You do want us to have a future together, don't you?'

Looking up into Hugh's eyes, Sally realized he was in earnest. There was just time for a whispered, 'Oh, yes,' before she felt his lips on hers.

Making two mugs of hot chocolate, Sally glanced at the kitchen clock; it was almost two o'clock in the morning.

'What do you intend to do now then, go back to Vivienne's?'

'No way! As I said in the church carpark, I intend to spend Christmas day with you. Don't worry, I'll ring Charles first thing in the morning. I really don't want to disrupt their Christmas any further. Serena will no doubt stay with them and I will stay here. Simple, really.'

Sally grinned and handed Hugh a mug of chocolate.

'What's so funny?'

'Everything, when you come to think about it. A short while ago Roz was convinced Bernard was the father of my baby. Then when she arrived tonight, I thought the cat was really out of the bag, but of course she still thinks you can't have children. So while I'm worrying about what Roz is thinking, you're in the middle of a row with Serena, who thinks you're gay, and there's poor Laura, gaping open-mouthed as I head off into the night with you!'

Returning to the settee, Hugh sipped his hot chocolate and reflected thoughtfully, 'Mmn. Put like that, I suppose it does seem amusing, though at the time I found being screamed at by Serena anything but.'

'I'll tell you what *will* be amusing... our Christmas dinner! Do you realize as I was going to be spending Christmas with Laura and Marion, I've hardly any food in the house - unless you fancy a spaghetti Bolognese? I made a couple of those last week for the freezer.'

'Spaghetti Bolognese would be wonderful and we can pretend my poinsettia is the Christmas tree.'

'Speaking of which, Roz was curious to know why you didn't buy a red one. Am I correct in assuming you remembered what I'd said about red roses?'

Nodding, Hugh helped Sally to her feet. 'Come along, let's go to bed. You look exhausted. We can discus things in greater detail tomorrow.'

'Don't you mean today?' She yawned sleepily.

*

Hours later, preparing her Bolognese, Sally removed a stray bay leaf from the sauce. Her thoughts turned automatically to Stanley. 'Hugh... did you ever decide what to do with Stanley's ashes?'

'No, it was something I always wanted to discuss with you, only I've never got round to it. Too painful to think about I suppose.'

'So where are they?'

'In the mahogany cabinet in my office. Why do you ask?'

'I was thinking... perhaps once the lawn is laid and I start planting out some shrubs, perhaps we could scatter Stanley's ashes round the bay tree... that's if you'd like to?'

Encircling his arms round her, Hugh thought lovingly of his loyal and faithful friend. 'I'd like that very much. I'm sure Stanley would have approved of the idea, too.'

CHAPTER 21

Watching a fine drizzle fall on the newly laid turf, Sally turned away for the window and switched on the DVD player. The midwife had told her the baby's head was engaged, so it seemed a good time to run through the birth tape again. It would help take her mind off the fact Hugh was on his way to meet Charles. An *unofficial* meeting to discuss the divorce, Hugh had said.

With the DVD drawing to a conclusion with its rather dramatic birth sequence, Sally was almost relieved when the doorbell rang.

'Terry, what a lovely surprise. Is Julie with you?'

'No, he's out delivering flowers, but he asked me to give you these.' Terry held out the first of the new season's daffodils and followed Sally through to the kitchen.

'Thank you, they're lovely and the perfect reminder that spring is just around the corner. Mind you, it doesn't look very spring-like out there. Look at the mess.'

Terry peered from the window and whistled. 'Bloody hell! What happened there? It looks like the battlefield of the Somme!

'The men picked today to lay the new turf. I know January isn't exactly the best time of year for it but as we had such a mild autumn… I didn't think they were going to make so much mess. They even managed to knock over Stanley's bay tree and practically demolished it with the roller.'

'Wasn't the bay tree where you planned to scatter Stanley's ashes?'

Sally nodded tearfully. 'Hugh's going to be terribly upset.'

Terry patted her hand and added brightly, 'Don't worry about the mess. Julie and me will pop round one day when it's not quite so wet and clear up a bit. As for the bay tree, it doesn't look too healthy to me. Tell you what, when I go to the wholesalers I'll see if I can find a replacement.'

'I'd really appreciate that. Now, how about a cup of tea.'

Insisting on carrying the tray, Terry placed it on the coffee table just as the DVD came to an end. 'Oh, sorry, was I interrupting a film or something?'

'Or something is right, Terry! It's the birth DVD I borrowed. Luckily you called at the right moment. They were just getting to the actual birth.'

'Then can I have a look – that's if you don't mind?'

'Are you serious?'

'Yes, I've always wanted to see a baby being born, but with things the way they are with Julie and me it's not as if we're likely to have any, are we?'

'No, I suppose not,' said Sally, pressing the start button.

Terry stared in wonderment at the television screen, where in the final stages of labour, the baby's head began to emerge. Feeling a lump rise in his throat, he whispered, 'That's amazing, I never realized…' Turning to Sally, he asked, 'Aren't you frightened? I know Julie's sister's terrified.'

Sally nodded and patted her bump. 'I have to admit I am. Still, it's too late to change my mind now.'

Stirring his tea, Terry fixed her with a sympathetic smile. 'Yeah, I guess it is. Will Hugh be with you at the birth?'

'I doubt it. Our timing wasn't very good I'm afraid. The baby's due at about the same time as Hugh and Serena's silver wedding party. Considering Serena doesn't know about the baby *and* she still thinks Hugh is funding Julie's sister's pregnancy… I can hardly ring her and ask her to send Hugh to the hospital for me!'

'They're still going ahead with that party? That's barmy! I thought Serena wanted a divorce.'

'She does, though she remains convinced Hugh is having an affair with Julie – I hope you don't mind us going along with that, by the way?'

Terry chuckled and shook his head. 'Not at all. Julie and I think it's a scream. Anyway Serena deserves it, especially after poor old Stanley and the other business…'

'And this other business,' said Sally shifting uncomfortably in the chair, 'will quite possibly be making its presence felt soon if the past twenty-four hours are anything to go by.'

'You're not going into labour!'

'No, don't worry. I've just been getting what they call Braxton Hicks contractions. Not the real thing… but still pretty uncomfortable.'

Filled with renewed concern, Terry reminded, 'Don't forget what Julie and me said last week. You've only got to ring us when things start to happen.'

'I know. In fact I have Pots and Posies cards with your phone numbers, landline and mobile, stuck up in every room. And when things start, Terry, I'll expect you to come and hold my hand!'

'Right, you're on!'

'I was only joking…'

'Well, I'm not!'

Sally contemplated the prospect of Terry being with her at the hospital. Nobody could stop her having him there, could they? Besides, if Hugh couldn't make it and as she didn't want to drag Laura and Marion from the gallery… This being a first baby and because of her age, labour could go on for quite a while. If Terry were to hold her hand and support her in the early stages, giving her sister time to deal with Ben and Nathan, then she supposed it was an option…

'Are you really sure?'

'Positive!' said Terry, beaming from ear to ear. 'After all I've seen it on the DVD, so I know what to expect.'

Getting up to leave, he suddenly remembered, 'By the way, you never quite finished telling me about Hugh and Serena's anniversary party. Why are they still going ahead with it?'

'Ah! That's quite a long story, but apart from all the expense and the problems if they cancel, they both have their own reasons for doing so.'

'Meaning?'

'Meaning Serena, according to her sister, who in turn told Hugh, is planning to announce to their assembled guests that Hugh is a homosexual, which is why she's divorcing him!'

'The bitch! And what about Hugh, what's he going to say?'

'Oh, he's proposing to tell her that she's gravely mistaken in her assumptions, before he makes a speech to celebrate the twenty-five years of their marriage and its inevitable end.'

'And will he tell them about you and the baby?'

'He's still undecided.'

'Oh, Sally. If only I could be a fly on the wall!'

*

In Thornhampton, Charles welcomed Hugh into his office and motioned him to a chair. 'It was good of you to come, Hugh. I, er…'

'Look, Charles, before you begin, can I say that I fully appreciate how difficult this is for you. And if it will make things any easier, try and pretend I'm not family.'

'Can't do that, old chap.'

'Why not?'

'Because as far as Vivienne and I are concerned, you are still family.'

'It's kind of you to say so, Charles, but if you are acting for Serena, you know we really shouldn't be meeting like this in the first place.'

Charles clicked the top of his silver ballpoint in and out. 'I know, and Serena's making the whole thing deuced awkward for me.'

'And you still maintain this is an off-the-record meeting?'

'You have my word, Hugh.'

'What exactly do you want to know, then?'

Charles sucked in his cheeks. 'It's about this homosexual business, though of course it wouldn't matter to Vivienne and I if you were, but truth is

Hugh, we don't believe it for one little minute. But Serena – well, you know Serena.'

'I most certainly do, and much as I deplore her behaviour in recent months, I still don't want her to make a complete and utter fool of herself in court.'

'You don't?'

'Of course not. I can't dismiss twenty-five years of marriage with a mere flick of the fingers.'

'Yet she's adamant about you and this – um – Julie.'

Reaching into his wallet for the Pots and Posies card, with Julie's message written on the back, Hugh pushed it across the desk. '*That*, Charles, is the sole basis for Serena's accusations. So, tell me, where on that card does it say that I'm gay?'

'Nowhere.'

'Exactly and do you think a barrister would be prepared to stand up in a divorce court and use that as evidence?'

Charles shook his head. 'But Serena seems to think you've spent evenings at Julie's flat.'

'Of course I have! Julie and his partner Terry – and for your information *they* are both gay – invited us to dinner on numerous occasions.'

'You mean you and Serena?'

'No, I mean me and the person I intend to marry, when the divorce comes through. And shall I tell you what we've been celebrating every time we go there for a meal?'

Charles moved the Pots and Posies card back in Hugh's direction. 'Even if I said no, I still feel you'd go ahead and tell me.'

'How well you know me, Charles.'

'Well, we do go back a long way, don't we? I feel as if I know you almost as well as I know myself, which is why I didn't believe Serena.'

'Unlike me, who did!'

'Afraid you've lost me there, Hugh.'

'I believed her when she told me about the baby. All those lies about an adoption, remember...?'

'How could I forget?' Charles broke in. 'That awful day in Thornhampton Park, Hugh. I'm so very, very sorry that it had to me who… I remember going home to Vivienne, thinking how could two sisters be so close and yet so different. Vivienne, who'd give a home to every damned waif and stray in the neighbourhood and….'

'Serena, who wouldn't,' Hugh finished for him.

Deeply embarrassed, Charles shook his head, surprised when Hugh made as if to leave. 'You're not going because I've upset you, old chap, by talking about…'

'No, not any more,' Hugh said, reaching across the desk to shake Charles warmly by the hand. 'I'm afraid I have to dash. I've an appointment with my own solicitor in twenty minutes. Oh, yes, and by the way - as I never got to finish - the reason for the celebrations with Terry and Julie… I'm about to become a father!'

'You're *what?* But *how*? I mean *when*?'

Smiling, Hugh picked up the pen Charles had been holding and reaching for the desk calendar drew a circle around January tenth.

'But that's…'

'Precisely. That's a week from today, so do advise Serena not to do anything silly in the meantime.'

Completely stunned, Charles stood at his office window and watched Hugh run down the steps and across the market square with the energy of a twenty-year old.

'Well I never!' he murmured. 'Serena my dear, you are in for a very rude awakening!'

*

On the actual morning of their wedding anniversary, Hugh placed a small box by Serena's breakfast plate.

'What's this, a peace offering?' she said, her tone icy. 'Because if you think it will make me change my mind about the divorce, you're very much mistaken.'

'No, it's not a peace offering. Let's just say it's a joint anniversary and parting gift, shall we? I think you'll find it's the one you wanted.'

Serena forgot herself for a moment, and tore excitedly at the wrapping. 'Is it the one I saw when I went to London with Vivienne?'

Hugh merely nodded, poured himself a coffee and picked up the morning paper. Five rows, each containing five diamonds, sparkled in the glow from the angled spotlights, suspended from the ceiling.

'If you've changed your mind about it, you can always sell it. After all, you know how much it's worth,' Hugh said, turning to the financial pages.

Serena said nothing, and only twisted the ring on her finger as she stared into the ghostly and deserted winter garden. Aware of Hugh folding the paper, she turned to face him.

'Thank you,' she said numbly. 'It is the right one.'

Hugh rose from the breakfast table and made his way from the kitchen. 'That's good, and an appropriate choice if I may say so. One diamond for each of the twenty-five years; I suppose it's just as well it's not our golden wedding.'

At any other time, Serena would have thrown the ring and the box after him; however, even she wasn't that stupid.

Later, getting ready to have lunch with her sister, Serena was surprised to see Mrs Burt walking up the drive to the front door.

'What is *she* doing here today! I distinctly recall telling her *not* to come until tomorrow and why isn't she going to the back door?'

Angrily Serena walked downstairs and, opening the door, found Mrs Burt in her best coat and hat. In her hands was an exquisite flower arrangement.

'Mrs Burt, I wasn't expecting you.'

Holding forth the arrangement, Mrs Burt announced proudly, 'Happy Anniversary! I had it done special like to match your colour scheme.'

Completely taken aback, Serena found herself opening the front door wide and beckoning her cleaner into the house for a coffee.

'Only a quick cuppa then,' Mrs Burt insisted, 'because Mr Burt's coming for me in ten minutes. We're going into Thornhampton 'cos the sales are on and it's also market day. I always prefer to get my fruit and veg on the market. The green grocer's at the bottom of our road is dreadful. Not like where I got that.' Mrs Burt pointed to the flower arrangement.

'It's very beautiful, Mrs Burt. So delicate and the colours are simply perfect,' Serena acknowledged, surprised that her cleaner could have chosen something so exquisite.

'That's just what I said to Mr Burt; well not in quite the same words, mind you. And he agreed with me, you'd never think that was done by that pretty young man, would you?'

Serena felt her whole being go rigid. 'What do you mean, Mrs Burt?'

'That Pots and Pansies place I told you about.'

'I think it's Pots and Posies.'

Mrs Burt chuckled. 'Well, it's the same difference, isn't it? Come to think of it, you could say that about Julie and Terry. Julie does the flowers and Terry deals with the veg.'

Serena remembered her brief visit to the shop. 'And you know them both, do you?'

'Not really. I know Terry's mum better. She's had her stall on the market for years. Quite cut up about it she was, when her Terry came out of the cupboard, or whatever else they call it these days.'

'I think you mean closet.'

'Oh, do I? Anyways, as I was saying, Lily - that's Terry's mum – didn't like it at all, and when he moved Julie into his flat there were ructions. She refused to have anything to do with them.'

Pouring the coffee and keeping her tone casual, Serena enquired, 'And does she have anything to do with them now?'

'Apparently they all got together before Christmas and then buried the hammer, or is it hatchet, at New Year. Lily says that as Julie and Terry have been together for so long, and they're not causing no trouble to anyone, why not let bygones be bygones.'

'Why not indeed?' Serena heard herself saying.

Mrs Burt was still chattering away about Lily, her son and his flat when Mr Burt tooted the horn of his car to announce his arrival.

'It's small but beautifully furnished and decorated, Lily said, and it just goes to show what a small world it is, 'cos she said she thought she saw Mr Barrington coming out of the flat opposite, when she went at New Year. She knows him for the store, you see.'

The moment Mr and Mrs Burt's car was out of sight, Serena grabbed her coat and car keys and headed for Elmsmarsh. Driving past the small row of shops she searched the neighbourhood for blocks of flats, which courtesy of Mrs Burt and Lily's information, weren't too difficult to find.

Parking her car at the rear, Serena gazed up at the windows with their assorted drapes, nets and blinds. Which one belonged to Julie and Terry? Five minutes later she was studying the names on the letterboxes on the ground floor and filled with renewed enthusiasm, headed for the stairs.

'Julie and Terry,' she whispered loudly. 'Where are you?'

'If you mean the couple from Pots and Posies,' a voice cut in from the shadows, 'they're upstairs on the right, only you won't find them in. They'll be at the shop I expect. Why don't you try there?'

'Of course,' Serena replied, knowing full well that she had no intention of doing so.

Waiting until the coast was clear, she ran upstairs, located Terry's flat and then turned to face the one opposite. In trepidation she rang the doorbell. There was no reply. Totally dejected and disillusioned, Serena walked slowly back down the stairs, but not before making a mental note of the name outside the door. A. and M. Thompson.

Returning home, Serena pulled the Thornhampton telephone directory from the drawer and frantically scanned the list of Thompsons. There were so many it was like looking for a needle in a haystack. In disgust she threw the directory on the floor and only then remembered her lunch date with her sister.

*

For the umpteenth time, Vivienne looked up as a cold draught heralded the arrival of yet another diner. When at last she recognized her sister's flustered features, she waved her arm and called out, 'Serena, over here!'

Making her way to the table, Serena cast a sideways look at the other customers, hoping there would be no one she recognized. It was the last thing she wanted.

'I thought perhaps you'd forgotten,' Vivienne said, passing the menu across the table.

'No, I had to go to Elmsmarsh unexpectedly.'

At the mere mention of the name, Vivienne's eyebrows shot up. Though Charles had refused to tell her anything of his meeting with Hugh, Vivienne had her own suspicions as to why her sister had gone to Elmsmarsh.

'Oh, Serena. I hope that doesn't mean you've been trying to see…'

'If you mean the boyfriend, no I haven't. But I have been to see where he lives – if you can call him a "he"?'

Vivienne shook her head sadly. 'My dear, you really have no proof that Hugh and….'

'Julie!' snapped Serena. 'No. Perhaps not, and *maybe* I jumped to the wrong conclusions, but I'm convinced there's a connection one way and another. Why else would Hugh have his card with that cryptic message on the back?'

'It needn't be cryptic at all. It could be a perfectly innocent message.'

'Hmph!' muttered Serena after giving her order to the waiter. 'The way Hugh's been behaving recently, I hardly think innocence has anything to do with it!'

Vivienne watched as Serena drummed her fingers of her left hand on the table. 'And is that new ring anything to do with Hugh's behaviour?'

Serena gave a sly smile, 'At least I got that out of him. It was the one we saw in London – remember?'

Initially, Vivienne declined to comment. By the end of that day spent in London, Serena's credit card—or should that be Hugh's—was red hot. All that money spent on clothes, shoes and fripperies and now they were talking of a divorce. Eventually, taking a deep breath, she said discreetly, 'Serena, it's a truly beautiful ring, and I'm sure Hugh wouldn't have bought it for you unless… I mean… does it really have to end in divorce?'

'According to Hugh it does. He gave me this as a parting gift.'

Vivienne practically choked on her spritzer. 'That's a parting gift!'

'Apparently so,' Serena said, flashing the ring and sending myriad rainbows darting on the crystal glassware.

Saddened by the disclosure, Vivienne picked at her seafood pancake and watched her sister stab at a black olive on a bed of radicchio. 'Serena, I honestly think you should consider the situation very carefully.'

'Why? What do you know? What did Hugh tell Charles?'

'I can't tell you.'

'You meant you won't!'

'I mean I don't know, and even if I did, I wouldn't be at liberty to say.'

Vivienne covered Serena's be-ringed hand with her own. 'Look, I'm your big sister and I don't want to jeopardize our relationship. Can't you see, it's your future we're discussing here.'

'So!'

'So it could be a future without Hugh. Have you thought about that?'

'Of course I have, because he'd have to pay me a pretty decent settlement. I'd certainly want my fair share of… Whatever's the matter, Vivienne? Why are you looking at me like that?'

As in their younger days, unable to cope with Serena's obdurate nature, Vivienne finished the rest of her meal in silence.

*

Uneasy at parting on such a discordant note, Serena was nevertheless determined to pursue her quest, that of locating A. and M. Thompson via directory enquiries.

'I'm sorry, madam,' came the clipped and precise tone of the operator, 'we have no one of that name listed at that address. Perhaps they prefer to use a mobile phone.'

'Could they be ex-directory?'

'If they are, I wouldn't be able to give you their number.'

Sensing the operator was about to terminate their conversation, Serena said hurriedly. 'What about a new listing? What if they've only just moved in? That might explain why the number isn't in the book.'

'Perhaps, but with everything being computerized…'

'Look! I don't give a damn about computers! Could you just check if the Thompsons are under a new listing or do I have to contact your supervisor?'

'No. That won't be necessary. I'll see what I can do.'

'Christ! It's like dealing with a bloody robot!' Serena announced when a number eventually echoed tonelessly down the line. Scribbling the six digit number, she dashed to her bedroom and picked up the phone. It was safer to ring from there, in case Hugh arrived home unexpectedly. Moments later, and to her delight, a young and confident male voice answered.

'Hi! This is Andy Thompson. I'm sorry Melanie and I aren't here to take your call. If you'd like to leave your name and number...'

'Damn,' hissed Serena, hanging up the phone while studying the number on the square of paper. 'Well, as I've certainly not heard Hugh mention an Andy or a Melanie, I shall just have to try you both later.' With two days to go until their anniversary party, there was still time to surprise Hugh and maybe Andy Thompson himself. She doubted if he'd be sounding quite so confident if he discovered that his wife had been having an affair with Hugh!

CHAPTER 22

Early on the Saturday morning with the caterers setting up the table in the dining room and Hugh discussing the wine and champagne, Serena took herself off to the tranquillity of her bedroom. Assuming the Thompsons to be a young working couple, she hoped she would find them at home for the weekend.

'Hello… Andy Thompson…'

'Oh! I'm sorry to bother you Mr Thompson, and I do hope you weren't still in bed as it is rather early… but I'm trying to trace the previous owner of your flat - a Mr Hugh Barrington.'

'Sorry, I think you've got the wrong flat. There was a woman living here before us but that wasn't her name.'

Serena heard Andy Thompson yawn noisily down the phone. 'Why don't you try directory enquiries.'

'I already have, that's how I got your number.' Serena was beginning to get desperate, someone was calling for her from downstairs, presumably a member of the catering team. Perhaps if she were to ask this Andy if she could speak to his wife? After all, if Melanie was having an affair with Hugh, her husband was hardly likely to know about it. 'Perhaps if I spoke to your wife, she might be able to help me. It's very important, you see.'

Still half-asleep and angry at being woken so early by a complete stranger, Andy turned to his wife. 'Mel, I have absolutely no idea who's on the phone. The woman's probably a complete nutter, but she's asking about a Hugh somebody or other. I keep telling her there was a woman in the flat before us…'

Catching only the tail end of this conversation, Serena was delighted when a female voice murmured down the line, 'Hi… can I help you? My husband says you're looking for someone called Hugh…'

'Yes, that's right, Hugh Barrington,' Serena simpered, 'and I really wouldn't have troubled you so early if it wasn't important. I'm planning a surprise, you see, and I did want this special friend of the family to be part of it. I was told he used to live at your address, someone even saw him there at New Year.'

Melanie rubbed the sleep from her eyes. 'Well, as there was a woman living here before us, and Andy and I moved in here the day after Boxing Day, I don't really see how we can help you… unless you mean the man with the keys.'

'The man with the keys?'

'Yes. That's the only person I can think of. Although the previous occupant was a woman, and she left just before Christmas, I remember the estate agent ringing to say a man would call with the spare set of keys for the flat. To be honest, he did give his name, but as we were knee-deep in packing cases… I didn't take much notice at the time. I only know it sounded like that mountaineering chap.'

Initially disappointed that Hugh's name had done nothing to unnerve either Andy or Melanie, Serena clung to the telephone in anticipation.

'Andy,' Melanie called, 'who was that guy who wrote The Everest Years?'

'Chris Bonnington,' came the muffled reply from beneath the duvet.

'That's it!' Melanie said brightly, 'Bonnington. Wasn't that the name you mentioned?'

Bonnington, Barrington, Serena thought to herself. Well, if you were completely thick, as the Thompsons obviously were… Hardly daring to ask what this man with the keys looked like, Serena couldn't believe her ears when Melanie broke in. 'He was quite good looking too, in a distinguished sort of way, a bit like that actor my gran always drools over in South Pacific. Not the young one, the older one – with the nice voice – who sings *Some Enchanted Evening*, only it wasn't him singing, was it? It was someone else.'

Hardly in the mood to discuss Rogers and Hammerstein, Serena had at least gleaned one snippet of information. Hugh had turned up at the Elmsmarsh flat with a spare set of keys, though quite why was still a mystery. However, as it appeared that Melanie Thompson had now woken up and was in full flow, why not take advantage of it? Could she perhaps add another piece of the puzzle?

Erring on the side of caution, Serena ventured. 'It's just a thought, but if the person, who lived in the flat before you left a forwarding address, perhaps she might know where I can find Mr Barrington.'

'I can certainly help you there,' Melanie chirped, 'although I haven't got it here in the bedroom. We've been away all week you see, trekking in Snowdonia; we're all-weather climbers and didn't get back until late last night, but as we're still getting post for , erm, Mrs Palmer…'

'Palmer? Do you mean Sally Palmer?'

'Yes, that's right. Gosh! Do you know her too?'

'Yes, but I haven't seen her in ages...'

'In that case, why not pop round for her post - as there's been loads while we've been away – then you can kill two birds with one stone. If you go and see Sally and she can give you your friend Hugh's address, you'll be able to surprise them both. Won't that be fun?'

Choking back a sob, Serena said huskily. 'Yes, why don't I do that? I'll ring you before I come just to make sure you're in.'

'What a good idea,' Melanie replied in all innocence, hanging up the phone.

'Good idea indeed!' Serena spat, slamming down the phone and storming into the en-suite for her hidden cache of cigarettes. 'Sally Palmer! You've got to be joking! I don't believe it. You bet I'll go round and pick up her post – I'll – I'll certainly give her a *nice* surprise, one she won't forget in a hurry. My God! How long has this been going on?'

'About a year,' Hugh said softly, appearing in the doorway.

Startled, Serena spun round to face him. 'How long have you been there!'

'Long enough to hear your scheming plans… and your so-called surprise for Sally.'

'Too damned right I'll give her a surprise! Just you wait until I tell her.'

'Tell her what Serena?'

'That she's destroyed our marriage.'

Walking over to his wife, Hugh lit the cigarette she had wedged between her lips. He then took her by the hand and led her back to the bedroom. There he sat her on the bed, while he chose the dressing-table stool.

'Serena, let's get one thing straight, shall we? Sally didn't destroy our marriage – you did.'

'I did? How dare you? When I think about…'

'Oh, dear. Is this where you bring up that one very brief affair I had over twenty years ago, while you were swanning around the Bahamas, spending money that neither I nor Barrington's could afford?'

'You said you didn't mind me going on holiday because you couldn't…'

'Yes, I couldn't what?'

'Give me a baby. You said you felt guilty about it.'

'Hmm… at the time, I well remember feeling guilty about that, even ashamed and humiliated. It wasn't easy when people kept asking me when they were going to hear the patter of tiny Barrington feet. Later of course I became even more humiliated when I discovered how you behaved whenever you went on holiday with your sister.'

'So, Vivienne's been dishing the dirt on me, has she? The bitch! Just wait until I see her!'

'Goodness, you are going to be busy, Serena, first Sally, then Vivienne, not to mention several members of the catering staff who have been asking for you. That's why I came to find you. For your information it wasn't Vivienne who told me. Your sister has always been extremely loyal to you. Not that you deserve it.'

Studying the lengthening ash of her cigarette, Serena reached for a blue Wedgwood dish and flicked the ash onto the figure of a horse. Watching her exhale a thin column of smoke into the air, Hugh turned and went to open the window. From below came the sound of excited voices unloading food and glasses.

'What I can't understand,' Serena said angrily, crushing the remains of her cigarette on the horse's head, 'is why you let me go along with all this – the anniversary and inviting all our closest friends. Don't you realize what we've done? We haven't invited them to a wedding anniversary celebration at all. We've invited them to a Whitehall farce!'

Hugh nodded in agreement. 'It was, after all, what *you* wanted Serena. I was never keen on the idea. You've known for months how things have been between us since Stanley died.'

'Good God! You're never going to blame the breakup of our marriage on that bloody dog!'

'No, let's just say having Stanley put to sleep unnecessarily was almost the final straw.'

'Almost. What's that supposed to mean? And who said it was unnecessary, your wonderful Sally? If you hadn't been away sleeping with her, your precious dog might still be alive. Perhaps you should have stayed at home that weekend!'

'I spent all of that weekend with Bertram in Harrogate and well you know it!' Anxious to protect both Charles and Vivienne, Hugh declined to be drawn further. 'Anyway, as I said a while ago, people are looking for you. The catering manager wants to discuss the seating plan.'

'I don't give a damn about the seating plan.'

'Really, and there was me thinking you want everyone sitting in the right place for when you declare that I am having a homosexual relationship with a local greengrocer!'

Studying the disturbingly inflexible set to Hugh's jaw, Serena felt her face redden. Nervously she fingered her new diamond ring, slipping it up and down her knuckle until she wedged it back in place next to her wedding ring.

'I *will* go and see to the seating arrangements, Hugh, but believe me, you haven't heard the last of this!

'No, I don't suppose I have, Serena, and neither have you.'

Serena shot him a withering look and sashayed downstairs. Her appearance in the dining room resulted in the sound of raised voices and the grating of furniture as it was moved from one side of the room to the other.

*

At Elmsmarsh, Sally stretched lazily in her bed. For once, she'd not bothered to set her alarm. She knew that unlike previous Saturdays, Hugh would not be coming to see her.

He'd called in yesterday lunchtime, and spying fresh vacuum tracks in the carpets and smelling lavender polish, had admonished her severely. 'You are supposed to be taking it easy, not leaping around like a mountain goat.'

'I'd hardly put myself in the mountain-goat category. At the moment I feel more like a beached whale.'

Taking her in his arms Hugh had cautioned, 'Sally, you must be careful. The baby is due today. I call in and expect to see you resting and what do I find?'

'I don't feel like resting, in fact I feel positively energetic. I haven't felt this good for weeks. Besides, though today is my due date, first babies are always late.'

'Always?' asked Hugh, his voice full of concern.

'Let's say mostly…'

Now almost twenty-four hours later she was beginning to regret the vigorous spell of early spring-cleaning, her back ached and she felt distinctly uncomfortable.

Running a warm bath, she thought of Hugh and Serena and wondered what was happening in the Barrington household. Hugh's vivid description of recent events made the whole business sound utterly ludicrous, almost like hounds baying for the kill.

'Don't worry, Sally,' he'd reassured with a smile, 'even though I feel the adrenalin rising, I can assure you there won't be any killing, only a few bruised egos.'

Stepping carefully into the warm scented water, Sally studied her own bruise. The one on her right hip, the result of an over-zealous push of the vacuum cleaner, and a collision with the bedside cabinet. Running her hands from her bruised hip to her now heavily pregnant form, she was filled with an overwhelming sense of wonderment and love. Wonderment at the miracle growing inside her and love for the father of her baby.

*

'It will be a blooming miracle if we ever get to lay the table, let alone serve the food!' the catering manager muttered angrily to her assistant. 'First she wants a horseshoe table, with her and her husband sitting side by side. Now she wants one long table with her at one end like the lady bountiful and her husband at the other.'

'All I can say is, best let her have her own way then. She looks a pretty hard bitch if you ask me.'

'Yes – and quite possibly used to having her own way. OK, folk, start shifting the tables and get the places laid asap, before she changes her mind again.'

When Hugh popped his head round the dining-room door, a sea of faces looked anxiously in his direction. 'Oh, what happened to the horseshoe?'

'Madam changed her mind about it,' came the reply.'

'Did she? Fine, just so long as I know. Carry on then.'

Breathing a sigh of relief, nimble hands smoothed out starched white damask tablecloths and folded ice-blue napkins into fans.

*

Freshly bathed, Sally prepared herself some lunch, flicked through a magazine and settled down to watch *While You Were Sleeping* on the television. She'd watched it a least half a dozen times before, having first seen it with Roz, years ago. She'd cried then and no doubt would cry again this afternoon, it being both happy and sad in places.

Three incoming phone calls later, she got up and switched off the television. 'What's the point,' she sighed, tracing her fingers over her Stanley bump. 'I shan't have any peace until you arrive. Don't you realize all these people keep ringing to find out whether or not you are on your way? Perhaps we should leave them a message and go out for a walk instead?'

Slipping on her coat, and reaching for her handbag, it was no surprise when the phone rang for a fourth time. 'Well, who's it to be?' she asked her reflection in the hall mirror. She'd already had calls from Jackie, Roz and Laura. This meant it could only be Marion.

'Sally.'

'Hugh! What are you doing, ringing me now? I thought you'd be busy with…'

'My darling, I am, but not too busy that I can't ring you.'

'Where are you ringing from and what about Serena?'

'No need to panic. I'm ringing from the garden on my mobile and Serena doesn't even know I've left the house; she's far too busy giving the caterers hell.'

'Oh dear. It doesn't sound much like a celebratory occasion.'

'Don't you believe it! Everything's going swimmingly,' Hugh chuckled. 'In fact it couldn't be better.'

'Hugh, have you been drinking?'

'No, I haven't touched a drop. I want to be sober when the fun and games start.'

Sally frowned hard, "fun and games?" She wasn't so sure about that.

'What exactly do you mean, Hugh?'

'Put simply, I don't intend to drink as much as my guests so that when I tell them about you, they'll all be completely pie-eyed and probably cheer me on my way.'

'Hugh! You must be mad. Why tell them about me, today of all days?'

'Because… my dear sweet Sally, if I don't, Serena will!'

Recovering from the shock of this announcement, Sally steadied herself against the banister rail and lowered herself onto the stairs. 'Are you saying you told Serena about me?'

'No. I didn't have to. She found out quite by chance this morning. You've got to hand it to her… her timing was perfect.'

Unable to share Hugh's enthusiasm, Sally made no response. She merely sat undoing and refastening the buttons of her coat.

'Anyway, my darling, as long as you and baby Stanley are OK, that's my main reason for ringing. You haven't been tearing about like a whirling Dervish today, have you?'

'No, nor a mountain goat.'

'That's good. I'll ring you later tonight then, when they've all drunk me out of house and home. Take care, remember I love you.'

'I love you too,' she whispered as Hugh switched off his phone and returned to Serena's ravings.

Opening her front door, Sally was glad to be going for a walk. She needed some fresh air following Hugh's revelations.

Nodding to the new neighbours, who were busily hanging curtains, she walked past the row of unfinished houses in the direction of Elmsmarsh village and the shops. Then, remembering it would soon be Roz's birthday, she called at the newsagent's for a card.

Contemplating whether to send a pretty or humorous one, Sally found herself wondering whose name or names would be on the card. Would it be just hers or hers and the baby's? But what name, that was the problem.

As yet, she and Hugh were totally undecided over names. To them, the uncomfortable bulge, now pressing on her bladder was still baby Stanley.

Leaving the newsagent's, and feeling a desperate need to spend a penny, Sally looked about her. It was too far to walk home. The only solution was to call in at Pots and Posies. There she found Terry weighing out potatoes, while Julie was taking some daffodils from a bucket on the floor.

'Do you think I could just use the loo?' she whispered to Julie.

'Sure, but mind how you go through, the floor's a bit wet from the sap of these daffodils.'

Manoeuvring herself past sacks of potatoes and onions, Sally reached the safety of the toilet. It was only when she went to close the door that her foot slipped on a piece of cabbage leaf and she found herself propelled clumsily onto the lavatory seat.

'Just in time,' she sighed, struggling with her panties and tights. Relieved to have the pressure taken off her bladder, she attempted the reverse struggle with her undies, only to be stopped short by an excruciating pain shooting through her back.

'Damn. I must have pulled a muscle when I slipped.'

Waiting for her to wash her hands, Julie held up the teapot.

'Fancy a cup of tea? Terry and I are just going to have one.'

Rubbing her back, Sally nodded and reached for a stool.

'Hey! Are you all right?' Julie asked, passing her a mug. 'Only you look a bit pale.'

'Mmm, I'm fine. I think I overdid it with the cleaning yesterday and I must have twisted my back just now, I slipped on a piece of cabbage.'

'What's that?' Terry called, coming through to the backroom for his tea.

'Sally slipped on a bit of cabbage. She's also been overdoing it with the cleaning.'

'I know. Hugh told me.'

'He did? When did you see Hugh?'

'Yesterday. He called in after he'd been to see you.'

Sipping her tea and wondering why Hugh should have gone to see Terry, Sally felt another surge of pain. As one hand gripped the stool, she tried to steady her mug with the other. Watching her place her tea on a nearby ledge, Terry cast an anxious eye in Julie's direction.

'Sally – is anything the matter?'

'I don't know… I mean I'm not really sure. It can't be the baby, can it?'

'And you're asking us…?' Terry grinned

Forcing a weak smile, Sally eased herself from the stool. 'Do you think one of you could walk home with me, just in case…?'

'Walk home with you! You've got to be joking! Julie, shut the shop!

'You can't shut the shop just like that,' Sally pleaded.

''Course we can!' said Terry, throwing Julie a bunch of keys.

Helping Sally into the white van with its green Pots and Posies emblem, Julie turned to Terry and whispered, 'What are we going to do?'

'First we're going home to fetch my car, then I'll take Sally home so she can ring the hospital and fetch her bag.'

'You, Julie, can follow us back to Sally's in the van and stay there in case Hugh calls.'

'No, Terry! I don't want you to tell Hugh. It's their anniversary party.'

'Hmph! Wake, more like, from what Hugh was telling me yesterday. Anyway, let's not bother about that now. Let's get you home.'

'While Sally was on the phone to the hospital, Terry frantically scribbled some instructions onto the back of an envelope and thrust them in Julie's hand, putting a finger to his lips as he did so.

'I understand. Mum's the word.'

'In more ways than one, I reckon,' Terry said, watching Sally walk uncomfortably into the room. 'What did the hospital say?'

'They say I can go in if I want to, or I can stay at home until the contractions become more regular.'

Terry helped her to the settee. 'And what would you prefer to do, love?'

'At the moment, I don't really know. Hospitals terrify me, yet I don't want to leave it too late, do I?'

'Hmm. Well, from what I remember of that DVD we watched together, and looking at you now, I'd say it's safe to stay at home a little while longer. Would you like me to rub your back?'

Sally made a grab for Terry's hand as another contraction began. 'You will stay with me, won't you?'

'Of course. Like I told you, I'll stay with you now, then take you into hospital when you're ready and remain with you until the baby arrives, if that's what you want or until reinforcements arrive.'

'What do you mean, reinforcements?'

Terry gave a nervous shrug of the shoulders. 'I thought, um, your sister or maybe your friend Roz…'

Concentrating on timing her contractions, Sally merely nodded.

Watching all this from the far end of the room, Julie became distinctly uneasy. He'd always been squeamish, and it bothered him to see Sally in distress. Casting an anxious look in Terry's direction, he motioned to the door.

'That's all right, Julie. If you can go and see to those last deliveries… Don't forget to take the mobile and I'll call you later.' Completely oblivious to the wink that Terry gave Julie, Sally closed her eyes and breathed in deeply.

CHAPTER 23

At seven-thirty on Saturday evening, just as Serena was applying the finishing touches to her make-up, Terry collected Sally's bag from the nursery and helped her into his car.

'Are you sure you don't want me to ring Hugh?'

'Positive,' she gasped, struggling through another contraction. 'They'll have barely started the canapés. Regardless of what Serena thinks of me, I don't want to spoil her evening. Promise me, on no account will you ring Hugh.'

Grim-faced, Terry agreed to her request and switched on the ignition. 'I'll drive as carefully as I can, but you must tell me if you want me to stop along the way, if it makes dealing with the contractions any easier.'

Arriving outside the hospital's maternity unit, Sally fixed him with frightened eyes, 'I really don't know if I can do this. The minute I get that first smell of disinfectant or whatever else it is they use, I simply go to pieces…'

'You take it from me, Sally,' Terry said, taking her arm with one hand and her bag with the other, 'I have no intention of letting you go to pieces.'

Watching her force a smile, Terry took a last deep breath of crisp January air. Moments later, the same familiar smell that Sally dreaded so much, hit his nostrils.

'Hello, Sally! So we're on our way at last then,' a kindly voice said in greeting.

Relieved in some small part by the sight of her midwife, Sally paused for breath.

'Terry, can I introduce you to Sue, my midwife.'

Nodding in greeting, Terry was aware of the questioning gaze in his direction, 'Oh, Terry's not the father, Sally explained, 'He's my neighbour and he's offered to stay with me. That's OK, isn't it?'

'If that's what you want, my dear, that's fine by me. As long as he doesn't pass out on us at the crucial moment.'

'No way! I've watched the DVD, so I know what to expect. I've even been practicing rubbing Sally's back, but she seems more comfortable walking than sitting.'

Sue smiled kindly. It seemed strange Sally should arrive with a neighbour – and a male one at that, but as he seemed extremely conscientious… Hers was not to reason why the father of Sally's baby wasn't with her, or hadn't put in an appearance at ante-natal classes. Today's

mums-to-be often turned up with a variety of friends and family for support.

'He seems very keen,' Sue whispered, when she led Sally away for an examination.

'Oh, he is. He's really looking forward to the birth, providing he's standing by my shoulder and not the delivery end. I only wish I could share his enthusiasm.'

With the internal examination completed, Sue laid a hand on Sally's tummy to gauge the strength of the contraction. 'I'd say you've a while to go yet before the cervix is fully dilated. If you do want to go for a walk… Just don't go charging about like a mountain goat.'

Sally laughed. 'That's exactly what the baby's father said the other day. By the way I haven't told him I'm in labour. He has a family celebration this evening that's why Terry's with me.'

Puzzled, Sue shook her head, watching Terry take Sally's arm and head off for a walk along the corridor. 'And what's this then, if it's not a family celebration?'

*

Hugh tapped on Serena's bedroom door, which she opened almost immediately.

'I was wondering if you are ready, I can hear the sound of cars in the driveway.'

'No doubt Clive and Belinda!' Serena said tersely. 'They're always the first to arrive, the first to get drunk and the last to leave.'

Hugh refrained from asking why these people had even been invited, and turned his attention to Serena's appearance instead. As Sally had predicted, swathed in sumptuous black velvet she looked lovely.

Looking up with an expectant smile on her face, Serena waited for Hugh's reaction. 'Well,' she said, 'what do you think?'

Using Uncle Bertram's expression, he replied, 'I think you look stunning. Now, are you ready to greet our guests?'

Hugh held out his arm to a slightly bewildered Serena. Yes, she did look stunning, but at the same time he felt no familiar stirring as her hand clasped his elbow. Any such feelings had long since disappeared.

Walking down the staircase decorated with garlands with Serena by his side, Hugh contemplated the past twenty-five years. Yes, they had shared some good times together in the early years, but somewhere along the way, and at that precise moment he couldn't pinpoint exactly when, they had begun to drift apart. And, if they were to be entirely honest with each other, it was probably long before Sally and Stanley.

Sweeping past the two waitresses standing in the impressive entrance hall holding trays of Bucks Fizz, Serena fixed a smile on her face and greeted Belinda and Clive with open arms. 'Darlings! How wonderful to see you! So pleased you could come.'

'Just you try and keep us away, old thing,' Clive said, plonking a wet kiss on Serena's cheek.'

'Less of the old if you don't mind!'

Clive chuckled and stepping back shot Serena an admiring glance. 'Quite right, I stand corrected. You look even lovelier than ever, doesn't she,

Belinda?'

Belinda cooed in Serena's direction and brushed her hand gently against her shoulder. 'Lovely, darling. The dress is simply divine. Velvet again, I see, just like you had on your wedding day all those years ago. Hugh, my dear, how delightful to be with you again. How are you?'

'Very well as you can see, Belinda. Allow me to offer you both a drink.'

Hugh watched Clive gulp at his Bucks Fizz. 'You'd probably prefer it without the orange juice, but the night is still young and as I'm relying on you to get the party going with a swing after dinner…'

'Your wish is my command. You know you can count on me,' Clive replied. Draining his glass and reaching for another, he watched as Serena and Hugh stepped forward to welcome yet more guests.

*

Studying the distress on Sally's face, Terry reached for the small triangular-shaped sponge, moistened it with water and applied it to her mouth and forehead. 'Keep going, Sally, it can't be much longer now.'

'I hope not,' she whimpered. 'To be honest, I've already had enough. I don't think I can cope with much more of this!' Her eyes pleaded in Sue's direction.

'You're doing fine, Sally, how about trying the gas and air again? Trust me, it will help, you know.'

Sue turned aside to Terry. 'If you can, try and persuade her to persevere for a bit. She really is doing well. And in a while I'll be able to give her some pethidine which will help.'

At the mere mention of pethidine, Sally's face brightened as she reached for the gas and air. 'Oh, thank goodness, that's the injection I was telling you about earlier.'

Terry's face went suddenly white. Injections! He hated injections; both having them or watching other people on the receiving end. Year ago, when he was at school, and they'd all lined up for their BCG injections, he'd even passed out!

'Would you mind if I went out while you had your injection, Sally? They do for me what the smell of hospitals does for you.'

Coping grimly with a contraction, Sally shook her head and in between her controlled panting, urged Terry to have a cup of coffee while he was out of the room.

'No way, I'm not staying away longer than I have to.' Squeezing Sally's hand reassuringly, he added, 'I'll be back in a mo. Don't run away.'

'Fat chance of that!' Sally cried, tossing the gas and air mask to one side. 'Just wait until I get my hands on Ben! It's his fault I'm having to go through this! If he hadn't taken those condoms…'

'Who's Ben? Her partner?' The trainee nurse asked Terry, as he moved towards the door. Spying the needle in Sue's hand, Terry simply shook his head and ran.

Smiling, the nurse watched as he scooted off down the corridor for the gents' loo. At first she'd thought Terry was the father of Sally's baby, yet in his T-shirt and jeans, complete with designer stubble and earring, he seemed a most unlikely partner. As for why Sally was blaming someone called Ben for her predicament, when he also wasn't the father… Confused, the young nurse took Terry's place by the bed, murmured further encouragement and began rubbing Sally's back.

*

Giving Hugh a hearty slap on the back, Clive returned to his seat at the table.

'A great meal, Hugh! Now what about your speech? We're all waiting and hoping you're going to put an end to all these rumours.'

'Rumours?' Hugh frowned, looking in Serena's direction, where she sat at the far end of the table.

'That you're retiring from Barrington's,' Belinda explained.

'Oh, you'll never get Hugh to retire,' Serena called back icily. 'He's just like Pa-in-law used to be—married to the wretched place!'

There was polite murmured laughter and Vivienne looked anxiously in her husband's direction. As she'd whispered to Charles, only minutes ago, the atmosphere between Hugh and Serena was becoming decidedly more strained as the evening wore on.

'Perceptive as ever, my dear,' Charles said, squeezing his wife's hand. 'But I shouldn't worry about it too much, if I were you. Some of the guests haven't seen Hugh and Serena for quite a while, and the rest of them are probably too well-oiled to sense otherwise.'

Vivienne's gaze rested on Clive as he banged noisily on the table in preparation for Hugh's long awaited speech. 'Order! Order!'

'Be quiet now, Clive!' Belinda hissed to her husband.

Adjusting his bow tie and straightening the cuffs of his dress-shirt, Hugh rose to his feet.

'Before I begin, may I just thank the delightful team of ladies who have served us this evening and ask them to refill your glasses. Then at least, if you think my speech is going on for too long, hopefully you'll all be too polite to complain.'

'Or too drunk,' Serena hissed under her breath, looking directly at Clive.

Hugh nodded as the waitresses, dressed in black with white frilly aprons, stepped forward with yet more bottles of champagne. Dismissing them good-naturedly, he donned his reading glasses and began.

'Ladies and gentlemen, dear family and friends, as we've known each other for what must be the best part of twenty-five years, I expect you'll be wanting me to begin my speech with what makes a happy marriage. To that end I do not intend to disappoint. The secret to a happy marriage as I see it, is lust!'

Ribald cries of, 'Good old, Hugh,' came from Clive's direction and the faces of some of the female guests filled with horror. Serena meanwhile simply emitted a snort of disgust.

'However,' said Hugh, 'before I upset the fairer sex any further, let me borrow a phrase from that well known television series *Star Trek*, and say *lust*, but not as we know it.'

'Beam me up Scottie!' a voice echoed, amidst the laughter.

'L. U. S. T.,' continued Hugh, 'as I interpret it stands for Love, Understanding, Soulmates and Trust. Although there are of course many other words I could have used, and in a different order, only they wouldn't have held your attention in quite the same way, would they?'

Across the table, Hugh noticed people nodding in assent while others sipped at their champagne. So far so good, he thought; at least everyone seemed suitably mellow. There was even a beginning of a smile playing on Serena's lips. Raising his glass in her direction he continued.

'I'm sure most of us have shared all these qualities in our marriages, otherwise we wouldn't be here now. Let's face it, with one in three marriages ending in divorce, we've not done too badly between us, have we?'

Waiting for the cries of 'Hear, Hear!' to subside, Hugh fixed his eyes on Serena. 'There's also another word beginning with 'S',' he began softly. 'Secrets, and who among us hasn't had secrets? Ladies, I expect you've all had that little number in your wardrobe, knowing full well it wasn't the amazing bargain you made it out to be and gentlemen, isn't it strange how all those unexpected business meetings involved taking along the golf clubs?'

'Or in Clive's case, the golf clubs and a little blonde!' Belinda said, draining her glass of champagne.

There was an embarrassed silence, which to everyone's relief was broken when Hugh began speaking again.

'On the subject of secrets, this is where Serena and I share one of our own. You all think you were invited here to celebrate our silver wedding - which is after all partly correct – but at the same time Serena and I wish to announce the end of our marriage as well. As civilized beings we also thought why not have a double celebration. So… if you'd all like to join me, I'd like to propose a toast, not only to our past but also to our future.'

Ignoring the silence pervading the room and his wife's withering look, Hugh walked to her chair holding two glasses of champagne. Leaning forward, he kissed her ashen-faced cheek, offered her a glass and then raised his own in the air. 'To the past and the future, Serena.'

'The past and the future,' she said numbly, her own response drowned out by fifty other voices.

With the waitressing staff back in position to clear the tables, and guests heading for the drawing room, Hugh was approached by the catering manager.

'Excuse me, Mr Barrington but someone's just arrived with a bouquet of flowers for you.'

Hugh looked at his watch. It was eleven o'clock. 'Flowers at this time of night, surely not?'

'Yes, sir, they've just this minute arrived.'

'Then they must be for my wife, not me.'

'No, Mr Barrington. I distinctly heard the young man ask for you. The funny thing is, I thought he said his name was Julie but he must have meant the flowers are from Julie.'

'Julie!'

To the rest of the guests it appeared Hugh was calling a member of the waitressing team; only Serena, Vivienne and Charles knew otherwise.

Leaving the table, Serena followed Hugh into the hallway while Vivienne requested yet more coffee and liqueurs for the guests and Charles began a rendition of *The Lion and Albert.*

Giving Julie a welcoming hug, Hugh motioned him into his study.

'I'm so sorry to disturb your evening, Hugh, only Terry's just rung from the hospital and insisted I came to see you with the flowers.'

'The hospital! You mean Sally...?'

Julie nodded. 'Things started this afternoon when she called at the shop. Terry took her home and stayed with her until about seven-ish, then he took her in...'

'Seven-ish! But why didn't she ring me? Why didn't *you* ring me?'

'Because Sally made Terry promise. In the end he got desperate and rang me. He suggested I come straight here and put a message in with the flowers, in case I didn't see you personally. That way he didn't actually break his promise...

Hugh moved towards the bouquet, but Serena, who had been hovering in the doorway, was there before him. Snatching at the envelope with its rose decorated card and message, she gave a loud gasp.

'"Sally in labour, can you come?" What the hell does this mean, Hugh!'

'Exactly what it says, Serena! Sally is in Thornhampton hospital giving birth to my child, so if you'll excuse me, I have to go.'

'That's preposterous! You can't have children at your age!'

'Correction, Serena. *You're* the one who can't have children, or had you forgotten?'

'But you can't leave, Hugh! What about our guests?'

'I'm fed up with *can't*, Serena. As for our guests, they've been wined and dined this evening at considerable expense to myself and whether they want to celebrate the end of our marriage or the birth of my first child is up to them.'

'The end of our marriage,' Serena repeated, wishing she hadn't drunk so much this evening.

'Yes, it's what you wanted, isn't it? What you've been talking about for weeks. So I'll just bid our guests a fond farewell and leave them in your capable hands. Didn't you say the other day there was so much you wanted to tell them tonight?' Hugh nodded in the direction of Julie, who was still standing nervously by Hugh's desk.

'Just give me a few minutes, Julie, if you'd like to wait in the van and get the engine started…

Hurrying from the room, with Serena in pursuit, Hugh found his way barred by Clive.

'Sorry, Clive, I'm afraid I have to go.'

'Go? You mean to say you're leaving? But it's your party and the night is still young.'

Not as far as Sally's concerned, Hugh wanted to say. His beloved Sally had been in labour for hours and… 'I know Clive, and I must. Still, I shall be leaving you in Serena's capable hands. No doubt if you twist her arm, I'm sure she'll entertain you at the piano. Don't forget Serena and Vivienne do a wonderful rendition of that old classic *Sisters*.'

As if on cue, Vivienne appeared by Hugh's side, and nodding in Serena's direction, he whispered in her ear, 'Take care of her, please Vivienne, and I'll ring you tomorrow.'

Climbing into the Pots and Posies van, Hugh was aware of someone running from the front door.

'Hugh!' Charles called breathlessly, 'I take it the baby is on its way. Good luck, old chap!' Shaking Hugh firmly by the hand, Charles added,' You will let us know, won't you?'

'Yes, Charles. I'll let you know, and thanks for everything.'

Watching the white van disappear down the gravelled driveway, Charles went back inside the house where he heard the opening bars of *Sisters* echoing into the hallway. Serena, once more the centre of attention, had begun to play.

Feeling particularly smug with himself, Terry walked back into the delivery room just as Sally burst forth with a string of expletives, which included not only his name but also Ben and Hugh as well.

'No need to look so alarmed,' Sue said, 'It's a really good sign. It's what we midwives call transition and a sure indication that baby's almost here.'

'But Stanley can't come yet!' Terry declared. 'Hugh's not here!'

'Terry!' Sally cried, forgetting her shallow breathing, 'you promised you wouldn't ring Hugh.'

'I didn't, I sent Julie round to fetch him.'

'You did what! But how did Julie know where to… Oh, my God! I think I want to push!'

With the midwife urging Sally to wait for the next contraction, and then not to push too hard, the young nurse exchanged places with Terry, all the while aware of a commotion going on in the corridor outside.

'No! Terry is *not* the father, *I* am! So will you please let me through!'

As Sally started pushing, and she and Terry looked towards the door, the trainee nurse, seeing Hugh – a picture of elegance – did a double take. It was the man from Barrington's department store. Only tonight he wasn't wearing a lounge suit and a yellow rose in his lapel, he was wearing a dinner suit and a bow tie!

'Sally, my love!' Hugh cried. 'Why didn't you send for me?'

Unable to reply, Sally reached desperately for Hugh's hand and followed Sue's instructions.

'That's fine, Sally, half the head is there, so stop pushing for the moment and just do as I say… gently now…'

Awestruck, Hugh and Terry gazed in wonderment as with a final groan, and Sue's expert guidance, Sally pushed her baby into the world.

'Oh! My God! It's head's all blue,' Terry called, keeling over.

'All babies are like that until they take their first breath,' Sue explained, offering Hugh the scissors to cut the baby's umbilical cord.

With misted eyes, Hugh kissed Sally's cheek, stroked her damp hair from her forehead and caressed the tiny, wrapped bundle in her arms.

Swallowing hard, he whispered, 'I can't believe it. I simply can't believe it. Has this really happened, Sally?'

'Oh, yes,' she said, shifting uncomfortably, 'I can assure you it has!'

'I'm just *so* sorry I wasn't with you all the way through.'

'You were here for the most important bit, Hugh, and that's all that matters. And Terry was marvellous—by the way, what happened after you picked him up from the floor and led him out? Where is he?'

'Hopefully at home by now with Julie. I told them not to wait for me. I think it all got a bit too much for him in the end and…' Hugh got no further as at that moment a tiny hand wriggled from the blanket and clasped his finger. Gazing adoringly, he whispered, 'we're not really going to call him Stanley, are we? Shouldn't we think of something more suitable?'

Smiling, Sally carefully peeled back the blanket. 'Yes, I think we should—think of something more suitable, I mean. S*he's* really not going to thank us for calling her Stanley, is she?'

'But I thought it was a boy! You mean it's a girl—but that's wonderful!'

'You're not disappointed?'

'Gracious, no! If she turns out to be anything like her mother, how could I be disappointed?'

Watching Sally cover up his baby daughter, Hugh sighed contentedly and looked at his watch. It was gone midnight. 'I suppose I'd better go and order myself a taxi and let you both get some sleep.'

'Will you be going home to Ser-?'

'No. That's no longer my home. Serena will stay there of course and I'll probably go back tomorrow – or should that be today – for a change of clothes. If it's all right with you, I thought I'd go back to Elmsmarsh.'

'That's fine. The keys are in my handbag, in case you don't have your set with you.'

Hugh reached in his pocket and jangled some keys. That's OK, I came prepared.'

'But not for delivering babies. You have a stain on your shirt.'

Hugh laughed and stroked her hand.

'What's so funny?'

'I seem to remember that's how all this began – with me getting make-up on my shirt… do you remember?'

Sally blushed at the memory… she in her bathrobe and Hugh in her kimono.

'My goodness, but it was worth it,' Hugh said, brushing a hand gently against the baby's head before he stood up. 'Who would have guessed?'

'Who indeed,' Sally said, as Hugh kissed her goodnight.

CHAPTER 24

Hugh woke early next morning, wondering if last night had been simply a dream. Driving past Terry and Julie's flat, he noticed the curtains and blinds still drawn. Not to worry, he thought, he would call them later.

Pulling into the driveway of his house, he recognized the caterer's vans and assumed they would be clearing up from yesterday's party. It also meant Serena wouldn't be alone in the house, either, which in some ways came as a relief.

It had been one thing waking up with that wondrous feeling of euphoria, knowing that overnight he'd become the proud father of a beautiful baby daughter, and quite another knowing that he still had to face Serena. Inserting his house key into the lock, Hugh felt the door open without effort.

'Charles! I didn't expect to find you here.'

Charles put a finger to his lips and beckoned him inside. 'Vivienne and I thought we ought to stay over with Serena.'

'She's all right, isn't she?'

Charles smiled ruefully. 'Oh, yes. She's just a bit hungover that's all.'

'I see, and where is she?'

'Still sleeping. So are you going to come and tell Vivienne and me the good news?' Charles studied Hugh's dishevelled appearance. He was still wearing his dinner suit. 'It is good news, I hope?' he asked anxiously.

'Oh, yes, Charles. Wonderful news, I have a beautiful daughter!'

Vivienne looked up at their approach, from where she was reading the Sunday paper. Her eyes brightened when she saw him. 'Well…?'

'A baby girl, quite tiny in fact, only six pounds but perfect.'

'Oh, Hugh, my dear that's simply wonderful… and is the mother…?'

'Yes, Sally's fine, just very tired. She'll be staying in for a little while longer. It was all a bit of an ordeal as you are only too aware, Vivienne.'

Vivienne nodded in agreement, remembering back to all those years ago when she'd given birth to Gareth. Giving Hugh a warm hug, she whispered, 'And are we going to see your beautiful daughter?'

Hugh looked warily towards the drawing room door. 'Of course. But aren't you worried about Serena? She might not approve.'

Shrugging her shoulders, Vivienne announced. 'Concerned, yes, but not worried. Still, we'll think of a solution, I'm sure. From what Serena was saying last night, she's already got her future mapped out.'

'Yes,' broke in Charles, 'but she was also very drunk.'

'Mmm, so she was. Perhaps I'd better go and make us some fresh coffee. Hugh, will you stay for a cup?'

'Vivienne, this is Hugh's house, remember?'

'I know, Charles, but I doubt very much if he's staying, are you Hugh?'

Hugh shook his head. 'Not for long, I only came for a change of clothes. I can't really go back to the hospital looking like this. However, I would very much appreciate a cup of coffee.'

Packing a suitcase, Hugh became aware of the aroma of freshly ground coffee wafting up the stairs and the murmur of voices from further down the landing. Presently there was a gentle tap on his bedroom door.

'Hugh, I've brought you a tray, as I didn't know how long you'd be. I thought I'd also let you know Serena is awake. I told her you were here and about the baby. I hope you don't mind.'

'No,' he said, taking the tray. 'She has to find out sooner or later. Perhaps it was easier coming from you, Vivienne—who knows?'

'The old man of the mountain knows, that's who!' Vivienne laughed, 'I'm sorry, you probably haven't a clue what I'm talking about. It's a line from a song our grandparents had on one of those old 78 records. It was about a little boy called Sparky who lost his echo, hence the old man of the mountain helping him to find it. Sparky also had a magic piano. Serena and I used to love listening to those records when we were small and we used to have tea with Grandma and Grandpa. Mind you, they were very strict and we had to sit up straight at the table and behave properly.'

Hugh was finding it hard to think of Serena as an innocent child, let alone behaving properly, when Vivienne broke into his chain of thought. 'Do you know,' she said, 'I'm convinced we still have those old 78s somewhere in the attic - and a record player. 'Perhaps when your little girl is older… By the way, you never said, what are you going to call her?'

Hugh took a pile of shirts from the drawer. 'To be honest, Vivienne, we haven't decided, We'd been calling her Stanley until she arrived. She, er, was conceived the day after Serena had Stanley put to sleep.'

'Oh! I see… Well, thank heavens some good came out of such an unpleasant episode. I know Serena's my sister, but she behaved…'

Hearing Serena's bedroom door open and close and footsteps on the landing, Vivienne said in hushed tones, 'I'd better go down, Hugh. Look, if we don't see you before you go, all the best, my dear. And if you think we're being anti-social when you do come down, we're simply doing it for Serena's benefit. OK?'

'OK,' Hugh agreed.

As expected, moments later Serena burst into Hugh's bedroom. Still in her bathrobe, with her hair uncombed and probably for the first time ever, traces of smudged make-up around her eyes, she appeared strangely vulnerable.

Any feelings of pity that Hugh might have had for her diminished rapidly when she walked right up to him and sneered. 'Hmph! I gather you've got a daughter. She couldn't even give you a son!'

Exasperated, Hugh reached for Serena's chin and tilted it until he was looking straight into her eyes. 'And what did you give me, other than a pack of lies about adopted babies and my dog! In case you're wondering, you will have this house and you will be well provided for. And doubtless it will be your story our friends hear first, but I can live with that. What I won't live without, however, is Sally… and by the way, in answer to your earlier bitchy comment about my daughter, which is what I've come to expect from you, all I'll say to that is perhaps Sally and I will have a son next time!'

Snapping shut his suitcase and walking briskly downstairs, Hugh noticed the drawing room door ajar. No doubt Charles and Vivienne had heard everything.

'I'll call you,' Charles mouthed silently.

*

Still fuming from his encounter with Serena, Hugh paused outside Sally's room. Put it all behind you, he told himself, reminded of something Sally said months ago, while trying to comfort him. 'That was then and this is now.' Exactly! Now showered and shaved, he was ready to greet his daughter.

Spying the empty cot, Hugh turned towards the bed where the baby lay sleeping quietly against Sally's naked breast. Overcome with emotion, he found himself unable to move, as if trying to freeze-frame the delightful scene. Sally looked up and smiled. 'Aren't you coming in to see us?'

'Yes, yes, of course.'

Moving to the bed, Hugh bent and kissed her, before stroking his index finger down the baby's cheek. 'How is she?' he whispered.

'Greedy.'

Hugh grinned. 'And how are you, my darling?'

'A little bit sore but blissfully happy.'

Hugh sat on the bed. 'I must say you're looking infinitely better than when I last saw you.'

Taking the sleeping baby from her breast, Sally placed her in his arms. 'Stanley, I think you should get to know your daddy.'

Alarmed, Hugh asked, 'Are you sure? You mean it's all right?'

'Of course. After all, you only held her briefly last night, or should that be this morning?'

Watching Hugh tenderly cradle his daughter, Sally asked, 'Speaking of this morning, how did it go with Serena?'

'Let's just say it wasn't particularly pleasant, but Charles and Vivienne were wonderful. They can't wait to meet you both. Anyway, we don't have to discuss such things now, do we? More importantly, I think we should discuss the matter of this young lady's name. Uncle Bertram was most concerned to discover we're still calling her Stanley.'

'I'm glad you managed to ring Bertram and tell him our good news.'

'I did more than that, I called in to see him before I came to the hospital. Oh, and by the way, he asked me to give you this.' Gingerly, so as not to wake the baby, Hugh reached in his jacket pocket and brought out a long thin box.

'What is it?'

'I'm not sure. Apparently he bought whatever it is years ago, for a very special lady, only he left it too late to give it to her.'

Opening the dark green box, Sally lifted out a perfectly formed string of pearls and held them against her cheek.

'They're beautiful, but why give them to me?'

'We already know that he highly approves of you. It might also have something to do with the day I took you to meet him. Weren't you talking about Freya and the mistletoe?'

'Of course! Freya's pearls.'

'Speaking of pearls, this little one is about to dribble all over my shirt. Do you have a tissue or something?'

'And there was me thinking you were used to females ruining your shirts!' Sally said, dabbing at the pearl of milk forming on the baby's rosebud mouth.

Hugh looked thoughtful as his eyes met hers. 'You know that could be a possibility for a anme.'

'What ruined shirts!' she grinned.

'No! I mean Freya. What do you think?'

'I don't know. Freya…' Sally said softly. 'Yes, I suppose it does go with Barrington. The only names I've thought of so far are Rachel and Katherine. Perhaps I could ask Roz. She asked if she could come and see us before we go home.'

'Then perhaps I'd better go. I take it she still doesn't know I'm your mystery lover.'

'No, but I expect your time is running out, mystery lover. Any day now, you and Roz are going to come face to face.'

'I shall look forward to it immensely,' Hugh said, carefully handing back the baby.

*

Roz stood by the side of Sally's bed and peered into the cot with tear-filled eyes. 'She's beautiful and so perfect, just look at her rosebud mouth, and she's even got hair!'

Removing her glasses to dab at her eyes with a handkerchief, she turned to face Sally. 'I do hope you didn't mind me coming in, only I simply had to see you, you clever girl.'

Roz grabbed hold of Sally's hand. 'Tell me,' she urged, 'was it truly awful? Donald said I wasn't to ask, but I'm dying to know. Was he, I mean the father, was he with you for the birth?'

'Let's just say it wasn't a bed of roses, and yes, he was with me to hold my hand when she was born.'

Roz slumped on the bedside chair with an enormous sigh. 'Thank God for that! I can't tell you how anxious I've been. By the way, speaking of roses, just as I was coming into the hospital I could have sworn I saw the boss man with a beautiful bouquet of roses. He was standing in one of the telephone booths. I didn't know Serena was in hospital. Still, if she is, I expect I'll have all the news when I go into work tomorrow.'

'Yes, I expect you will,' Sally said.

Moments later, when the door opened and Hugh walked in (minus the roses), he called brightly, 'Mrs Hughes, how lovely to see you, and what do you think of my beautiful daughter!'

*

Sally chuckled as Hugh helped her and the baby into the Jaguar.

'Poor Roz! If only I'd had a camera to record her reaction. It wasn't really fair of you, you know.'

'How else was I going to tell her? I didn't think she'd stay with you that long. At the time, it seemed the only way. Anyway, you have to admit my timing was perfect.'

'Yes,' Sally sighed, 'in fact, it always has been when you come to think of it.'

'Like finding you and Roz collapsed on the stairs in a fit of giggles that afternoon when she was drunk.'

'I wasn't actually thinking of that occasion.'

Drawing to a gradual halt outside the house, Sally was surprised to see Terry and Julie in her front garden. They were tying pink ribbons onto a mini-avenue of clipped bay trees in pots.

'What are they doing?'

'It was supposed to be a surprise,' Hugh said. 'I wanted to make up for the ruined bay tree where we were going to scatter Stanley's ashes. Then Terry suggested having an avenue of them and Julie got carried away and came up with the idea of blue ribbons.'

'But it's pink for a girl.'

'I know. But it was only this afternoon I realized that Terry and Julie still thought you'd had a boy. If you remember he keeled over just before I cut the umbilical cord. That's why Roz saw me near the telephone booth. For once I didn't have my mobile and Terry had to race back to Pots and Posies for some pink ribbon.'

Sally watched as in a swirl of pink ribbon, Julie rushed to the very last bay tree, still tied with blue, 'Julie, no! Don't!'

Confused, Julie stepped aside as Sally, holding the baby, approached the blue beribboned bay tree. 'Please, if you don't mind, can you leave that one exactly as it is? I'd like to keep that bay tree for Stanley.'

Swallowing hard, Hugh walked back to the boot of the car and brought out the bouquet Roz had mentioned earlier. Sally gave a gasp and clasped her daughter tightly to her breast – Roz had never mentioned the colour. Through tear-filled eyes she saw Hugh coming towards her, carrying a sea of red blooms. Putting his arms around her, he whispered lovingly, 'What was it you once said about red roses for commitment?'